ALSO BY GINNY BAIRD

Right Girl, Wrong Side

The Holiday Mix-Up

Christmas Eve Love Story

GINNY BAIRD

Published by Sourcebooks Casablanca, an imprint of Sourcebooks
P.O. Box 4410, Naperville, Illinois 60567-4410
(630) 961-3900
sourcebooks.com

Cataloging-in-Publication Data is on file with the Library of Congress.

Printed and bound in the United States of America.
KP 10 9 8 7 6 5 4 3 2

For John

ONE

On the first Christmas Eve

ANNIE JONES HURRIED OUT OF the snow and in through the employee entrance at Lawson's Finest in her red knitted pom-pom hat and peacoat, clocking in on her department store app, and—*ahh!*—almost mowing down Santa. She startled, jerking back. *Where did he come from?* She blinked at the jolly old elf, who seemed jollier—and maybe stockier—than the Santa she'd seen here before. His beard was very real looking too. It matched his bushy white eyebrows and the fluffy fake fur on his red tunic's sleeves.

"Hello"—he smiled, and his rosy dumpling cheeks rounded—"Annie." Her pulse spiked. She reached for her name tag. But no. That was under her coat.

She tugged on her neck scarf with her mitten. "How do you know my name?"

"Ho ho ho!" He tapped the side of his cherrylike nose. "Santa knows everything. Haven't you heard?"

"Ha. Yeah." Talk about being into a role. But still. She felt... What? Strangely peaceful inside? She slid her cell phone in a coat pocket, and a wave of calm washed over her, bathing her in *comfort and joy*. Which was…really, really weird. But reassuring somehow.

"I hope this is your best Christmas yet." His baby-blue eyes twinkled, and she was swept back in time to that one special Christmas when she was nine. She'd gotten the prettiest snow globe with Santa's sleigh inside it. A sign in the snowy white yard said: *Believe*.

Her heavy shoulder bag slid off her arm, hitting the terrazzo floor. *Nooo!*

Her purse jettisoned out of it, popping open. *There goes my lip gloss tube, twirling away toward the elevators*. She chased after it in her snow boots, dragging her bag along with her.

Ding-ding. An elevator chime sounded.

Great. Now one of her winter-white work pumps had toppled out of her tote.

What did Santa do? Curse me?

Wait. Where'd he go?

She bent to retrieve her shoe, and the elevator's doors opened. Out walked a pair of shiny black men's shoes, very official-seeming, with tied-tight laces. The toe box on one of them rose up—and came down—trapping her rolling lip gloss tube.

Annie slowly looked up—past those regulation navy-blue pants legs and—*whoa*—well-supplied duty belt, holding a flashlight, baton, radio, and—she gulped—a gun. Her gaze swept past his flat stomach and buff arms—in that blue button-down shirt with shoulder patches and a gleaming silver badge stating "Security." He'd clipped a mic to a spot below his collar and above the center of his *obviously* rock-hard chest.

Her stomach did a tiny twirl.

This guy's seriously built and—ooh—very handsome, with wavy dark hair and bright-blue eyes. He reached for the lip gloss tube and handed it to her. "This yours?"

"Ahh, yeah, thanks!" she said, a little breathy. Because, well. She didn't have these kinds of run-ins often. As in, never. The only great-looking guys she spoke with these days were the ones in here shopping for their girlfriends or wives. She shoved the lip gloss tube in her coat pocket and yanked off her bright-red mittens, using them to dab her brow.

"No worries." He smiled, and a dimple settled in his chin.

Her pulse hummed.

What? No! Stop that. No humming allowed. Especially not here! Not at Lawson's. She had work, work, work to do. She stood upright, grabbing her canvas bag off the floor. Her second work shoe plopped out of the bag, landing by her feet. *Groan.* She picked it up, her face steaming. Not a super start to her workday. Though it *was* a continuation of her awful morning.

The security guard handed her the other shoe, after stealing a peek at its heel and maybe judging her. But hey! She liked looking nice on the job. Apparently, so did he. Wow. She crammed her things back in her bag, going slightly lightheaded. Likely from the glare of holiday lights. The store was all decorated for Christmas, and swags of greenery were everywhere. She grabbed on to an endcap fronting the toy section and held on tight.

He studied her a moment. "Have we met?"

She scanned his name tag: Braden Tate. Where had he been hiding? She definitely would have noticed him. He cut a stunning image against the backdrop of the jewelry counter, with its glittery rubies and emeralds on display. A fair number of engagement rings too. *As if.* Not with her record.

"Er, no. I don't think so," she said, refocusing her energy. She was a young professional woman, moving forward, *and* about to get promoted. She didn't need old what's his name any longer. *Roy, his name's Roy*, an annoying little voice in her head said. Maybe it was good to remember some things. That way she could avoid repeating her mistakes. She sighed and let go of the endcap, prepared to stand on her own two feet. Annie looked down. It would be nicer if she wasn't wearing ancient snow boots that had faded from red to dusty rose, but she *had* ordered new ones.

Braden shook his finger at her, like he'd put something together. "You're our window dresser, right?"

She proudly squared her shoulders. *Lawson's soon-to-be Lead Visual Artist.* "Um, yep. That's me! I was just talking to..." She glanced around.

"Talking to...?"

"Our new store Santa." A few sales associates strode toward their departments or opened registers. Annie craned her neck looking for Santa, but she didn't see him anywhere.

Braden crossed his arms. "He's not the one we had before?"

"No, I don't think so." She undid the brass buttons on her suddenly too-toasty coat. "This one's *very* good."

"So, maybe he's the real deal?" Braden teased her with a grin. "You're never too old to believe, I hear." Snowflakes swirled through her mind, and she felt all mixed up inside, almost as if she were in that snow globe herself. Silly.

"Erm, that's what I hear too." She made a feeble stab at banter. "I mean, I'm sure he still comes to *some* people." Annie rolled her eyes. "The *nice* ones on his list."

"Right." His mouth twitched. "The naughty ones get coal and switches."

She gasped. "What? *No*. Santa's always forgiving and kind." This impromptu exchange was fun, almost flirty. Not that she flirted—much. Anymore. She was probably out of practice.

"Ah, so you *do* still believe," Braden said deadpan.

Think. Think. Think. Witty repartee!

She drew a total blank.

Definitely out of practice.

"Um, sure?" She searched his eyes. "Don't you?"

Annie bit her lip at Braden's amused look. "I'd say the jury's still out on that one."

He peered toward the front of the store and past mounds of sales tables piled high with *gifts for him, them, or her*. "You did a great job with that window, by the way. Love your 'Night Before Christmas' theme." She was pleased that he'd noticed. *And glad he'd changed the subject.*

She'd created a holiday window design in the long street-side window beside the main entrance. It portrayed a Christmas Eve living room scene, with a Christmas tree and a stocking hanging from the hearth's mantel. "Thanks." She made a show of reading his name tag, acting like she hadn't done it before. "Braden."

He grinned at her.

"Hi. I'm Annie."

"Nice meeting you, Annie." Braden stepped aside as more people exited the elevators.

"Yeah, um-hmm. You too!" So what if his eyes sparkled when he smiled, and he was handsome—and well, apparently, nice. She was twenty-four, and he was—what? Not yet thirty. Late twenties maybe. He was also probably married.

Quick ring check.

Ahh, nope!

All right then. He had to have a girlfriend at least. The good ones were always taken, according to Tina. Her heart gave a painful twist. She'd been the jerkiest person on earth, taking Roy's word over Tina's. Now the rift between her and her former best friend was too deep to repair.

Annie had to get her head out of this space. She was not in one of those rom-coms she binged on, and Braden was not her hunky hero. Besides that, Braden wasn't interested in her and she wasn't interested in him. Even if he *was* very attractive and maybe available. Also, maybe not. Most likely not.

She glanced at a wall clock, seeing it was nearly nine fifteen. Arriving late was not the best look when you were up for a promotion. "Sorry. I'd better—"

"Yeah. I've got to stop by the security office." He eyed the far side of the salesfloor and the customer service area, beyond which the security office was located.

Braden turned as she pivoted toward the elevators.

They nearly collided.

His neck reddened. So did the tops of his ears, making him look cuter than ever with his face gone ruddy. "Ahh, sorry about that," he murmured, and she went warm and fuzzy inside. He smelled super sexy too, like lemon and spice—and *everything* nice. She swooned just a little.

"Yeah, uh. Me too." What if he *wasn't* seeing anybody? Didn't mean that he'd want to see her though. Still. Didn't mean that he wouldn't want to either. She licked her lips when her mouth went dry. "Well. Guess I'll see you. I mean, hope so!" *Awkward. Why not just throw yourself at him and take his number? Gee.*

His eyes danced. "Same, Annie. See ya around." At least he took it well. He'd probably joke about her with his girlfriend later. Random woman at work hitting on me. Who wears high heels and believes in Santa. Which she did *not*.

An elevator's doors opened, and Annie jumped. "Santa!" *This guy's all over the place.* He nodded and walked by her, heading for his workshop. This was turning out to be a *really strange* day. She boarded the empty elevator and spied Braden staring at her. She waved. Then, feeling stupid about it, she yanked her hand back down. She fumbled with her scarf. Her coat. Her bag. He squinted at her, like he didn't know what she was doing. *Thank goodness* the elevator doors clamped shut.

She ripped off her pom-pom hat and her staticky brown curls crackled, fanning out around her shoulders. She face-palmed and moaned. If she could get *one thing right* today, that would be spectacular. Maybe her day would improve? Because honestly—she glanced at the lighted floor numbers above the elevator doors—the only way to go from here was up.

Patrice motioned Annie aside when she returned from her lunch break. Patrice's crimson-colored pantsuit nicely complemented her complexion and tawny hair. Annie guessed she was in her fifties. "Have you got time for a little chat?" Annie's spirits lifted. She'd been waiting for this meeting all day.

"Um, sure," Annie said, following Patrice into the conference room. The employee break room and locker area were on the third floor. The first two stories of the building housed salesfloors connected by an escalator in addition to two elevators. A large stockroom adjoined each salesfloor. Business offices were up here. Patrice closed the door behind them, and they were alone in the claustrophobic space.

Annie's heart lurched at her boss's thin smile. It didn't look exactly congratulatory. "I know you were expecting good news"—Patrice adjusted her large-framed red glasses—"and I'm really sorry not to be able to give it to you."

Annie's nerves churned. Wait. She was *not* getting promoted? *Why?*

Patrice crossed her arms and her blazer bunched up. "As you know, Veronica Lawson's made several changes around here since inheriting the store from her grandfather."

Annie was keenly aware of those changes. Reporting time was now nine instead of nine thirty, even though the store didn't open until ten, and employees went *off the clock* for lunch, with shorter break times. When Oliver Lawson had been alive, things at Lawson's Finest had been different. Employees used an old-fashioned time clock to clock in rather than a high-tech cell phone app with a built-in GPS locator. The atmosphere here had been congenial, friendly, and not so extremely focused on productivity. "Yes. And?"

"I hate to have to tell you this, but Lawson's is not doing well financially."

"What? Since when?"

"Since online shopping developed a stronghold. It's getting harder and harder for independent businesses like ours to compete." Patrice frowned, and lines formed around her mouth and eyes. "The sad truth is Lawson's is looking to cut back."

Annie's anxiety spiked. "Cut back how?"

Patrice sighed. "By eliminating some of our regular employees and hiring freelancers." Meaning Lawson's could pay those individuals an hourly wage, without needing to carry the overhead costs of employee benefits, like health insurance.

Annie walked to the conference table and dropped down in a chair. She stared up at Patrice. "Are you saying the visual artist team—?" It was tiny as it was, consisting of only three people: one full-time lead—and that slot was vacant, a full-time assistant—her, and their part-time intern, Kira.

Patrice hung her head. "I'm afraid so."

Annie's thoughts raced. "But why us?"

Patrice pulled out a chair and sat beside her. "Ms. Lawson is aiming to trim staff wherever she can, and she's not convinced our current displays are up to snuff. She claims they're a bit"—Patrice shrugged apologetically—"old school, out of touch."

That couldn't be right. Annie had learned from the very best. Their former Lead Visual Artist, Julio, had primed her for this job before his move to Chicago. Once she'd assumed his position,

Annie was supposed to get to hire her own full-time assistant, and she already had her top candidate in mind. Kira was gifted at her job and could do even more with additional training. Annie was sure of it. "But my work here—"

"Has been nothing short of stellar in my opinion. Unfortunately, it's not only my opinion that matters."

Annie gaped at Patrice. "How long have you known?"

Patrice removed her glasses and folded them in her hands. "Only since yesterday. Ms. Lawson reviewed our seasonal numbers, and I regret to say she wasn't impressed."

Queasiness roiled through her. Not only was she *not* getting promoted, Annie was on the cusp of getting canned. She'd been counting on this promotion and pay raise to help cover Leo's vet bills. The cat was elderly, so his options were limited. But his *forever home* was already with her. Her stomach ached. Apart from her job, Leo was *all* she had.

"But I'm good," Annie insisted. "Customers love my displays."

Patrice's dark eyes glistened. "Retail is down, Annie."

"But *not* because of my windows. It can't be that." Doubt trickled through her. "Not only that?"

Patrice strummed her fingers on the tabletop, and her many rings glinted in the artificial light. "You know those electronic door gizmos Lawson's installed? The ones keeping track of the number of folks entering the store?"

"Yeah? So?"

Patrice crossed her legs, and her black ankle boot tipped up, its toe pointing skyward. "When foot traffic goes down, so do sales."

Annie shifted in her chair. "Lots of factors contribute to foot traffic. Advertising, competitive pricing, marketing, promotions." She glanced toward the hall, grasping for straws. Something. Anything. "The *weather*."

Patrice's ankle boot bobbed up and down as she stared at Annie. She uncrossed her legs and leaned forward. "Look," she said kindly, "nothing's been formally decided regarding the lay-offs, and won't be until after the holidays. I— Well. I just wanted you to be prepared. And hey," she said, her tone brightening, "maybe there's still time for you to come up with something—new? Groundbreaking. Fresh!"

A pang of dread gripped Annie. Without a job, she might lose Leo. Steady employment was a requirement at the rescue, and she'd merely been fostering him so far, meaning to apply for adoption after getting her raise. "But it's already Christmas Eve. Isn't it too late?"

Patrice shook open her glasses, sliding them back on her nose. She peered through them and straight at Annie. "We'll have our post-Christmas sales figures to consider, and those can be a huge revenue booster." Patrice turned up her palms. "You're very talented, Annie. Maybe there's still a way for you to pull a rabbit out of this hat?"

Right. And there's really a Santa Claus too.

Annie braced herself against the table and stood on wobbly knees. If ever there was a day when she wanted to crawl back into bed and start over, this was it. "Thanks," she said with more confidence than she felt. "I'll work on it." Just how, she wasn't sure. Her eyes burned hot. But no. She wouldn't cry. What good would that do? It would only make Patrice feel worse, and she clearly felt horrible enough. "Have you talked to Kira?"

"I'm speaking with her next." Patrice stood and smoothed down her slacks. "I'm sorry, Annie. Really, I am."

"It's okay, Patrice. None of this is your fault. I appreciate you telling me."

Patrice walked toward the door and turned with her hand on the knob. "Oh! One more thing," she said as an apparent afterthought. "I meant to ask you earlier to check your front window display. It seems the Christmas tree lights have gone out."

Annie shut her eyes.

Of course they had.

TWO

BRADEN STOOD BY THE MAIN entrance at Lawson's Finest, greeting new arrivals and wishing happy holidays to those departing. He saw Annie powering toward him in those towering white heels of hers. She held a large package in her arms. Likely Christmas tree lights for her display window, since those had gone out. They were LED lights, so that wasn't supposed to happen. Just like he wasn't supposed to be on the floor today. Normally, he worked the night shift, but he was filling in for Carlos, who was out sick.

Annie's voice rose above the hubbub of the crowd as she got closer. "Excuse me!" She scooted past a pair of women holding shopping bags, her long hair bouncing behind her. "Incoming!" she warned a passel of teens, swooping by on the kids' left side. She was a woman on a mission, and totally in charge. Unlike she'd been this morning while scrambling after her lip gloss in that impossibly bright-red pom-pom hat. When she'd stared up at him with her big brown eyes and professed her belief in Santa, he'd nearly lost his mind over her incredible cuteness.

Not that he was thinking of her in any interested way. She was just a coworker at Lawson's, and he'd simply been observant.

It was pretty impossible not to pay attention to Annie, especially when she was right there in front of him.

"Whoa!" She sprang back, and a younger man in a tweed coat lifted his fancy jewelry bag in the air. The shiny black bag had two gold-embossed letters on it, an L and an F for Lawson's Finest. "Sorry!"

"No problem." Annie shot him a flustered look and kept going. "We're good."

On the far side of the salesfloor, kids and adults lined up at Santa's Workshop to see the jolly old elf, but the clock on wish-making was ticking. Lawson's was closing early today—on account of the brewing storm. People everywhere wore panicked looks, loading up on gifts from tables holding holiday knickknacks and scurrying to checkout counters.

Braden kept a careful eye on his surroundings while two of his colleagues patrolled the floor. Two more security officers were stationed upstairs. The clothing departments were on the second floor, including Bridal. He saw Annie coming toward him, a vision in white.

No. Braden. Just no.

What was he thinking? *Not* about holy matrimony. With anyone—much less a coworker he barely knew at all. He wasn't ready for serious. Not even casual. He'd been on a break from women for a while. Ever since leaving the army. He shook off the scent of smoke and the sound of sirens blaring in his head.

"No, Dylan! Let me!" A young boy raced past Annie, darting through Homewares.

Braden's senses went on high alert, his muscles tensing.

Another kid yanked on the boy's arm, scooting in front of him. "No, Marcus! Me first!"

Braden's hand shot to his mic when he saw their mom wildly chasing after them. "Dylan! Marcus!" she shouted, in hot pursuit of her sons. They appeared to be twins maybe, or at least brothers and born very close together. Both had brown hair like their mom's and bright-pink faces. They wore puffy coats over holiday sweaters and munchkin jeans.

"But I want my Robo-bot!" Marcus hollered.

"Santa! Santa!" Dylan cried. "Wait for me!"

Braden cut a glance at the workshop, seeing Santa depart for his break. The kids were running amok, darting through swarms of shoppers. If they weren't stopped soon, somebody was going to get hurt. He took leaping strides toward the boys. He'd head them off at the pass with outstretched arms and a staunch warning.

Their mom got to them first, grabbing for the hood of one boy's coat. "You won't get *anything*," she shouted, "if you don't"—her eyes got huge—"*stop*!"

Marcus bumbled into Dylan, tackling him into the retractable belt cordoning off the window. Both kids landed in the fake snow, pulling the belt down with them. One black steel pole anchoring the belt lurched past them with a clatter—hitting the Christmas tree with force! The tall structure teetered this way and that.

Braden broke into a sprint, racing toward it. Annie dropped her package and started running too. The tree keeled over—its star topper smacking against the front window and yanking free a strand of icicle lights—before walloping the faux fireplace and sweeping three singing angels off the mantel. *Whoa*. It hit a tray holding cookies and milk for Santa on its way down. A china plate shattered, and sugarplums and snowflakes twirled above the wreckage.

Annie groaned under her breath. "What a disaster."

The mom pulled her kids to their feet. "Boys!" she said with an embarrassed look. "*What* were you thinking?" She stared at Annie and Braden, abashed. "I'm so sorry." She opened her purse and took out her wallet. "Listen, whatever it costs—"

Annie met the woman's eyes and said graciously, "Oh no, we can't let you do that. Lawson's will cover it." Braden knew that was the store policy for accidents. The customer was always right at Lawson's Finest, even when their offspring had done *really, really wrong*.

The boys hung their heads and looked up. They had to know they were in huge trouble. Especially with the guy keeping *the list* nearby. The store Santa stood a few feet away wearing a frown. "You were coming to see me?"

Marcus nodded.

"He pushed me!" Dylan said.

Santa scratched his snowy-white beard, weighing the situation. Annie'd been right about him. He did seem different. More like the genuine article. *If* there was such a thing.

The mom nudged her sons. "Apologize."

"We're sorry!" they told Santa. The mom turned to Annie and Braden, noting their name tags. "And to them."

The children frowned and spoke in unison. "Sor-ry."

Braden set his hands on his duty belt and spoke to the curious onlookers who approached. "It's okay, folks. Everything's under control." His commanding manner caused most of them to back off, thankfully. He put in a quick call to the security office to let them know what had happened and request a replacement on the door. Not that they probably hadn't already seen it all on CCTV. He'd have to make a full report on this later.

Santa spoke to the mom, glancing at the boys. "Mind if I have a word?"

She blew out a breath. "Be my guest."

Santa crooked a finger in his white-gloved hand and the boys crept toward him. He motioned the boys closer and bent down to talk with them. They listened wide-eyed, solemnly nodding their heads. Whatever he was saying, this Santa was making a *big* impression.

Braden sensed it too. Some sort of odd holiday mojo seeping off this older guy. He experienced a joyful lift in his heart, like everything was merry and bright. Just like it had been when he was a kid, all those years ago when Christmas had felt as cozy as a warm woolen blanket on a cold winter's night. But that was absurd. This Santa was simply an actor. A good one, but still. Nobody was good enough to make Braden believe in fairy tales. Life had dealt him enough hard knocks to keep him fully apprised of reality.

"Remember what I told you," Santa said to the boys as they walked away.

"Yes, Santa!" they answered together.

Santa winked at their mom, his baby-blue eyes twinkling. He really was very jolly—a great fit for the part. "They're good lads at heart."

The mom blew out a breath. "Thanks for being so understanding." She marched the kids out in front of her, and Santa leaned closer, whispering behind the back of his hand.

"Be sure Marcus gets that Robo-bot, and Dylan wants a rocket drone."

"What?" She blinked like she couldn't believe it. "After all—"

Santa chuckled. "They know-ho-ho-ho better now." He nodded in a self-assured way. "It won't happen again."

Braden hoped not. Wow.

The family departed, and Annie turned to Santa. "You were very good with them."

He laid a finger beside his nose and winked. "All in a day's work."

Santa toddled off toward the elevators, and Annie whispered, "Boy, that guy's good. *So* into it."

Braden's heart thumped. *Slow down there, buddy.* But then it thumped again. He cleared his throat, willing himself to dwell on the situation at hand, and not on Annie's incredibly beautiful brown eyes. They were a mixture of caramel and khaki—darker near the center and lighter around the edges of the irises—and unlike any he'd seen. *Captivating*. Braden knew better than to be captivated by a coworker. Although he'd failed majorly at that when they'd first met this morning.

He waded into the fake snow and picked up a train engine that had been thrown off its track when the tree fell over. Its barred wheels churned up and down. He found the switch and turned it off. It would take Annie forever to clean this up alone, and they had extra security staff here today anyway. "You've got an awfully big mess here," he said, handing her the toy engine. "How about I help you pick up?"

She blushed. "Don't you have patrolling or something to do?"

He chuckled at her choice of words. "I'll be all right." He patted the two-way radio on his duty belt. "If anything comes up where someone needs me, they can reach me here."

"Well, um, thanks!" Her eyes met his, and his neck warmed.

He righted the holder for the retractable belt, nodding toward the fallen Christmas tree. "So. Should we stand that up first?"

"Good idea." She crouched down and repositioned the star tree topper, and Braden settled his grasp around the tree's trunk. She held on from the other side, and they pushed the tree into its upright position, steadying it on its weighted base. Several ornaments dropped off, Christmas balls breaking with sharp pings against the wooden platform in the window.

A circular rug lay between the tree section and the fake fireplace, and heavy bolts of glittery fake snow hugged the window's perimeter. With the tree skirt bunched up against the disjointed train track, the space directly under the tree was bare. Except now it was littered with colorful pieces of shattered glass.

Braden read Annie's down look and tried to cheer her up. "Looks like most of this can be salvaged," he said. He straightened some Christmas tree limbs, which were made of bendable metal and plastic. "This tree's still in decent shape." He pointed to the icicle lights dripping from the window. "And those just need to be secured with some nails."

Annie stooped to examine the train cars and the track that was supposed to run around the base of the tree. She set the toy engine down beside them. "You're right. I don't think any of this is broken." She checked the wooden angels, placing them back on the mantel. "These guys either." She'd definitely need a new plate for Santa's cookies. Although those—and the glass of milk—appeared to be fake.

She got down on her knees to plug in the extension cord that ran to the tree, which had gotten jerked from its outlet. Ironically, replacing these lights was now the least of her worries.

Braden frowned. "No good?"

She sat back her haunches. "No good."

"Looks like we'll have to start over."

Annie's forehead wrinkled sweetly under her long mop of curly brown hair. "Looks like." If he could help make things better for her, he was determined to do so. With the two of them working together, they'd get this cleanup finished in no time.

Two hours later, they'd mostly gotten it done. Santa paused on his way out the door as Braden tacked up the icicle lights. "Looking good, you two!" He smiled at Annie. "Just needs a little something." More? They were just about to call it a night.

Santa stroked his snowy-white beard. "I know. How about a touch of tinsel?"

Somehow, Braden could see it. *Tinsel could be nice. Glittery.* Judging by her grin, Annie liked the suggestion too. "Got any of that in back?" he asked her.

"I think I do." She turned away to hide her blush. Maybe it was too much to hope that was about him, but he seemed to have that effect on her. Admittedly, it was mutual. "Thanks for the tip," she said to Santa. "Have a great night!"

"Going to be a busy one." Santa adjusted his tunic beneath his open overcoat. "Always is." Braden glanced at Annie, who held in a giggle.

She peered over her shoulder toward the stockroom. "I'll be right back."

Annie returned with two packages of tinsel, and Braden moved his ladder in front of the tree. She climbed its rungs, daintily laying fine silver strands across the Christmas tree's spindly branches. She was such a natural at this. *Of course. She decorates stuff all the time.* She smiled down at him. "This is looking great!"

Braden held the second package in his hands, draping tinsel over the tree's lower branches. "Yeah, things are really shaping up."

She reached for a top branch and slipped. "Oh!" She grabbed the ladder's handle and Braden gripped her waist, steadying her with his hands. She smelled all perfumy and light, like wildflowers in a springtime meadow.

"You all right there?" His throat went scratchy, and the words came out rough.

She sounded all breathy. "Yeah, thanks."

He realized he'd been holding her for too long, and that she'd already found her footing, even in her towering shoes—probably not the *best* choice for climbing ladders. She wore them nicely though, and her legs were long and trim in those white stretch pants, leading all the way up to her snowman-patterned turtleneck, that cute black vest—and her heart-melting grin. He abruptly let her go. "Careful there."

"Right. Thanks." She tucked a lock of her hair behind one ear and climbed back down the ladder as he struggled to get his bearings. What was he doing? Not thinking of becoming involved with a coworker. No. He was more like...rolling the idea around in his mind. Testing it out. The concept intrigued him, honestly. *Assuming she's single.*

Braden folded the ladder. "I guess that's a wrap." In a way, the display *was* improved by the addition of that tinsel.

She looked around, smiling happily. "Thanks for your help."

"My pleasure." He acknowledged the possibility—no, really, the *likelihood*—of her being in a relationship. She was beautiful and charming. So the chances of her having a boyfriend were fairly high. Still. That didn't mean they couldn't have a friendly cup of coffee together—so he could find out for sure. "Hey, Annie?" He stared out at the blustery evening, deciding to brave it. "Feel like going for a coffee?"

She blinked. "What? Now?"

He raked a hand through his hair. Maybe he'd made a wrong move. "Just a merry Christmas Eve cup? There's a place near the subway." She hesitated, and his pulse pounded. For an instant, he thought she might say yes, but she grimaced apologetically.

"I can't risk missing my train. I mean, if things shut down—"

"Right." He picked up the ladder, hiding his disappointment. "I gotcha."

"And honestly—I've got errands to do."

Great. Now she was making excuses. He'd overstepped his bounds. She probably *was* involved with someone. Either that, or she simply wasn't interested in him, and now he'd made things uncomfortable for her.

"All righty. No worries." He studied her one last time, thinking about that potential boyfriend of hers and what a very lucky guy he was. They probably had holiday plans together, which was cool. Braden had his own plans too. “I hope you have a very happy holiday.” His heart thudded in a dull ache as he strolled away, which was highly unnecessary. They’d only spent a few hours together, and he’d just met her today. He barely knew Annie at all.

It’s not like she’s my destiny.

He was already passing through accessories when he heard her lilting voice call after him. “Merry Christmas!” Somewhere high up in the sky, and far above the store, Braden thought he heard sleigh bells. But no, that couldn’t be. His mind had to be playing tricks on him.

THREE

ANNIE APPROACHED HER BUILDING THROUGH the driving snow, taking care on the slick sidewalk in her snow boots. An older man clambered up the steps. He grasped on to a walker with one hand in front of him and tugged at a large suitcase on the step below. She'd seen him once or twice, she thought. He lived in a bottom unit in her building.

He teetered on a step. Oh no! She hurried toward him. "Sir! Wait!"

His foot slipped, and he jerked his hand toward the railing, letting go of his walker. It clanked against the steps in front of him while his suitcase tumbled backward down the stairs.

Annie set down her grocery bag and raced toward the older man, scooting around the suitcase on the sidewalk. She caught him a split second before he fell.

"Oomph!" He turned in shock. "You saved me." He was tall-ish but slender. His slight body quaked in her grip.

She didn't let go. Not yet. "Are you all right?"

He nodded and picked up his walker. His hand trembled on the handle, and she helped him. "This doesn't look safe."

"I normally do all right, when it's not icy out."

Snow covered his coat and dusted his gray hair.

Annie glanced at the sidewalk. "Let's get you inside, then I'll grab your suitcase."

He was too shaken to argue with her. "Thank you, young lady."

She held him tighter by the elbow, bringing his body in close to hers.

"If you hadn't happened by..." His shuddery breath clouded the air.

But the good thing was she had. She got him to the landing, and he pulled his keys from his coat pocket, but the key stuck in the lock. Annie reached over to help him get it open.

"I keep asking our super to fix this," the man groused.

Annie commiserated. "Yeah, me too."

He scooted ahead of her into the hallway using his walker, and she spun back toward the street. A young guy with a backpack motioned to the tipped-over suitcase and her groceries. "These yours?" A swath of black hair dipped out from under his forest-green stocking cap.

"The groceries, yeah. Suitcase belongs to Mr.—" She glanced at the older man.

"Harrington," he said.

"Mr. Harrington," she told the younger guy, who picked up the suitcase in one hand after nabbing her groceries. He deposited both in the entryway.

The older man thanked him. "First name's Harrington. Last name's Bryte."

"Eric Park." His dark-brown eyes crinkled when he smiled.

"I'm Annie Jones. I live in 3-A." They all exchanged hellos, and Harrington unlocked his apartment door, shoving it open ahead of his walker.

"My flight almost didn't make it in," he said. "Runways closed down at LaGuardia."

Annie smiled at Harrington. "Glad you made it home safely." She helped him indoors, and Eric scooted his suitcase over the threshold.

"Me too!" Harrington turned around on halting footsteps, using his walker for support. "Thank you both for your help. Merry Christmas, all."

"Merry Christmas," Eric said, and so did Annie.

She climbed the stairs to her apartment, her thoughts racing. That could have been *such* a bad scene. She shuddered, envisioning coming home to Harrington lying on the sidewalk, maybe even unconscious. She was grateful that hadn't happened, and that she'd arrived when she had.

So, see! The day hadn't been a total bust. She'd been able to help in some small way, and helping had felt good. So had spending time with Braden, honestly, and allowing him to help her. There'd been something awkwardly sweet in their goodbye, or maybe she'd imagined that telling sparkle in his eyes. Part of her wanted to hope Braden was interested in her. He *had* suggested getting coffee, after all.

But another part of her said, *Take it easy, Annie. He was only being nice.* What kind of a chance would she stand with a guy like him anyway? He seemed so great and really kind. Plus he was sexy looking. It wouldn't take much for another woman to snag him away from mundane her, especially if the lady in question was more outgoing and glamorous than she was. That included most of the females in New York City.

She entered her apartment, and Leo blinked at her from his sentinel-like post in the foyer.

"Hi, Leo."

The big cat sat up straighter, exposing his fluffy white chest. He had large gray splotches on his back, and his gray eyes matched his tail and cute kitty ears. But wait, a small white remnant of some sort hung from his mouth. "*What* have you been up to?" She stooped down to tug free the tiny piece of paper dangling from his tooth, rubbing it between her thumb and forefinger. Toilet paper. "Oh, Leo, not again!"

Annie huffed and carried her grocery bag into the bathroom with Leo close on her heels. Shredded toilet paper was everywhere. He'd completely unwound the roll! "Lucky for you I bought some more," she scolded the kitty.

He slunk back behind the doorframe, aware that she was cross with him. But she wasn't really that mad. More like annoyed. She'd just bought him loads of kitty treats at the discount store, figuring she'd fill his stocking. "Maybe you should be getting coal and switches, instead?" she teased, thinking of her playful conversation with Braden. She knew her cat had only misbehaved because he'd been lonely. Leo wasn't normally that destructive. He never clawed at things besides his scratchy box—thank goodness—and, well, obviously, toilet paper rolls.

"Come on." Annie waved him along beside her into the

kitchen. "Let's feed you." He mewed, seeming happy about that. He really was precious—when he wanted to be. She set her grocery bag on the counter and glanced down at him. "Spoiled kitty." He'd get spoiled a little more tomorrow. He'd have her around all day.

She fed Leo his dinner and removed her damp coat, draping it over a kitchen chair. She laid her scarf, hat, and mittens across the radiator to dry and started putting her groceries away.

"Guess who's coming tonight?" she asked Leo.

The cat looked up, licking his chops.

She giggled at his cuteness. "Santa! That's who!"

She dug into her grocery bag, extracting a box of candy canes and setting it on the counter. They'd caught her eye at the store, and although she hadn't bought any in years, she'd decided this Christmas Eve *owed her*. She'd also bought a frozen turkey dinner for her Christmas meal tomorrow and a few other essentials, in case she got snowed in for a while.

Annie opened the box of candy canes and carried it to the small table in the living room, plugging in the lights on her miniature Christmas tree. She set down her candy cane box to admire the snow globe that sat beneath her tree. Though she didn't decorate her apartment much, she got this special memento out every year. She picked up the snow globe and shook it. Tiny snowflakes skittered everywhere, dancing and twirling around Santa's sleigh and his reindeer team, and showering over the candy-cane-striped North Pole. Annie sighed at the sign in the snowy white yard: *Believe*.

Yeah, she'd done that more than once, but her belief had been shattered to bits like those Christmas tree balls crashing to the floor at Lawson's. A distant memory swirled around her, coming into focus.

Annie's mom pulled a wrapped candy cane off the tree. It was eleven days after Christmas, and they still hadn't taken down their holiday decorations. Her mom loved this time of year and always dragged her heels when it came to putting things away.

"This is for Annie's cocoa later." She handed the wrapped candy cane to their teenage sitter, Debbie, and her short brown curls bounced. Annie'd gotten her mom's hair, but not her dimples. "Would you like one too?"

Debbie shrugged breezily. "Sure." Debbie was so cool. Annie wanted to be her one day. The ponytailed teenager took the candy canes from Annie's mom and smiled at Annie. "Ooh, chocolate and mint. That sounds delicious. Maybe we can have some while we play cards?" Annie loved playing cards with Debbie. She looked up to the older girl, who was a neighbor in their modest, middle-class neighborhood. Debbie was smart and going to college, Annie's parents said.

Annie bounced on her heels. "Can we play rummy?"

Debbie shot her a thumbs up. "You got it."

Annie's mom gathered her purse and car keys off the table by the front door. She was all bundled up in her fancy church coat and had makeup on. Annie's dad looked nice too. Aunt Susan and Uncle Bob stood with them, ready for their outing in the city. The four of them were headed to Manhattan for a Broadway show. The tickets were an early birthday gift from Annie's mom to her sister, Susan.

"Why don't you let me drive?" her dad offered.

"Thanks, Cash." Annie's mom shook her head. "Tonight's my treat. I don't mind it."

"But it's snowing, Nancy."

"I'm good with the snow," Uncle Bob intervened. "We can take my SUV."

"It's not that big a snow." Aunt Susan laughed. "Only flurries." A mild discussion broke out among the adults, and Annie thought of the flurries in her special snow globe. She tugged on Debbie's sweatshirt sleeve. "Want to see what I got for Christmas? It's something really cool."

"Sure." Debbie held out her hand so Annie could lead her, and Annie excitedly tugged her back to her bedroom. She carefully lifted her snow globe off her dresser by her mirror and shook it, handing it to Debbie. "See?"

Debbie acted suitably impressed. "How awesome is that? It's Santa and his reindeer! All eight of them. And whoa, the North Pole looks like a real candy cane." She looked up. "Who knew?"

Annie giggled, so happy to have Debbie over. She didn't have any brothers or sisters, and she sometimes wished for an older sister like her.

"Annie! We're leaving!" her dad said. He poked his head into her bedroom. "Oh, there you are."

Her mom appeared behind him and smiled. "You two have fun."

"You too," Debbie said. "Drive safe!"

"We'll text when we're on our way home," her mom said. She winked at Annie. "Behave."

"I think the word is 'Believe,' Nancy," her dad teased, retreating into the hall. "Our Annie always behaves."

Debbie's eyes lit on the painting hanging on Annie's bedroom wall. "Way cool." She stared at the snow globe, returning it to Annie. "Did your dad do that?"

"Yeah." She heard their footsteps fading, and panic gripped her. "Wait!" she cried, shoving her snow globe back at Debbie. Debbie caught it, holding it tightly, and Annie raced into the hall. She stopped her parents in the foyer, staring up at them with sad eyes. "You didn't say good night." Her aunt and uncle were already outside, warming up their SUV.

"Oh, honey. We're sorry." Her mom stooped down to hug her. She smelled of flowery perfume, so pretty. "Good night, baby." She kissed Annie's cheek and held her back by her shoulders, smiling tenderly. "I love you."

Her dad kissed the top of her head. "I love you too."

A shock of blue awoke Annie from her slumber hours later. The lights were going around and around, blindingly bright in her dresser mirror, and casting an eerie sheen across her snow globe. Annie jumped out of bed and ran to her bedroom window, her heart pounding. She peered through the falling snow, and her heart lodged in her throat. A police car sat in her driveway.

Annie opened her bedroom door and Debbie stood in the foyer, white like she'd seen a ghost. Tears streamed down her face, and she scrubbed them back with her fists. A woman police officer glanced at Annie, and Debbie nodded. "Yeah," she said, blubbering out the words, "that's her."

Tears slid down the dome of Annie's snow globe, leaving glistening trails. Leo stared up at her with concerned eyes like, *What's the matter, Mama?* Annie dried her snow globe with her shirt sleeve and set it down, wiping back her tears. "Hi, big boy." She picked up Leo, holding him close. "It's just you and me this year." *And we're going to make the most of it.*

She glanced at her laptop on the coffee table, knowing what would brighten her mood. She'd stream a holiday rom-com and savor a cup of hot cocoa. Maybe it wouldn't taste as good as she remembered, but she craved it, nonetheless. She hugged Leo tighter, and he dissolved into a purring puddle of love. *No one's taking you away,* she said in her heart. *They'll have to fight me first.*

A few hours later, Annie snuggled down in her pj's with her laptop, and Leo nestled beside her. Winds howled outdoors, creating loud echoes in the light well, and snow blasted against the living room windowpanes, but at least she and Leo were inside and dry. They were blessed to have heat and electricity too, and hopefully those would hold.

The closing credits rolled on her movie, and someone knocked at her door. *Unusual at this time of night. Has to be someone in the building.* She set her cocoa mug on an end table and the partially melted candy cane slid sideways. "Stay right here," she warned her kitty. Leo lazily lifted his head, clearly not interested in leaving his nest in the soft sofa blankets.

Annie peered through the peephole in her door. The lady who lived across the hall stood there dressed in a long purple bathrobe. An array of metal clips pressed down her auburn locks, holding them in place. Annie had only seen her in passing a couple of times. She opened the door partway. "Yes?"

"Sorry to bother you," the woman said, noticing Annie's flannel pajamas. They were blue and covered with playful kitten pairs chasing skeins of yarn and tumbling over one another. "But—with the weather getting worse—I'm not sure I'll be able to get out to the store, and it's probably closed by now anyway."

Annie opened the door farther, and the woman held up a clear glass measuring cup. "Would you happen to have a cup of sugar I can borrow?" Creases formed around her mouth and eyes. "I'm making a sweet potato casserole, and I hadn't realized I'd run so low."

"Of course," Annie said. The woman passed her the measuring cup, and she took it, having the instinct she should invite her neighbor in, but the woman didn't budge, standing firmly planted in the hall. "I'll just be a second."

The woman nodded. "I'll wait right here."

Annie returned a few moments later with a full cup of sugar. "Are you sure this will be enough?"

"Oh yes, fine. Thanks so much." She bowed, and her bathrobe's tattered hem scraped the floor. "Merry Christmas."

"Merry Christmas," Annie said, shutting the door.

FOUR

On the second Christmas Eve

FA-LA-LA-LA-LA. LA-LA. LA—LA!

Annie rolled over and groaned, silencing her cell phone on her nightstand. She'd downloaded a ringtone for "Deck the Halls" to serve as her alarm. But she wouldn't be decking any place further today. She was exhausted from Christmas Eve, and now it was Christmas! Yay! A full day off! She yawned, staring down at her phone.

Wait.

Dec 24

Winter Storm Warning

She sat bolt upright in bed and peered around her room, shifting Leo on the covers. He blinked and started purring. She patted his head and closed her eyes. She must have read the date wrong. Of course there was a winter storm warning. The storm that started yesterday was predicted to rage all day today. Annie took a deep breath and opened her eyes.

There! Better!

Ahhhhh!

She threw back the blanket, and Leo tumbled onto the floor, landing on his feet. Still looking a little stunned though. "It is *not* December 24," she told him firmly. Ugh. Her phone was messing up. *Merry Christmas to me. Now I'll need a new phone.*

She grumbled and got out of bed. "Great way to start—ow!"

She hopped on one foot and sat back down. She'd stepped on one of Leo's toys, a wand handle attached to a feather, and the tip of the handle had pricked her instep. She scrunched up her lips at the cat. "Merry Christmas to you too, boy." She'd filled his stocking with goodies last night. She should probably pick up some of his many other toys before saddling him with more.

But first! Coffee! She strolled to the kitchen window and opened the blinds, expecting a blanket of white. She'd gone to bed amid howling winds and driving snow. There had to be nearly two feet by—*Noooo!* Sparkly stars danced before her eyes, and she went hot all over. *This can't be. No way.* The sidewalk out front was clear—and the sky cloudy and gray? *What?*

She dashed to the table and checked her computer.

Dec 24 7:08 AM

She sprang back against a chair, nearly knocking it over. Maybe her phone *was* messing up, *and* her computer too? Those things happened, right? Doubt clawed at her gut. Those were very coincidental technology glitches.

Okay, Annie. Think, think, think.

I'm dreaming! Yes.

Right. Makes sense.

She eyed her pour-over coffee setup, which included a ceramic cone seated on top of her favorite Christmas mug, and walked to the counter in a daze, switching on her electric kettle. She loaded the filter in the cone with a hearty scoop of espresso grounds, and the water would take less than two minutes to heat.

Annie reached into her refrigerator for the milk. Weird. The carton felt light. She peeked back in the refrigerator, but it was almost bare. Some jam, a half stick of butter, a yogurt, and a few apples. So, what? She *hadn't* been to the store?

She latched on to the freezer door handle and yanked it open, searching for her frozen turkey dinner, but—nope. Nothing was in there but two paltry plastic ice cube trays, and those were cracked at the corners. Her breath quickened, and her temples throbbed. *Okay, Annie, calm down. You know this isn't happening.* She was dreaming, right?

She shut the freezer door, and a lump formed in her throat. A refrigerator magnet held a photo of her laughing with Tina. Tina's reddish hair and freckled face lit up the shot as they rode on the Coney Island Ferris wheel. Puffy white clouds hovered above them, with a bit of the beach and the ocean visible below. They'd been tighter than tight back then. That blue-sky day at Coney Island had been blustery and bright, mid-April with cherry blossoms blooming in the city.

Tina stood beside the large glass case holding the fake genie Zoltar with his golden-turbaned head and pointy dark beard. She'd just paid for Annie's fortune.

"Go on," she said when Annie pulled the thin paper card from the machine. "What does it say?"

Annie laughed and flipped over the rectangular yellow card proclaiming "Zoltar Speaks." His seemingly pencil-drawn genie face sat inside a Zodiac wheel. The short paragraph on the other side warned Annie against false flatterers but promised happiness in store. She relayed the upbeat closing line, "You will scale new heights."

Tina glanced at the Wonder Wheel and grinned. "Today's the day."

"Oh no!" Annie held up her hands. "Not getting me up on that thing." She'd never liked amusement park rides, or anything that made her feel out of control. She'd endured enough jolts of the unexpected in her short life.

"Come on, Annie." Tina coaxed with her winning smile. "Be brave!"

Annie backed away, but Tina latched on to her arm. "But, Tina," Annie wailed, though she was giggling. "You know I'm afraid of heights."

"The best way to fight your fears is to face them," Tina said, dragging her along.

"I faced down a Nathan's hot dog earlier, and that just might come back up if you don't watch it."

"Ha-ha," Tina retorted, undeterred.

Annie reluctantly let Tina pull her into the short line. They'd come here on a workday to avoid the crowds. Tina had gotten a better editorial position at a different publishing house, along with a boost in pay. She'd taken a week off between jobs, and Annie had taken the day off to help her celebrate.

They settled into a car, and the attendant shut the gate in front of them with a clank. Annie's stomach lurched, and she gripped Tina's arm.

"It will be okay," Tina said. She settled back in her seat and wrapped an arm around Annie's shoulders, hugging her tightly. "Just wait until you see the view at the top."

"I'm going to close my eyes."

Tina laughed. "No you won't, and I'm going to take a selfie."

That had been one of the best days of Annie's life.

Annie poured the steaming-hot water over the espresso grounds by making circular motions with the hand holding the kettle, desperately missing her best friend. If Tina were here, Annie knew just what she'd say: *Go back to bed, Annie!* Wait. Her hand froze, and she tipped up the kettle. Hadn't she wished—? *No, no, no, no, no, no!*

She added milk to her coffee, and it dribbled down to its very last drop. Annie stared at the empty milk carton and shook it. *Hang on. There's no cocoa mug in the sink either.* Maybe she *hadn't even made* cocoa last night, since she hadn't had the—she gulped—milk?

Don't panic. She wiped her hot forehead with her pajama sleeve and took a quick sip of coffee, and another. Caffeine always brought clarity. *I can't wait.* She took one more long drink from her mug and set it down on the counter, her hand trembling.

"I did have Christmas Eve, I *did*," she told the ceiling, rolling her eyes. She was making too much of this. Seriously. Everything was cool. Everything was fine. She'd also filled Leo's Christmas stocking! She specifically recalled saying to Leo, "Guess who's coming tonight?" right before she put candy canes on the— Annie dashed into the living room with Leo following behind her, and her heart slammed against her chest. His kitty stocking looked *empty*, and there wasn't a single candy cane on the tree. *Ooh. What's happening?*

Maybe some sort of fugue state?

Right! She'd snap out of it soon enough.

She chuckled at her silly nerves, and she had absolutely nothing to be nervous about. She'd had a difficult day yesterday, but it was over. Maybe she should have gone for coffee with Braden, after all? But this wasn't the season for second-guessing. Christmas was the time for being merry and bright! She shut her eyes, thinking Zen thoughts. She was good. No, great! She had her job. She loved it—*and wanted to keep it*. She had her apartment, which was—she opened her eyes and glanced around—*okay*. She had Leo. *Aww. He's the sweetest*. She wanted to keep him too, except he nearly tripped her on her way to the kitchen by snaking his way around her ankles. *Hungry boy*.

Leo meowed loudly as she opened his canned food and she wrinkled up her nose at the fishy smell, but he purred to beat the band. "You're welcome," she said, setting down his metal bowl. He lunged forward and—*nooo*—the bowl slipped from her hand, landing on the floor with a *plop* and a *ting*.

Again? Annie's pulse skittered. Just like yesterday. Wait.

Her intercom buzzed by the front door, and she froze.

Not that too?

Annie held up a finger for Leo to wait and pressed the intercom button. "Yes?"

"Package for you!" a gruff voice said. "Lock's sticking! Can't get in."

She punched the intercom button and answered, "Be right down!" She winced at the cat food mess in the kitchen. Leo was trying to nose his way under the bowl, scooting it along and smearing stinky cat food across the linoleum. *As soon as I clean up here.*

"Come on, big boy," she said, lifting the cat.

Oof. So heavy.

She shut him in the bedroom and walked back to the kitchen. This was *way too familiar*. These things had all happened before. The weather alert on her phone. The spilled cat food. The package delivery. *No. Impossible, right?*

She laughed to herself and stared up at the walls' higher sections. Also at her small kitchen bookcase, which contained the cookbooks she'd inherited from her mom, and which she'd mostly kept for sentimental reasons. She strolled casually into the living room and lifted a cushion off the sofa and then another. She didn't know what she was looking for. Hidden cameras? Hidden by whom? She was a nobody. So nobody would prank her.

Okay, she was being absurd. But—if it *was* December 24—she'd have to go in to work. Hopefully not to face *that* day again. She returned to the kitchen and cleaned up the cat food mess before letting Leo out of the bedroom and squirming into her snow boots. She shrugged into her coat over her pj's and traipsed down the stairs from the third floor, arriving in the foyer with its line of six brass mailboxes.

If this was the same package for the woman in Apartment 2-A, she was going to lose it. She balled her hands into fists. No, she wouldn't. There was a logical explanation for everything, including this. She needed to focus on the positives here and stop spinning off in so many nail-biting directions. If she was dreaming, at least she was lucid dreaming, so completely aware of how outlandish this was. That also meant she'd wake up soon. She hoped.

Annie pressed open the building's front door, battling against the winds. Icy gusts whooshed through her, chilling her to the bone. Her skin stung from the cold, and her eyes teared up. She hugged her arms around her heavy peacoat's sleeves and stared up and down her tree-lined street. Large mounds of snow sat curbside, darkened from vehicle exhaust and grime. Some snow still clung to rooftops or stayed wedged into gutters. But, for the most part, the earlier blast of winter weather had cleared, and now New York City was expecting another big storm tonight. No, wait. That was yesterday. She was *so* confused.

An oblong package sat on the stoop, and she bent to retrieve it.

Whomp!

Something hard hit her from above, and icy streams raced down her neck under her coat collar. She pushed the snow dump off her head and scowled, shaking out her hair. "Seriously? Again?" She trudged back inside with the package, which was—yep—for Jane Sanchez, Apartment 2-A. This was great, really great. She *was* dreaming. *Lucid, or not.* Had to be. She pinched her wrist to check. *Ouch, that hurt! Okay, not doing that again.* Still. Something super weird was going on. Annie stared around the foyer, and winds wailed against the building. *Deep breaths. All I have to do is drop off this package and crawl back under the covers.* Then, she could wake up for real and start this day right!

She reached Apartment 2-A, and the door popped open. *Ahh, this part is new.* The woman looked roughly Annie's age. She had amber eyes, wore her charcoal-colored hair in a top-knot, and had on a medium-blue uniform of some kind. "Can I help you?" *I definitely didn't meet her yesterday.* Could you dream-invent people? Annie didn't think so. But maybe? That meant—*nooo*—that department-store Santa—and Braden—were figments of her imagination? She held out the package. "This came for you," she said, "but the delivery guy buzzed me by mistake."

The woman eyed Annie's pajama bottoms tucked into her boots. "I'm sorry he woke you."

"Oh no! I was up." In a manner of speaking. She was still technically sleeping, probably, but no need to overshare.

The woman accepted the package and studied the return label. "*Yes.* I've been waiting for this."

Annie nodded, preparing to go and dive back into bed, but the woman kept talking. "My little girl," she whispered. "Caridad. She wants this for Christmas." She frowned. "Well, not *this* this. The real Amazing Agatha."

"Amazing Agatha?" she couldn't help but ask.

"The doll." The woman stepped into the hall, keeping her voice down. "Ridiculously expensive because of all the accessories. She has a cell phone, computer, home office."

"What?"

The woman nodded. "The little printer even prints!"

"Prints what?"

"Clues. Agatha is a real estate agent who solves mysteries in her spare time. Mystery of the Missing Cat. Mystery in the Mint Garden. Et cetera."

Whoa. She'd never had anything that fancy as a kid. "So this is a fashion doll?" Annie asked, completely sucked in. Merchandising these days was over the top. Still, it kept her employed. So. She wanted to stay that way too.

The woman nodded. "Fashion plus function. Fully accessorized."

Annie thought other dolls set high-bar expectations. "Okay."

"I've told Cari real life's not like that. No one has everything, *and* is beautiful, and has a detective boyfriend named Dean."

Annie chuckled.

"But she doesn't care. And what can I say?" The woman shrugged. "She's eight. So, if she wants to have her dreams..." She snapped herself back to attention. "Why not?"

"Yeah," Annie said, thinking of Braden. Her dream guy. Literally a dream. *Yesterday did not happen, Annie. Okay? I knew he was too good to be true.*

"Look at me! Holding you up." She backed into her apartment. "I'm sorry." She lifted the box. "And thanks for this. Thanks a lot."

Annie turned around before the woman shut the door. "So. Today is?" she asked, just to be sure. It never hurt to check.

The woman smiled. "Oh yeah! Merry Christmas Eve."

Yikes. Annie's pulse raced.

"I'm Jane, by the way," the woman said with a smile.

"Annie," she whimpered before hurrying upstairs. How was this happening? *How? How? How?* Didn't matter. Seemed it just was. A Christmas Eve do-over? No. It was more likely that yesterday had never happened, and *that* had been the dream. Sure! That's all this was. She'd had some sort of freaky dreamlike premonition about a horrible day. But what about that package? And the spilled cat food? Leo's empty Christmas stocking? No. She had to stop cycling this around in her brain or she'd drive herself nuts.

Maybe if she dressed and went in to work like everything was normal, it would be? She'd take a stab at it anyway. The moment she got to Lawson's, things would be better. She hoped. If it really *was* Christmas Eve, maybe her job wasn't actually in jeopardy—and the disaster with her window display hadn't happened. She might even be able to prevent it. Yes!

Annie reached into her closet for a fresh outfit, but her snowman-patterned turtleneck, black vest, and white slacks hung neatly from their hangers. She could have sworn she'd tossed them in her hamper yesterday, but no.

She exhaled slowly.

Christmas Eve! Okay, good. I'm on it.

She dressed and gathered her work bag off the sofa, stuffing her high-heeled shoes, lunch, and purse inside the tote, but where was her name tag? She strode back into the bedroom, so sure she'd left it on her desk.

A kitty tail twitched beneath her bed. "*Leo*," she said. "You didn't?" She got down on her hands and knees, peering under the box spring. Leo crouched by the wall, his two front paws pressing her name tag to the floor. He goggled at her with guileless cat eyes, but she wasn't fooled one bit. "At it again, huh?" Somehow, he'd pieced this together. Most times, when she ran out for errands, she returned quickly. When she put on that name tag, though, she was gone for at least ten hours.

She lowered herself further to the ground and dropped her right shoulder, extending her right arm under the bed and stretching out her fingers. Leo snapped up the name tag in his teeth and scooted out on the other side. "Leo! No!" He darted around the bed and shot out the door before she could get to her feet. Annie stood up, grumbling, and tugged at her rumpled vest. She smoothed out its wrinkles and traipsed into the hallway. "Oh, Leo!" she said in singsong tones. "Santa's watching!"

He peeked his head around the corner from the kitchen, and Annie set her hands on her hips. "You know I have to go in to work. It's how we pay our bills." Leo backed away and watched her as she came into the kitchen, hunting around. *Where, where, where?*

Ah, there! Underneath the radiator. Annie knelt and grabbed her name tag, attaching it to her vest above her holly wreath pin.

Leo pranced over to her and meowed.

"All right"—she scooped him into her arms—"one last hug, but *promise* you'll be good"—she held him closer—"for the whole rest of the day."

He blinked as if to say, *Of course.*

She carried him into the hallway and closed the bathroom door, putting him down. "Behave."

Twenty minutes later, she dashed down the concrete steps to the subway in her coat and snow boots. She had to catch that train. Had, had, had to. No! It was loading. She raced for the platform as people squished themselves inside, drawing in their bags and elbows. The train's doors closed. *Argh.* She wasn't going to make it. *Again?* This day was feeling very déjà vu–like in the worst possible way. But she was just having a moment. It would pass.

Please let it pass.

Please, please, please.

Annie sat down on a bench on the near-empty platform. Another train would be along in ten minutes if she was lucky. She checked her watch. Today was a busy day. Christmas Eve always was. If it *really* was Christmas Eve. Maybe she should ask someone else to be sure? The woman in her building could have been mistaken. A long shot, but still.

"Excuse me?" she asked a teenager walking past her. He pulled one of his earbuds from his ear. "Can you tell me what day it is?"

He squinted at her like she'd lost it. "Uh, Tuesday?"

"No, I mean, the date."

The guy backed away. "December 24."

A man sat down on the bench beside her and shook out his newspaper. The same date was stamped on the front page of the paper. "Okay," she told the teen, who seemed to want to put space between them. "Thank you." *Ooh, her head hurt.*

This was so bizarre, she wished she could share it with someone. Wouldn't Tina get a laugh out of this? Me freakishly dreaming I'd already had the day which I obviously haven't. Tina was so clearheaded, she'd have things analyzed in a flash.

She took out her phone and opened an app. She could text Tina, yeah. But what would she say? Sorry I ghosted you? You were right about Roy, and I was wrong?

Annie's spirit ached as she recalled their last conversation.

"I'm not saying this to hurt you." Tina sat at the bar beside Annie at their favorite after-work drinks spot. They both drank white wine. "I just thought you should know." Tina had said she'd seen Roy at a lunch place looking cozy with another woman, but Annie couldn't believe it. She and Roy spent nearly all their free time together. There was no way he could be involved with someone else.

"No." She shook her head. "That's not Roy."

Tina set down her wineglass. "Not the Roy you think you know, maybe." She leaned closer. "Listen, I know this is hard, but I've been worried about you for a while. There've been other things too."

"Things?" Annie asked, taken aback. "What things?"

Tina lowered her voice. "The way he talks to you sometimes. Like he's in charge of your every little decision. It's not—right."

Annie experienced a niggle of concern, but she dismissed it. Sure, Roy was a little opinionated, but he had his good points, and he'd made her feel so good in the beginning. That would come back, it had to. Of course it would. They were just going through a rough patch.

Annie picked up her drink. "Roy just knows what he likes, that's all."

"What he should like," Tina said, "is the person you already are, not someone he's trying to turn you into—just to please him."

That sliced into her heart like a knife. So out of left field. "I can't believe you said that, Tina. Roy is the man I love, and he loves me." Hurt bubbled up inside her along with a sense of betrayal, but not at Roy—at Tina.

"I love you too"—Tina laid a hand on her arm—"which is why I'm saying, maybe you'd be better off without him." Tina stared at the mirror in front them where shelves held liquor bottles. "I mean, just look at us, Annie." She turned to face her. "We used to be so close, but now we barely see each other anymore."

"That's because you have Lloyd," Annie said defensively.

"No." Tina frowned. "It's because you have Roy."

She'd thought about texting Tina hundreds of times, but the more the weeks flew by, the harder it became to bridge that divide.

A new train's lights appeared in the tunnel, and Annie shot to her feet.

She was *not* missing this one.

FIVE

ANNIE PUSHED THROUGH LAWSON'S EMPLOYEE entrance, unwinding her snow-covered scarf and clocking in on her department store app. The bottom dropped out of her stomach. Dec 24 9:08 a.m. This day was *not happening* again—her pulse pounded—was it? If it was, it seemed to be happening sort of differently. This morning she'd met Jane. Still. Spilling Leo's food and missing her train had gone pretty much the same.

She rounded the diamond jewelry counter, hunting for Santa. Various sales associates strolled toward their stations and arranged merchandise, but Santa was nowhere in sight. Neither was Braden. Maybe this day would cut to the chase with the bad stuff, and she'd head straight into her upsetting meeting with Patrice before having the kids wreck her display?

That was *not* the do-over day she wanted. Why not get all the good parts, instead of the bad? Annie skulked out of the elevator on the third floor, scanning the area for Patrice and hurrying down the corridor to her locker. Maybe their uncomfortable chat wouldn't happen again, and she'd get promoted instead? A girl could dream. No, wait.

"Good morning, Annie."

Annie slammed shut her locker. It was him again. Old Saint Nick. Who seemed to turn up everywhere when you weren't looking. This was for sure the same guy as yesterday with his very real-looking beard. He waved cheerily as he left. "Hope you have a great day!"

She locked her locker, hyperventilating. Had Santa cast some sort of spell over her? No. He was just an old man in a red suit. He didn't have those kinds of powers. She thought of her snow globe and how Santa had seemed to teleport her back to her ninth year. And then, he was gone. Just like that!

"You okay there?" Braden. Looking as devastatingly handsome as yesterday. Her heart thumped happily. *So he is real.*

"Oh yeah, ha-ha. Just having kind of a weird morning, that's all." Super, super weird.

"Sorry about that." He put his jacket his locker and closed it. "Here's hoping for a better day." Wait. He doesn't recall asking me out for coffee yesterday? No. Today. *Ahhh. My head. Head. Head.* Her temples pounded. Maybe that was a *good thing*, as far as Braden went. Because—that way—he didn't remember the lip gloss episode. Or her awkward attempt at flirting. *Saved by the do-over! Yes!* He stared at her curiously. Maybe he *was* remembering too. That would be a breakthrough. And extremely embarrassing. "You're the lady who does the windows, right?"

Okay. Starting fresh. She could do this. "Ah, yep! That's me." *The person you spent two hours helping yesterday, remember?* No. He clearly didn't.

Braden cocked his head. "Nice job with those. Love your theme, 'The Night Before Christmas.'"

"Yeah?"

"Yeah."

She grinned, feeling all fluttery inside. That part was no different. Her intense attraction to Braden. In some ways, it seemed worse. Better. Whatever.

"The Nutcracker one was great too. But honestly?" He rubbed the side of his neck. "'Winter Wonderland' was one of my favorites. Those ice-skating polar bears were really something."

Warmth pooled in her belly at his admiring tone. "Oh. Well. Thanks!" she said, trying not to sound as giddy as she felt. He was *super swoony* with that dimpled chin and those always-sparkling eyes. He was also going to be her knight in shining armor by racing to the rescue later and helping her clean up that mega mess. Unless she could find a way to keep that from happening to begin with, and she was going to try.

Okay. If he asked her to have coffee again, she was one hundred percent going. Assuming he was single. She'd have to devise some nonobvious way to find out. Then, if he didn't ask her, because the day changed up some more or something, she'd ask him! Yeah! Her heart beat double-time. She heard Tina's voice egging her on.

You can do it, Annie. Be brave.

He grinned. "I'm Braden, by the way. I don't believe we've met."

"Annie." That felt so surreal saying it again.

"Annie." He nodded. "Nice meeting you."

"Yeah, uh-huh. You too!"

"So"—he shifted on his feet—"I guess I'll see you around?"

"Hope so!" *Ugh. Again?*

His eyes danced. "Yeah, Annie. Hope so too," he said, walking away.

As much as she believed yesterday had happened, maybe it hadn't? She didn't have one shred of evidence to prove it. Nothing in her apartment had changed, and her morning had gone pretty much the same, with a few minor modifications. Maybe she should check her window display to see if those Christmas tree lights were still on, because she and Braden had *most definitely* replaced them. *Or, um. Hopefully.*

She made her way down to the first floor and approached her Christmassy living room scene at a fast clip. She could see the Christmas tree's lights aglow all the way back from accessories. *Whew!* So, either she and Braden *had* fixed those burnt-out lights, *or* they'd not yet gone out. Maybe they'd never go out, and her display would never be trashed!

That's thinking positive. Yes! I'm in a brand-new day, and yesterday was not a day at all, just some wickedly twisted fantasy-like dream that had somewhat foretold the future! That had to mean she could still get promoted. She'd met Braden now, too, in a somewhat less humiliating fashion. So that boded well. Her whole day was looking up!

She quickened her steps, needing to verify things up close and personal. But, when Annie reached the window, she covered her mouth and gasped. The Christmas tree's colorful lights shone brightly, and silvery strands of tinsel dripped from the tree's many branches. *How* was that possible? She hadn't added any tinsel on the twenty-third. She was sure of it. She'd only done that last night.

All signs kept pointing in the same direction. She peeked at Santa's workshop. *Today is some kind of freaky repeat of yesterday.* Santa saw her goggling at the tree and winked, laying a finger beside his nose like he was about to work some magic.

Or maybe, he already had.

Patrice stopped Annie by the employee lockers. "Do you have a minute?"

Annie's jaw clenched. "For an uh—little chat?" She'd been hoping to avoid this part.

Patrice adjusted her glasses, appearing astonished. "Why, yes." The uncomfortable conversation was no more pleasant the second time around. The fact that Annie knew what was coming only made things harder. She tried to speed things up a bit. Maybe if she ended their talk sooner, she'd be able to prevent those kids from wreaking havoc with her window.

"I understand foot traffic's been down," Annie said, sitting at the table.

Patrice's ankle boot bobbed up and down. "That's right." She peered quizzically at Annie. "It has. Which is why—"

"Don't worry, Patrice," Annie said. "None of this is your fault."

Patrice frowned. "None of what—exactly?"

Annie exhaled sharply. "Lawson's is in financial trouble, right? Aiming to cut back."

"I'd hoped to break it to you gently." Patrice removed her glasses, folding them in her hands. "Annie," she said kindly, "about your window—"

"Old school. Yeah, I know." Annie shook her head. "I'm afraid I disagree." Very strongly, but she didn't need to belabor the point. Patrice was on her side, after all. It was Ms. Lawson who was the problem. "Still!" Annie said brightly, "I intend to work on it." She swung her fist through the air. "Make it—groundbreaking! Fresh!" She was still figuring out how, but Patrice didn't need to know that.

Patrice pursed her lips. "Okay, well. Good. That's great!" She stood, seeming strangely disconnected, like she was trying to make sense of their abbreviated conversation, but Annie didn't have time to explain. She had to get downstairs. Patrice stopped her when she reached the door. "Um, Annie! I meant to tell you—"

"Christmas tree lights, right!"

Patrice's mouth hung open. "But, how did you—?"

"See you later, Patrice! Thanks for the chat!"

Annie hurried to the second-floor stockroom to grab more lights. Though she kept most of her display supplies downstairs, all electronics were up here. She scrambled down the escalator to the ground floor, turning sideways and deftly scooting past customers. "Coming through. I'm sorry!"

She nabbed two king-size bed pillows from the Linen Department next, intending to hold the pillows out as buffers when the boys barreled toward her window. She wasn't very muscley, but she was strong due to all the lifting and physical work she did at Lawson's. She'd catch those rascally boys like two flyballs in gigantic baseball mitts!

"Excuse me." She wound past a couple of women holding large shopping bags, stepping sideways through the crowd.

"Eeep!" She jumped back when a man nearly flattened her leaving the jewelry counter.

"Oh! I—" His face was all flushed. "Sorry about that." She should have seen that coming. Seriously. The snow dump this morning too. She was questioning everything. Including how odd she must look shimmying through the store holding an armful of pillows and a jumbo package of replacement—

"No, Dylan! Let me!" A young boy raced past her, darting through Homewares.

What? Already?

She peered down at her watch—which had stopped. *Arghh.*

Dylan yanked at the other kid's elbow. "No, Marcus! Me first!"

Please, no. Please. Please, please. No.

"Dylan! Marcus!" their mom called, chasing after them.

But, yeah. There they go!

"I want my Robo-bot!" Marcus hollered.

"Santa! Santa!" Dylan cried. "Wait for me!"

Her temples throbbed. *No way.*

Their mom wailed in desperation. "You won't get *anything*, if you don't"—her eyes got huge—"*stop!*" The kids evaded their mom's reach, stumbling toward Annie's display, and the entire sequence unfolded in unbearably slow motion.

Oh nooooo!

Annie and Braden raced toward the tree, but it smacked against the front window, upending its skirt and knocking the train off its track before clobbering the wooden angels on the mantel, and—*ahhh!*—demolishing Santa's cookies and milk. At least Annie had replaced the Spode china plate with a plastic one. Still.

Annie dropped her pillows, and the package of lights collapsed on top of them.

Braden's jaw unhinged. "Oh, wow." He had an astonished look on his face.

Yeah. Annie couldn't believe it either. Lightning didn't strike twice. Not unless you were doubly cursed. This was *not* her lucky day. So, naturally, she had to repeat this one. Why couldn't she have had that brilliant day at Coney Island with Tina? Or one of her early dates with Roy, when he'd been attentive and kind? Or even her ninth-year Christmas? *There are so many other choices, and all of them better than this.*

The kids' mom tugged them to their feet, and Santa came and went. Braden offered to help her pick up, and she embarrassingly answered, "Don't you have patrolling or something to do?" Annie gritted her teeth. *What am I? On auto-repeat?* She should have improved on that line, but she seemed to have trouble improving her lines around Braden. It was like she knew what she was going to say before she said it, but still said it anyway, like rehearsing for a play.

Maybe this *was* all a dream, or maybe she'd dreamt up yesterday? All she knew was she regretted saying no to coffee when Braden asked her, and she wasn't going to make the same mistake twice. Not if she learned he was single. *Hey, if I'm dreaming, this is my dream. I'm owning it.* She did need to find out about the girlfriend though. Because. History.

"What are the pillows for?" Braden asked, eying them curiously.

Nothing she could say would sound right. Would he even

believe her about her repeat day? She half didn't believe it herself. "I—was just on my way to return them." He nodded, seeming to buy that. Customers changed their minds on purchases all the time, sometimes setting items down in completely different areas from where they'd found them.

They righted the Christmas tree, and she plugged in the extension cord for the lights. Even though they'd worked just fine this morning, not a one of them was glowing now. Braden held up the replacement package of Christmas tree lights. "Looks like we'll have to start over."

He grinned, and Annie's pulse fluttered. While she normally wasn't comfortable around strangers, it wasn't like they were *total strangers* anymore. Not in her mind anyway.

Annie glanced at the littered floor. "We should probably sweep up first."

Braden held down the dustpan, and Annie swept the glass shards from the broken Christmas tree balls into it. "You're really good to help me do this," she said. There was a calm steadiness about him, something so solid and good. Not that he'd be interested in her romantically, and she wasn't exactly angling for a romance either. *Fine. All right.* Maybe a romance with Braden *had* entered her mind once or twice last night when she'd been watching her movie. Okay, possibly three times. No, four. It was a rom-com! Who was counting? Oh yeah, she was. And dreaming about his swoony dimpled chin and bright-blue eyes. She quickly switched her attention to her broom, gripping its handle.

He stood and dumped the refuse into a waste can. "Glad to."

"Are you new here?" she asked as she began sweeping up again.

He walked back over to her, crouching down and holding the dustpan. "New? No. Why?"

She shrugged and kept sweeping, pushing the debris toward the dustpan. "I don't remember seeing you around before today."

"That's because I generally work nights," he said matter-of-factly. "I've spotted you a time or two."

"Oh?"

He grinned up at her. "Working on your windows with a shorter woman and older guy."

She nodded. "They would be Kira and Julio."

"Haven't seen Julio in a while."

"No, he took a job in Chicago."

"The windy city!" he said.

Annie laughed. "Bet they're getting snow there too."

"Snow's not such a bad thing"—his eyes sparkled—"when you're inside and warm."

"Or, outside playing in the snow," she countered.

He dumped some more of his trash as she kept sweeping. "You like playing in the snow?"

"I've been known to hold my own in a snowball fight," she said, enjoying their banter. How long had it been since she'd felt carefree, like a kid again? Too long. Forever.

"Good to know," he said, crouching again with the dustpan. His muscles tensed beneath his work slacks and shirt, outlining his well-built frame. She could see him in the snow all right. Only, in her fantasy world, they weren't snowball-fighting. He took her in his arms and held her close, snowflakes swirling around them.

Her broom bristles caught in some of the fake snow lining the side of the window. "Oh!"

Braden squatted lower to untangle them, and she simultaneously bent down, jamming her hand into the blob of fake snow. Their fingers brushed and, suddenly, they were almost nose to nose, his flickering blue eyes peering into hers. His neck turned red. But his mouth looked the hottest of all. *He could probably work some real holiday magic with those lips.* Annie fell forward, clutching the broom handle, as his mouth drew nearer. *Lemon and spice and everything nice—and ooh, she wanted to taste him to tell for sure.*

SIX

"WHAT HAPPENED HERE?"

Annie jumped up so fast, she nearly fell over, stabilizing herself on the broom. Ms. Lawson! Yikes! *Okay, this dream is now officially a nightmare. What* had she been thinking? Not about kissing Braden—right here, in the store, in her front window. *Gah.*

Ms. Lawson surveyed Annie warily like she was wondering about that too. The attractive blond wore a green felt hat with a big black feather on it. She looked like a fashion model in a fitted emerald-colored dress with a wide belt, and high-heeled black boots. She held an animal-print coat in one arm and stood ramrod straight in a position of authority, though she couldn't have been much older than Braden.

He straightened his knees, springing to attention too. A tiny whisp of fake snow dangled from his watch. "We, uh. Had a minor customer incident with the window, ma'am." He raked a hand through his hair, appearing as flustered as Annie felt.

"Goodness!" Ms. Lawson cried. "Looks like a major catastrophe to me." She tamped down her hat, casting a glance at Annie. "No one was hurt. I hope?"

"No," she said, but her voice squeaked. *Why, oh why* was

Ms. Lawson here *now*? She almost never came into the store. "We're making it better too!" Annie promised her. "Working on improvements."

"Improvements, that so?" Ms. Lawson grimaced at the totaled display as if she were trying to imagine—unsuccessfully.

"Things will be better than new by the time Lawson's reopens after Christmas," Annie assured her. "You might even say—groundbreaking! Fresh!"

Ms. Lawson read her name tag. "You're—?"

"Annie Jones, Assistant Visual Artist."

"Ah yes." Her light eyes glinted dimly. "Now I remember."

Braden shook her hand. "Braden Tate. Nice meeting you, Ms. Lawson." He noticed the fake snow stuck to his watch band and plucked it off, dropping it in the waste can.

Ms. Lawson smiled, and the tense vibe eased. "Veronica." She cocked her head at Braden and Annie. "Both of you, please."

"All right," Annie smiled. Good to be on a first-name basis. Maybe that would help? Although the state of her window was not winning bonus points from anyone.

Veronica studied the window one last time. "Well!" she threw up her hands. "I can't wait to see what you do with it."

No kidding. Me either.

Veronica walked away, and Annie moaned under her breath, "Today of all days."

Braden noticed Annie watching Veronica ride the escalator to the second floor. "I'm sure she doesn't blame you."

"Maybe not for this." She swept her hand over the mess. "But for how things looked before?" She shrugged. "I'm afraid so."

"Hang on. Are you saying she's not pleased with your display?" He sounded dumbfounded, and Annie was heartened by his support.

She took the lone Christmas stocking that had stuck to the side of the tree and hung it back on the mantel. "She thinks they're 'old school.'"

He held open his hands. "Well, old school can mean classic, can't it?"

"Thanks, Braden." He was such a nice guy. How come she hadn't met him before? Oh yeah, she had. Yesterday. But today could still be salvaged, depending on whether or not Braden was dating anyone, and also—on her degree of nerve.

Later that evening, Santa paused on his way out the door. "Looking good, you two!" He smiled at Annie as Braden tacked up the icicle lights. "Just needs a little something."

What? Annie shot him a cheery grin. "We added tinsel!"

"Delightful, yes." Santa nodded. "I know." He held up a gloved finger. "More snow."

"Snow?"

Santa gripped his big belly. "Ho ho ho, fake snow! The window could use a touch more."

More snow could be nice. Sparkly.

Braden seemed to like the suggestion too. "Got any of that in back?"

"Sure do." Annie led Braden to the first-floor stockroom. She reached for a box of fake snow, but it was up too high.

"I think I can get it." Braden extended his arm, tapping at the corner of the box with his hand. It moved slightly, then a bit more. *Whoa!* Suddenly it came crashing down on top of them. The two of them caught it together, and Braden's fingers laced over hers.

"Oh!" She bit her lip when his eyes twinkled.

"Close save," he rasped, and tiny tingles shot up her arm before spreading out all over.

"Good thing this box is light," she joked.

"Yeah."

Her heart skipped a beat. "Braden?"

"Hmm?"

Do it. Do it now before you lose your nerve. Braden stared at her with his bright-blue eyes, and her heart beat harder. "Er. About Christmas?" she asked above the drumming noise in her ears.

"Yes?" He looked so adorable, so handsome. He had to have a girlfriend.

Still, she had to ask. "Are you planning to spend it with someone?"

"Are you inviting me somewhere, Annie?"

"Gosh, no." Humiliation swamped through her. "What I mean is—"

He smiled. "I'm spending it with my mom."

"Nice." She tucked a lock of hair behind her ear, acting like she'd not been prying.

He grinned, sensing what she'd been getting at. "Just the two of us. No girlfriend."

"Ha!" She wanted to sink through the floor. "That's not why I asked."

His face said he thought it was though. He took the box from her, and she released it. "What are you doing for Christmas?" he asked as they walked back to the window display.

"Me?" she asked meekly. "Erm, plans."

"Plans?" She couldn't admit she had no friends. *No life.* The truth stung a little, even though she only had herself to blame.

"Yeah," she fibbed. "Loads and loads of 'em."

"Cooking for a crowd, huh?"

"Er." She and Leo didn't exactly qualify. "It will be more intimate."

"Ah. Gotcha." His face fell. "You've got a boyfriend."

"No, I don't!" she said too quickly.

His eyes danced. "Oh great."

"Great?"

"No. Not great. What I mean is"—he blew out a breath—"good to know." They were going for *most awkward conversation of the century*, but she was liking him so much. He was sweet. And kind. And single. *Yes.* As far as she knew. She didn't think he was pulling a Roy, but a woman could never be too sure. *Proceed with caution.*

But, come on, if she was dreaming, maybe she could dream a little more and investigate over coffee by getting to know him? She checked her phone for the time, seeing she had twenty minutes to spare compared to where she'd been at this time yesterday. Their cleanup had seemed to go more quickly, maybe because they'd done it before. Not that she'd anticipated doing this again. She hadn't.

They arrived at the window, and Braden opened the box. "So," he said, digging into it. "Snow?"

Annie grinned. This was great. This was all new and hadn't happened before. This was progress. Her confidence surged. Didn't matter that those kids had trashed her display again, and forget the fact that Veronica Lawson had showed up unexpectedly. She and Braden had fixed the damage, and in record time too. Despite its redux nature, this day was moving forward in ways that were generally positive.

"Snow!" she said, scooping a batch of the fuzzy white fluff into her hands. She added extra snow along the low backdrop dividing the display area from the salesfloor, and he taped some to the front window beneath the icicle lights.

"I like it!" he said. She did too.

Her heart gave a happy leap just as it had during every other interaction they'd had today. She didn't know how it was possible, but he somehow seemed even more appealing than he had previously. She was appreciating more about him too. His easygoing nature. How solid and self-assured he seemed. His smile—that called her to him like a beacon on stormy seas. And oh, how she'd wanted to drown in his kisses, so badly. But yeah, most definitely, the moment had *not* been right.

Still, she didn't *think* she'd imagined his attraction to her. Her heart beat harder. Could be that Braden wasn't after fashion-forward? Maybe snowman-patterned turtlenecks were more his jam? There was only one way to find out, and that was *not* by chickening out again.

"So, Annie," he said, folding up the ladder. "I was wondering—"

"Coffee?" She couldn't miss getting back in time to help Harrington though. "I might have time for a quick cup!"

His grin lit her up from the inside out. "How did you know what I was going to ask?"

SEVEN

BRADEN SAT ACROSS FROM ANNIE at the Blue Dot Diner, very glad she'd accepted his invitation for coffee. He'd gotten them both paper cups of coffee with coffee sleeves and lids, and a couple of donuts from the counter. This place was informal. Self-serve, and you took a seat wherever you wanted. They picked the only empty booth available, one in back with peeling leather benches and a faded Formica tabletop covered with turquoise pebble-like spots.

She accepted her coffee. "Thanks for this. You didn't have to buy."

"My pleasure. You've had quite a day."

He held out the donut bag, but she declined. He'd gotten powdered jelly filled. His favorite. He worked out to be able to eat the way he did. Coming from a big Italian family, group occasions were heavily focused on food.

He took a bite of donut. "These are delicious."

She giggled. "Big on sweets, huh?"

He couldn't lie. "You don't want to see me around my mom's cannoli. That is *heaven.*"

She smiled, not seeming to mind his appetite. "You have family in town?"

"Just my mom." He chewed the tasty morsel, all powdery sugar and sticky raspberry goodness, and wiped his mouth. "My sisters are still in Philly. That's where they grew up."

"They, but not you?" She wore a fun snowman-patterned top under a black vest, and the red-and-green holly wreath pin he noticed earlier. All ready for Christmas and those major plans of hers.

He shook his head. "My sisters are all a lot older. Ten, twelve, thirteen years. I was the caboose."

"Ahh. The baby brother."

He enjoyed the shimmer in her pretty brown eyes. "Yeah."

She spun her cup around in her narrow fingers. They were tapered and delicate seeming, a lot like she was. Though he detected an inner strength. It radiated from a quiet place within her, as if she were a resilient person. Braden recognized that in others, having been through a few things himself.

"So, if not in Philly, where did you grow up?" she asked him.

"For the most part, in Brooklyn." Braden pushed back in the booth, the heels of his hands against the lip of the table. "My stepdad moved us here for work when I was eight." He took a sip of coffee. "What about you? Brothers? Sisters?"

"Nope. Just me," she said. "And Leo."

He smiled at the name. "Let me guess. Your cat?"

She laughed. "Yeah. He's a sweetie. Big boy too, nearly twenty pounds."

"Whoa, that's bobcat size."

"He likes to eat."

Braden chuckled. "A feline after my own heart." He peeked in the donut bag but decided he'd better not overdo it in front of Annie. So he folded the paper bag flap. "Where'd you grow up?" he asked her.

She took a small sip of coffee. "Red Bank, New Jersey."

"Nice place." It was also close to Belford and Atlantic Highlands, two towns Braden had been eying for his big move someday. When he was a bit farther along and thinking about having a family.

Her smile looked a little sad. "It can be." Braden intuited she didn't want to say much about her family, and he understood. Certain family dynamics were complicated, and maybe hers were too. He glanced around the packed café as more folks took cover inside and out of the building storm.

"Well, I'm glad we got it fixed," he said, changing the subject. "Your window display."

"Thanks for all your help with that."

He shrugged. "Didn't mind it. Glad to help."

She set her coffee cup aside. "So. How long have you been at Lawson's?" He guessed she hadn't been paying as much attention to him as he had to her, but that was all right.

"Going on my second year."

She blinked in surprise. "Really? I've been there three. And before Lawson's?"

"U.S. Army," he said.

She sat up a little straighter. "Thanks for your service."

"You're welcome."

"Did you like being in the army?"

"There were good parts to it," he said, "and bad." He frowned, not particularly interested in thinking about those. Not when he had a pretty woman's company. "My good buddy Harper's still in Germany. We're like brothers." Seeing as how he hadn't had any, Harper was as close as he'd come. "You know how it is with good friends," he continued. "They're like family."

Her expression changed, and he wondered what he'd said.

"Harper sounds nice. Where did you meet him?"

"Baghdad. We were in the same platoon."

She read something in his eyes. "Rough tour?"

He shifted in his seat. "A little."

"Sorry," she said, looking like she was. "Maybe I shouldn't have asked that."

He shut his mind off to the shellfire and the bomb blast in his head. He wasn't perfect at blocking things out, but he was getting better at it. One day at a time.

"You got a bestie like Harper?" he asked her. "I mean, someone close?" Her eyes glistened and, for the second time in two minutes, he felt like he'd stepped on a land mine.

"There's Tina. But she and I—" She stopped and caught her breath. "It's just been a minute since I've seen her, that's all."

"So hey, reach out." He shared an encouraging grin. "It's Christmas."

"You know what?" she said. "You're right." She squared her shoulders. "I think I will reach out tomorrow. First thing." She smiled. "Just to say merry Christmas."

"There you go!" He toasted her with his coffee cup. "Here's to Tina and to you—spreading your Christmas cheer."

She tapped her paper cup against his. "Here's to Tina wanting to accept it."

"Aww, come on," he said. "Who wouldn't like hearing from you?"

She rolled her eyes. "Do you want the whole list?"

"Is that a nice list, or a naughty one?"

Annie gasped playfully. "All my friends are nice."

"You've got bunches of 'em, huh?"

She bit her lip. "Er. Some."

"Maybe you'd have more if you weren't so choosy," he teased.

"Choosy? What?"

He leaned toward her. "Why not let some of the naughty ones in?"

"Depends on your definition of naughty."

"That could get subjective," he said, rubbing his chin.

Her whole face went red. "Are we talking about you now?"

He laid a hand on his chest. "What? Nooo. I'm as good as gold, Annie—almost all the time. Although, even when I'm not"—his mouth twitched—"the ladies seem to like that."

She shook her head. "Stop."

"Stop what?"

"Congratulating yourself on your appeal."

His ears perked up. "I've got appeal now, do I?"

She toyed with her hat and mittens on the table. "You've got—something, all right," she smirked lightly. "It's called an ego."

"Ha!" He sat back against the booth and drank from his cup.

"I'm actually pretty modest, if you must know." Which was the truth. He'd only been trying to elicit her pretty smile. She'd seemed so down about her estranged friend Tina.

She laughed, and a new sense of ease settled between them. "I'm sure you are." After a moment, she picked up her coffee and said, "I can't wait for some time off. How about you?"

"I've always liked the holidays. Yourself?"

She shrugged. "I've always liked having a vacation."

She had a sly way of turning a phrase, and he liked her sense of humor.

She checked her phone for the time. "This has been a *really different* day."

"Oh yeah?"

"I guess I've been working too hard." She sighed. "That's what Tina would say."

"Your Tina might have a point." He sipped from his coffee, recalling the long hours she'd pulled. The front window display got changed out every six to eight weeks, except for the fancy Christmas one. That went up in October and lasted through New Year's. He'd seen the team working on salesfloor displays too, in different areas of the store.

"For a moment, I—" She shook her head. "Never mind."

"Go on," he asked, intrigued. "What is it?"

She slid a little lower in her seat. "I almost felt like today was a do-over of sorts."

He nodded. "I've had those rat-on-a-wheel days too. Everything keeps cycling around and around. No matter how hard you work, it's never done. You can't seem to get ahead."

"It's not really that." She hesitated a beat. "It's more like the feeling that I've been here and done this before."

"Déjà vu? Yeah, I get that too. It's kind of eerie when you have those sensations."

"Yeah, but normally it's just about one thing, right? A certain thing you say, maybe a conversation you've had?" She grimaced. "Not like a *whole day*."

"You've felt like that all day today?"

She fidgeted with her holly wreath pin. "I know it sounds a little out there."

"Not to me, it doesn't." He set his hands on the table. "Hey, seriously. It sounds like you need a break. Tomorrow's Christmas. The R&R will do you good. Today was not the most calming Christmas Eve at Lawson's. It was a zoo in there. That's probably where those feelings came from. You were reliving the stress of other days like it. Not the actual events, but the emotions attached to them. That kind of thing has happened to me too."

She smiled softly. "I'm sure you're right. Thanks, Braden. You're very easy to talk to."

He raised his cup. "You too."

She glanced at her phone again. "Oh gosh. I'm sorry." She buttoned up her heavy wool coat. It was navy blue with red piping and big brass buttons that had anchor emblems on them. "I really need to get going." She frowned and added, "I don't want to be late."

Disappointment seeped through him. She was meeting someone, of course she was. She hadn't told him the details about her Christmas plans. It was possible she was meeting friends or might even have a date. Just because she said she didn't have a boyfriend, that didn't mean she wasn't seeing someone casually. And if she was, that was her business and not his.

"Which way you going?" Braden asked as they stepped outdoors. Snow blew across the sidewalk and into the busy street, where vehicles crawled along bumper to bumper, their windshield wipers beating back the snow. It seemed all of New York City was out and about trying to tie up their seasonal shopping. Festive decorations hung from lampposts, and holiday lights brightened the dusky sky.

She named a subway stop, saying she had grocery shopping to do before heading home.

"I'm going in that direction too." His station was the next one up. "Okay if I walk with you?"

Annie nodded and tugged down her red hat. The big pompom on it bounced, making her look the cutest. "Thanks for the coffee. It was a great idea."

"You're welcome. I enjoyed it." He snagged a quick glimpse of Annie, painting such a pretty picture against the mob of unseen faces hustling by. Her snow boots looked old, like she'd had them a while, but they obviously did their job. The thick layer of snow on the sidewalk made it slick, and more kept pouring down by the minute.

They trudged past decorated storefronts, brisk winds circling around them. One place had cell phones wearing Santa hats in its front window. Another displayed mechanical gingerbread people with waving arms. She viewed these appreciatively, maybe getting ideas for future designs of her own. Her cheeks reddened in the cold, the bridge of her nose turning bright pink. His face was chilled too, but he didn't mind the nip in the air or the icy swirl of snowflakes.

"I love this time of year," he said. "Everything just seems—merrier and brighter, hopeful. You know?"

"I like Christmas too," she quipped. "It's when I do my best windows." Her smile seemed a little flirty. Or maybe he was just wishing. He laughed at her self-congratulatory statement, not minding it at all. It was good that she took pride in what she did. He admired that in her.

"That's true. You do." It was too bad Veronica Lawson couldn't appreciate Annie's talent, because he sure did.

She shook her head in wonder. "I still can't believe you remember my polar bears."

"I remember all your window displays, Annie."

She peered at him. "All of them?"

He nodded. "'Autumn in New York'? That was amazing. 'Fun in the Summer Sun' was cool too. Mannequins with surfboards and wearing sunglasses! You trucked in real sand."

"You *have been* paying attention." She playfully shoved his arm, and his face heated.

"It's my job to notice things."

She studied his uniform and grinned. "Yeah. Guess so."

He looked up and down the street at the festive decorations. This time of year always took him back, and the memories were happy ones. "We lived in Brooklyn but came into the city a lot, especially at Christmas, to see all the gorgeous windows. My folks weren't rich by any means, so it was more like window shopping than buying. But it was always so fun. You know what I mean? Like looking into these cool and magical worlds."

Her eyes danced, and he knew he'd struck a chord. A happy one. "I really do. That's why I like designing them so much. Each window is like its own little universe. Special."

"Yeah," he replied. She was awfully special too, and talented. "So, you live where in Brooklyn?" They'd reached the entrance to her subway line.

"Crown Heights."

"Oh yeah. It's nice over there. I know it. My mom lives over that way, not too far from the library."

"Oh yeah? I'm near the museum."

He nodded.

"What about you?" she asked.

He shook the snow from his jacket's sleeves. "Sunset Park."

"That's not too far away." They stood at the top of the concrete steps that led underground.

"No." He smiled. "But a bit of a walk on foot."

"Well, anyway!" She checked her phone. "I'd better go."

"Sure." Snow pounded them harder, coating her long eyelashes, and she brushed them off with her mittens. Man, she was a beautiful woman. He was so tempted to ask her. What? If she'd like to see him again? Sometime after Christmas? But they worked together so, no. She might not like that. Feel like they were crossing a line, although neither of them worked directly with or for the other. So that part was okay. But then, he lost his nerve. "Take care, Annie."

She grinned sweetly. "Hope you have a merry Christmas."

"Yeah, Annie. You too."

She scooted down the stairs, getting swallowed up by throngs of fellow commuters, and his soul gave a funny lurch. *Which makes zero sense.* He'd scarcely gotten to know her.

He heard sleigh bells and squinted up at the sky. Braden shielded his eyes with his hand. *Jingle. Jangle. Jingle.* Wait. That was closer. He scanned the area, spying the bell ringer dressed as Santa on the corner, collecting donations for charity. He blew out a breath. *Of course.*

What had he been thinking? Not about *real* Christmas magic and Santa.

About Annie though? Yeah, maybe somewhat.

Liar.

Fine. Maybe a lot.

EIGHT

ANNIE DROPPED HER GROCERY BAG and raced toward her building. "Harrington!"

The old man startled on the steps, grasping the railing as his walker clanked forward. She reached him in a flash, steadying him in her arms. He glanced over his shoulder.

"Where did you come from?"

"Down there." She gestured toward the street. "Are you all right?"

He nodded, his breath clouding the chilly air. "Will be now." He stooped forward and righted his walker. "Thanks to you."

"I'm Annie," she said, helping him along. "I live upstairs."

"As in, in the Kingdom?"

She laughed, grateful that he could joke. "No. In apartment 3-A."

"Could have fooled me," he said. "I thought you were an angel." Hardly. She'd nearly missed his fall. She thought she'd timed this so well. Next time she'd—

Wait. She experienced a freak-out moment.

There wasn't going to be a next time.

Was there?

"I'll go back and get your suitcase, or—maybe someone will come along," she said, spotting Eric ambling down the sidewalk. He saw her and Harrington on the steps and picked up his pace, jogging toward them.

"Hey!" he called to her, pointing to the suitcase on the sidewalk and her bag of groceries. "Need help with these?"

"Sure! Thanks!"

"Just one question." Harrington scooted in the door and turned to her. "How did you know my name?"

Oh, right. How?

Her pulse pounded.

"You must have mentioned it before."

He dragged a hand across the top of his head, wiping off some snow. "Did I?"

Eric arrived, setting down the suitcase. Annie reached for her shopping bag, and Eric passed it to her.

"Thanks, young man," Harrington said. He nodded at Annie. "Thanks to you both. It was such a bad trip. Dicey with the storm."

"Oh no." Annie worriedly scanned his eyes. "Your plane ride?"

He scratched his head. "And how did you know about that?"

Think fast. "Your suitcase! I just assumed."

"Oh. Yes. Yes." His face creased in a frown. "I was in Florida visiting my brother. He's in a nursing home now, and things don't look good."

Annie's heart ached for him. Losing people you loved was so hard. "I'm sorry."

"Can I do anything?" Eric asked. "Bring your suitcase into your place?"

Harrington viewed him gratefully. "That would be very kind."

"I'm Eric," he said when Harrington opened his door. "Eric Park." He had a backpack on his shoulder, and it was open partway, due to its broken zipper. Paperback books were stuffed inside it. The top one's title was *Leaves of Grass*, Walt Whitman's poetry. Melting snowflakes dampened the volume. Annie and Harrington introduced themselves as she helped Harrington over the threshold. He still seemed a little shaky from his fall.

"You in school here?" she asked Eric.

Eric nodded. "NYU. Master's program in English."

"Nice."

"Yeah." He glanced back toward the street. "Would have been nice to get home for Christmas too."

Annie wrinkled up her nose. "The weather?"

"Cash flow." Eric set his chin, looking down about it. "Or lack thereof."

"Where's home?" Harrington asked him. He nodded toward a door, and Eric took the suitcase into a bedroom.

"Los Angeles," Eric said, returning.

Harrington whistled. "Coast to coast."

"Yes, sir."

Annie glanced around Harrington's sparsely furnished apartment. The kitchen appliances were old, but they looked barely used. "Do you have something to eat tonight?" she asked Harrington. "I'm not sure how much longer the stores will be open."

Harrington turned toward her using his walker. "I've got some canned spaghetti in the cupboard. Soup too."

She nodded, thinking she should do something more, but not knowing what.

Eric shrugged. "Well, I guess I'd better get going. Merry Christmas, everyone."

"Merry Christmas," Harrington said. Annie left the first floor, wishing them both happy holidays. But when their apartment doors shut, lonely echoes filled the hall.

She entered her apartment, and Leo scooted away from the door, scampering back into her bedroom. Odd move. "Leo?" she called, switching on the light. "What are you up to?" She walked forward and her toe smacked a roll of toilet paper. Ugh. A toilet paper trail ran across the length of the living room. Annie set down her grocery bag and picked up the toilet paper roll, winding it up as she strolled toward the bathroom located directly in front of her. The coat closet was on the left, and her bedroom to the right. She glimpsed a swath of Leo's tail, twitching back and forth, just over her bedroom's threshold. "*Leo.*" She seethed with frustration. "How could you?" He glanced over his shoulder and darted under her bed.

Annie shook her head and carried the toilet paper into the bathroom, placing it on the roll holder. He'd somehow popped its spring, causing the contraption to drop down on the floor. He'd taken advantage from there. Annie closed the bathroom door from the outside and pressed lightly against the knob. The door sprang open with very little resistance. Great. She peered at the latch and tried again, but the latch wasn't catching. Add another item for the super! The apartment rents here were likely the lowest ones on the block. There was a reason for that too.

She entered the bedroom and peered under the bed. "It's all right, kitty."

Leo's eyes widened.

"I know you didn't mean it." *Or maybe you did, you little sneak*. She'd have no problems with him tomorrow. She'd be here herself to prevent any kitty mischief. Though that wasn't as likely to occur when she was home. Leo seemed to adore having her around. "Come on, Leo," she coaxed gently. "It's dinnertime."

That got his attention, and he scampered out from under the bed.

"What am I going to do with you?" Annie picked him up and hugged him. *Love you and keep you, I guess*.

Annie fed Leo and put her groceries away. This time, instead of a frozen TV dinner she'd bought herself a turkey breast and boxed stuffing with canned cranberry sauce, deciding to treat herself right. *So what* if she couldn't eat it all, or even most of it? She'd get good leftovers out of her meal and could always freeze what was left. Now seemed like the right time to make this meager self-care gesture. After the Christmas Eve she'd had—twice now—she couldn't wait for a bit of self-pampering at Christmas.

She hadn't cooked much for herself since before her breakup with Roy, and—even when she'd been with him—they'd mostly ordered takeout because he'd been critical of her cooking.

Roy set down his fork and frowned. "What's this supposed to be?" He had light-brown hair and eyes with a permanent three-day beard. He worked selling suits at an upscale men's shop and had no shortage of pricey clothes in his closet. That's one of the things that had attracted her to him, initially. He'd dressed well and taken her on fancy dates, then the day-to-day had kicked in.

"It's an Italian sausage and potato casserole." Annie's throat went raw and tender. "Like my Grandma Mable used to make." She'd also added frozen peas and butter, and slow-cooked it until everything was savory and golden brown. It was a low-cost dish, and Annie was on a much stricter budget than Roy. Before Tina had moved in with Lloyd, she and Annie had shared an apartment. The rent was a lot cheaper here but still steep for Annie to handle solo. She'd planned to get a roommate to help make ends meet, but Roy had talked her out of it. He didn't want strangers around when he was over. He wanted her all to himself.

He slid his plate across the table, landing it in front of her. "Babe, you know I can't do a ton of carbs." He sounded exasperated, even though he'd merely said he was cutting back and not eliminating carbs entirely. He was trim enough as it was.

"Fine," she said mildly. "I'll fix us some eggs." She stood to clear their plates, no longer hungry.

Suddenly, Roy changed his tune. "Hey, come here." He was like a weather vane these days, pivoting in this—and that—direction. Annie was weary of never knowing which way the wind would blow. And yet, having someone was better than having no one at all. She was still unsettled by her wine date with Tina, and she hadn't heard from her since.

She walked toward him, holding their loaded plates.

He pouted artificially. "I apologize, really, I do. I know you loved your Grandma Mable"—hurt welled in her heart—"and I'm sure it's good, just not for me. Tell you what." He slid his arm around her waist. "We'll order takeout. All right?" He peered up at her and said soothingly, "You can get lo mien, and I'll order sushi."

Lo mien wasn't her favorite, but she couldn't say so. He gave her that soft smile that always reeled her back in, like a fish on a line.

"I'll even buy." He pulled her closer. "What do you say?"

"Yeah, uh-huh. Good." She'd been scared to mention Tina's allegation to Roy. What if he blew up and got mad at her? Or worse—what if she hurt his feelings with an unfounded accusation? Still, she'd sleep better if she knew.

She set their plates on the counter and ventured casually, "I saw Tina the other day."

"Did you?" She turned to see his face had tightened. "When?"

"Wednesday. We went for a drink after work." He'd been working late that night, closing shop.

"Funny you didn't mention it."

"I, um." Annie tucked a lock of her hair behind one ear. "It was kind of last minute."

His eyes narrowed. "Were you hiding something from me, Annie?"

Her heart pounded. "What? No. I just. It's funny." She licked her lips. "Tina said she saw you out to lunch last week."

He crossed his arms. "Yeah, so?"

Annie swallowed hard. "And that you were with someone." Her words came out so softly, it was like she'd nearly lost her voice. "A woman."

"What?" Roy's eyes flashed, but then he laughed. "Oh! Eileen?"

Annie shrugged.

"We work together, Annie." He shook his head. "She's a colleague and a friend."

"Funny you didn't mention her."

"Wait." He wore an angry scowl. "Don't tell me Tina suggested—?" He raked both hands through his hair and bellowed a rough laugh. "That woman's got quite the imagination."

Annie sucked in a breath. "So, no?"

He held open his hands. "Who are you going to believe, Annie? Tina or me?"

Annie fixed her hot cocoa, pushing thoughts of Roy aside. At least she didn't have to deal with him any longer. That still didn't take the sting out of being lonely, but she didn't need a guy to be good to her, not when she was perfectly capable of doing nice things for herself. She'd started by fostering Leo. Roy had been against her owning a pet, coming up with a million and one reasons why she shouldn't, but this was her life now, not his.

Annie was glad to have a new rom-com to distract her. The hot cocoa was a soothing balm as well. But her greatest comfort came from the loving kitty nestled up against her side. Leo made a tiny bit of mischief sometimes, but that only added to his personality. She couldn't fault him for becoming bored when she was at work, and he was so good for her when she was home. Truthfully, they were good for each other. She petted the cat's head, happy for his company. His low rumbling purr said he was grateful to be here too.

When her neighbor in 3-B knocked on the door, Annie was ready with her sugar container on her kitchen counter. She set her mug of hot cocoa on an end table and her laptop on the coffee table, gently nudging Leo aside and standing from her cozy spot on the sofa.

The woman held up her measuring cup. "I hate to bother you—"

"Borrow sugar? Of course."

The woman blinked and stared down at her measuring cup. "Ah! The tip-off."

Annie accepted the empty cup. "Not a great night for going to the store."

"I'm hoping it won't be too bad tomorrow." Annie didn't comment. Everyone in the city was talking about this Christmas storm. The woman's face brightened. "I'm going to my daughter Caroline's house in Queens."

"Oh, nice."

She grinned proudly. "Got two grandkids, a boy and a girl."

Annie smiled. "I'm Annie, by the way. I don't believe we've met."

"Beatrice Holly," she said, "but my friends all call me Bea."

"Ms. Holly."

She shook her head. "No, no. It's Bea, please."

A tender feeling settled over Annie, and she thought of her Grandma Mable. "Bea," she said. "Please call me Annie."

Bea laughed. "That's what I intended."

Annie turned to get the sugar and spun back around. "Why don't you come inside?"

Bea entered her apartment, closing the door behind her as Annie walked to the kitchen. "What a cute little Christmas tree!" she said, admiring the decoration. Leo leapt off the sofa and gave a soft meow. "Well, lookee here." Bea bent down and held out her hand. Leo cautiously crossed the room and sniffed her outstretched fingers. The cat butted his head against her hand, and she petted him. His purr was so loud, Annie giggled.

"Leo likes you."

"And I like Leo." Bea patted his back and stood. "He's an older fella, isn't he?" she asked softly.

Annie's heart thudded. "Yes, eleven. How did you know?"

Bea smiled down at Leo. "I worked as a vet tech for over twenty years."

"How nice." She motioned for Bea to follow her into the kitchen, where she filled Bea's measuring cup with sugar. "Did you like it?"

"Loved it." Leo pressed himself up against Bea's long bathrobe, and she looked at Annie. "Aww. He seems happy. I can tell he's found a good home."

"He has," Annie answered. She was determined to keep him here too.

They walked back into the living room, and Bea spied Leo's loaded Christmas stocking by the radiator. Annie had filled it before starting her movie. Bea smiled at the cat. "Looks like someone's been a good kitty this year."

Not exactly, but she was cutting him some slack.

Annie smiled. "How did you know it was for him?"

"I just figured." Annie passed her the sugar, and Bea thanked her. "Caroline's got a cat, and she has her own stocking too."

Annie was glad not to be the only one who incessantly spoiled her pet. "What's Caroline's cat's name?"

"Luna. She's all black with a little white star right here." She pointed to a spot below her neck.

"I'm sure your grandkids love her."

"Oh. They do."

"How old are they?"

"Kyle is six and Gina's nine. Kevin—that's Caroline's husband and the kids' dad—brought Luna home as a present to them last Christmas. The kids had been wanting a pet for a while."

"Aww. Was she a rescue?"

Bea nodded. "She was." She stole a peek at the door. "I guess I'd better get back to my baking. They'll be expecting my sweet potato casserole tomorrow."

"Sure." Annie hated the thought of Bea getting disappointed. Her family too. But the odds of Bea making it to Queens tomorrow were poor if the bad weather continued.

Annie walked with Bea into the hallway. "Let me know if you need anything else."

"Thank you. The sugar's great."

"Hope you have a very merry Christmas tomorrow."

"Thanks, Annie. You too."

When she disappeared into her apartment, Annie recalled seeing an older man who lived there with her. Now that she thought on it, she hadn't seen him in a while. She hoped nothing bad had happened to him, but it was impossible to know, unless Bea said something about him later. Annie could ask, but she didn't want to intrude.

Naturally, her neighbors all lived their separate lives, but she'd never considered that very much until now. Each unit in her building represented its own little world, sort of like her uniquely designed windows. But here, you couldn't see through to what was going on inside. Everybody kept to themselves, like Annie.

She picked up Leo and cradled him in her arms. "How did you like Ms. Bea? Pretty nice lady, hmm?" She rubbed him under his chin, and he purred. "Yeah, I think so too." Her other neighbors seemed nice as well. Harrington and Eric. Jane. She'd never seen whoever lived in the other apartment on the second floor. "You know what I think?" she asked Leo. "I think this has been an okay Christmas Eve."

Leo blinked and purred louder. He obviously agreed.

Despite the bad news from Patrice and those kids running amok through the store, the day had had its bright spots. One of the brightest spots had been spending time with Braden. She hadn't minded going through that twice. Whatever had caused this weird time glitch, she had those memories to hang on to—even if she never ran into him at Lawson's again. Although she hoped she would.

She continued her conversation with Leo, swaying him gently. "I *also* think tomorrow's Christmas, and one big boy I know needs to go to beddy-bye. Otherwise"—she giggled—"Santa will never come!"

Annie set Leo on the floor, and he padded away on heavy footfalls, obediently heading for the bedroom while she deposited her empty hot cocoa mug in the kitchen sink. When she reached the bedroom, he was up on the bed and had tucked himself into a curl. She had him very well trained, *and* she was tired too. She checked her phone making sure the alarm was turned *off* and walked to her window and peeked through the blinds.

Winds howled and snow poured into the alley beside her building. Nearly a foot of snow piled up on the fire escape in the blustery night, and more kept cascading down. If this continued, no one would be going anywhere tomorrow. Including her.

NINE

On the third Christmas Eve

FA-LA-LA-LA-LA. LA-LA. LA—LA!

Wait! Annie sat bolt upright in bed grasping her phone. She did *not* set her alarm last night. She was positive. Her pulse pounded, and she shut her eyes. Still, she had to brave it. She peeked out of one eye and then the other, opening them both—extra wide.

Noooo!

Dec 24

Winter Storm Warning

She threw back the covers and Leo flopped onto the floor, landing on his feet and looking stunned. Poor kitty!

"It is *not* December 24," she told him surely. *Not again.*

She leapt out of bed and hopped on one foot. "Ow! Ouch, ouch, *ow*!" She'd stepped on Leo's wand toy again. Annie dropped down on the bed, holding the kitty toy in her hand. Her head spun, and she caught her breath.

What's hap-pen-ing???

She left the cat toy on her pillow and strode to the window, yanking up the blinds. The fire escape had a few icy spots on it, but no piles of snow. The sky was cloudy and gray.

What?

She dashed into the kitchen and checked her computer.

Dec 24 7:08 AM

She sprang back against a chair, nearly knocking it over on her way to the window.

Not great. The sidewalk out front was clear too.

Okay, Annie. Think, think, think.

I'm dreaming! Yes.

Right? Noooo.

Wait.

Recurring dream?

Yeah.

Maybe?

Annie gasped. Was she stuck in a time loop? Her heart thud-thud-thudded in her chest. She laid a hand across it, afraid it might burst out of her, and walked into her living room. This was totally—nuts. Not possible. No way. Leo wound himself around her ankles and meowed. He wasn't bothered in the least. She goggled at his empty Christmas stocking. *Oh, nooo.* He hadn't gotten anything from Santa. But wait, look! *Yes.* Candy canes hung from her miniature tree. She went over and counted eleven, meaning—she turned toward the kitchen—she'd had one last night in her hot cocoa.

So. This wasn't a *total* time loop. Only a mixed-up partial one?

Some things from yesterday had moved forward. She stared at the snow globe beneath her Christmas tree, and her heart pounded. *Believe*. Yeah, but what? That she was losing her grasp on reality?

Leo meowed, wanting his breakfast.

"Right. But this time, we're not spilling any on the floor."

Annie fixed herself some coffee first, checking the contents of her refrigerator. It looked pretty bare, with no turkey breast in sight. The freezer was fairly empty too, so no frozen TV dinner. Ugh. She was also now out of milk. She'd have to go the store. If only she was one of those people who loved shopping. Fact was, she didn't. Wait. An empty cocoa mug sat in the sink, and she'd just used up the milk in her coffee. So *how* had she made that cocoa?

Annie opened a cabinet and took out the box holding individual cocoa packets. It was the instant kind, so you could add milk—or water. She tallied the packets, and there were a few of them missing, but she had no idea how many there'd been to begin with on Christmas Eve. So, okay. She could have made the cocoa last night, in either case. She stared at the melted candy cane smudges in the mug. *Somewhere along the line I did buy those candy canes though*. Her temples throbbed. None of this made sense.

Time loop? Not a time loop?

Sleepwalking? She took a long sip of coffee. *Probably not.*

Leo head-butted her shin.

Very hungry cat. She picked up his food bowl and filled it on the counter. "You," she commanded, "stay put." She bent to feed him, and Leo lurched forward, but she was ready. She pushed his head back with one hand and placed his food bowl on the floor with a flourish. *Whew!*

Her intercom buzzed. Annie's finger trembled when she pressed the button. "Yes?"

"Package for you!"

Of course it was—*not*.

"Be right down, thanks!"

She drew in a calming breath and took a sip of coffee, glancing around. Okay. This wasn't happening. However. If it *was*... She could certainly do better than yesterday. Just look at Leo happily eating his cat food! And the kitchen was mess-free. Annie shrugged on her coat and wiggled into her old boots, descending the stairs to her building's front door. Would be nice if the package actually *was* for her. She desperately needed her new pair.

She reached for the oblong box and remembered—jumping back.

Whomp!

She missed getting clobbered by the snow mound by a split second. But she *had missed* getting clobbered. Which meant—yes! Maybe she could avoid another catastrophe at Lawson's with her window display and even have a different sort of meeting with Patrice, one with a more positive outcome? Assuming everyone else still thought this was Christmas Eve. She clutched the package to her chest and climbed the stairs, knowing she'd find out soon enough. If it was Christmas Eve again, Jane would say so, like she had the day before.

Annie knocked lightly on the door, and Jane opened it.

"Hi there!" Jane observed the package. "Is that for me?"

"Yeah. The delivery person buzzed the wrong apartment."

The conversation flowed exactly like Annie expected, right down to the details about Amazing Agatha. When Jane was about to shut her door, she introduced herself, and so did Annie. A beeper sounded inside Jane's apartment. "That's my coffee." She peered over her shoulder. "Would you like to have a cup?"

Annie hesitated on the landing. That sounded nice, and maybe Jane was lonely, despite having a daughter. She didn't see why she couldn't have her second cup of coffee here, rather than upstairs. "Sure, I'll take some."

"We'll have to sit in the stairwell," Jane said, "if that's all right? Cari's still sleeping. I'll have to wake her soon to get her to her sitter's before work."

"Where's that?" Annie asked her.

"Brooklyn Museum. You?"

Annie smiled. "Lawson's Finest."

Jane nodded. "Busy time of year."

Annie shoved her hands in her coat pocket. "Today's one of the busiest." She put that out there, leading Jane a bit.

Jane took the bait. "Christmas Eve," she said. "Bet so."

So there was Annie's confirmation. She was destined for another do-over day. A jolt of understanding hit her. *Time loop, not a time loop?* No. That was too black and white, and this was in Technicolor. She was in a time loop, all right.

A time loop with loopholes.

Annie's heart beat faster. That meant she had to try to make the most of each day until she could find a way out of it.

Despite her best efforts, Annie missed another train. It was almost like the train schedule kept changing ever-so-slightly to vex her. She sat on a bench, and the man with the newspaper sat down beside her as the teenager wearing earbuds walked by. Annie pulled out her phone and opened her text app, staring at the icon of a hand holding a writing pen. This time loop with loopholes was tricky. It was also uncannily precise when it wanted to be.

What would Tina even think if Annie texted her about this now? Maybe if they'd been in closer touch over these past few months, Annie contacting her wouldn't seem so surprising. It would still be hard to explain what was happening, because Annie didn't have a full grasp on it herself. She couldn't open with an odd pronouncement about time loops. No. She needed to make things up to Tina first. Annie bit her lip, her heart pounding, and typed a short note.

> Hey Tina! It's Annie.
>
> I know we've been out of touch—

Although Tina hadn't reached out either. Annie swallowed past the lump in her throat. Maybe she should take that as a sign? Maybe Tina didn't even want to hear from her?

The man beside her stood, folding his newspaper, and Annie saw a new group of commuters clamoring toward the train. She dashed through its open doors, somehow knowing she'd arrive at Lawson's at 9:08 a.m. exactly. *Again.* She hoped this day would bring more good things, and fewer bad.

Forty minutes later, Annie scurried past the escalators at Lawson's, her hat and coat covered in snowflakes. A fancy package caught her eye, and she stopped short. No way, but it was. Amazing Agatha in all her glory. Annie paused to examine the rectangular box containing the doll and her basic office setup, along with that crafty little printer. The box for Detective Dean sat next to it on the display shelf. There were others too, all with different outfits and jobs, but Agatha was clearly the star of the show with her amateur sleuthing prowess. Annie picked up the box and checked the price tag. *Whoa. That's a lot to blow on a doll.* No wonder Jane had gotten the knockoff. The woman clearly wasn't made of money. None of the people in Annie's building were.

"Morning, Annie." She saw a swath of sturdy red pants legs and glossy black boots…his thick round middle and his baby-blue eyes.

"Santa!" The box slipped in her hands. Someone else grabbed it to keep it from hitting the floor. A sexy scent washed over her, *lemon and spice and everything nice*. Braden had a habit of turning up unexpectedly too. He handed her the package, and Annie placed it back on the shelf. "Er, thanks!"

Santa glanced at the doll display. "Buying for someone special?" he asked Annie.

"Oh no, I was—just looking."

"She's the hot ticket this year," Santa said informatively. "Amazing Agatha."

Annie nodded. "That's what I hear." Did Braden remember

anything about her at all? Helping her yesterday? Having coffee at the Blue Dot? And what about Old Saint Nick? She peeked out of the corner of her eye at the jolly old elf. What did he know about any of this?

Braden smiled at the older man, clearly amused. "Bet you've been keeping careful track of who's been naughty and nice."

"Ho ho ho." Santa's big, round belly jiggled when he laughed. "Indeed. Although everyone's nice"—he winked—"in my book."

Braden smirked playfully. "If you say so, Santa."

Santa patted down the cuffs on his tunic's sleeves. "I most certainly do." He turned toward Annie and Braden. "I hope you both have a very merry Christmas."

Annie stopped him before he left. "Santa, wait!"

Santa spun back around. "Yes, Annie?"

What could she say? She couldn't very well ask him if he'd thrown her into a time loop with loopholes. Thrown *all of them* into one. Not in front of Braden. How would that sound? Santa might call security. She darted a glance at Braden. *Oh yeah, right.* "Er. Hope you have a very merry Christmas too."

"Why, thank you." He bowed his head, and the pom-pom on his hat swung forward.

Braden shook his head as Santa waddled down the aisle. "That guy's *something else.*" His eyes shimmered in that sexy way that made her heart pound. Because. Of course. He was so attractive and kind, and she knew that even more clearly now.

"Yeah, he is." Her pulsed hummed when she recalled the way Braden's mouth had been so close to hers seconds before Veronica Lawson had interrupted. *Hello! We were at the store! It's not like something could have happened.* Her mind took that little road trip anyway.

"If I didn't know better," Braden joked as Santa walked away, "I'd swear he's the real deal." He picked up the box for Detective Dean, scanning its contents.

Annie watched Santa approach his workshop, chatting with his elf assistant. "Just wait until you see him later."

Braden looked up from the box, somewhat distracted. "Who? Santa?" Detective Dean looked a little like Braden with dark hair and blue eyes, and Agatha slightly resembled her. Annie held her breath. She was *not* playing dolls with Braden, or house either. Sadly.

"Yes," Annie said. "With the kids, I mean. I have this *really strong hunch* he'll charm them all later—a certain few, especially."

"Hmm, I'm sure you're right." Braden turned the package around, holding it toward her. "Look at this guy." A grin tugged at his lips. "He's got a badge and everything."

"Ha! Yeah." Annie's gaze shot to Braden's badge, dropping to his duty belt. She jerked it back up again to Braden's sparkling blue eyes. He put Detective Dean back on the endcap and she read his name tag, pointing to hers. "Hi. I'm Annie." A small part of her hoped he'd remember. No, okay. A large part. Very, very huge.

He hooked his thumbs over his duty belt and grinned. "Nice meeting you, Annie. I'm Braden." *So much for leaving a lasting impression.*

She shifted her canvas bag handle on her shoulder. "You too."

"Hey." He rubbed his dimpled chin. "Aren't you the lady who—?"

"Yep! That's me."

Braden folded his arms. "How did you know I was going to ask about your windows?"

She shrugged meekly. "I, er, guessed?"

"Well, you, Annie, are a really good guesser." *If only you knew.* He grinned and shook his head. "I bet you get comments about them all the time."

"Um. I do!" *Including from Ms. Lawson.* Unfortunately, her comments hadn't been glowing.

"Well, you do great work."

"Thanks!" She checked the time on her phone against her watch. She really needed to get to work if she was still hoping for that promotion. Maybe since this was her third try, she'd find a way. "Sorry, I—"

He glanced toward the back of the store. "Yeah, I've got to stop by the security office." He tried to move out of her way when she attempted to step around him, and both sprang back. Annie's bag slid off her shoulder, its handle hitting the crook of her arm. She grabbed for it, and it gaped open. Out plopped one of her winter-white pumps, plummeting to the floor.

Braden bent to retrieve it. "Looks like you dropped something," he said, standing and handing her the shoe. She grabbed the toe of it, and he had the heel. Both of them froze. His blue eyes widened, appearing more sparkly and bluer than ever. He shook his head, bringing himself out of his trance, and shoved the shoe toward her. "Hey, have we—?"

"Ah no. No, I don't think so," she said, cramming the shoe back in her bag.

"No. Of course not. That would be weird." He backed up a step. "Well, okay"—he licked his lips—"better run!"

"Uh-huh, right. See you around!" She inched away from him, nearly trampling over some folks exiting the elevators.

"Yeah, Annie. See ya!"

Hope so.

Her heart pounded.

At least she hadn't said that out loud.

TEN

THAT AFTERNOON WHEN PATRICE CALLED her in for the meeting, Annie arrived with her replacement package of Christmas lights. Maybe if she cut this meeting even shorter, she'd get to her window display before Dylan and Marcus.

Patrice frowned. "Annie, I'm sorry to have to—"

"Don't worry, Patrice," Annie said, preempting her before either of them could sit at the table. "It's not your fault."

Patrice blinked. "What's not?"

"About Ms. Lawson, or my promotion."

"But how did you—?"

"Foot traffic is down, right?"

"Why, yes."

"She blames my window displays."

Patrice pinched the bridge of her nose. "Have you been talking to Carl?" she asked, naming their Human Resources Manager.

"No"—Annie set her chin—"I just had a feeling."

Patrice removed her glasses, folding them in her hand. "Maybe it's not too late? Maybe there's still time?"

"There could be more time than you know."

Patrice's face screwed up. "What's that mean?"

Annie's shoulders sank. "Just that I'll work on it."

Patrice stared at the package of Christmas tree lights in Annie's hands. "Oh yes, one more thing..."

Annie held up the lights. "On my way!"

Annie spotted Kira on the salesfloor, neatening up a table of sweaters on sale. She sorted and folded the various items by size and color, the butterfly tattoo on her wrist peeking out from beneath her long black T-shirt sleeve. "Kira," she said in low tones, "I don't want you to worry about anything."

Kira's eyebrow bar rose beneath her spiky purple hair. "Worry?"

"About your meeting with Patrice." Annie held up crossed fingers. "I'm hoping everything will be okay."

"Wait. What?" Kira rasped quietly. "Are you *not* getting promoted?" Kira knew her promotion was dependent on Annie's. They'd already talked about it.

Annie drew in a breath and hurried away. "I'm not sure, but I'm working on it!"

The man leaving the jewelry counter beelined toward her, and she recoiled when he drew near. One disaster averted. No, two! Three! Counting Leo's cat food and this morning's snow dump. Now she was going to prevent a fourth. Annie hastened her steps across the salesfloor, darting through the crowd. If things went as planned, she'd still be replacing that burnt-out strand of Christmas tree lights, but she would *not* be dealing with—

"No, Dylan! Let me!" A young boy raced past her, darting through Homewares.

Another kid yanked on his arm, scooting in front of him. "No, Marcus! Me first!"

Wait! Where did they even *come* from? She stared down at her watch and moaned. *You're kidding me?* Her watch hands had frozen—again. She'd put in a new battery too.

Annie goggled at the boys as they raced ahead, like whirling dervishes.

"Dylan! Marcus!" their mom called, chasing after them.

"But I want my Robo-bot!" Marcus hollered.

"Santa! Santa!" Dylan cried. "Wait for me!"

Annie reached into the janitor's closet, shaking her head. Why couldn't she fix this when she'd fixed everything else? Well, not *everything* else, but some things. And *this thing* was an enormous thing not to fix.

"Annie." Braden stood by the door. He had his grip around the handle of a rolling wastebin. "Are you okay?"

"Yeah." She stared at him, dazed. "That was just—just a lot."

"I know it looks bad, but hey." He smiled, and his blue eyes glimmered. "We'll make it better, all right?"

When he said that she wanted to believe him, and somehow deep in her heart she did.

"You know it's funny that we only met today, because somehow I think I know you. You're just"—he searched the ceiling and looked at her—"very familiar."

"Yeah. I, um—sense something too."

He snapped his fingers. "You're not from Philly, by chance?"

"Originally, no." She held on to the broom handle, resting her weight against it. "Red Bank, New Jersey."

He grinned. "Nice town. Lots of galleries and such."

Annie's heart pinged. "Yeah, my dad was an artist there."

"No kidding?" Braden stood up straighter, resting a hand on his hip. "That's very cool. Would I have heard of him?"

"Sadly, he never really took off. My mom sold his work though. She had a small gift shop in town." A magical memory came back to her, and she saw her mom's storefront gleaming with a pretty holiday display. "She did the best windows."

"So, you come by it honestly then."

"What?" Ahh, she got it. "Oh, yeah, guess so." Though Tina had pointed this aspect out to her, Annie hadn't considered her mom's influence over her work in a long time. Maybe both her folks had influenced her. Her dad had been artistic and her mom great at retail space design.

He leaned his shoulder against the doorframe, and the taut muscles beneath his shirt sleeves showed. "They still live there, in Red Bank?"

Painful memories flooded her, but—though it throbbed and felt sore—her heart grew full. She'd known what is was like to be cherished by her folks and loved by her grandparents. "No. They both passed when I was little. Car accident."

"I'm sorry, Annie. Really I am." He frowned. "Bet they were really special."

Annie's eyes misted. "They were." She studied him. "How did you know?"

"You're pretty special yourself." He winked. "Apples don't fall far from the tree."

She teemed with embarrassment. "You don't even know me."

"No"—he shared a puzzled grin—"you're right. Still. I've got good instincts."

Annie lifted her broom. "And *my* instincts say we'd better get busy if we're going to finish up in time for New Year's."

Braden connected a new string of lights to the one on the tree and passed the end of it to Annie. He was unassuming but caring, and *ooh so easy on the eyes.*

"So. Where'd you work before Lawson's?" he asked her. She named the major New York City department stores where she'd apprenticed. "That must have been exciting."

"Yeah, it was." But not half as exciting as what was happening now—making small talk with a super-handsome guy who was probably thinking up the best way to ask her to coffee. Butterflies flitted around inside her as she settled the lights on the midsection branches of the tree before passing him back the strand. "But I like Lawson's best. It's homier somehow."

"Yeah, I get that," he said. "Old man Lawson used to run it very well." He shook his head. "But there's been a bit of a different vibe here lately."

"I think Veronica Lawson means well," she said, taking the charitable view. "She's trying to save the store."

"Save it? Is Lawson's in trouble?"

Annie held her breath. "I'm probably not supposed to say anything."

He stopped threading his strand of lights through the tree. "Well, if that's the case, I'm sorry to hear it."

She decided to confide in him. Braden always seemed to know the right thing to say. "My job might be on the line, to tell you the truth."

He stared at her in disbelief. "But why?" He glanced at the street and the walloping storm, driving snow against the window. "Wait. Is this about Ms. Lawson thinking your work is old school?"

She settled more lights on the tree, weaving them in and out of the prickly branches. "That's part of it. The other part is the store is looking to cut back on staff. Hire out freelancers."

Braden grumbled. "Well, no one could do better windows than you."

She appreciated his support. "Thanks, Braden." She stretched up on her tiptoes but couldn't quite reach the upper branches, despite her high heels. Braden held out a hand, and she passed him the end of her strand of lights. Their fingers touched again, and she blushed. He didn't comment on that or his own very ruddy complexion. Instead, he wound his way around the tree, accomplishing his job, but even he couldn't reach the very top.

Braden opened the ladder and set it in place. "I'm really sorry you got bad news," he said, obviously still stewing over it. "Especially right before Christmas."

"Doesn't have to be bad news." Annie set her hands on her hips and surveyed their handiwork. They'd gotten nearly everything done. "Patrice said nothing will get decided until after the holidays."

He nodded and climbed down the ladder. "Well, here's hoping all goes well." He smiled, and her pulse fluttered. "I'm holding good thoughts."

"Thanks."

He walked over to the armchair where they'd set some new boxes of Christmas tree balls and picked one up.

"Wait!" Annie scurried to the side table meant for Santa's cookies and milk. Those were on the mantel for the time being, and the side table held boxes of Christmas tree ornaments. She picked up the box on top, which also contained Christmas tree balls, only these were fashioned from unbreakable plastic rather than made of glass. They weren't as shiny as their glass cousins, but they were certainly sturdier. She handed Braden the box and picked up another for herself. "Might be safest for us to use these."

Braden winked. "Good thinking."

"Yeah." Especially if she was faced with another do-over day. Though she hoped to prevent that, she wasn't certain that she could. So best to be prepared.

Santa paused on his way out the door. "Very nice, you two." He studied the window display. "Just needs a little something."

Annie set her hands on her hips. Tomorrow, she'd have to find a way to be ready for this. *If* tomorrow was another Christmas Eve. She couldn't believe she was already planning for it! She motioned toward the tree. "We added tinsel." She pointed to the fake snow. "And have plenty of the white stuff too."

"Hmm, yes I've got it!" Santa adjusted his red velvet hat

with its thick white brim. A white pom-pom bounced from its tip. "Maybe a nutcracker or two?" Annie giggled at his harmless request. Seriously. What would it hurt?

Braden folded up the ladder, turning to her. "Got any of those in back?" The ones she had were large and wouldn't really fit in here. They did sell smaller sets of them in Homewares though. She could borrow one to place on the mantel alongside those singing angels. "I think I can rustle up a pair."

Santa sent her a cheery thumbs-up. "Ho ho ho! Merry Christmas!"

Braden chuckled as Santa left. "That guy's good."

"*So* good," Annie added. "Yeah."

Braden shook his head as Santa darted down the snowy sidewalk, disappearing into the night. "I wouldn't be surprised to see him riding in a sleigh"—he gestured toward the window with his hand—"all the way down Fifth Avenue."

Annie giggled. "Funny. I can kind of imagine that too."

"So, Annie?" he said. "I was wondering about later—"

"Coffee at the Blue Dot?" she asked, and he grinned. "I'd love to."

ELEVEN

BRADEN SET THEIR COFFEES ON the table, and they both slid into the booth. He held the paper bag of jelly donuts in one hand. "Donut?" he asked, prying the bag open. Annie unwound her neck scarf and folded it up, tucking it in the canvas bag beside her.

"No thanks, but you go right ahead."

He was glad he'd stayed late to help her clean up. There was something about Annie that was just so special. She was unique—yet familiar, in a way he couldn't place.

She took a sip of coffee. "Thanks for this. It's really good."

"Yeah, the coffee's great here." He picked up a donut and took a bite. "Hmm. Very tasty." Braden pulled a napkin from the dispenser, wiping his fingers. "Sorry. These can get a little messy."

She shrugged. "Sometimes messy is good, right?"

He thought of her totaled window display. "Sometimes, sure." He polished off the donut in another two bites and closed the bag. "Other messes though?" He frowned. "They're best to be avoided."

"Like those kids wrecking my window."

"Exactly." Suddenly, in his mind's eye, a sandstorm whirled

around him, and he was caught up in a swirling brown cloud, which was *not* where he wanted to be at the moment. Where he wanted to be was present with Annie. He pulled himself together and pushed the donut bag aside. "Sounds like you stayed busy before Lawson's," he said, picking up his coffee. "Was that how you got your training—through those apprenticeships?"

She wrapped both hands around her coffee cup and grinned. "It was."

"Well, you seem to be a natural at it. It's nice when someone finds their work fit."

"How about you? How'd you wind up at Lawson's?"

He stared down at his coffee, not sure he wanted to go there, but he didn't want to be rude. "Ah, I was in the service for a while."

She nodded. "Army, right?"

He pushed back in his seat. "Wow, yeah. How did you know that?"

She fiddled with her mittens on the table, setting them on top of her hat. "I just—had a hunch?" She looked like he'd called her out on something, but there was no real way she could have known. Maybe it was a fair assumption, given his current job. A lot of former service members made similar transitions. She looked adorably embarrassed for having put two and two together. He gave her credit for her sharp analytics.

He playfully shook his finger at her. "You, Annie Jones, are a very good guesser." He slumped back in the booth and crossed his arms. Wait. That felt strangely déjà vu–like tripping off his tongue. *No. When would I have said that?* He blinked, clearing his head.

"I was in the army, yeah, but I didn't work for a while before coming to Lawson's." He heaved a breath, not sure why he should hide it. "I was at a hospital in Germany recovering."

"Recovering?"

He rested his forearms on the table and slumped forward. "Broke both my legs on a mission in Iraq and got airlifted out."

She put down her cup. "Oh, Braden. That sounds awful."

"It wasn't great." He frowned and stared out the window, the flurrying snow carrying him far, far away. Evening commuters hurried by, along with shoppers holding brimming sacks. Most had their heads ducked against the snow. Some held umbrellas. A wind gust turned a few umbrellas inside out. "But, you know"—he shrugged—"I survived it." His mind plodded through gusts of sand and plumes of choking black smoke.

She gently squeezed his arm. "What happened?" Her words were low and tender, and he experienced a tug on his heartstrings. "Sorry." She winced. "Didn't mean to pry."

Strangely, it didn't feel like prying coming from Annie. Even more strangely, he felt like telling her. His gut twisted at the memory. It wasn't a pretty one. Still. Somehow he felt safe with her. She was timid, but she was kind. She was also strong. He could sense that.

He swallowed past the burn in his throat. "I was in charge of my squad," he said, "and getting us to the rendezvous point with rest of our platoon. Unfortunately"—he stared at her, spiraling into the darkness—"our convoy got rammed by a truck carrying explosives." He pulled himself back from that ledge, aware of her touch. Her support. Her caring.

She tightened her grasp on his arm. "Ambushed," she gasped.

He steadied his voice and continued. "My vehicle crunched up like an accordion, the steering column and everything got pushed back. Honestly? I'm lucky to be alive. Not everyone"—he brought his fist to his mouth; it was still pretty raw—"was so lucky."

A moist sheen coated her eyes. "Oh, Braden. That's really hard," she said, still hanging on to him.

"Anyway." He sat back against the booth, and his arm slid out from under her grasp. "I decided I'd had enough of the army after that. My mom had recently lost my stepdad and was on her own in the city, and I'd always liked New York. So." He shrugged. "I decided to come home."

"Well, I—for one—am very glad you did." Her expression was so sincere, it was almost heartbreaking. What was he doing, laying his worries on her? Shame washed through him, and he held open his hands. "Just look at me chewing up your time with my sob stories. I'm sorry, Annie. Really, I am. What a way to say merry Christmas! Bah-humbug on me."

"No," she said softly. "Don't be. I'm just sorry you went through that." She scanned his eyes. "Thanks for telling me." She really was an incredible person, so unlike anyone he'd ever known. And yet, he couldn't shake the feeling that he did already know her.

Annie walked alongside Braden in silence, both of them perusing the storefront windows. She was headily aware of the attractive man beside her. This had felt so much like a date, but of course it hadn't been a real one. Braden didn't even remember meeting her before this version of her day. And still. He'd been comfortable enough around her to open up about his very personal past. He cut her a sideways glance. "I hope I didn't overburden you back there at the Blue Dot."

"Absolutely not," she said as they strolled along. "I've liked spending time with you." *Lots and lots of time, more time than you know.* Her heart ached. *Oh, if only you remembered it too.*

"Yeah, Annie," he said huskily. "I feel the same."

He looked around at the bustling crowds and the snarled up traffic, gazing at the decorated lampposts and squinting his eyes against the snow. "I've always liked the city at Christmas. My folks used to bring me here to look at—" They passed another window display and he blinked. "Huh. That's *so weird*."

"What is?"

He cleared a powdery layer of snowflakes off his hat. "I just had the strangest sensation that I'd told you that before. *And* about me, and my mom and stepdad moving to New York from Pennsylvania."

Annie was unsure of what to say. He appeared to sometimes remember some things, but only very vaguely. If only he could recall all of it, like she did—treasuring every moment. "You mean like déjà vu?"

"Yeah, I guess you could call it that. But no." He paused and stared at her. "I mean, we never even talked before today, and I know I didn't mention that at the store, or at the café."

"That's why déjà vu's such a mystery." She shrugged. "Nobody's totally sure where it comes from." *Except for me, in this case. Because you did tell me about moving here as a kid earlier.* "There are other mysteries in the universe," she said broaching the topic lightly. "Relating to time travel and such." What if he believed in that stuff? That could give her an opening to talk about time loops. Maybe she could tell him then?

He hooted a laugh. "What?"

Or maybe not.

Braden shot her the side-eye. "Hang on. You're not serious? About time travel? I mean, ah. It's very fun in fiction."

It wasn't technically *travel* if you kept traveling back to the same day, was it? Or maybe it was, sort of. *A time loop with loopholes. Great.* Of course she didn't get a normal one.

A muscle in his cheek flinched. "Annie?" He searched her eyes, and Annie wanted to die. Time loops? Ha! He thought she was the loopy one. And honestly? She didn't blame him.

"Nooo!" she lied. "Just kidding! What I meant was, 'There are more things in heaven and earth, Horatio.'"

He quirked a grin. "Shakespeare."

"Yeah."

This seemed to intrigue him. "You like the theater?"

Her bag slipped on her shoulder, and she fixed it. "I do."

"Cool." They reached her subway stop. "Maybe we could go sometime?"

"I'd like that," she said.

He nodded, and she noticed the Christmas bell ringer dressed as Santa behind him on the corner. Maybe he'd been there all along, and she'd just now seen him. Sort of like she hadn't noticed Braden at the start. He had her full attention now.

"Hope you have a very merry Christmas, Annie."

She smiled, sad to say goodbye. But that was silly. If this time loop with loopholes held, she'd be seeing him tomorrow, and the day after that possibly. Chances of them getting to the theater at this point were slim. "Thanks, Braden. You too."

TWELVE

LEO PRANCED TOWARD ANNIE WHEN she flipped on the light. She'd made it home in time to help Harrington and meet Eric, just as she'd planned.

"Hi, big guy," she told him. "How was your day?"

He meowed.

"Yes, I can see you're exhausted from all the work you've done around here. I hope you behaved." Annie perused the living area, surveying her small tree. Eleven candy canes were still on it, like they'd been this morning. Good sign.

But wait. She spotted something on the floor. A long white sheet of toilet paper ran across the hall in front of her, seemingly emerging from the bathroom—and what?—disappearing through her open bedroom door? "*Leo*," she said in exasperating tones. "What did you do now?" She'd thought she'd outwitted him by taking the toilet paper off the roll holder and setting it on the shelf above the toilet. How had he reached that? He had to be a jumping superstar. At eleven? Maybe it was a good thing she hadn't gotten him as a kitten. Who knows what he would have been capable of at that age.

She left her groceries in the kitchen and peered into the bathroom. He'd evidently knocked the roll to the floor and nudged it with his head somehow—or maybe his paws—shoving it into her bedroom and—where? Oh, there! "Nice going, big guy," she said as he watched her dig the roll out from underneath her bed. Or more like, what was left of the roll. Great. He'd partially shredded it too. "You're very lucky Santa's forgiving and kind."

She returned to the kitchen to unpack her groceries. Leo meowed like she'd forgotten him, but of course she hadn't.

"Okay, okay." She smiled indulgently, because—honestly—he was the only friend she had, and he kept her good company—when he wasn't being a little devil. "I'll feed you first and *then* put the groceries away." Although a few of them weren't going anywhere except for straight into a cooking pot. She fed Leo and took out the skillet she'd use to brown the beef. She went to the kitchen bookshelf loaded with the old cookbooks that used to belong her mom. One was really a recipe folder with handwritten index cards inside clear plastic sleeves. The pages were clamped together in a three-ring binder.

"You know what?" she told Leo, taking off her coat. "I think I'll look up Mom's recipe." She waited for that angsty feeling to wash over her. The one that always consumed her when she remembered cooking with her mom. She waited a minute more.

Nothing happened.

Annie removed the recipe holder from its shelf. She flipped open its pages, and her heart stilled. All the recipes were in her mom's very tiny and precise printed handwriting. Her throat went raw, but the moment passed. She traced a finger across the cool plastic page covering the recipe she sought: "Nancy's World-Class Chili." Annie's dad had always complimented her mom's cooking, saying it was world-class. "World-class dinner tonight, Nancy." He'd said that about everything from tuna casserole to meatloaf. He'd been a good husband, Annie saw that now, and a really great dad.

A drop of moisture splashed against the clear plastic page, and Annie realized she'd shed a tear. But no. She didn't need to feel sorry for herself. What she needed to do was cook for Harrington. If she could remember how. Roy had questioned her culinary capabilities, along with so many other things. When she'd finally gotten up the nerve to leave him, she'd never seen him looking so shocked.

"You don't mean it, Annie." He glowered at her. "You'll be back." No. She didn't want this any longer. As scary as it was, she was better off on her own.

She stuffed her things into her backpack with her laptop and zipped her backpack, putting it on her shoulder. Roy's apartment was muggy with summer air, and all the windows were open. He stood in the foyer between her and the door, but she was done with being blocked by Roy.

She walked right up to him, channeling her Grandma Mable. "Don't let anyone make you feel small," her dear grandma had said. "Remember who you are: a girl with a big heart." But her heart was bleeding, and Roy was squeezing the life out of it. She'd thought he'd really loved her, but no. She'd learned that this morning when the text message from Eileen popped up on his phone. Apparently, a lot more than sewing went on in that tailoring room.

"Please get out of my way."

"Come on, Annie." He put on his soft tones. "Let's talk."

But there was nothing left to say. "Roy," she grated out his name, "move."

He threw up his hands. "Okay, okay!" He stepped aside. "But you'll regret this."

What she regretted was believing his lies in the first place.

Annie landed back in the present, staring down at her mom's recipe. Enough. Roy was history now, and she was her own person. She could order whatever she pleased off a menu, and cook exactly what she wanted as well. Roy had never liked her chili. She couldn't wait to fix a huge batch.

She set all her ingredients on the counter and glanced at Leo, who'd finished his food. "What do you think, boy?"

He meowed loudly.

"You're right," Annie agreed. "I've got this."

An hour later, she lifted a spoonful of piping-hot chili to her lips and blew on it to cool it. Steam rose off the hearty mixture, and savory aromas wafted toward her. She took a tentative taste, appreciating the complex flavors. *Hmm, not bad.*

She finished the taste on her spoon, and her tongue tingled with sensation. Annie smacked her lips. "Okay," she told Leo. "This passes the test. I'm taking it to Harrington." But first, she'd set aside a mugful to have for her own supper when she got back.

Annie carried the covered casserole dish of chili down the stairs. She knocked on Harrington's door, and it didn't take him long to answer. A television was on in the living room. It was the old tube kind. From the depression in a sofa cushion and the plaid throw blanket that had been pushed aside, it looked like he'd been sitting there watching a show.

"Annie?" He stared down at the casserole dish and leaned into his walker. "My, that smells delicious."

She grasped the heavy container with her oven mitts. "It's a homemade chili. I don't know if you've eaten?"

His cloudy eyes glistened. "You made that for me?"

"It's my mom's recipe." She swallowed hard. "My late mom's."

Harrington donned a compassionate frown. "I'm sorry about your mom, young lady." He studied the dish in her hands. "But how kind of you to think of me."

"Can I set this on the stove for you? It's still hot."

Harrington tugged on his cardigan sweater. "My mouth's watering already."

"It's not too spicy," she said because she hadn't been sure if he had any restrictions. "If you'd like spicy though." She dug a bottle of hot sauce out of the pocket in her apron. The apron had belonged to her mom, and it was her first time using it. She'd worried that it would feel morbid, but it didn't. More like comforting, as if her mom had been right there with her.

"My. My. My." Harrington shook his head. "You have thought of everything."

She placed the hot sauce bottle on the counter beside the stove.

"This is very good timing," Harrington said, easing his way toward the kitchen. "I was about to fix myself a late supper." She noticed a mug with a teabag tag dangling from it on the coffee table.

"Well, good." She smiled. "I'm glad I got here in time."

"You certainly did."

"Don't worry about the container. You can return it whenever. Just let me know and I'll come and get it." But how would he contact her? He definitely couldn't climb more stairs. Not all the way up to the third floor, unassisted. Much less carrying a casserole dish. "Tell you what," she said. "Why don't I give you my number, and you can text me—"

He waved a hand. "I'm afraid I don't do that."

She smiled, spotting his landline. "You can call me then. If I don't answer, leave a message."

He nodded. "And they say this old world is going to rot."

She set one hand on her hip. "Who's they?"

"The great 'they.'" He dramatically swept a hand through the air. "Those know-it-alls who say the world isn't the place it used to be." That was just because they didn't live in *her* world, where every day was *just like* the last. But she knew what he meant.

"I guess we're all kind of in it together," she said. "We're doing the best we can with what we have."

"Yes."

Annie let herself out. Before she closed the door, Harrington stopped her. "I wasn't wrong in what I said before." He grinned with a solid assurance. "You really are some kind of angel."

"Don't give me too much credit!"

"Merry Christmas, young lady!"

"Merry Christmas."

She nearly bumped into Eric when she spun toward the hall. He'd retrieved a stack of mail from his mailbox and held a few packages. "Oh, Eric! Hi!"

"Hi, Annie."

"Looks like you got a lot of special deliveries."

"Yeah. I ordered some stuff."

She had too. *Where* were those snow boots?

"Christmas stuff?"

"Not exactly." He lifted the heavy packages. "Books for next semester."

"You like to read hard copies, huh?"

"Yeah, when I can. I spend lots of time—writing," he finally said. "So being off the computer for a while is a nice break."

"That's cool. What is it you're writing?"

"A novel." He lifted a shoulder like it was no big deal. "Not sure if it's any good."

"I'll bet it's fantastic."

"Hope my profs think so. It's for my master's thesis. The others in my program are writing one too."

"Well, I think that's awesome. I can't imagine writing anything that long. I'm lucky to complete a grocery list."

He laughed, seeming more at ease. "What is it you do?"

"I work at Lawson's Finest designing their window displays."

"Now *that* sounds cool and creative."

She stood up a little straighter. "It has its moments." Images of that careening Christmas tree flashed through her mind. "Most of them great ones!" she added when he looked perplexed.

"Ah, nice. I'm glad you like it."

"I do like it," she said, understanding just how much. "I guess I'm lucky to enjoy my job." She'd be even luckier to get to keep enjoying it. If only she could dream up a way to help Ms. Lawson see her window in a new light. "Anyway," she said. "Good seeing you!"

"You too, Annie. Merry Christmas."

If she had a dollar for every time her neighbors wished each other a merry Christmas around here, she'd be a very rich woman soon. Of course none of them recalled saying that yesterday. Neither did Braden or any of her other coworkers at Lawson's, including that department-store Santa. *Wait.*

She relived that mysterious twinkle in his eyes when he'd said, "All in a day's work." No. There was no Santa Claus. Not actually. And the jolly old elf couldn't cast spells either. Or could he? *For goodness sakes, Annie!* She shook her head, continuing up the stairs. Next, she'd be hearing reindeer prancing on the roof!

Later that evening, Annie passed Bea a cup of sugar in her kitchen. "I was just about to have some cocoa," she said, nodding at the pot on the stove. Tonight, she'd made it authentic with melted chocolate and real milk. "Would you like a cup?"

"Oh, that sounds delicious, but I'm baking."

Annie couldn't help trying again. "I made it from scratch," she said, tempting.

"Well in *that* case," Bea said. "Maybe I'll have to." Leo pressed up against Bea's ankles, purring.

"Leo's happy about that," Annie said.

Bea smiled and bent down to pet the cat. "Me too."

Annie fixed them both a mugful, and they carried their drinks into the living room. She glanced at the candy canes on her tree and said, "I've always liked adding a candy cane to my cocoa. Makes it minty." She turned to Bea. "Want to try it?"

"Why not?" Bea held out her hand, and Annie gave her a candy cane. They both sat and unwrapped their treats, dunking them in their drinks.

Bea made herself comfortable in the armchair, placing her house key on a silky red ribbon on the coffee table. She stirred her candy cane around in her mug a few times and took a sip of cocoa. "Ooh, this is delightful."

Leo jumped up beside Annie on the sofa and curled himself into a ball. "It's my mom's recipe."

Bea placed her mug on the side table. "Does she live nearby?"

Annie's heart pinged. "No. Unfortunately, I lost both my parents young."

Bea frowned at the news. "I'm sorry, honey."

Annie rolled back her shoulders. "It's all right, but thanks." She stared at her tiny Christmas tree and the snow globe sitting beneath it. The cocoa was great. It tasted so much like home. "Do you live alone?" Annie asked, although she suspected she knew the answer.

"Do now." Bea picked up her mug, staring down at it. She looked up, and her eyes seemed sad. "I lost my Harry a little over a year ago."

Annie's heart went out to the older woman. "I'm sorry. Were you together long?"

Bea nodded. "Thirty-six years."

"That's amazing," Annie said.

"Yes," Bea answered. She got a fond look on her face. "It was."

Before they knew it, an hour had passed with Bea telling Annie so much about her late husband and family. Annie shared a few minor details about her life too, but mostly kept the conversation casual and focused on her work at Lawson's.

"Well, thank you for the Christmas Eve cocoa," Bea said. "This has been lovely." She stood and looked around, scanning the coffee table. Nothing was on it but Annie's closed laptop. "Now that's odd."

"What is?"

Bea shoved her hands in her bathrobe pockets, rummaging around. "I could have sworn I put my house key on that table."

Annie frowned, noting the cat's empty spot on the sofa. She hadn't even realized he'd stealthily gotten up and moved. "Leo!" she called. She stood and smiled at Bea. "Hang on. I have an idea." Annie strode into the bedroom and peeked under her bed. Sure enough, Leo had Bea's key pinned down by his paws. Part of the red ribbon hung from his mouth. "Rascal." Annie snagged the key away from him. "Found it!" she called out to Bea.

Leo obviously liked Bea as much as she did.

He'd wanted her to stay.

THIRTEEN

On the fourth Christmas Eve

FA-LA-LA-LA-LA. LA-LA. LA—!

Annie popped up in bed like a jack-in-the-box, grasping her phone.

She stared down at its screen as light peered through her window.

Dec 24

Winter Storm Warning

This time she didn't blink. She pushed back the covers, nudging Leo onto the floor. He landed on his feet and meowed.

"I know, I know," she told him. "*You* don't remember yesterday, but *I* do."

She swung her feet to the floor, pulling her right foot back as she reached down and picked up Leo's wand toy. She shook it in her hand. "Not this time." She set it on her nightstand and stood, heaving a deep breath before striding to the window.

Okay. No snow on the fire escape, which meant there'd be none out front either.

And there wasn't!

Leo's stocking also wasn't filled. She stepped around a cat ball in the kitchen with a tiny silver bell in it. *As if he needs more toys.*

Her open laptop sat on the table.

Yep.

Dec 24 7:08 AM

She spotted the candy canes on the tree and something else. One of the cookbooks was missing from the bookshelf in the kitchen, leaving a rectangular gaping hole. *Yes.* There it was! Beside her electric kettle. So, Harrington? Could she hope that he'd really gotten that chili?

No. He couldn't have. If this was Christmas Eve, he still hadn't returned from Miami. Hang on. She peered into the sink basin and jumped! Only one empty mug sat in the sink, the telltale remnants of hot cocoa left in its bottom. What about Bea's mug? Annie was certain she'd had her over. She was equally positive she'd had new conversations with Braden yesterday. Not only with him. With Harrington too, and Eric. Plus Jane.

But since it was the twenty-fourth, she'd have to start over again with everything. Her pulse skittered. *Don't panic.* She could do the day over and do it *better*. Of course she could. Whether anybody else remembered it or not, she would. And, if today wasn't good enough—

Noooo!

Annie caught her breath.

She couldn't possibly be stuck here forever?

Her throat closed up.

Could she?

Leo wound himself around her ankles and meowed.

"Okay," she said. "I'll feed you." She did that carefully, responding to the intercom when it buzzed, announcing her package delivery. In a strange way she was looking forward to this day. Sure, it had its downsides, but there were upsides too. Annie felt like she was on a teeter-totter that was tilting in the opposite direction. It was enough to make her wonder whether enduring the bad parts of this time loop had been worth it.

No, Annie. Stop!

Seriously. What was she thinking? Nothing could have been worse than the chaos that unfolded at the store and having Veronica Lawson—of all people—happen upon it. Thank goodness she and Braden had been able to rectify the damage. Her heart fluttered when she recalled them working together, so seamlessly in tandem. She remembered her mission. The package, right, and coffee with Jane. *Not romance with Braden.* Although a few lilting thoughts hovered over that notion too.

Annie slipped into her coat and boots, remembering about the toilet paper. She walked into the bathroom and got the toilet paper roll, setting it on a high shelf in the bathroom linen closet. That door closed with a click. She grumbled to herself, "This is ridiculous." She grabbed her name tag off her desk in the bedroom, pinning it on the black vest hanging in her closet. That door closed with a click as well. Leo followed along, watching her every move. "Not this time, Leo." Today, she'd be better prepared for other things too.

Annie sprang back when the snow mound cascaded onto the stoop and picked up Jane's package. A short time later, she sat in the stairwell with Jane outside Jane's apartment. Jane handed her a coffee mug, and Annie remembered the candy canes in her coat pocket. "Oh hey! I brought us something."

"Brought us?" Jane asked. "What do you mean?"

"Erm. I've got these." She pulled out the two candy canes, and Jane laughed.

"Look at you, a walking-talking Christmas elf."

Annie handed Jane one. "I used to stir these in my coffee back in high school."

"Did you?" Jane stared at her treat. "Was it any good?"

"Delicious!" Annie unwrapped her candy cane and plopped it in her coffee.

Jane grinned. "All right. I'll try it."

"You weren't kidding about Amazing Agatha," Annie said. "I saw the doll at work. She's pricey."

Jane rolled her eyes. "Super pricey. We're talking a whole week's worth of rent." She unwrapped her candy cane, adding it to her coffee as well and stirring it around a couple of times. She rested her coffee mug on her knee. "Well." She shrugged. "If people will pay it."

"Yeah," Annie said. "Guess so."

Jane drank from her coffee. "If only there really was a Santa Claus."

Annie thought of the Santa at Lawson's, but no. He wasn't *the* Santa Claus. At best, he was some sort of wizard. She wouldn't tell Jane about that, though, or mention time travel either. She'd learned her lesson about that from Braden yesterday. "That would be epic."

"How old were you?" Jane asked her, "when you stopped believing?"

"Me? Oh." Annie's heart hurt. "Probably around nine."

Jane nodded. "Guess that's a typical age, though some kids wise up sooner." She must have noticed the storm clouds rolling across Annie's face. Jane leaned toward her. "Okay. Truth time. What did I say?"

"You?" Annie asked. "Nothing." What did it hurt to give this tidbit up? Jane wouldn't even remember it tomorrow. "I just"—Annie paused—"what I mean is, nine was a hard age. I lost my folks then."

Jane's eyes watered. "Oh, Annie. I'm so sorry."

"It's all right." Annie picked up her coffee and took a sip. "Life went on."

"Did you...?" Jane winced. "Go to live with relatives? What?"

Annie's memories tugged her back in time.

Blue lights flashed in the driveway, painting streaks against the living room windows as heavy snow fell outdoors. Her sitter Debbie sat beside her on the sofa in silence, hugging her elbows to herself. Debbie's mom sat in an armchair, and the lady police officer stood in the hall, while a second officer waited in their cruiser.

Tires crunched on the snow, and a car door popped open, slamming shut. Seconds later, Grandma Mable arrived in the living room, her coat and white hair dusted with snow and her face long. "Annie. Sweetheart." She held out her arms and hugged Annie, but Annie couldn't move. Or speak. She could barely think. All she could do was wish with all her might that none of this was real. Just a terrible, terrible dream—and that she'd soon wake up.

Jane laid a hand on Annie's arm, and Annie turned toward her. "My Grandma Mable took me in. She was my grandma on my dad's side, and the only relative I had in Red Bank at the time."

"New Jersey?"

"Yeah." She shrugged out of her coat. "My mom's parents were still around, but they were older and in ill health, plus they lived in Canada. I guess the family thought that move would have been too big a change."

Jane set her chin. "Sounds like that was the right call?"

Annie nodded. "I was able to stay at my same school and keep my friends—for a while." Annie folded over her coat, setting it on the step beside her. "But, later in elementary school, that friend group pretty much faded away. I was the odd one out, I guess, and it was awkward for the other girls that I didn't have parents—or even divorced parents, like some of them. Things got a little rough in middle school. The only one who never made an issue of my home situation was Tina. We met in the seventh grade."

"Are you still in touch with Tina?"

Annie frowned. "Not at present. We sort of had a falling-out."

"Ugh. Sorry. And your Grandma Mable? Is she still in Red Bank?"

"No. She died the year after I graduated from high school. I came to live in the city after that. Tina was in school here, and she encouraged me."

"Jeez"—Jane stared at the ceiling—"and there I thought my childhood was rough because my brothers picked on me." She said it lightly, like it hadn't been a serious big deal, and Annie was glad for the turn in the conversation. Anything to take her mind off Red Bank and those difficult early years.

"Did they?"

"Only until I learned to whip their tails." Jane held up her arm and flexed a muscle. "Brown belt in judo."

Annie chuckled, liking Jane so much. This also made her feel a little guilty about Tina, but she wasn't replacing their friendship. She was simply making a new friend, she hoped. Tina had always had other friends besides her, and Annie had understood. Maybe she'd been too dependent on Tina without realizing it. "Good for you!" She thought on this. "Do you get along with your brothers now?"

"Oh yeah," Jane said easily. "We're tighter than tight." She winked at Annie. "That's because they respect me."

"Ha! Bet so."

Jane took another sip of coffee. "Mmm, this is really good." She grinned. "Minty."

Annie's tensions eased. "Peppermint-y, yeah." She blinked when it hit her. She *was* tasting the peppermint—very strongly, and it was super good. She wondered about Jane and what her story was.

"I'm lucky, I know." Jane's face fell. "It's just hard sometimes being on my own with Cari."

"So Cari's dad isn't—?"

Jane shook her head. "We had a thing back in high school. When he found out I was pregnant, he wanted nothing to do with it."

An arrow shot through Annie's heart. That sounded terrible. So callous.

"But I understand," Jane said. "We were just kids ourselves."

"But aren't there laws?"

Jane's eyes were rimmed with sadness. "To what? Force him to participate? Make him want to be her dad?" There was no anger in her voice, only sorrow. This moved Annie.

Jane sighed. "I make more money than he does anyway, and his life hasn't been good. He's had trouble—with things." Annie wondered with what. With the law? With drugs? She didn't dare ask. She was touched that Jane was confiding in her.

"I'm sorry, Jane."

"Life's not all gloom and doom." She looked up with an impish grin. "My ex's parents are involved, and I've got Sam."

"Boyfriend?"

Her grin broadened, and she got a salty look in her eyes. "Girlfriend. We've been together five months now."

Even though she didn't know Jane well, it did Annie's heart good to know that she had someone. "So Sam's in Brooklyn?"

"Sadly, no. Akron." Jane crossed her arms. "We met online like pretty much everyone these days and are trying to make it work."

"If it's meant to be, it will happen."

"Hope so," Jane said. "Because I really like Sam. She's stable. Caring. Plus, the kid loves her."

"Well, that says a lot."

Jane nodded. "It does." She studied Annie a moment. "How about you? Got someone special?"

"I...did? But we were a bad fit."

"Bummer." She raised her coffee mug and took a sip.

"Roy had—opinions."

"Uh-oh," Jane said, clearly not liking the sound of that.

Annie blew out a breath. "At first, I thought it was good, you know? He was a little older, and I wrongly thought wiser. I was kind of adrift after losing Grandma Mable, and newish in a big city. Then along came Roy, promising to solve everything. In retrospect, he probably caused more problems than he solved," she said, stewing over her painful rift with Tina.

"Sounds like he *was* a bad fit, in that case." She toasted Annie's coffee mug with hers. "Here's to moving on."

"Yeah." Annie smiled, feeling stronger about that.

"How long ago was this?"

"We broke up last summer."

Jane nudged her with her elbow. "So, hey. Maybe someone else will come along?"

Annie's pulse fluttered. *Someone tall, dark, and handsome with bright-blue eyes.*

"Wait one New York minute!" Jane grinned. "Or maybe they already have?"

"Not sure," she said shyly. "Maybe?"

Jane winked. "Good things happen at Christmas."

"That's what I hear."

If only she could get there.

FOURTEEN

"HOLD THAT ELEVATOR!" BRADEN. STRIDING toward her and looking like a dream wearing his lopsided grin. Annie mashed the button on the elevator panel, stilling the door's retreat, and Braden stepped inside the cramped space, his lemony-spicy scent filling the air.

No one else was on the elevator but them. Still. Annie tried not to stand too close. He radiated so much hotness, she feared she might combust. He didn't know he was going to offer to help her later, and ask her out for coffee, but she did. And the knowledge was killing her. It was like knowing what he was going to know before he knew it. Or something very confusing like that. This was their fourth Christmas Eve together, and each time she saw him she only liked him more. It was probably too much to hope he recalled something of their previous conversations.

She hoped anyway.

He narrowed his eyes at her. "Have we met?"

So much for that! "Er, no. Nope. Don't think so. I would have remembered you." *Ack!* She'd said that out loud?

"Ah, yeah. Right." He raked a hand through his hair. "I

normally work nights." Didn't she know it. She also knew he was going to spend part of this night with her. At least, she hoped they'd still go to the Blue Dot. That outing had been fantastic. So had their walk to the subway. Although her second coffee date with him had seemed a bit more serious, she intuited they were growing closer. Even if their recollections of that were slightly one-sided.

He held out his hand. "I'm Braden."

She squeezed his grip and swooned. Touching him was like falling into a time warp—or out of one. Whatever was happening, it always felt so good. He tucked his hands under his arms and stared at the ceiling, then around at the elevator's walls. Also, down at his feet. He finally looked up, surveying her outfit.

"Cute pin," he said, commenting on the decorative holly wreath jewelry on her vest.

Annie grinned tightly. "Thanks! Nice…" She studied him, searching for a way to return the compliment. Badge? Silly. No. "Uniform," was all she could think of. Her face flamed—*ouch*—so hot.

He scratched his head. "Standard issue."

Annie mentally face-palmed. "Well, you wear it *very* well."

His ears went red. Great. Overly personal.

She had to fix this. *Divert. Divert. Divert.*

"I mean, er." She pointed to his duty belt. "You seem really well equipped."

He arched one eyebrow, and her cheeks steamed.

Gah! Way to make it worse. Frying pan into the fire.

"What I meant to say was"—Annie bit her lip—"you have so

much junk there!" Oh. My. God. She did *not* just say that while apparently staring at his crotch. Annie tugged at her too-tight turtleneck. "I uh—meant *st-stuff*." Boy, it was stuffy in here. She fanned her burning face with her hand, but it honestly didn't help. She pointed to his flashlight. "Guess that comes in handy in power outages!"

"It can."

Her view bypassed the handcuffs. No, she wouldn't dare. "And I see you've got a baton."

"Yep."

"What's that?" she asked, noting the dual containers.

"Mag pouches."

"Mag?" Oh. "*Ohhh*." She glanced at his holster. "Right." She stared at the elevator floor numbers above the door. This was the slowest ride on earth. "Not much call for that at Lawson's, I guess," she said lightly.

"Not usually."

Sweat broke out on her brow. "And that one?" she asked, pointing to a smallish canister.

"C.O."

"What?"

He peered into her eyes, and her skin tingled all over. "Pepper spray."

Ouch. That did not sound fun.

She was not, not, not going to ask about his gun.

They reached the ground floor—*finally*—and he gave her a curious grin. "Are you aiming to make some trouble, Annie?" His thumb grazed over his handcuffs.

She wanted to *die, die, die*. "Who, me?" her voice squeaked. "No." She wiped the sweat from her temples. Gross. She cut him a glance, prepared to make her escape. "It's just nice to know we're in good hands, here at, ah—Lawson's."

The elevator doors opened, and she scurried out of there as fast as she could go.

"Bye!"

She got halfway through Homewares and held her breath, daring to peek over her shoulder. Braden seemed to be mumbling to himself and walking away. She was sure she'd made a great impression.

You wear it very *well. Gah!*

Although—honestly—he did. Maybe he wouldn't remember this tomorrow? In any case, if it was another redux day, she was *not* getting back on an elevator with him.

She obviously couldn't handle it.

Annie walked past Patrice in Bridal carrying her package of jumbo lights. "Got it!" she said before Patrice could say a word.

Patrice blinked. "I was just about to tell you—"

"No problem! I'll fix it."

"Annie, wait!"

Annie spun around to face Patrice by the second-floor escalator fronting the shoe section. "I'd like to have a minute"—Patrice pushed back her glasses—"upstairs." Meaning on the third floor in the employee conference room.

"For a little chat?"

Patrice gaped at her. "What?"

Annie couldn't spare the time. "Hold that thought!"

Patrice lowered her voice. "Is something going on, Annie?"

Annie blew out a breath. "I've got to save my window before Ms. Lawson gets here."

Patrice blinked. "Ms. Lawson's not expected today."

"Oh yes, she is!" Annie said, wheeling back around.

"Annie!" Patrice called.

"I'm sorry, Patrice," Annie said over her shoulder. "I'm trying to save my job."

She almost bulldozed Kira in Juniors. "Kira! Oh! Sorry!"

"Annie?" Kira scooted out of Annie's path, yanking the headless mannequin toward her. She'd been dressing it in a sparkly red top and jeans. One of its arms fell off, but Kira caught it. "*Where's the fire?*"

Annie raced down the escalator two steps at a time, taking care with her footing in her heels. "I'm trying to put it out!"

Annie weaved through the crowd, circumventing the ladies with their shopping bags. *Here comes the guy leaving the jewelry counter.* He moved aside just as Annie did, stepping right in front of her. "Ooh! Sorry!" He shifted to one side. The same side as Annie. She tried to get around him, but he got in the way. What was this? A dance?

"Sir. Uh, excuse me."

"Sure, sure." He finally stepped back so she could get through.

"No, Dylan! Let me!" The young boy raced past Annie, darting through Homewares.

Another kid yanked on his arm, scooting in front of him. "No, Marcus! Me first!"

"Dylan! Marcus!" their mom called, chasing after them.

You've got to be kidding me.

Annie scurried toward her display window as Braden turned, noting the commotion.

Noooo!

She dropped the lights and raced for the falling Christmas tree, the same time as Braden. It slipped through their grasps…and they stumbled forward. Both of them landed in a heap in the fake snow, with Annie on top of Braden, her chest bearing down on his.

Ooh, it's rock-hard. Solid.

Every. Inch. Of her broiled.

"Are you all right?" he asked with his arms around her.

"Yeah, uh—" She pushed back on his shoulders and tentatively patted herself down—the parts of her that she could reach that weren't smashed up against him. "Fine."

His heart pounded against hers, and his hard duty belt pressed up against her. At least she thought it was his duty belt. His face went beet red, and she scrambled to her feet. Braden pushed himself off the ground and dusted off his pants. His uniform shirt, as well. He snatched a peek at her, turning away to report the incident to the security office. "Mike, we've had a little incident down here."

Mike's chortle crackled back through the radio. "Yeah. We got it all on CCTV," he teased. Mike cleared his throat. "But seriously, I'll send Charlie to assist and get Lou on the door."

"Thanks, Mike."

Annie's pulse raced. First, she'd nearly kissed the gorgeous guy in front of Veronica Lawson. Now, she'd landed smack on top of him right here in her window. *Talk about making a display*. Maybe the camera footage wouldn't keep? She couldn't keep doing this day after day.

"Boys!" the dismayed mom shouted. "What have you done?"

Santa strolled over, addressing the boys with arms akimbo. "You were coming to see me?"

Annie avoided Braden's eyes as the blur of events unfolded. Every instant she was around the incredible guy, she kept falling for him harder, but could she just get through one day with him—without things becoming incredibly awkward? At this particular moment, the answered appeared to be *nope*.

FIFTEEN

ANNIE BROUGHT THE TRAIN TRACK pieces over to the Christmas tree, and Braden carried the engine and three of the boxcars. They'd set these things by the front of the window earlier while cleaning up and re-dressing the tree. "This should make easy work," Braden said. The toy train itself wasn't that big. There were six boxcars altogether and the bright-red caboose.

Annie squatted to connect the track pieces until they formed a wide circle around the base of the Christmas tree and its skirt. She smiled up at him. "Yes, we're almost done!" The icicle lights had been secured over the window, and the decorations were all back on the mantel.

"Everything's shaping up." Braden set down the engine and boxcars, going back to get the rest of the boxcars and the caboose. He handed them to Annie, and she held up an empty boxcar, peering into it. "It would be fun to fill these with something."

"Any ideas?"

"I'll think on it."

He passed her the caboose, and Annie chuckled. "Guess that's you!" she said, holding it up.

"Sorry?" He glanced over his shoulder, stealing a peek at his bum.

"Oh! Um. Not that— What I meant was—" *Think. Think. Think.* "Didn't you say something about being the baby brother?"

"Did I? When?"

"Uh, earlier?"

"Earlier?" He scratched his head. "But not today?"

"I, er—think we spoke at the"—she peered at the shimmering lights on the tree—"holiday party!"

She could tell he was searching his mind and drawing a blank. "That's funny," he said. "I don't remember seeing you there."

"That's because I was only there briefly. Very, very briefly, like in the blink of an eye!" She batted her eyelashes at him.

"If you say so," he said, still looking unsure.

Enough about the party you didn't go to, Annie! "So, erm"—she lifted the engine and a boxcar, one in each hand—"should we hook up?"

Braden blinked. "Well. Annie." He cleared his throat.

Noooo. "No, gosh, no." She scrambled to her feet. "Not *hook up*."

He set one hand on his duty belt, dangerously close to those handcuffs.

Annie's chin jerked up. "I mean, *n-n-not yet*." *Eeep! Did you actually say that? Please, floor, open up and swallow me now.* "Or-or probably ever!"

"Never?"

She couldn't exactly promise him that. But he did *not* need to know about her fantasies. She'd already blabbed enough. "What I meant was! Ha!"

"Ahh, gotcha." He stared down at the track. "You want us to put the train set together."

"*Yes.*" Thank God. She kept her eyes glued to the floor as they did that, not daring to peek at Braden. First the elevator, then the window tackle, now the hookup talk? What was wrong with her? She was making a mess of this day, and it wasn't like she hadn't had practice.

They attached the train cars, and Brandon switched on the engine. It took off circling around the tree, merrily pulling the other cars along. They both stood and dusted the fake snow glitter from their pants. She peeked at Brandon and caught him staring at her. Who knows what he thought of her now. But maybe this wasn't a bad thing. In a very weird—and okay, okay *awkward*—way, they were bonding.

Braden shifted on his feet. "Cute train."

"Yeah, er. It looks really sweet!" She straightened her vest. "Braden?"

"Hmm?"

"Thanks for breaking my fall earlier, when"—she shrugged—"you know."

"Glad no one got hurt."

"Plus, nothing got broken!" she said.

He nodded with amazement. "Good thing about Santa's cookies and milk all being fake, and that plate made of plastic. Those Christmas tree balls too." He grinned at her. "You really planned this carefully."

Maybe not the first time. Annie heaved a breath. "Yeah." Keeping this alternate reality from Braden just felt *wrong*. She'd tried talking to him about it earlier, but there didn't seem to be any great way to explain things so he'd understand. Still. She seemed to be punching holes through this time loop bit by bit. She was spending more time with her neighbors, and obviously with Braden too. If only all the people she was getting to know better, were also getting to know her better back—so they were truly connecting.

Santa stopped to examine the window. "Nice job, you two!" He adjusted his Santa hat.

"Wait for it," Annie whispered to Braden. "He's going to say something isn't quite right." Even though she'd majorly embarrassed herself in front of him, many times now, she was growing more comfortable around Braden. Maybe it was *because of* those moments that they felt more like kindred spirits? He'd never judged her negatively in any way, and all her assessments about him had been heart-poundingly favorable.

Santa eyed the table holding the fake cookies and milk. "Still. This display could use a little something."

Braden repressed a grin. "How did you know?" he asked under his breath.

"I'm a very good guesser." Annie winked, feeling emboldened and maybe a tiny bit flirty. And flirting with Braden felt good, like she should have done it a little more.

Oh yeah, right.

She had.

Duty belt, hook up, gah.

"I've got it!" Santa snapped his gloved fingers. "Those cookies! They're not quite right."

"Cookies?" Annie asked. "They're not real ones, Santa."

"No, but what kind do you have there?" He ambled over to get a closer look.

Annie retrieved the plate and took it to him. "Fake sugar cookies and gingerbread people."

Santa clicked his tongue. "That's what it is!" He smiled at Braden and Annie. "Everybody knows Santa's favorite cookies are oatmeal raisin." Annie didn't want to argue with the older man, but she'd never heard that one before.

"You don't possibly have any of those in back?" Braden asked her.

Annie thought on this. "The box of prop cookies is a variety pack."

"Aha!" Santa said. "You see there? Should be simple enough to add some." Annie winced at Braden. She felt kind of caught, but what did it matter in the scheme of things?

Braden held open his hands. "Why not?"

True. Everything Santa had suggested had helped improve the window display. She wasn't sure what oatmeal raisin cookies would add, but she decided to humor Kris Kringle. "Sure, Santa," she told him. "Really great idea, thanks!"

Braden followed her into the stockroom and chuckled. "Man, oh man. That guy thinks he's the real deal."

"Maybe he is the real deal?" Annie teased.

"Now, Annie. Don't go getting any ideas." Her nerves skittered happily at the thought of them spending more time together.

She really hoped they'd get to go to the Blue Dot. Maybe she shouldn't chance it? Why not ask him?

Come on, Annie, Tina's voice egged her on, *be brave.*

"Aha! Here it is!" She pulled the cookie box from a shelf and examined its contents through its clear plastic window. There were four of each kind of the different varieties and—*yes*—oatmeal raisin was included. She slid out the plastic tray holding them and removed two oatmeal raisin cookies. She passed Braden the oatmeal cookies and he held them. "The only idea I'm getting," she said, "is that I'd like to finish this up so we can go get coffee." Annie flushed. That came out so *direct. So different* from how she was—normally.

But maybe this was her new normal? Every day was changing ever so slightly. Maybe she was too?

Braden cocked his head, looking pleased. "Are you asking me to coffee, Annie?" At least that was tamer than what he'd thought she'd been suggesting earlier.

She slid the cookie box back on the shelf. "Might be."

"Only if you'll let me buy."

"That hardly seems fair—when you've done so much to help me."

"How about this?" He smiled. "You can buy next time?"

Her heart pounded so, so hard. *Next time? Yes.* She'd love that, she really would. Annie wanted there to be a "next time" with all her heart. "All right," she said, like her pulse wasn't racing and her mind spiraling off in all sorts of directions. Braden seemed so nice. Outgoing and kind. He'd probably make the very best boyfriend someday.

Don't get ahead of yourself, Annie.

You'll have to get out of this time loop first.

Braden held open the stockroom door. "So. About that coffee," he said as she walked past him. "Where were you thinking?"

"The Blue Dot has great jelly donuts, I hear. "

He grinned, and his voice went husky. "I *love* that place."

SIXTEEN

BRADEN OPENED HIS PAPER SACK, offering Annie one of the two jelly donuts he'd gotten.

"Oh no, those are for you." Still, she looked tempted.

She wasn't as shy as he'd first suspected. She had a subtle sassy side that could be very direct. Like when she'd invited him out for coffee. And he was awfully glad she had. Otherwise, he'd been prepared to ask her. "You're the one who mentioned the jelly donuts here."

She shrugged. "I thought you might enjoy them."

"You're *such* a good guesser," he teased. "And you're right. These are the best."

She reached for the bag. "I'll take half." She broke one in two. A burst of gooey red jelly stuck to her fingers.

"I'll take that." He accepted the morsel before she could return it to the bag. She nibbled on her treat, and so did he.

"Mmm." She smacked her lips. "Delicious!"

She had little white powder dots stuck to her lips, making her look adorable. He motioned with his napkin, and she got it, wiping her mouth.

She took a sip of coffee. "I haven't had a donut in—well, a really long time I guess."

"Why not?"

She shrugged. "I'm normally not huge into..." He thought she was going to say sweets. Some people were like that. Having more of a salt tooth than a sugar one. Instead she said, "food."

He frowned. "Really?" That was such a foreign concept to him.

"I mean, I haven't been. Typically." She finished the rest of her donut half, gobbling it down. "At least not for a while."

He wondered what she meant by that. "So. You used to be more into donuts and such?"

"Oh yeah, hugely when I was a kid." She took a small sip of coffee. "In high school, I was in the baking club."

"There was a baking club?" he asked, amazed.

"I wasn't into it at first. My friend Tina made me join, thinking if I learned to make tasty treats, I'd ultimately enjoy them."

"But no?" he asked, dumbfounded.

Annie shook her head. "Not so much, but it was fun watching others drooling over our goodies. We met once a month and tried out new recipes. There was an anonymous vote to see whose dish was the favorite."

"How was it anonymous?"

"All the cakes, pies, or whatevers, were laid out on a table and numbered—no names. People tasted a small sample of each and voted on their favorites. Sometimes, teachers stopped in 'by coincidence,' asking if we wanted their opinions too."

He chuckled at this. "Sneaky teachers."

"We didn't mind. There was always more than enough."

"So. Always sweet stuff? Desserts?"

She nodded. "Generally. We did a holiday party with lunch foods too, and another one like it at the end of the year."

He leaned back on his bench and patted his tummy. "That sounds like my kind of club."

"Yeah. You mentioned cannoli."

"What? Did I?"

Eeep. "At some point, I think so? Is your family Italian?"

"Yeah, third generation. Tate was my stepdad's last name. He formally adopted me after marrying my mom, since I was the only little kid at home. My sisters were all a lot older and out on their own."

"And your dad?"

He shrugged. "He died when I was so little, it's hard to remember a ton about him. Other than his laugh—he had a great one, and his smile—really kind."

"I'm sorry about that."

"It's fine," he said, meaning it. "My stepdad Fred was really good to me. That's why we moved to the city, me and my mom, after my mom married him."

Annie nodded, seeming to process this. "What else were you into back in high school?" he asked her. He liked learning about her past.

"Working on set design for the high school plays. Tina was the thespian. I got her into that."

He smiled. "Sounds like you two were good for each other." He studied her a moment, understanding her interest in visual aesthetics went way back. "So window dressing isn't such a stretch."

"No." She shrugged happily. "It was a natural fit. And you?" she asked him. "What were you into as a kid?"

"Sports. Music."

"Music? You mean like favorite bands?"

"I mean I was in a band. Garage band. Except we didn't have a garage, so my buddies and I practiced in the alleyway next to our apartment building."

She smirked teasingly. "Bet your neighbors loved that."

"Ha, yeah." He smiled at the memory of all the heavy-duty power cords streaming out of windows. "We never went anywhere, other than to play at a few high school parties."

"That's pretty cool."

"You might not say that if you'd heard us."

"Come on." She grinned. "I'll bet you were good. What did you play?"

"Electric keyboard. My folks were very tolerant." He shook his head. "They were also glad when it ended." He laughed. "So were the neighbors."

She seemed to be eying the donut bag. "We do have another," he said. "If you want one more?"

"Oh no, I couldn't. Really. If I eat that, that will be my dinner."

He whistled. "That's a very light dinner in my book."

"You're right. And anyway, I won't be eating until later."

He opened the bag and split the second donut with her, enjoying their snack and their conversation. "No?"

"I'm making chili for my neighbor, Harrington."

A muscle in his cheek flinched. He wasn't jealous, of course not. Annie had her own life. Still, he asked, "Harrington?"

"He's a gentleman in my building." Annie read his probing look. "A *much older* gentleman."

His tension eased, though he didn't know why. It wasn't like he was dating Annie. Not even close. "That's nice of you to look out for him."

"He lives alone," Annie explained. "Lost his wife some time ago." She shrugged. "So I thought it would be nice to do something."

He viewed her admiringly. "Do you know your other neighbors?"

"Most of them. Another guy lives on the ground floor, same as Harrington. That's Eric. He's younger and in grad school at NYU. Then there's Jane. She's the sweetest, and a hardworking single mom. I've just started getting to know her, and Bea."

"And Bea is?"

"She's the older lady who lives across the hall from me. Not 'older' older like Harrington, who's more like old enough to be my grandpa. I'd say in her late fifties or so."

"That's cool you know the people in your building," he said. "I don't know any of them in mine. I pass folks walking their dogs occasionally and we say hi, but that's about it."

"It can be hard to reach out," she said, like she knew a lot about it. Although that was hard to believe. She'd so easily impacted him with her kindness.

"So, tell me about Tina." They'd chatted some while redressing Annie's Christmas tree at Lawson's, and Braden was curious to learn more.

She blinked in surprise. "There isn't much to tell."

"You said at the store you'd had a falling-out. When we were talking about best friends, and I told you about Harper and his family."

"Ahh, it's a long story, and"—she glanced at the snowy scene outside and people hustling by on the sidewalk—"we don't have much time."

"Maybe give me the short version?" He didn't know why he was encouraging her to share. It wasn't like they were that well acquainted. Still. He sensed that she needed another friend. Maybe he did too.

She hung her head. "Tina said something to me about Roy."

He could pretty much guess Roy was an ex. "What did she say?"

"She hinted that he was a player. Unfaithful. And also, bad for me in other ways."

Braden set his jaw, not liking the sound of that. "Was he?"

"Unfortunately, yeah," she said sadly. "The thing is, I refused to believe Tina."

"I see."

"I really regret it now." She frowned. "But so much time has gone by."

"How much time?"

She whimpered. "Months."

"Annie." Braden reached out and took her hand on the table. "It's never too late to make amends."

Her chin quivered. "In this case, I'm afraid it might be."

He held her hand tighter. "You won't know until you try?"

She exhaled a shaky breath. "I'm sure you're right."

"It's Christmas, hey," he said. "Good things happen."

Her laugh was a little melancholy. "You're the second person who's said that to me today."

"Let me guess," he ribbed. "The other was Santa?"

"No." A smile graced her lips. "Jane."

He couldn't resist the banter. "Guess I'm not the great guesser you are, huh?"

This made her chuckle again, just as he'd hoped.

She squeezed his hand and released it. "Thanks, Braden."

His heart wrenched when she let go, like he'd inexplicably lost something. Whoa. That was weird. He barely even *knew* Annie. He folded his napkin over on the table, hunting for something else to say. "So!" he said, looking up. "Santa likes oatmeal raisin cookies! Who knew?"

"I know, right?" She leaned toward him. "At least he should be happier with our display tomorrow." Braden liked the way she'd said *our* display, like she'd let him into her world and he'd been a part of it.

But wait. "Tomorrow? Isn't that Christmas Day?"

"Oh, right!"

"So, our guy Santa will be very busy."

"No," she corrected lightly. "He'll be busy tonight."

SEVENTEEN

A FEW HOURS LATER, ANNIE stood at her stove using Leo as her culinary consultant. He sat watching her from the living room after becoming bored with his tiny chipmunk toy. "What do you think, Leo? Not enough chili powder?"

He meowed.

"All right," she said. "We'll try it." She added another dash of the ingredient and stirred her wooden spoon in the pot. She grabbed a fresh teaspoon from a drawer, taking another sample. The chili was hot and smelled aromatically delicious. She slurped carefully. Flavors burst onto her tongue. This was so much better than yesterday's. Yum! "Your idea about adding a pinch of cinnamon was genius."

Leo blinked as if to say, "You're welcome."

Though it really wasn't his idea at all. Her mom's recipe was amazing, but suddenly Annie was spurred to arrive at one of her own. It was a little like her window designs. She sometimes took inspiration from what other visual artists did. Though her displays were unique, it was informative to see how others put their windows together. Their individual twists encouraged her to come up with her own themes. Just like she was doing with this chili recipe. She'd stayed up late poring over recipes online, getting to bed just before midnight.

She paused in her work, setting the wooden spoon on a spoon rest.

Of course! That's what she should do!

Stay up until midnight.

Annie groaned. Why hadn't she thought of that earlier? That way she'd break through into Christmas. *Yes.* And tomorrow would be another day!

Annie turned off the gas burner, believing the chili was just right. Not too spicy, but with exactly the right amount of heat. She couldn't wait to take it to Harrington, and when she did, he was so appreciative.

As she gave him her phone number to call when he was ready to return the casserole dish, she said, "Maybe you should put my number in your wallet?"

He leaned into his walker, seeming perplexed. "I won't be taking your chili pot with me to the market."

She smiled. "No, but you never know? Maybe you'll be out somewhere, and—" She'd been about to say "need help," but that would only make him feel helpless, which he wasn't. Besides that, Harrington was clearly a proud man.

"And?" His forehead creased below his short-shorn gray hair.

"Need something," she said. "Say. If you're on a trip. Visiting your brother or something, and want to know what the weather is like back home?"

"That's what the weather forecast is for."

"Those are sometimes local." She knew he didn't own a smart phone or a computer, so he could hardly check the weather on those.

"If I didn't know better, young lady, I'd say you were hitting on me." He held a mischievous gleam in his eye, and Annie knew he was joking.

She smirked. "I've always liked mature men."

"In that case, I'm right in that category."

"Come on now." She handed him her number on a piece of paper. "Keep it with you. Just in case. You might get stuck somewhere. Need someone to call a car."

"Seems to me I could do that rather than phone you."

"Harrington, please take this. And call me. If you need anything. I mean it. I'm in and out of here almost every day for work, and—even during my days off—it's easy enough for me to run a quick errand." She passed him the paper, and he took it. "There's no need for you to go all the way to the store if I can grab something for you when I'm there anyway." Annie was aware there were grocery services that delivered, but they were pricey, and it seemed Harrington lived on a budget.

"It's good for me to get out," he said, being stubborn. "That's how I keep my youthful figure."

She cocked an eyebrow, and he relented.

He folded the piece of paper with her number on it and tucked it in his wallet. "Thanks for this," he said, waving his wallet in the air before sliding it into his hip pocket. "And thanks for the chili too. I know I'll enjoy it."

"What did you do?" she asked him, curious. "For a job back when you worked?"

He smiled proudly. "I was a conductor for the MTA."

"You drove the trains?"

He nodded. "Yes, ma'am, I did. For a good forty years."

She noted a framed black-and-white photo of a young couple on an end table by the sofa. Wait. That face. She glanced at Harrington. That was him—years younger. With a broad smile and beaming dark eyes. The woman with him was gorgeous.

"That's me with my Gracie," he said, seeing her eyes on the picture. "She was my everything."

Annie's heart ached at how he'd said that.

Harrington hung his head. "Lost her six years ago in May. Mother's Day weekend too."

"I'm so sorry. Did you and she—?"

Harrington peered up at her with red-rimmed eyes. "No kids. We wanted them. But life?" He shrugged. "Had other plans."

"I'm sorry."

"She was a very gifted woman," he said. "Worked at Our Savior of Peace as their administrative assistant. She also played the organ."

"How nice. Did she sing?"

He appeared lost in a happy fog. "Beautifully."

"May I?" she said, asking permission to pick up the picture.

"Go right ahead."

She admired the couple and how happy they seemed, a well-matched pair. "How about you?" she asked, looking up. "Did you sing too?"

"Not so much." Harrington chuckled. "I tried joining the choir, but they asked me to leave."

Annie gasped. "You're kidding?"

"The choir director was very serious about the music there."

Annie couldn't believe it. "I know, but still."

"It's all right." He grinned. "I'd only done it to capture Gracie's attention anyway. That's how we met—in church."

So this was historic data. "How long ago was this?"

"Ooh." He tapped his chin. "Going on fifty years now."

Annie teasingly chided him. "So you were hitting on *her*."

"I suppose I was." He chuckled. "In a godly way."

Annie carefully set the photo back on the end table. "Maybe the Man Upstairs had something to do with getting you two together?"

"Hmm. Maybe?" He smiled. "That's what Gracie and I always believed."

Annie knew she had to go. She wanted to see Eric in the hall and be ready when Bea came by later. She really liked Harrington though. He was such a nice man.

"Thanks, Annie." When she opened the door, he stopped her. "You really are some kind of angel, you know."

But she knew that she wasn't. Not really. She was merely being a good neighbor, something she maybe should have thought of being before. She nearly missed Eric as he ducked in his door, holding his stash of mail. "Oh hey!" she said. "Good to see you."

"Oh yeah, Annie. You too." He stared at the door behind her. "Checking on Harrington?"

"Yeah. Took him some supper."

"That was nice. How's he doing?"

"Better than before."

Eric nodded, preparing to go.

"Eric!"

He peered over his shoulder.

"What was your favorite treat on Christmas morning?"

"That's easy," he said. "Cinnamon rolls."

Great. That gave Annie an idea.

She got ready for bed that night, humming a happy Christmas tune. While she'd not made it out of the time loop, she'd made the most of each day, to the extent of her abilities. Leo snuggled down on the covers, and Annie reached into her closet for the extra pillows she kept on her closet shelf. A canvas caught her eye in the darkened corner. The painting was one of her dad's, and he'd made it years ago when she was a girl. The colorful oil stood seventeen inches tall by twelve inches wide and was whimsical in its own way. Her dad had painted her Christmas snow globe, and tiny snowflakes drifted inside it. The sign in the snowy white yard said: *Believe.*

Annie hadn't dared to dwell on it for years. And yet, it had been impossible to part with this gift from her dad's heart. She reached for the frame with trembling fingers and lifted the piece out of the closet, setting it on her desk, propped against the wall. Hurt welled in Annie's throat and in her eyes. When she'd gotten that special snow globe for Christmas, she'd loved it dearly, believing with her whole heart that it had been made for her by Santa's elves. But it was made from real glass and not plastic, and she was worried sick she might break it.

Having a kind and sensitive heart, her dad had created a special painting capturing the essence of the snow globe, so that—no matter what happened throughout the years—the lovely image would always be hers. He'd given it to her the morning that he and her mom went out with Aunt Susan and Uncle Bob to the show. "If anything ever really does happen to your snow globe, Annie," her dad had said, "you'll always have this." He'd winked, and his longish dark hair had dipped forward.

Her dad held out his arms, and nine-year-old Annie raced toward him, getting embraced in his big, strong hug. He smelled of sandalwood and sawdust. Apart from painting oils, he did woodturning too. "I love you, Annie"—he lightly stroked her hair—"and always will."

Her eyes filled hot to brimming.

Annie sniffed and grabbed a tissue from her nightstand, wiping her tears.

"Don't cry, Annie." It was her mom's voice, soft and faint like the distant tinkling of sleigh bells. "We're here." Annie clutched her hands to her chest and stared around the room.

"Mom? Dad?" Her voice trembled.

Leo lifted his head from his spot on the covers, but all she heard was the fierce whistling wind blustering up against the window.

"Yeah, boy"—she blew out a breath—"I need some rest."

But she wasn't going to sleep before midnight, because now more than ever she wanted to get through to Christmas Day—so she could text Tina and do something nice for her neighbors. Move past those boys trashing her window design and find a way to salvage her career. And maybe, just maybe, develop a future with Braden. She felt a sharp tug on her heartstrings. Oddly, she was going to miss their store Santa. But he never worked after Christmas Eve, for obvious reasons.

Annie considered her dad's painting. Though she'd had it in her childhood room at Grandma Mable's, she'd never put it up here. Maybe she'd bring it into the living room tomorrow and leave it out for the whole day. It would be a way to keep her parents present, and maybe it was time. She fluffed a couple of pillows against the headboard, settling in to read the new book she'd borrowed from the library. It was a rom-com like those films she liked to watch. That made her think of Braden.

What if they *were* meant to be together after all this craziness ended? Even if her repeat Christmas Eves never stopped, she ached to continue seeing him again. He was so tender and caring in a way that made her feel more positive about the world. Like she could conquer any calamity and maybe even finally get her own merry Christmas after all.

EIGHTEEN

On the fifth Christmas Eve

FA-LA-LA-LA-LA. LA-LA—!

Annie muted her phone, holding it up in front of her.

She squinted at the date. *Oof. Of course.*

Dec 24

Winter Storm Warning

She closed her eyes and groaned. She'd tried to stay up—so hard. But, by eleven thirty, she'd been exhausted and must have drifted off. Annie peered down at the floor where her paperback book had slid off the bed, landing beside the feather-and-wand cat toy. She reached over and switched off the lamp beside her bed, picking up the book and cat toy and setting them aside.

Leo "made biscuits" beside her, purring loudly and pressing his claws against her duvet.

Okay, Annie.

Think, think, think, think, think.

This was what? Her fifth Christmas Eve? Was this going to be her life? Day after day of all the same things?

Her lungs seized up.

Don't panic.

Her view landed on her dad's painting of her snow globe leaned up against the wall, and her mom's soft whisper haunted her. *We're here, Annie.* But they weren't. So what did she have to believe in? Not the sad past she couldn't change. Or her loneliness and isolation. But in the Blue Dot with Braden, the world had seemed a different place. One filled with light and possibilities. Annie fell back against the pillows and moaned. *This is so hard!* No matter how her day changed up, Braden seemed to be as constant as the North Star. So did other important people in her sphere, including her new acquaintances in the building.

When she saw Jane this morning, how would she behave? On friendly terms like they'd chatted before, or like they were complete strangers? And what about her other neighbors, including Harrington? Her interactions with the older man had seemed deeper last night. She hadn't had much opportunity to chat with Eric though. But she *had* confirmed about his penchant for cinnamon rolls—and she was going to make him some for Christmas. Annie sat up in bed. If only she could share what she was going through with someone—anyone—and not have them think she'd lost it.

She reached for her phone and opened her message app, selecting Tina from her contacts.

Hey, it's been a while...

No. She erased it.

Merry Christmas!

Wrong. She couldn't ignore certain facts, like the hurt she'd caused Tina.

I want to apologize—

Better, but—a lump wedged in her throat—she needed to do that in person. Only, Tina wouldn't be around at Christmas. She and her husband always went to his folks' place in Maine. They did Thanksgiving with her family in Long Island.

Annie pushed back the covers.

Might as well get this day started and see what it brings.

Leo pounced off the bed and followed her to the kitchen. They passed through the hall, and she peered into the living room. His Christmas stocking was empty—naturally. And, naturally, she'd filled it. Maybe tonight she'd just *give* him his treats on Christmas Eve? Although that would take some of the fun out of it.

She stared at the candy canes on her tree, and her mind whirled with confusion. There were still eleven of them, meaning only one was missing. The one she'd put in her cocoa on that first Christmas Eve. She pushed back her hair, sweeping it over her shoulders. There had to be some reason certain elements of her day repeated while others didn't.

Her "good touches" had lasted, like the augmentation to her Christmas window at work. But making chili for Harrington had been a good thing too. She strode to the refrigerator and tugged it open. *Argh*. No sign of the groceries from last night. The kitchen window revealed bare sidewalks and a gray sky, and a lone mug from the hot cocoa sat in her sink.

Annie prepared her coffee and sat at her kitchen table.

Leo watched her and meowed.

"Don't worry. I'll feed you in a minute." *Before the intercom buzzes, for sure.*

Annie spun her coffee mug around in her hands and glanced toward her door. Last night, Bea had talked more about her late husband, Harry. Her daughter, Caroline, in Queens too. She clearly loved her grandkids and looked forward to seeing them at Christmas, but Annie doubted she'd get there with the storm. Maybe Annie should ask Bea over, if she had no place to go? To what? Share a turkey breast and boxed stuffing? Maybe that was better than nothing. Bea could bring her sweet potato casserole.

Annie shook her head at a gloomy thought. Maybe she'd never get to Christmas Day. At this rate, it seemed doubtful. Leo meowed again, winding himself around the legs of her chair. But no. She had to push on. She couldn't give up now. Not with so much good stuff waiting on the other side of Christmas Eve. Building relationships with her neighbors and possibly even dating Braden. Hopefully saving her job somehow, and reconnecting with Tina. Those things would be so wonderful if they happened. "But how can we do that?" she asked Leo. *How, how, how, how?*

A lot of this day seemed to be out of her control, and yet she had this murky feeling that moving forward was just beyond her reach. If she could just do *something*. Get one part of Christmas Eve exactly right.

The cat released a plaintive meow.

"Right," she said, standing. "I promised."

She fed Leo without spilling his food, and her intercom buzzed. She put on her coat and boots, shoving two candy canes in her coat pocket. If only she could think of someone to ask. Someone kindly enough to listen and not judge her. Not Jane, that would be too much. She couldn't saddle any of her other neighbors with this either. Patrice? No way. They were cordial but not close, and she'd never play this head game on Kira.

Braden? She kept itching to tell him the full truth, but something inside held her back. She'd mentioned her déjà vu feelings and he'd been supportive, but she hadn't pushed things beyond that because she feared—what? Damaging their fledgling relationship? Having him walk away altogether? Although part of her sensed he wouldn't do that, another doubting voice caused her to question what she would think under different circumstances, if—to her, the day seemed normal—and he tried to tell her the same things.

She wanted tell Braden everything, and she would. But first, she wanted a clearer-headed idea about what was actually happening, and why. If only she had someone else's perspective. *Yeah, right. That person would have to believe in time loops and magic too.*

A light bulb went off in her head.

Santa.

Annie hurried through the entrance at Lawson's, but Santa and Braden were nowhere around. She checked her front window first. Right. The living room scene had all the new touches she and Braden had added—up to what they'd included last night: the fake oatmeal raisin cookies. She started to head for the elevators but thought better of it. Whatever she did today, she was not riding an elevator at the same time as the unnervingly attractive guy. She'd totally put her foot in her mouth yesterday. She'd ride the escalator to the second floor and take the stairs to the third.

Annie stared up the set of moving steps, spotting a familiar figure. *Eeep! There he is! Braden.* Riding down the escalator on the other side. They passed each other with her riding up, and him going down. He did a double take and backed up a few steps. She'd removed her coat and held it in one arm.

"Hey, you!" He met her eyes. *Yay! He remembers.*

"Hi." She gripped the strap of her shoulder bag extra hard. Because, well. He was just as dreamy as always. And now she'd finally left an impression.

"You're"—he squinted at her name tag—"Annie, right?" *Or not.*

Her hand shot to her name tag. "Ah, yeah. That's right." Since she kept ascending, he backed up some more. His balance was *very* good. He didn't even look down. He *was* holding the handrail though, to be fair.

"And you're"—she snatched a peek at *his* name tag—"Braden." He backed up another few steps and grinned. He was doing a dance now, almost in a rhythm. At this pace, he'd never make it to the ground floor.

He shook his finger, like he'd had an aha moment. "You do the windows." He cleared his throat. "I mean, design them."

"Yep! That's me." She spied the Juniors Department cresting over the plexiglass wall beside her.

"Well, they're really great ones. Nice work." He kept walking backward, stepping up, up, up the Down escalator.

"Excuse me!" That was Kira scooting around him and giving him a strange look. She shot Annie the side-eye, like *what the heck?* Annie wasn't sure why, but Braden was obviously stuck on something. Probably too big a stretch to hope he was stuck on her.

"Thanks!" He gave her a lopsided grin. "Nice work—security guarding!" *Security guarding? What?* Her face burned hotter. *At least I didn't hit below the duty belt by commenting on it. Gee.*

"Thanks, I try." He started moving away from her, descending toward Homewares. He changed his mind and backed up quickly, jogging backward up the escalator to the top. The man was seriously fit. When she got there and stepped off, he said, "I—just thought of something I wanted to tell you." He shook his head. "But then it was gone. Poof!"

"Yeah, funny. Ha! Sometimes happens to me. I mean, I think about you *all the time*." *What did I just say?* She removed her too-hot pom-pom hat, and her hair stood out in a frizzy halo. *Groan.*

"Wait." He looked enormously pleased. Not with her hair though. Blessedly, he hadn't seemed to notice that. She patted it down, but it bounced back up. She wanted a refund for that hair product: Silky Satin Curls. Yeah, right. "Do you"—his eyebrows formed a V—"think about me?" His lopsided grin melted her heart. "Why?"

"Because, uh." Annie held her breath. She glanced at his duty belt. No. "Safety is a priority here at Lawson's!" *It would be safest if you just kept your mouth shut, Annie.*

"That's true. Thanks for noticing"—he saw her eyes on his duty belt, and her chin jerked up—"that." Braden's neck went red, and so did his ears.

What is wrong with me? Seriously?

Foot-in-mouth disease?

He stared at her a moment. "You and I—" He motioned back and forth between them with his hands. "We've never met before, have we? I mean, before Lawson's?"

"Ah, no. I don't think so."

"No, right. Of course not." He wore a puzzled frown. "I was overseas."

Annie nodded. "In Germany."

Braden laughed. "Yeah, wow. How did you know that?"

Oh boy, oh boy, oh boy. "I—guessed?" she said with a little squeak.

"Well, you, Annie Jones, are a very good guesser."

"Ha. Yeah." What would he think? That she'd been spying on him? Looking him up on social media? Which she had done just a tiny bit. She hadn't been able to stop herself from sneaking peeks at his accounts over the last few days.

No, this day. *Today.* Christmas Eve redux.

She'd seen photos of him with a friend, who she thought was Harper, since he had a sweet-looking wife and a cute kid. She'd also seen pics of his big Italian family, from what appeared to be one of his sister's weddings. Everyone wore broad smiles and looked all huggy and chummy with each other.

He seemed to be thinking up something else to say when Santa walked past them, approaching the down escalator. "Good morning!"

Braden watched Santa stride away. "There's something *very familiar* about that guy." He considered Annie. "And you too, actually."

"Ha!" Secretly though, she wondered if anything was coming back to him. Like memories of him asking her out for coffee and—later—on a date? "I suppose we've seen each other around the store?" Annie's spirits flagged at his confused expression. How could he not remember any of it so far? Not even the elevator? As badly as she'd wanted him to forget that exchange, she was stupidly discouraged that he had.

"Yes, right," Braden said. "I'm sure that's it."

Annie pulled her cell phone from her purse by her locker, and her text app stared her in the face. She'd told Braden twice now that she would text Tina "tomorrow" which was technically today in her world. *But not.* This was seriously so messed up. But the look in Braden's eyes just now had been so dreamy, she couldn't help dreaming that he was also thinking good things about her. Today, when they had coffee—

Wait. Annie's chest tightened. What if they *didn't* have coffee because they never got there? Without Braden helping her pick up her window, he might never ask. Annie released a burst of pent-up breath. No. They could have coffee one way or another. She hoped. And if not today, on account of her display—

Noooo.

She didn't even know if there'd be a tomorrow, in the traditional sense. Which meant she had to make the most of *right now*. She opened her text app and accessed Tina's icon.

Hey there! It's been a while!

Yeah, like six months. She erased that.

Hey Tina! It's me!

Captain Obvious. Because. Tina had Annie's number in her contacts.

Unless.

Her throat felt raw.

She'd blocked it.

Annie quickly tapped the back button with her thumbs and closed her text app. She'd text Tina later. Maybe on her lunch break. Or tonight when she got home. *After* she'd made Harrington's chili and invited Bea in for cocoa. The realization hit her with a jolt. For a typically isolated woman, her social calendar was really filling up. She'd even had coffee with a friend this morning. At least Jane was beginning to feel like a friend, in some sentimental and interesting fashion. But right now, she couldn't dwell on that. She had to find the jolly old elf and ask him a question.

"Hey, Santa!" Annie caught his attention before he left the toy aisle.

"Yes, Annie?"

"Do you have a minute?"

He glanced toward his workshop, where his elf assistant was neatening up, preparing for the day. "Sure."

She shifted on her feet, not knowing how to phrase this. "This has been a bit of an odd day."

"Has it?" He checked his watch. "The day's only getting started in this time zone."

"Ha. Yeah." She straightened her holly wreath pin. "That's just the thing?" Her voice rose on the statement like it was a question. "This day, um. Seems to be—dragging on."

Santa smiled. "Impatient for Christmas. I know. Even grown-ups feel that way."

She was more than impatient. She was starting to feel *desperate.*

Santa peered into her eyes. "That's not quite it though. Is it?"

She leaned toward him and whispered. "Something really weird is going on."

"Weird? How do you mean?"

If she told him the truth, would he report her to management as someone losing her marbles? No, that wouldn't be very Santa-like. He was kind and understanding. Even when people were misbehaving, and she hadn't done anything wrong. She got an uncomfortable feeling. So, yeah. She'd lost touch with Tina. And sure, she tended to keep to herself, but those weren't major transgressions. They were minor ones. Also, extremely personal. She drew in a breath and answered Santa. "What I mean is, today has felt off in a way that seems—redundant. Like it's happening over and over again."

Santa frowned. "I'm sorry you're unhappy, Annie."

What? Me? "I'm not, not unhappy," she said, feeling a painful tug at her heartstrings. Lonely, maybe. Closed off—until now. A little. Unhappy though? She wasn't some grumpy old Scrooge. That wasn't her.

"You know what Mrs. Claus always says?" He studied her kindly. "The best way to find happiness is to search your heart." Santa peered at the sparkly tinsel hanging on the tree in her window. "Look for those silver linings." He turned to go, but Annie stopped him.

"But Santa! Wait!" Nothing had been solved here.

He glanced over his shoulder.

"About my display," she said. "You keep saying it's not quite right."

"I think you'll know when it is, Annie." She felt as deflated as a week-old helium balloon. Well, what had she thought? That some store Santa was going to hand her all the answers? "I'm not just some store Santa, you know."

Her heart pounded. Wait. How had he heard her think that?

Someone touched her arm. "Annie?"

She turned to see Braden standing beside her in the toy aisle. Santa was already halfway to his workshop. "Oh Braden, hey!"

"Hey." He grinned, and for an instant she forgot all about the prescient Santa and being stuck in this repeat day. He held out a cell phone. "This was on the floor behind you. Is this yours?" Annie's hands shot to her hip pocket. Her phone! It *was* gone. He passed her the phone, and she flipped it over, examining its back and front. Fortunately, its protective case had kept it from cracking.

"Yeah, it is. Thank you."

"Santa Claus giving you some tips?"

She forced a laugh. "Ha, yeah."

Braden perused the store as the various sales associates took up their positions, some of them opening registers. "Hard to believe it's Christmas Eve already. This time of year, the days just fly by." What she wouldn't give to get a ticket on that plane.

"Annie." He stared down at her. "You're sure we've never met before Lawson's?"

"Very sure, yeah."

"Maybe you're one of those people," he said. "The kind folks meet and immediately believe they've known all their life."

That had never been Annie's experience.

Until now.

With Braden.

He was staring at her like he was trying to figure her out, and—ooh—how she wanted to tell him the truth. But he'd never in a million years believe her. She was still wrapping her head around everything herself, including her humiliating performance in the elevator yesterday. And that extremely embarrassing incident during which she'd landed smack on top of him. She hadn't exactly improved her situation with her hook-up talk, or by taking the escalator either. If she was dreaming, this was one super-elaborate dream, complete with totally humiliating parts. Be nice if she could skip those.

She tucked a lock of her hair behind one ear. "Most people don't even notice me," she said, speaking her truth. Annie was often overlooked in a crowd, like she had been back in high school.

She didn't mind that normally. She liked hiding in her own little corner. Staying out of the spotlight. Being on stage was not for her. She was a behind-the-scenes kind of girl.

"I've noticed you." The flirty glimmer in his eyes pleased her.

"Have you?"

"I've seen you setting up your displays, sometimes late into the night."

"My work's important to me. I like to get things right."

"You're a perfectionist."

Yes, but what wasn't she getting right this time? "Braden?"

"Hmm."

"Thanks for giving my phone back." She bit her lip. "And thanks most of all for noticing."

He winked, and her skin tingled. "Any time."

NINETEEN

AT TWENTY PAST TWO, ANNIE darted out in front of Marcus and Dylan like a linebacker.

"No, Marcus! Let me!"

She dodged this way and that, her hands cupped forward and shooing them away from the window. "Boys! Please!" They scuttled around her in a brutal offensive. Annie's shout overlapped their mom's. "*Stop!*"

Dylan tumbled into the retractable belt, taking Marcus with him.

And there went her whole display.

Down. Down. Down.

Down.

"Let me guess?" Annie asked Santa wearily as she and Braden finished fixing her trashed window. "Something's missing?"

Santa strode to the cookie plate beside the chair and picked it up.

"There are two oatmeal raisin cookies!" she announced.

"I've heard they're Santa's favorites!" Annie's pulse raced. Was she *ever* going to break out of this time loop, or have Braden remember?

Braden wore a puzzled look. "Wait. What?"

This was so disheartening in so many ways.

Santa lifted a fake oatmeal raisin cookie off the plate and evaluated it closely. "Hmm, yes. Nice touch. But!"—Santa held up a finger—"Isn't there generally a note?"

"A note?" asked Annie.

Braden stepped forward, taking the cookie plate from Santa. He stared down at it and glanced at Annie. "He's right," he said. "Kids still do that, don't they?"

Annie wasn't totally sure. For all she knew, there was now a Santa app of some kind, and they texted him. "Well, I supposed they could?" She turned up her hands.

Santa placed the fake oatmeal cookie on the plate as Braden held it. "Well, I for one think the idea is grand. I always love hearing from little ones." He winked at Annie and Braden. "Big ones too." Annie wasn't sure how a note for Santa was going to majorly improve her display, or more greatly impress Veronica Lawson, but—at this point—anything was worth a try.

Braden followed her to the Stationery Department, surveying a wall of individual note card choices. "What kind do you think?"

Braden nodded to another wall holding Christmas cards. "Maybe one of those?"

What a great idea. "Of course!"

He selected a card out from the rack, turning it to face Annie. "How about this one?" The illustrated card showed an old-timey

Santa with his reindeer team poised on a rooftop. Santa was out of his sleigh and had a big sack of toys slung over his shoulder. Smoke curled from the chimney of the house, and sparkly stars lit up the wintry night sky.

"I think that's perfect." This area of the store was quiet with the rest of Lawson's shutting down. She carried the card to the register and rang it up using her employee code, putting it on her store account, like she did for work supplies. She hunted around for a pen.

Braden grabbed one from the counter, handing it to her. "Looking for this?"

She smiled. "Thanks." The pen slipped through her fingers, plummeting to the floor. "Oh!" Braden grabbed it, handing it to her. His eyes locked on hers, and Annie's heart raced.

"I can't help having the feeling we've done this before." His mouth was so close, Annie thought she saw stars. No. Those were the bright holiday lights on the fake tree by the register. "Annie," he said, standing, "level with me."

She stood and held on to the counter. "Hmm?"

"When we met this morning on the escalator, how did you know about Germany?"

"I, er." She bit her lip. "Braden," she said, all breathy. "I think you told me."

"Did I?" he asked. Still, he drew nearer. "When?"

Yeah, when? Think, think, think, think.

"Er, maybe at the holiday party?"

He blinked. "You were at the holiday party?"

"I, uh—arrived very late."

"Yeah." He stared at the mini Christmas tree beside her and back in her eyes. "That's probably it."

"There were a lot of people there! Gobs and gobs!"

"Yeah, but *you*? I think I would remember."

Not accurate, but okay. Also not your fault.

She opened the card and set it on the counter, her heart pounding. Keeping this enormous secret from Braden was getting next to impossible. It was even more impossible to think of sharing it with him. The man didn't even believe in time travel, so Christmas magic and Santa spells were kind of a stretch.

"We could probably leave it blank," Braden told her. She looked up and he shrugged. "I mean, who's to know?"

She gasped, but she was playing. This was one of the things she loved best about being around Braden, their flirty banter. And she was getting better at it. She hoped. "We'd know." She put on teasing tones. "And maybe so would Santa." She nodded in the direction of Santa's workshop, and Braden laughed.

"With *that guy*," he said, "you never know."

Annie paused with the pen hovering above the open card. It was blank inside. "Hmm. What should we say?"

Braden laid a hand on the counter. "How about"—his eyes sparkled devilishly—"'Thanks for making our Christmas'?"

"We're writing the note to *him*?" She glanced at the workshop, and Braden smirked.

"Why not to *him*? He's the closest thing to Santa we've got."

Annie dropped her voice in a whisper. "Who's to say they're not one and the same?"

Braden chuckled and shook his head. "The jury's still out."

"All right," she said boldly. "Why not?" She wrote *To Santa, Thanks for making our Christmas!* with a flourish and looked up. "Do we sign it?"

Braden smiled. "Of course." He nodded for her to go ahead. "You first." This was such a silly game, but she was enjoying playing it with Braden. "Hey, Annie," he asked as she stuffed the note card into its envelope. "Do you maybe have time to grab a coffee?"

"A merry-Christmas-Eve cup?" She smiled, her heart so light. At least she was getting to repeat the good parts of this day, and not just the bad. In some ways, the good parts kept getting better. If only she could let Braden in on her secret. But how?

Annie sipped from her coffee at the Blue Dot, gathering her nerve. She wanted to tell Braden what was going on and have him understand. So badly. Since Santa hadn't helped her, maybe Braden would. It was hard to know how he'd react, but her heart said she should risk it.

Braden closed the donut bag, folding over its flap. "I'm really sorry you had such a rough day." He frowned. "Getting your window totaled was a tough break after you worked so hard on it. Then to have Veronica Lawson come in, after she'd already hinted to your boss about your job being on the line. Man, oh man"—he blew out a breath—"talk about brutal."

"So, yeah," Annie said. "About that…?" She laid her mittens on top of her hat, stalling.

"Hmm?" He unzipped his jacket and looked up, meeting her eyes.

"Today's maybe been worse than I let on," she said.

"How so?"

"Braden, I—" She ran her fingers through her hair. How could she say this without sounding ridiculous? *Maybe I should just spill it.* "I feel like I'm stuck in a time loop. No. Not just *feel like.*" She exhaled a shaky breath. "I believe I am."

"It's been a very stressful day," he said soothingly.

"No! It's not about that." Would he ever believe her? "You're going to think I've lost it."

"No, I won't, Annie." His eyes glimmered kindly. "So, tell me. What's been going on?"

She lifted a shoulder. "Lots and lots of the same stuff, but different things too."

"Such as?"

"This morning when I woke up"—she viewed him askance—"it was December 24."

"Yeah," he said. "Me too."

"Braden, I'm serious."

He scanned her eyes, seeing that she was. "I'm listening."

"Everything that's happened today, it happened to me yesterday too. No. Wait. Not everything. But most things." She shook her head. "All I know is that—no matter what I do—when I go to bed at night, it's Christmas Eve and a storm is raging. But, the next morning when I wake up, the sky's all cloudy again, and the sidewalks are clear. It's like the whole day before never happened, and it's Christmas Eve all over again."

His eyes widened. "That does sound like a lot."

"You must think I'm the weirdest per—"

"No, Annie. I don't think that at all. What I do think is that you've been under tons of stress, and stress does things to us, makes it hard to think clearly sometimes. I get it." He reached out and took her hand. "How can I help?" The look in his eyes was so tender. So caring, she wanted to weep.

She couldn't believe her ears. "What?"

"I'm asking, Annie. How can I help you move past this?"

"I"—she caught her breath—"really don't know."

He gently squeezed her hand. "Look, I don't know what's going on, but I do know you're one special woman. A very capable person too. So, whatever's troubling you, there's got to be a way around it. And if I can help, I will."

Heat filled her eyes because he was being so awesome. "That's just it," she whimpered. "I don't even *understand* the problem—totally."

"You know what I think?" He took her other hand in his so both sets of their hands linked on the tabletop. "I think that sometimes it's good not to think too far ahead. That's happened to me when I've gotten stuck."

"You've been stuck?" she asked quietly.

He held her hands tighter, not letting go. "There was a bad scene in Baghdad." His face screwed up in anguish, and her heart bled for him.

She gently squeezed his hands. "You lost someone."

He nodded grimly. "More than one friend, and, I won't lie—afterward—things were rough." He blinked and looked away.

Annie's heart pounded. "It wasn't your fault."

He frowned. "Maybe it was? My troops trusted me. I didn't spot the ambush."

"Braden."

"I'd have nightmares," he went on. "It was like it kept happening, again and again. I couldn't break out of the cycle."

Her soul ached for him. "So what did you do?"

"The army sent me for counseling. All of us survivors, actually." Was he suggesting that for her too? "Counseling's not a bad thing, and it *can* help. If you find you can't get out of this rut, you might want to consider it." But she was petrified to tell a counselor about this. Who knew what would happen to her then? "In any case," he said. "You might not need it, but I did. I lost some special people."

"Me too." The words scraped from her tender throat.

"What's that?"

"I did too, I mean," she said quietly, keeping their conversation confidential in the busy diner. "Not to undermine what you went through, but I lost my parents—both of them at once." Did he recall her mentioning losing her parents previously?

"Oh, Annie." From his crestfallen face, apparently not. "How terrible for you, upsetting." He gripped her hands tighter. "How old?"

"Nine." Pain seared through her chest. It was always hard talking about it. This was one topic Annie didn't care to revisit time and again.

He nodded, and she continued. "I did see a counselor. Tons of 'professionals,' truthfully. My Grandma Mable kept sending me. They say talking about trauma helps. But, in my case, I didn't find that to be true. Talking about it only intensified the hurt."

"Yeah," he said gently. "I get it."

She met his eyes. "I'm sorry you went through that too."

"Thanks. It's getting better."

"Is it? How?"

He squared his shoulders, still holding her hands. "It helps not to look too far ahead. Take things day by day."

"Yeah, but"—she frowned glumly—"what if every day is the same one?"

He leaned closer and whispered. "Okay, hour by hour. Break it down. Baby steps." Baby steps. That seemed to make sense. Except that would only mean she'd be moving slower instead of faster, and Annie was so past ready to sprint to Christmas Day.

"Here's what I'd suggest," he said. She held on to his hands, as he extended a lifeline. "I'd suggest you not worry about waking up tomorrow or getting to Christmas at all."

"What?"

"Annie." His fingers tightened around hers. "Enjoy today. Think about what you'll be doing an hour from now. Plan for it, sure. And the hour after that. But here's the thing. Sometimes we can't always plan out everything because life throws us surprises." He smiled. "This morning, for example, I had no idea you and I would be going out for coffee. Did— Wait."

She grimaced. "I kind of did."

Braden blew out a breath. "Look. I don't one hundred percent understand what's going on with you, but it doesn't matter. Whatever this phase is you're in, I've confidence you'll get through it." His confidence in her made her want to be confident in herself too.

"Thanks, Braden."

He let go of her hands and pried open the donut bag. "So what do you say? Want to split this last one?"

Annie was famished and somehow feeling so much better. "You bet I do."

Braden turned to Annie as they walked toward the subway. "I hope I didn't lay too much on you back there." Snowflakes dusted his hat, and he wiped them off with his glove. "I mean, about my time in the military."

"Not at all." She nudged his shoulder with hers in a way that seemed chummy, and a pleasant buzz hummed through him. "I'm glad you told me. And hey, hearing about it did make me feel better." She pursed her lips. "Not that I'm happy in any way that—"

"It's all right. I get it." The shimmer in her eyes heated him through and through. He felt connected to her somehow, like they'd previously been through this together. But they couldn't have *actually* done that unless he bought into the same version of reality she did. "You know, it's funny about your déjà vu day, because sometimes I think I'm experiencing it too."

"What?" She gasped, appearing hopeful. "Really?"

He shook his head. "I'm not *all in* like you are, but it's sometimes hard to believe we only met this morning. I normally don't spill so much about myself right off the bat."

"But you seem so outgoing!" They scooted to the side of the sidewalk as a pair of women in a hurry scuttled by.

Braden held up his hand. "Outgoing? Maybe. But that's

me being friendly on the outside. When it comes to what's in here"—he patted his chest through his heavy jacket—"I'm typically more careful about what I share"—he dove into her eyes—"and with whom."

Annie smiled shyly. "In that case, thanks for sharing with me." He had a hunch she was much the same way, and he was touched she'd also shared personal things with him—about her falling-out with Tina and her job being on the line, and so tragically losing her parents. Murky memories tugged at him. He felt like he'd known some of that before. But how could he have? It wasn't like they'd been talking for *days*.

Or was it?

She trudged along in her worn snow boots. Ice coated the sidewalks, and store awnings hung heavy with snow. People everywhere scurried to get out of the weather. He stared at a window display of gingerbread men with waving arms and at another from an electronics store in which cell phones wore Santa hats. "I've always loved this time of year," he said. "When I was a kid—"

The glimmer in her eyes said this wasn't news.

Braden gawked at her. "Don't tell me. You already knew about my folks bringing me into Manhattan?"

They paused at a street crossing. "Each window is special," she said, "just like—"

"—its own little world." A wave of recognition crashed over him. He'd definitely said that before—or she had. Annie gestured toward the street, and he saw the pedestrian light had changed and that a group of others had mostly crossed over, leaving him and Annie behind. They walked quickly to catch up. Braden thought hard, pondering this day from the moment it began and when he'd first met Annie by the lockers. No, wait. Not there. In the toy section? Wrong. On the escalators—elevator. *A rolling tube of lip gloss spiraled toward him, and he trapped it with his shoe.*

Braden blinked.

When had *that* happened?

A frame scrolled forward, like one movie scene transitioning to the next.

Braden bent to retrieve Annie's shoe. "Looks like you dropped something," he said, standing and handing it to her. She grabbed the toe of it, and he had the heel.

Both of them froze.

"Hey"—he stared at her, dazed—"have we—?"

No, of course not.

What? Had he dreamed that part?

No, he hadn't been sleeping.

Daydreamed maybe?

"This is my stop," Annie said, and he saw they'd reached the concrete steps leading underground to her train.

"Oh, right!" He shook off his stupor, hearing sleigh bells. No, wait. That was a bell ringer on the corner. She grinned up at him. "Thanks for the coffee. It was great."

He nodded. "My pleasure. We'll have to..."

Her eyes sparkled prettily. "Do it again?" Snowflakes dusted her hat and covered her long eyelashes. Man, she was a beautiful woman and attractive in so many ways.

He smiled. "Yeah, I'd like that."

"After Christmas?" she asked, like she was daring him to

believe what she did about this whole time loop deal. He didn't. How could he?

But he didn't totally *disbelieve* her either. "Let's call it a date."

She winked. "*First*, we'll have to get there."

Braden's soul filled with understanding.

Get to Christmas, right.

TWENTY

On the sixth Christmas Eve

FA-LA-LA-LA-LA. LA—!

Annie dashed through the employee entrance at Lawson's, clocking in at 9:08 a.m. A few sales associates exited the elevators, but Santa and Braden were nowhere around. No matter. She'd see them later, as she had during every repeat of this day. Maybe Braden would even remember some of their conversation from yesterday, and—after having thought it over—would start believing her about the time loop? *That would be amazing!*

Careful, Annie. Don't cling to false hope.

Amazing Agatha caught her eye, and she backed up a step. The doll sure was pricey, but Annie recalled what it was like being a kid and having your heart set on something. She'd seen a fancy snow globe at a friend's house and had wanted one so badly. Her parents had said that maybe if she was good, Santa would bring one to her.

Sparkly snowflakes swirled around her, taking her back to that magical morning.

Nine-year-old Annie rushed into the living room, brown ringlets falling past her shoulders. Her parents were still sleeping, but their Christmas tree was all aglow, casting pretty ribbons of light across the darkened room. A new package was tucked beneath it. Annie squealed quietly and checked the tag.

To: Annie

From: Santa

She excitedly picked it up, holding it against her powder-blue bathrobe with puffy stitching. Her fluffy slippers matched and had silky blue bows on them. Annie stared at the hearth and grinned. Her stocking was loaded! A package of licorice whips and a giant candy cane poked out of the top of it. She dropped down onto the carpet to tackle her present first, pulling it into her lap and greedily ripping off the red ribbon. The wrapping paper had reindeer on it and wasn't the pattern her parents used. The elves had to have made it.

She bubbled with excitement as she tore the packaging apart. She didn't care what her friend, Amy, said. She still believed in Santa. He had to be real. She pulled the lid off the box and removed the extra tissue paper tucked inside. A shiny glass globe glinted up at her. Annie's heart pounded as she carefully dug her fingers into the box. Santa and his reindeer team were in a snowy white yard with a stand of tiny pine trees behind them. She held the snow globe up to her face and peered closer. Sweet! A candy-cane-striped North Pole stood by Santa's sleigh, and a sign in front of him said: Believe.

Annie shut her eyes and hugged the snow globe close. "I do believe, I do." Happiness washed over her, along with a sense of calm. She opened her eyes and kissed the snow globe. "I'm keeping you forever." She shook it up and down, and sheer magic happened. Baby snowflakes skittered everywhere, rising and falling in gentle twirls toward the ground. A metal tab brushed her pinky finger, and Annie turned the snow globe over, holding it carefully. There was a wind-up key in the bottom! It played music. She giggled and cranked the key.

The music box played a familiar tune. Its tinkling bells sounded like fairies dancing.

"It's Beginning to Look a Lot Like Christmas."

Annie grinned from ear to ear.

"That was a very good year."

Annie blinked and turned to Santa beside her. Wait. They stood facing her Christmas tree window display. Annie brought her hand to her mouth. *How* had she gotten here? Had she been that caught up in her reverie? She gaped at Santa. "Did I—walk here from the toy section?"

Santa nodded. "You did, indeed." He brushed a few snowflakes off his overcoat with his white glove. "Though you seemed to be distracted."

Distracted? Right. She was lucky she hadn't bumped into anything—or anyone. Hang on. Annie caught her breath. "Santa?"

"Hmm?"

"What was it you said about that being a good year?"

"Your ninth year, of course." He seemed very matter of fact about it.

Annie's pulse raced. "How... How did you know I was thinking about that?"

He heaved a *ho ho ho*. "Who do you think brought you the snow globe?"

Okay. Full stop. This was looney tunes.

I have to be dreaming.

"Yes, but!"—Santa held up a finger—"Sometimes dreams come true."

Now, he can hear what I'm thinking?

Panic gripped her and held on tight.

"Not always," Santa answered. He tapped his temple. "But sometimes I get vibes."

Annie's mouth fell open.

Okay, don't freak, Annie.

This isn't really happening.

"Vibes?"

Santa spread open his hands, explaining. "Like shortwave radio?"

She had no clue what he was talking about. That sounded old school for sure. She undid the brass buttons on her coat, shrugging out of it while shifting her shoulder bag from one side to the other. "Who are you?" she asked on a gasp.

"I think you know-ho-ho." He smiled softly and tilted his head. His Santa cap pom-pom swished to the side.

Annie clicked her tongue. "There's no such thing as—"

"—Santa?" Santa's lips turned down in a frown, taking his heavy whiskers with them. "Says who?"

Annie gripped her coat firmly. The strap of her shoulder bag too. "Why, pretty much everyone over the age of eight."

Santa winked. "You held on for a while."

"Well, of course," Annie babbled. "I mean, wait." She lowered her voice. "How are you doing this?"

Santa gestured toward her window display. "We all make a bit of magic in our own way. Take your windows, for example. Each one is special, its own little world."

Annie's heart pounded. "That's what I think too."

Santa nodded. "And this world keeps getting better."

Annie got that part. "But will it ever be good enough?"

Santa peered at her. He was a stout man, and a little shorter than she was. "I think you'll know"—he tapped the side of his cherrylike nose—"when that moment happens."

Her heart leapt with hope. "So it *will* happen?"

"Oh yes." He acted so certain, and she badly wanted to believe him.

"And Veronica Lawson?"

He tugged on his coat lapels, speaking authoritatively, "She'll be very impressed."

Braden walked past them, heading for his post at the main entrance. He stopped and stared at Annie.

"Braden." She smiled. "Hi."

"Hello"—he read her name tag—"Annie."

Nooo. "I think we might have met before?" she replied. *So disheartening.*

"Have we?" He seemed to search his brain. "Oh, gosh. I'm sorry," he said, but clearly, he was lying to avoid hurting her feelings. "Sure. Of course! I remember meeting you. At the—holiday party? Did we chat there?"

Annie shrugged. "Maybe?"

Braden studied her window display. "Oh yeah, right!" He snapped his fingers. "You do the windows!"

Disappointment weighed her down like a heavy wet blanket. Braden didn't remember their conversation? About the time loop? Anything? "Ah yeah, that's me."

He grinned approvingly. "Great job with those." His eyes fell on the note for Santa. "I see you don't miss a trick."

"Ha!" *Neither do you, since you helped me.*

This was hopeless. Would Braden *ever* remember meeting her before?

She watched him stroll away, her head pounding.

Santa leaned toward her. "Give it time."

The morning seemed to drag with a series of rote repetitions. Neatening her salesfloor displays, helping out at various registers, responding to customer inquiries by ushering them to the relevant section of the store. When Annie finally reached her lunch break, she felt all *out of time*—and patience. She'd been in this time loop for six days now and had made very little progress. Only baby steps toward changing up the day, and those small changes never seemed to matter, because when she woke up the following morning it was always Christmas Eve again. When she'd talked with Santa by her front window, he'd hinted she needed to work some magic of her own to move forward.

Awesome advice.

But how?

If she knew that, she'd be enjoying Christmas Day right now, instead of being stuck here at Lawson's Finest. Annie pulled her lunch bag from the break room refrigerator as Kira walked in to grab some coffee. "Oh hey, Annie!" Kira's eyes brightened. She dropped a cartridge in the coffee machine and pressed a button. It whined with life, caffeinated aromas filling the air. "Guess you'll be getting good news today." She winked at Annie. "And maybe so will I."

Annie shut the refrigerator door. "Hope so!" She just wouldn't bet on it. Kira left with her coffee and Annie fixed herself a cup, sitting at the long center table. She tended to eat later than most of the staff, so she often had her lunch alone. She dumped her peanut butter sandwich out of her bag and stared at it glumly. She wasn't hungry, but she needed the fuel to get her through the rest of the day. This day, especially.

Her phone sat on the table in front of her. She strummed her fingers across its screen, tapping open her text app with her thumbs and starting a message to Tina.

Wish we could talk.

No. Wrong.

Miss you and I'm sorry.

Better, but not quite.

"Hey, Annie." Her chin jerked up. Braden!

"Oh, hi."

He strolled into the break room, his muscles flexing beneath his nicely fitted shirt. Annie's heart skipped a beat at his lopsided grin. "Nice seeing you again." He opened the refrigerator, extracting a water bottle and a white paper sack. The sack was three times the size of the small brown bag that had held her sandwich. He shut the fridge and peered over his shoulder. "Sorry about earlier. I'm usually pretty good with a face, if not a name."

And still, he'd completely forgotten hers.

Annie's heart twisted, but she told herself not to be silly. Just because she was becoming attached to Braden, that didn't mean he was caring anything at all about her. He clearly didn't know her from Adam. If only she could change that. Help him understand and remember.

He pulled out a chair across from hers and gestured to the table. "Mind if I sit?"

Annie pushed back her hair. "No, please. Go right ahead." She flipped over her phone so it lay face-down on the table and unwrapped her peanut butter sandwich. He stared at it.

"PBJ, huh?" He uncapped his water bottle and took a swig.

"Nope, just the peanut butter part."

He shrugged mildly. "Whatever suits." Braden pulled a long package from his bag and unwrapped a giant Italian sub. He also took out a bag of chips and a big chocolate chip cookie covered in plastic wrap. He stared at her little lunch compared to his and chomped into his sub. Annie smelled oregano and salami. Probably pastrami too, and a hint of olive oil and vinegar... Her stomach rumbled.

His food looked *really good*—she glanced at her whole-wheat sandwich bread with a slathering of organic peanut butter inside it—although her lunch was healthy enough. She picked up her sandwich and took a bite. It was fine, and it would hold her until later when she wanted that jelly donut, assuming she and Braden would go to the Blue Dot again. She hoped so. That was one of her favorite parts of this day.

Braden put down his sub and opened his chips. “Like your pin.” He pointed to the holly wreath decoration on her vest. “Very Christmassy.”

She was *not* saying he wore his uniform very well this time. “Thanks, Braden.”

“Bet you’re ready for the time off, like I am. Even if only for a day.”

“Yeah, I’m looking forward to Christmas.” *Really, really looking forward, and hoping to get there.*

He narrowed his eyes. “You know, it’s funny,” he said. “I have this odd, persistent feeling I know you.”

“Ha, yeah. I know what you mean.” *So much more than you know.*

“You didn’t grow up in Philly, by chance?”

How could she tell him so that he’d believe? “No, Red Bank, New Jersey.”

“Oh yeah!” He grinned. “I’ve been there. Cool town.” Santa walked by in the hall, and Braden blinked. “That’s really so weird.”

“What is?” she asked, sipping from her coffee.

“Sometimes when I see that guy,” Braden said, “I get this really strange feeling.”

Annie placed her coffee cup on the table. “Like nostalgia or something?”

Braden thought on this, studying the ceiling. He took a sip of water. “Possibly something like that,” he said, not appearing convinced.

"But everyone knows there's no such thing as Santa."

"Some say you're never too old to believe."

"That's what I've heard too."

Braden blanched and pushed back in his chair, bracing his hands against the table. "Wh-what did you just say?" He relaxed his stance and leaned forward, whispering across the table. "Annie, level with me. Have we had this conversation before?"

This was her chance. "Actually, yes," she said in hushed tones, "I'm sure we have."

His eyes flashed with incredulity. "Hang on"—he raked both hands through his hair—"you're not joking."

Annie stared at Braden. *Do it, do it now.* "Braden," she said softly, "I have something to tell you, and I want you to keep an open mind."

He looked at her askance. "How far open?"

"Er. Pretty far? Like wide open. The Grand Canyon. The Hoover Dam."

"Okay, that's pretty wide."

TWENTY-ONE

BRADEN SAT BACK IN HIS chair. "All right"—he looked at her warily—"I'm listening."

Annie got up and closed the door partway, leaving it open enough that anyone passing by wouldn't think anything of it. She couldn't have her fellow employees thinking she and Braden had something going on, because—uh, they didn't—except for in her mind. *Oh, if only I can convince him.*

"Braden," she said, returning to her chair. She spoke firmly but kept her voice down. "We're stuck in a time loop."

"What?" he blubbered out a laugh but caught himself, carefully scanning her eyes. "You mean it."

"I know how it sounds," she said, "but I have proof."

He eyed her carefully. "Proof would be good."

She shoved her half-eaten sandwich aside, resting her forearms on the table. "You and I?" she said, with her shoulders hunched forward, "first met six days ago."

"Nooo." His eyes went wide, and he blew out a breath. "Yeah?"

She nodded surely. "Yes." Might as well admit the embarrassing truth. It might jog his memory. "I had a bad start to my day and dropped my bag. One of my work shoes fell out of it, and then the other."

Braden peeked under the table at her feet and slowly looked up.

"I dropped my lip gloss too!" She pulled it from her pants pocket and held it toward him.

He gave it a skeptical glance. "What do you want me to do with that?"

"Take it," she said, "and give it back to me."

He did, and his hand froze in midair when their fingers brushed. Current zapped to her wrist, traveling up her arm. Braden yanked back his hand like she'd electrically shocked him. "Did you, uh"—he pursed his lips—"feel something?"

Annie nodded. "Braden," she whispered, "we're somehow connected in this. I don't know why, but somehow."

He gave her the side-eye and burst out laughing. "Good one, Annie Jones!" He roared at the ceiling.

"Shh! Keep your voice down."

"What? I thought you'd want me talking louder for the cameras."

"What cameras?"

"What is this?" He scrutinized her face. "Some sort of Christmas Eve prank?"

She spied a glimpse of red in the hallway. Old Saint Nick was going the other way.

"Hey, Santa!" Braden called cheerfully.

Santa stuck his head in the room, and Braden asked him, "You in on this?"

Santa cocked his head in his Santa hat. "I'm afraid I don't know what you mean?"

Braden blew out a breath. "This Christmas Eve joke Ms. Jones is playing?"

Santa surveyed Annie. "I don't think Ms. Jones is the sort to play tricks."

She exhaled heavily. "Thank you."

"Wait!" Braden held up his hand, but Santa had already slipped away.

"I can prove it," Annie rasped quietly.

Braden crossed his arms. "Oh yeah, how?"

She was ready with her answers. "When we leave here, Patrice is going to stop me in the hall and ask me to have a little chat."

"For what?"

Annie frowned. "She might have to fire me."

"Ouch." Braden's face fell. "At Christmas? That's harsh."

"It has to do with Veronica Lawson taking over the store from her grandfather," Annie continued in low whispers. "Profits are down, and she's looking to make cuts. Unfortunately"—Annie blew out a breath—"I don't make the very best impression on her later."

This piqued Braden's interest. "Why not?"

"Because," Annie confessed, "she comes into the store right after my window display gets totaled."

"Totaled?" Braden uncrossed his arms. "By whom?"

"These rascally little kids."

Braden's eyes clouded over, and he blinked. "No."

"Wait," Annie prodded. "Did you remember something?"

"I—don't think so," he said. "It was more about a train."

Her heart skipped a beat. "A toy train?"

"Hmm. Maybe?"

"Braden." Her tone was urgent. "That's just it. You help me pick up later, and Santa keeps saying there's something missing from the window display—that it needs something more. And"—she bit her lip—"you ask me to coffee."

He laughed, but this was so *not* funny. "Oh yeah? Where?"

Annie was starting to get annoyed. "The Blue Dot."

"Hmm. I do like that place."

Annie collapsed back in her chair. Maybe this was futile.

Braden took a sip of water and recapped his bottle. "So, *if* what you say is true—and that's a big if, huge—why is all this happening?"

Annie lifted a shoulder. "I wish I could tell you, but I'm not entirely sure. I think it's something about us getting through this day by making things right."

"What have I done wrong?" he asked worriedly. "Other than doubt you."

"I think it's more about me than you, honestly."

"And yet"—he thumbed his chest—"I'm caught up in this too?"

Annie winced. "Sorry."

"Look." He softened his tone. "You're clearly going through something—very tough."

"Yeah, but—you're going through it too. So is everyone else at Lawson's Finest, and all of my neighbors."

Braden spread his hands on the table. "Maybe you're just

having a bad day, you know? Sometimes we get those déjà vu feelings over things that aren't really related at all. It's more about how the experience feels familiar, and not the actual events."

Annie clasped her hands together. "You might think differently later."

"Okay." Braden squared his shoulders. "Let's wait and see." His smile was more to humor her than comfort her. Great. He thought she was unhinged. Time to bring out the heavy artillery.

"Braden," she said. "I know things about you. You and I, we've spent time together. Chatted a bunch at the Blue Dot, and right here at Lawson's—on more than one occasion. Many more. I told you some personal things about my family, about losing my parents—"

His frown was sincere. "I'm really sorry about that."

Now that she was on a roll, she barreled ahead. "And you told me about Harper."

"Harper?" He blinked. "What? When?"

"And Beth," she said, naming Harper's wife, "and their toddler, Theodore."

Braden shook his head. "I'm not sure how you're doing this, or why."

She lowered her voice. "You also told me about Baghdad."

His face clouded over. "No. I wouldn't have. Couldn't have done that."

"We've been growing close." She reached her hand across the table, and he cautiously took it. The moment their hands linked, he squeezed hers. He seemed to do it instinctively, like muscle memory.

He met her eyes, and her heart pounded. "This is all really weird."

"I know."

"Maybe we're dreaming?"

"Both of us—at once?"

"Isn't that a thing?"

"Uh, I'm not sure. Maybe it can happen?" She squeezed his hand tighter. "But not with total strangers."

"But we're *not* total strangers—according to you."

"Will you at least wait and see what the day brings?" She felt like she was begging, but she badly wanted him on her side. "Maybe then you'll finally believe me."

He stared at her like he was in a trance. "Sure, Annie." He firmly held her hand, and hope bloomed in her heart. "I can do that."

Kira pushed open the door. "Oh, hi there," she said slyly. She looked pointedly at their linked hands, and the two of them broke apart. "Don't let me interrupt."

Annie stuffed her partially eaten sandwich back in its bag. "No, no. It's fine."

Braden rolled up his trash. "Yeah." His face was all red. "I was just going."

Braden kept trying to process what Annie had told him, but it didn't compute. Time loop? Sure. He would have known about that from the get-go, if it were for real. He dumped his trash in the waste basket and refilled his water bottle, popping it back in the fridge.

"So"—Annie turned to him on her way out the door—"guess I'll see you later." He couldn't help but have compassion for her. She seemed like a really nice person. But time loop? No. She'd clearly put in too many hours and was stretched thin.

"Yeah, Annie. See ya!" His pulse quickened. That sounded awfully familiar. He'd probably said that to her earlier when they first met on the salesfloor. No, wait. They'd met beside the lockers. An image of them both holding her shoe came back to him like a big blurry thought bubble. So did a flash of her rolling lip gloss tube and her staring up at him from beneath her bright-red pom-pom hat, and saying she believed in—*stop*.

He set his hands on his duty belt and trailed her at a respectful distance. A polished middle-aged woman stepped out of the conference room. She wore a cranberry-colored suit and matching large-framed glasses. "Annie," she said, capturing her attention. "Have you got a minute?"

"Er. Sure, Patrice."

Patrice stepped aside, motioning for Annie to enter the conference room. "For a little chat?"

Annie peered over her shoulder at Braden.

His heart thumped. He got it, but that was just one thing. Hopefully not the thing that Annie dreaded, meaning she was about to learn her job was on the line. Braden's cell phone buzzed, and he pulled it from his pocket, pausing in front of the elevators.

It was his mom. He took the call. "Hey Ma, how are you doing?"

"Good, sweetheart, how about you?"

"It's been an, um"—he glanced toward the conference room as Patrice shut the door—"unusual day."

"Busy, I bet! Christmas Eve at Lawson's."

"Yeah."

"I'm checking in about tomorrow, on account of the weather." She sounded worried he wouldn't make it, and he rushed to put her at ease.

"I'll be there, I promise. Rain or shine."

"Yes, but." The pause was deafening. "They're calling this storm a blizzard."

"I'm sure it won't be that bad," he said, not sure of that at all. The reports did look dire, but—worst case scenario—if public transportation shut down, he could get to his mom's on foot. She was on her own since losing Fred, and she would be lonely. "You still working tonight?"

She sighed. "They'll need me in the ER. Lots of folks slipping on ice, I'm sure."

"Hope not too many."

"Same."

His mom was a great nurse, and the hospital was lucky to have her. Her manner was so reassuring and calm. "If the snow gets too bad, hon," she said. "I don't want you to worry. I'll understand."

"I'll be there, Ma." And this time he wasn't letting anybody down. Hurt lodged in his throat as he relived the bomb blast. He'd been in the hospital when his mom had buried Fred, so he hadn't been there to support her. He maybe couldn't have avoided that, but he could prevent his mom from being on her own on

Christmas Day. Though she put on a brave front, she had a soft heart underneath. Sometimes lately, when he'd stopped by to see her, her eyes were red-rimmed like she'd been crying. Losing two husbands she loved had to have been hard.

"How about you?" he asked. "You going to be fine commuting home at o'dark thirty?"

"Our head nurse has a four-wheel drive. He's been known to drive home those of us who live in Brooklyn before. So, I'm sure I'll be fine."

"Well, call me if you aren't?" he said, pushing any dark thoughts away. The last thing he wanted was his mom—or anyone he cared for—getting hurt, ever again.

"Of course. I'll have my phone on me."

Braden took up his post at the main entrance to Lawson's, welcoming new customers and wishing happy holidays to those departing. The storm outside kept getting worse as predicted, and instead of closing at six, as it normally did on Christmas Eve, Lawson's was now shutting its doors at four. Shoppers scurried everywhere, scooping merchandise into their arms and rushing to checkout counters. *Here comes Annie.*

She was dressed mostly in white, painting a very attractive picture against the holiday decorations around her. She held a large package in her hands and wore a serious look, like she was on a mission. Braden glanced at her window display, where the lights on the Christmas tree had gone out, guessing what that mission was. She'd seemed so sure of everything when they'd talked at lunch. Had convinced herself entirely of this time loop idea, and yet it was ludicrous when you viewed things rationally.

Annie jumped back as a man leaving the jewelry counter nearly ran into her. "Oh! Sorry!" he said. The guy seemed to be in his thirties and was dressed very well in an overcoat over a business suit. He held a small black bag with embossed gold letters, L and F, for Lawson's Finest.

"Incoming!" Annie warned a gaggle of teenagers as she scuttled around them. Why was she in such a hurry? That Christmas tree wasn't going anywhere.

"No, Dylan! Let me!"

Two boys darted through the crowd, with their mom in hot pursuit.

"Dylan! Marcus! Come back here!"

Braden's senses went on high alert.

No way. They were zooming straight for Annie's window!

Braden cut Annie a glance and she blanched, dropping her box of lights. She raced toward the boys, and so did he.

"*Stop!*" their mom called, but it was too late.

The sequence unfolded in unbearably slow motion. The boys went down with the retractable belt. There went the Christmas tree! So did the icicle lights, everything on the mantel, *and* Santa's cookies and milk. Braden stared up at the snowflakes and sugarplums twirling above the wreckage.

Annie gasped. *What a disaster.*

A big whoosh of wind washed over Braden like an icy blast of artic air, and images raced past him at breakneck speed: the mom taking out her wallet, Santa speaking with the boys, Annie telling Santa he'd been so good with them...

"*What happened here?*" a shrill voice intruded. Santa strode toward his workshop, and the mom walked away with her boys, holding hands with each one on either side.

Annie shrank back. "Ms. Lawson."

Braden goggled at the stylish blond dressed in green and wearing a big fancy hat. "It was just an accident, ma'am." He caught his breath, getting his bearings, and mashed the button on his mic, reporting the incident.

"Roger that," Mike said. "We'll get Lou on the door."

Annie stood up straighter. "Don't worry," she said to Ms. Lawson. "We'll pick everything up." She glanced at Braden. "I mean, I will."

"No, no," he assured Annie. "You got that right the first time. I'll help you." He turned to Ms. Lawson. "It will all be good as new when Lawson's reopens after Christmas."

"Let's hope so." She scanned the window. "We have after-Christmas sales to think of."

Braden seized the opportunity. "I bet they'll go just great when customers get a load of this window."

"Yes! It will be better than ever," Annie said. "Even better than before." She peeked toward Santa's workshop and added, "You'll be very impressed."

Ms. Lawson eyed her quizzically. "Will I?" She glanced at Santa too, and her expression filled with whimsy. "Oh, right," she said as if she'd remembered something but wasn't quite sure what. "I, um." She stared at Annie. "I can't wait to see what you do with it. I'm Veronica Lawson." She extended her hand. "You must be our window designer."

Annie nodded and shook her hand. "Assistant Visual Artist, yes, ma'am."

Veronica considered the wrecked display before carefully climbing over the low divider and into the fake snow piled high on the floor. She bent and picked up an envelope, holding it up in her hand. "Is this a note for Santa?"

Annie grinned. "Yes, it is."

"Huh." Ms. Lawson thumped the envelope against her hand and carried it over and set it carefully on the mantel, propping it against the wall. She stepped over the fake cookies and milk and the upended train track, making her way back to the fallen Christmas tree. She pulled the Christmas stocking from it and carried it to the mantel, hanging it on a nail. "There!" She patted the stocking and gave a self-satisfied smile. "That's better."

She climbed out of the window and stumbled. A man held out his hand, catching her. Veronica startled. "Quinn?" Braden identified the man as the guy who'd nearly run into Annie while leaving the jewelry counter. "What are you doing here?" Her expression indicated surprise and maybe something more. Attraction?

He stealthily slid the gift bag behind his back. "I could ask the same of you, Ronnie."

She shifted the animal-print coat in her arms. "I thought I'd pay a Christmas Eve visit to Lawson's Finest. See how sales were going." She frowned at the window, and Quinn shook his head.

"Shame about that," he said.

"Yes," she agreed. "Shame." She smiled flirtatiously. "We still on for dinner?"

"How about we head out early?" Quinn nodded toward the exit. "Grab a drink along the way?" He extended his elbow, and she hooked her arm through his.

"Great idea," she said with a smile.

Annie watched them leave and heaved a breath. "Well, that was a positive turn—I think."

Braden studied her. "That didn't happen last time?"

"No." She shook her head. "Definitely didn't."

"So, wait." Braden's head went all fuzzy. "Are you saying certain things repeat themselves, and others don't?"

Relief flooded her. "*Yes.*"

He tried to wrap his mind around the concept, but logic kept putting up roadblocks. *Don't let her suck you into her fantasy, man.* That had to be what this was. Some sort of contagious delusion. Braden snatched a peek at Santa's workshop and, even from way across the salesfloor, Santa noticed Braden's eyes on him and waved. Braden's heart hammered.

Santa Claus is not real. Come on.

This guy did a pretty darn good imitation though.

Braden had a million questions as he helped Annie pick up, and she answered every one. It was still hard to fathom they'd reconstructed this very same window scene six times, although Annie was very clear to point out that they'd added something new and different to the display each day. The guy in the red suit paused on his way out the door as Braden tacked up the icicle lights. "Nice going, you two." He considered the scene. "Just needs—hmm."

"A little something more?" Braden asked him.

Santa held his big, round belly. "Ye-es."

Annie widened her eyes at Braden, and he had to concede, she'd been very right about everything so far. How could she possibly have known?

Santa snapped his gloved fingers. "Are you familiar with my biography?"

"Pardon?" Annie appeared amused, and Braden found this funny too. Did this actor imagine he was a celebrity?

"'The Night Before Christmas' some call it," Santa said. "It's a storybook and a poem."

"Oh sure, sure." Braden climbed down the ladder. "''Twas the night before Christmas, and all through the house...'"

Santa linked his hands behind him and bowed forward. "Not a creature was stirring..."

Annie wrinkled up her nose, trying to get what Santa was telling them. "You want us to add a mouse?" She flashed Braden a look, her eyes huge. She was right. That was looney tunes. Not a real mouse. Wait. Maybe that's not what Santa meant. "You don't happen to have a mouse—?"

"—in back?" asked Annie. "Hang on." Her face lit up. "I think I do!" She glanced at Santa and explained, "I helped Julio put together a window display for our baby nursery sale last June. Its theme was 'Hickory Dickory Dock.'"

Braden turned to Annie. "You got a spare mouse there?"

"Yeah, one or two." She set her hands on her hips. "I also happen to have some props I can use. A cute little blanket. A tiny bed."

"A stocking cap for a sleeping mouse?" Braden asked her.

She batted her eyelashes at him. "You're very good at this."

"Yeah?" He grinned. "So are you."

They both turned to Old Saint Nick. "Thanks, Santa!"

He departed with a ho ho ho. "Merry Christmas!"

Braden stared straight at Annie, and she stared back. "I think I'm going to need that coffee," he told her.

Annie nodded. "Me too." She pulled her cell from her pocket to check the time. "But it will have to be a short one."

"You got someplace to be?"

"I do." She nodded earnestly. "I'll tell you all about it when we go grab Mickey."

"Mickey?"

She grinned. "Our mouse."

He laughed, feeling happy all over. Maybe she *had* sucked him into her fantasy, but that was okay. This wasn't such a terrible place to be. And, if he was dreaming, or jointly dreaming with Annie, he'd wake up from it tomorrow.

Over coffee at the Blue Dot later, she filled him in on all the details of the past six days, telling him about things that had happened at Lawson's Finest and what their interactions had been, and weirdly a lot of her reports rang true. She also talked a lot about her neighbors, and they all sounded really nice. It was very cool how much she cared for these people she'd only begun getting to know. Sort of like he was starting to care for her.

"I'm sorry," she said, checking her phone. "I need to get going."

Braden gently touched her arm before they stood from the booth. "Hang on. I want to be sure I remember." He grabbed a napkin from the dispenser on the table. "You got a pen?"

She nodded and pulled one out of her purse.

He held out his hand, and she gave it to him.

He scrawled out his reminder and held up the napkin to show her. *Believe Annie*. He underscored it three times and returned her pen, tucking the napkin in his jacket pocket and zipping it up. It was better than anything else he could think of and, if this worked, he'd know for a fact he wasn't dreaming. Nobody's dreams were *that precise*, and Braden almost never remembered his.

"What's that for?" She wore a hopeful smile.

He patted his chest above where he'd stashed the note. "Insurance."

TWENTY-TWO

On the seventh Christmas Eve

FA-LA-LA-LA-LA—!

Annie stared at her phone, so ready for this day.

Okay, it was still happening. And today, she was trying extra hard with Braden. Maybe she'd break through. Leo lifted his head from his perch by her feet and started purring. "Morning, sunshine!" Annie sat up and petted him, and he purred louder. "Do you know what day it is?" She smiled at the cat. "Of course, you do. I do too." Annie swung her feet over the bed, pausing to grab Leo's cat toy off the floor without stepping on it.

Leo plodded into the kitchen and she followed him with a purposeful air, raising the kitchen blinds. The sidewalks were clear, the sky cloudy and gray. Annie peered in her refrigerator at the nearly bare shelves. Shame. That last batch of chili had been extra tasty. Oh well. She shut the fridge door. She'd get another try at that too.

Tina's smile gleamed in their Coney Island photo. Annie badly wanted to text her, but she never had the right words to say. Now, she could be out of a job.

Not if I can help it.

Annie set her chin, preparing her coffee. Her window display at Lawson's was definitely improved from where she'd started. The toy mouse in a stocking cap snuggled in his bed behind the tree leant it a magical touch. Maybe there were more ways to add magic to her window?

Leo meowed, and she chuckled indulgently. "Okay, okay, I'll feed you."

She did so carefully—and without incident—before her intercom buzzed.

"Package for you!"

Annie rolled her eyes at Leo. "We both know that's not accurate."

Later, at the subway stop, she didn't even bother to ask the younger guy what day it was. Instead, she sat down on the bench beside the man reading the newspaper. His eyes were glued to data columns that looked like stock market reports. She peeked at the date on the front page as he held it open: *December 24*.

The man noticed her staring and closed his paper. "Happy Christmas Eve," he said in a light British accent. He was much younger than she'd noticed before, with dirty-blond hair and deep-brown eyes. Nice-looking too.

Wait. She recognized that face. "Quinn?"

He blinked and set the paper on his lap. "Have we met?"

"I, er"—she twisted a lock of her hair around her finger—"not exactly, but I think I've seen you in the store."

He crossed his arms, and his very nicely cut suit creased in places. "Which store is that?"

"Lawson's Finest." How had she not put this together?

Though, to be fair, she'd barely seen—or spoken to—the man by the jewelry counter.

"Ahh, yes. Probably so." He smiled proudly. "My girlfriend owns the place."

Annie did her best to act surprised—and impressed. "You're dating Veronica Lawson?"

"Not just dating," he confided in low tones. "Taking things to the next level tonight." He chuckled softly. "Don't know why I'm telling you this, but the truth is I'm a bit excited." He folded up his paper and slid it in his backpack. "A little nervous too."

"So, you're...?" Annie grinned excitedly. She'd guessed there'd been something very important in his gift bag.

Quinn nodded. "Proposing this evening, that's right. Got the ring custom-ordered right there at Lawson's." He grinned. "Thought it was fitting."

Annie grabbed her bag's handle when she saw their train coming. "I'm sure she'll love that surprise."

They both stood and he asked her, "What do you do at Lawson's?"

She squared her shoulders. "I design the windows, among other things."

"You're the visual artist there?" His mournful expression said he knew something. Maybe Veronica had told him about her plans to scale back on staff?

"Yeah, one of them." The train whooshed out of the tunnel and stopped right in front of them. An idea hit her. "And here's the great thing!" she told Quinn, hoping he might share this with Veronica. "I'm working on something new."

"For after the holidays?" he asked as they waited for the train's doors to open.

"No, no," she answered. "For—right now!"

Quinn rubbed his square jaw. "Interesting," he said. "Well, good luck with it."

"Yeah." She smiled up at him as a throng of people swarmed out of the subway car and she and Quinn prepared to enter. "Good luck to you too."

Quinn squeezed his way deeper into the packed car, and Annie took a free seat that became available. She settled her bag in her lap, teeming with energy. Today was going to be such a good day. A great day for Veronica Lawson too. Annie snatched a peek at Quinn through the crowd, delighted with her secret. She had to share it with someone, and she knew exactly who.

Annie hurried out of the elevator at Lawson's, not having seen Santa or Braden on the first floor. She'd scoured around for them both, but it was Braden she'd been hunting for most of all. She needed to know if he still had that napkin and whether he remembered yesterday. She beelined down the hall, heading for the section of employee lockers. Braden stepped out in front of her, emerging from the break room. "Whoa!" He stumbled backward, and his full mug of coffee sloshed in his hands, splattering the front of his uniform.

Annie covered her mouth. "I'm so sorry!"

Braden grabbed some paper napkins and started dabbing at his shirt. "Yeah, uh. My fault. I should have looked." He peeked in her direction. "I didn't see you coming."

She eyed him worriedly. "Did that burn you?"

"No, I'm wearing a vest."

"What?"

"Ballistic."

"Ooh." Of course, he was. Security, duh. Her gaze fell to his duty belt and raced back up to his stunning blue eyes.

"Wait." He balled the coffee-stained napkins in his fist. "Do I know you?"

What? Noooo. "I'm Annie."

He tossed the napkins in the trash. "Right," he said, glancing at her. "You—do the windows?"

Arghh. Seriously? "Braden," she said. "We need to talk."

He viewed her askance, like she was some kind of random weirdo. "About?"

She fiddled with a button on her coat, her nerves building. "Just things!" She smiled, but then her face fell. "You don't remember meeting me before, do you?"

"Sure, I do." He screwed up his face. "At the holiday party, right?"

Annie sighed.

"You were standing by the—Christmas tree?" He checked his watch. "Look, I'd love to stay and chat." He grinned charmingly, and her pulse fluttered. "The thing is, I've got to go and change and get to my post. Lucky for me, I keep a spare shirt in my locker."

"Sure!" She couldn't hold him here against his will. She also couldn't force him to recall their prior interactions either. Darn it. Still. She had to give it another try. Santa was right about those silver linings. Maybe she could still find one with Braden by bringing him around. "Ahh, Braden!" She caught up with him, striding toward her locker in her overly hot pom-pom hat. She ripped it off and he stared at her frizzy, snow-wilted hair. "I was wondering what time you take lunch?"

"Lunch?" He shrugged. "Today, around one thirty? Two?"

"Great!" Annie said. "Maybe we can talk then?"

Annie was already in the break room when Braden walked in. "Well, hey there," he said, pulling his lunch bag from the staff refrigerator. "Nice to see you again."

"Yeah," Annie said. "You too." She stared down at her peanut butter sandwich, which somehow didn't seem like enough. Maybe she should have packed a dessert.

Braden sat across from her and unloaded his lunch, including that gigantic chocolate chip cookie. Annie's mouth watered. *That looks so good.*

He noticed her staring. "Like chocolate chip?"

"Oh yeah, pretty much any kind of cookie." Which hadn't exactly been the truth merely a week ago. Most treats had tasted like cardboard.

Braden grinned. "I can give you half?"

"Oh, would you?" She hoped she didn't sound too eager. "That would be great."

He cast a look at her sandwich. "You should probably eat your lunch first."

"It's Christmastime! We can make exceptions."

"Don't want to get on Santa's naughty list," he teased.

She sat up straighter. "Take it from me, I'm mostly nice."

"Oh yeah?" Braden took a bite of his sub and set it down. "That means you still get Santa?"

"Of course," she bantered sassily. "Don't you?"

He laughed, and happiness fizzed through her like champagne bubbles.

"I guess I would," Braden answered, "if I still believed."

Annie put on a play pout and said deadpan, "But you don't."

Braden's lips pulled up in a grin. "I'd say the—"

"—jury's still out on that one?" she finished for him.

Braden narrowed his eyes. "Yeah. But how—?"

She leaned toward him. "Braden, I have something to tell you, and I don't want you to judge me."

"O-kay." His eyebrows twitched. "I'm listening."

She recited her whole spiel, ending with the tidbit about meeting Quinn on the subway platform and about how he was about to propose to Veronica Lawson. She finished her last nibble of cookie and chased it with a sip of her coffee, which had gone lukewarm by now.

Braden stuffed his trash in his lunch bag. "That's an awful lot to process, Annie."

"I know it sounds out there," she agreed. "But, apart from what's already happened, I can tell you what's *going to happen*—later at the store. And Braden—when I explained things to you yesterday, you believed me."

He pushed back in his chair. "No," he rasped hoarsely. "No way." He shut his eyes for a prolonged beat. When he opened them, he asked, "Did you—lose your lip gloss?" He looked like he was trudging through a swamp, fighting his way through murky waters. "Drop it on the floor?"

"I did," she replied firmly, "and you picked it up."

He murmured to himself, trancelike. "The shoe...the tree... the train." He gaped at her. "How—are you doing this?"

Santa strode down the hall. He stopped and poked his head in the door. "Afternoon, you two!" he said without waiting for a reply.

"It's not me," Annie whispered. She rolled her eyes toward the hall. "It's him."

"Santa?" His tone was incredulous.

"Or Christmas, yes," she said. "Look, I'm not entirely sure. There's just something going on where we're stuck in this time loop, and the only way out seems to be by fixing my window display and making it better."

Braden massaged his forehead. "Because that's the only part of this day that changes?"

Annie shook her head. "Other things keep changing too. My interactions with my neighbors, for example, and"—her heart stuttered at the curious look in his eyes—"my conversations with you."

"So, you and I?" Braden motioned between them. "We're a thing?"

Embarrassing. "No, no! Not, er, um...*a thing*"—she blew out a breath—"exactly." In her dreams.

Braden set his elbows on the table. "Then what?"

"We're...well, friends." Annie licked her lips, wishing they were so much more, but it was very hard to explain that under the circumstances.

He searched her eyes. "You said you have proof."

"Not me," she answered. "You do."

Braden laid a hand on his chest. "What?"

"It's in your jacket pocket," she told him. "You wrote something on a napkin at the Blue Dot last night—I mean later today." Annie turned up her hands. "Whenever."

"Okay," he said, standing. "My jacket's in my locker. Let's take a look."

They nearly bumped into Kira as she entered the room.

"Oh!" Annie sprang back, bumbling into Braden. She spun around and he caught her, his hands bracing her upper arms. Annie's breath hitched.

"Careful there." He was such a sexy and irresistible guy. No wonder she was falling for him. Panic washed over her like icy ocean waves. She could *not* let herself fall for someone she'd never stand a chance with in this reality.

"Sorry to interrupt," Kira smirked with a knowing gleam.

"You're not interrupting." Annie steadied herself on her heels. "We were just—on our way." She glanced at Braden, trying not to sound breathy. "Thanks for the save."

He grinned, and her heart pounded. "No problem."

Oh boy, this is bad. Badder than bad. She had the major hots for a man she was stuck in a time loop with. A time loop with loopholes, no less. How would they ever have a future, or even a first date? Assuming he felt the same. Braden turned, wearing a concerned expression when she lagged behind. "You okay?" The twinkle in his eyes said maybe he did find her appealing. Her knees shook, and she steadied herself against the wall with one hand.

She gathered her resolve and followed along. "Um, yep!"

As okay as I'll ever be until I can figure this whole thing out.

Braden entered the lounge area with its assortment of employee lockers and opened his. He took out his jacket and unzipped a pocket, fishing around inside.

Please let him find the note.

Please, please, please. Please.

He checked the other pocket and shook his head.

"Sorry." He frowned. "Nothing's there."

Annie's heart sank like a stone but wait. "Not the outside pockets. An inside one?"

"Ah." He reached into his jacket's hollow and extracted something in his fingers.

He gawked down at the napkin. "I wrote this?"

Annie nodded. *Yes! He found it.*

His eyes flashed with understanding—or maybe a hint of a memory. "Yeah," he said roughly. "Yeah, I—did." Braden stared at her, flummoxed. "Holy wow, Annie, this is seriously messed up."

"I know," she whispered when she saw Patrice approaching.

"Annie!" Patrice called, striding toward her. "Do you have time for a little chat?"

Annie grimaced at Braden with her back turned to Patrice, and he apparently got her hint. This was just the first of many events she'd predicted that were about to come true. Annie spun toward her boss and answered, "Be right there, Patrice."

At around half past three, Quinn helped Veronica out of the fake snow, holding her hand. He grasped his gift bag in his other fist, hiding it behind his back. "You're the visual artist, right?"

Veronica surveyed Annie. "Oh? Is that right?"

Annie nodded sheepishly. "Yeah, that's me."

Quinn tried to make a joke. "When you said you were working on something new here..." He quickly scanned the mess. "I didn't imagine this."

"Ha!" Annie said. "Me neither."

Veronica darted a look at the window and frowned. "What a bummer thing to happen on Christmas Eve," she said to Annie. "Looks like you've got your work cut out for you with the cleanup. Have you got any help?"

Braden stepped forward. "I've volunteered." He smiled at Veronica. "It will be better than new by the time Lawson's reopens after Christmas."

Veronica slid her arm through Quinn's when he extended his elbow. "That's so nice of you"—she read his name tag—"Braden."

"No worries," he said. "Happy to."

Veronica noticed the sleeping mouse by the upended tree. "How cute is that? Look, Quinn! *Not a creature was stirring...*"

"*Not even a mouse.*" He smiled at Veronica. "Clever bit."

Veronica tipped her hat at Annie. "Love it."

Annie's heart soared. "Thank you."

The two of them left, and Santa appeared as Annie and Braden righted the tree. He stroked his snowy-white beard, staring at the mantel, where Veronica had re-hung the single Christmas stocking. "Something's not quite right there."

Not again. But yeah, of course.

"With the stocking?" Annie asked him. "What?"

"I know!" He snapped his gloved fingers. "It's *stockings*."

Annie stared at the faux mantel. "Sorry?"

Santa tugged on his hat. "'The stockings were hung by the chimney with care...'"

Braden got it. He glanced at Annie. "That's *stockings*. Plural."

She rolled her eyes at Braden. "You want us to add one more?"

"At least!" Santa grinned. "One for little Billy and one for Nell."

"Wait," Braden whispered to Annie, "isn't that from the song 'Up on the Housetop'?"

"Our Santa knows his Christmas lore." She spoke louder to Santa. "No problem! We'll do it!"

Santa nodded and waded into the window, his black boots buried in fake snow. He squatted down to grab the fallen plate of cookies, dropping a few of them on the plate. He held up a fake oatmeal raisin cookie last, and stood, studying it carefully.

Braden picked up the knocked-over end table, and Santa put the cookie plate on it.

"Glad you added my favorite kind," he said, still holding the cookie in his hand. He opened his mouth and took a whopping big bite!

"Santa!" Annie startled. "Don't eat that!"

"She's right." Braden approached Santa. "That's not even real."

Santa rolled the morsel around in his mouth and chewed on it. "Tastes pretty good to me."

"Santa, don't!"—Annie held up her hand—"Don't swallow that, you'll choke!"

He paid her no mind and ate the piece anyway. Santa placed the remainder of the cookie on the plate. It clearly was damaged, having had a big bite taken out of it. She'd have to get another one from the box in storage.

"No need to replace that." Santa nodded to the plate and Annie blanched. There, he'd done it again, invaded her head somehow.

"I didn't invade," he said mildly. "You left the door open."

Braden sent Annie a look, like *What was that all about?*

She'd tell him later.

"And anyway"—Santa pointed to the cookie—"this is where the magic happens."

"Huh?" Annie had completely missed something.

So, obviously, had Braden. "What did our store Santa mean by that?" he asked when Santa walked away. "And what was that invasion talk?"

"I have no idea," she answered. "And I'll tell you while we pick up."

Braden set his hands on his duty belt and nodded toward the jewelry counter. "You were right about Quinn," he said, sounding amazed. "I paid attention earlier when he paid for his purchase. The sales associate slid something into the bag that looked like a ring box."

Annie stared out the front window at the blustery night. "Happy evening for them."

Braden watched them walk away. "Assuming she says yes."

Annie gasped, not having considered this. "I guess you're right."

"She probably will though." He nodded knowingly. "I read their body language. They seem pretty tight."

It was hard for Annie to imagine being that close to someone. Considering marriage. She met Braden's eyes, and her heart skipped a beat. Maybe she just hadn't met the right *someone*. Until now.

Braden rubbed his hands together. "What do you say? Should we clean this mess up?"

Annie flipped back her hair. "Only if we can go for coffee at the Blue Dot afterward?"

Braden smiled. "Lady, I'm definitely going out for coffee with you."

Annie set her chin, feeling happy about that. "Good."

Braden took out his cell phone. "And also," he said casually, "can I have your number?"

Annie grinned cautiously. "You planning to call?"

He shrugged. "Text maybe? I mean, things could get dicey with both of us stuck in this time loop together. Might be good to reach out to a friend."

Annie's pulse pounded. "How do we know our phones will save the new contacts?"

He smiled. "How do we know that they won't?"

TWENTY-THREE

On the eighth Christmas Eve

FA-LA-LA-LA—!

Annie sat up in bed like she'd been struck by lightning.

She grabbed her phone and stared at the date.

Dec 24

Winter Storm Warning

This is where the magic happens. Yes! On Christmas Eve.

She shoved the covers aside, and Leo plopped onto the floor, lazily blinking his eyes. "Oh sorry, kitty!" She reached down to pet him, and he nudged his thick head up against her palm, purring. "Merry almost-Christmas." She plucked his cat toy off the floor and set it aside.

Magic, magic, magic.

Maybe it had come to her in a dream?

No, *this* was a dream. No, wait. Alternate reality. Was Braden in it with her? She pulled up the contact list on her phone scrolling down to the Ts.

Annie's heart leapt in her throat.

Braden Tate

OMG—squee! He's in there. Her breath came in fits and starts. *Calm down, Annie. Okay. Let's check this.*

She strode into her living room with Leo bounding ahead of her. Her sweet Christmas tree was all decorated, but it was missing only one candy cane. The one she'd dropped in her hot cocoa that very first night. Leo's Christmas stocking was empty too. Hang on.

She returned to her bedroom, remembering something. The painting her dad had done of her snow globe rested on her desk. She went and picked it up, carrying it into the living room, holding it up beside her actual snow globe nestled beneath her little tree.

Believe.

Yes, right. But seeing was believing, wasn't it? Belief was about faith, sure. But sometimes when there were signs an event had really happened, you believed it even more. Santa biting into that cookie had planted a seed in her mind, and somehow overnight it had grown into a bigger—but not yet completely crystalized—idea. Certainty coursed through her. She'd figure this out, yeah, she would.

Annie arranged her dad's painting behind the Christmas tree, propping it against the wall and steadying it against the Christmas tree's base. It looked great there, so cheerful—it brought a smile to her face and tugged at her heartstrings. She lifted the snow globe and shook it heartily. Tiny snowflakes flitted around inside the globe, cascading down on Santa and his reindeer team. *Believe.*

She'd once thought her belief had been shattered to bits, but had it been—really? Maybe there'd always been a miniscule part of her that had never totally given up, a hopeful part that yearned for the goodness that exists in this world, like narrow slivers of light—apparent even in the blackest darkness.

She glanced at Leo, who sat perched on his haunches near the kitchen. He was hungry, of course he was. She was a bit hungry too. She'd make herself some toast with her coffee and do that quickly before the intercom buzzer rang.

There were new things to gain, even—paradoxically—in a repetitiously rewinding day. And she had faith that new friends would be here with her. Her spirit danced. So would Braden. Then maybe, *somehow*, they'd make it out of this mess together.

Leo meowed, and she chuckled at his desperate face. "I'm starving you, poor kitty." She popped a piece of bread in the toaster and fixed her coffee, serving Leo his food. She didn't spill an ounce. Her thoughts churned over her window display and how to fix it. She knew it had to do with Christmas Eve having come—and gone. Excitement rose up inside her. She was onto something. Maybe Braden would have some ideas? Assuming he still remembered yesterday—and her, they could meet up and develop a plan.

The buzzer rang, and she crammed the rest of her toast in her mouth. She'd slathered it with jam and—*oh, this tastes so fantastic. Raspberry goodness on crunchy whole grain.* Annie pressed the intercom button, her mouth packed full. She covered it with her hand, although the guy couldn't see. "Um-hmm?"

"Package for you!" he announced.

Annie took a quick swig of coffee. "Be right down!"

"Door's stuck."

"Just leave it on the stoop!"

Annie shrugged on her coat and squirmed into her snow boots, spying her cell phone on the kitchen table. What if Braden *didn't* remember yesterday, *or her*—at all? Her heart clenched. That would be awful. She had to find out. Annie picked up her phone with trembling fingers. Part of her wanted to know for sure that Braden would answer. Another part was terrified he wouldn't. Maybe her contact number hadn't even saved in his phone?

One way to find out.

She texted him.

Annie

You up?

Three dots appeared on her screen, soon several more. Annie's pulse pounded.

Braden

Annie? That you?

She held her breath, hoping.

Annie

Do you remember yesterday?

Braden

Not everything.

More dots.

I thought I'd had a weird dream, then I found the napkin in my jacket.

Ye-es. Annie fist-pumped the air.

It wasn't total recall, but it was something. She'd take it.

Annie

I think I've had a breakthrough. Can you meet up at Lawson's?

Braden

Just say when.

Annie checked her watch.

Annie

Can you be there before nine?

Braden

Break room?

No. Too many early birds getting coffee.

Annie

Conference room.

Braden

Okay.

Annie shucked her coat, ditching it on a kitchen chair. "Change of plans," she told Leo. She hurried into her bedroom to dress for work. She needed to get to Lawson's and talk this through with somebody levelheaded and kind, and who actually believed her. That somebody was Braden. But first, she snatched the toilet paper roll off its holder and stashed in the bathroom linen closet, securely shutting the door.

A short time later, Annie jumped out of the way of the falling snow dump on her stoop and scooped up the package for Jane. She had her work bag slung over one shoulder as she carted the package upstairs. Jane opened her door.

"Oh hey!" Jane scanned Annie's face, noting the package. "Is that for me?"

"It is," Annie said, passing it to her. "Deliveryman buzzed me by mistake."

"Thanks!" Jane studied Annie's outfit. "Sorry to take you out of your way."

"No problem." Annie smiled. "It only took a second to bring it upstairs."

Jane nodded and narrowed her eyes. "You live in the building, yeah?"

"Apartment 3-A." Annie nodded. "My name's Annie."

Jane scratched her head. "Have we spoken before?"

"Um, maybe once or twice?"

"Yeah," she said. "Must have." Jane stared at her again. "That's so funny. I somehow feel I *know* you."

"Yeah?" Annie answered. "I weirdly sense that too."

"Maybe we're friend mates?" Jane joked.

Annie laughed. "What's that?"

"Don't know." Jane shrugged. "Destined to have coffee?"

Annie grinned from ear to ear. "I'd like that, Jane."

"Great."

Annie turned, and Jane shouted. "Hey, wait!"

Annie paused on a lower step.

Jane viewed her curiously. "How did you know my name?"

Annie didn't miss a beat. "It's on the package."

Annie hurried down the stairs and stepped into the blustery cold, scuttling toward the subway as chilly snowflakes doused her hat and hair. She made it through the turnstile and onto the subway platform and squeezed into the loaded subway car, just in time. When she peered through the glass portion of the door, she saw Quinn racing for the train. He stopped and—for a split second—he stared at her, while Annie stared back. He shook his head, as if he'd mistaken her for someone else, and traipsed over to a vacant bench and sat.

Annie grabbed on to a handrail, and the subway car whooshed away.

Braden got to Lawson's first, stationing himself in the conference room. Annie burst through the door like a big gust of wind, wrapped in her red scarf and snow-speckled peacoat. "Sorry I'm late," she said catching her breath. "My train got stuck in a tunnel!" She clasped her hat and mittens in one hand and held on to the shoulder strap of her bag with the other. "I swear I've not been able to get here earlier than 9:08 on any of these days, no matter how I try." Her eyes seemed bigger and browner than ever. His heart thumped at her anxious look. She didn't appear so much nervous as excited, and her up mood was contagious.

"No worries," he said. "We still have a little time." He checked the clock on the wall above the door, seeing it was almost 9:15. He did need to stop by the security office, but that could wait five minutes, maybe ten.

Annie undid her brass buttons. "Wish we had more of it though." She grimaced. "Just not on Christmas Eve."

"Ha, yeah." He tucked the "Believe Annie" napkin in his jacket pocket. He'd been staring at it while waiting for Annie to arrive, trying to decipher this very strange puzzle. Even though he didn't know her well, he did trust Annie. She had no reason to invent the story she had, and some of the things he recalled happening couldn't possibly have transpired if today was Christmas Eve for the first time.

She deposited her bag in one of the chairs at the conference table, peeking back at the door and keeping her voice down. "Maybe we should shut it—at least partway." Braden nodded and closed it gently, leaving it open a smidge.

"What's this about an idea?" he asked, joining her at the table.

"Braden," she said. "I think Santa was giving us a clue."

"The store Santa, you mean." Braden's emotions went all jumbled. This entire notion of Santa being *Santa* was absurd. He was an actor employed by the store. Both of them knew that. They could joke that he wasn't but couldn't seriously pretend otherwise. "Annie," he whispered hoarsely. "There *is no* Santa, really."

"Of course, I know that. Only… What if there is?" Her

eyelashes fanned wide, and he thought of how they'd looked dotted with snowflakes. She really was an incredibly attractive woman. He was surprised she didn't have a boyfriend. And yet—when they'd caught that falling box… Wait. When had that happened? Not yesterday. Maybe the day before? Scattered images collided and blurred. He raked a hand through his hair.

He'd researched scientific theories relating to time travel last night. So, the notion of time bending back on itself was something he could possibly buy into. Nobody'd seriously studied the veracity of there being a Kris Kringle who lived at the North Pole though. Come on. That would mean believing in flying reindeer and elves, and all sorts of other fanciful stuff.

"So, ideas?" Braden asked. "I'm guessing you were talking about a way out of this time loop, for you and, uh"—he exhaled sharply—"me, because it really seems I'm in it?"

She thumped the table with her hand. "I think what San—" She stopped herself, then continued, "The old man meant has to do with that cookie and the fact he'd taken a bite."

"That part was a little scary."

"I know," she said. "But still, I feel like it was a hint."

"About your window display?"

"And improving it, yes."

"But we added another Christmas stocking."

"Braden," she said dead seriously. "This could go on for days, weeks, *months*. Can't you see? We can't keep waiting for Santa to suggest things, because he always will, piece by piece. What if he suggests a certain kind of ornament?"

Braden leaned forward. "Like the tinsel?"

"Like that, but something else. Shiny baubles! Candy canes!" She shook her head. "His list could never end."

"So how do we stop it?"

Annie tugged on her vest. "By taking the lead. Coming up with ideas first."

Braden crossed his arms. "That could take forever too."

Annie sat up straighter. "Not if we're strategic."

Braden turned her suggestions over in his mind. "You're saying we should be proactive—rather than reactive."

"Yes." Annie's face brightened as she pulled a small, spiral bound notebook out of her bag. The cover had sparkly gold letters on it that said *Make Magic Happen*.

"What's that?"

"My notebook." She took out a pen. "I use it to brainstorm ideas sometimes on the subway."

"And?" He was intrigued.

"This morning." She tapped the pen against her pretty mouth and smiled. "I thought a lot about Christmas, and how it was when I was little. The fun parts of my discovery on Christmas morning."

Braden chuckled, getting her vibe. "Finding a loaded stocking. Yep. That was cool."

"Presents under the tree!"

Braden grinned. "I once got a note *from* Santa."

"There you go!" She high-fived him, and sparks shot into his palm. He had to have imagined it. Annie wasn't any kind of live wire, but she did look incredibly animated. "Tell me," she said gleefully, "what else?"

He stroked his chin. "I guess Santa did eat some of the cookies we left out, after all."

"See," she said, as if that proved something. "We're getting somewhere!"

Braden clicked his tongue. "What are we going to do with all this, Annie?"

She smugly crossed her arms. "Show the magic's happened."

That resonated with him. "Oh, ho!"

"Oh, ho ho ho." Her eyes twinkled so merrily, he wanted to what? Kiss her? No. Not here, not now. *Not especially if she doesn't want that.*

Except, she licked her lips. "Braden?"

"Hmm?" He suddenly saw that his face had dipped lower, his mouth hovering near hers. He started to pull back, but she latched on to his upper arms, squeezing hard.

Man, she has the strength of a lion.

"I think we can do this."

He wanted to *do this* with Annie and so much more. He also wanted to help her save her job. Could fashioning her window into a "Christmas Morning" display do that? He recalled the happy glow on Veronica's face when she'd discovered the snoozing Christmas mouse. Hmm. Maybe so.

"Can we make all these changes today?"

Annie pursed her lips. "I'm not sure. I still have to get home for Harrington."

"The older man who slips on the steps?"

"Yes, him." She nodded. "Bea too, and I've got cinnamon rolls to make, and chili."

Braden grinned. "You've carved out quite an evening. Thanks for penciling me in."

She shoved his arm. "You're written in in ink."

"Really?" He was unbelievably pleased.

She opened her notebook. After a list of ideas concerning her window, she'd written down "Blue Dot with Braden."

Warmth spread through his chest. "I'm honored."

"Me too." Her voice trembled when she said it, and her lips slightly quivered. If he pressed his mouth to hers, he could show her he was steady, a stand-up sort of guy. The rock she could lean on—and wrap her arms around.

She latched on his gaze and held on tight, so tightly he felt like he'd tumbled off a cliff and into the canyon of her pretty eyes. It was a place he could get lost in for ages. He'd put down stakes and stay there forever if she'd let him.

"Oops! Sorry!" The door opened wider, and there stood Kira, her arms loaded down with file folders. "Didn't mean to interrupt."

TWENTY-FOUR

ANNIE COULDN'T WAIT FOR LUNCHTIME. Braden entered the break room and grinned, observing Annie sitting at the table with her peanut butter sandwich. "Light lunch," he said.

Annie smiled. "Yeah. Maybe I'll share your cookie?"

His forehead scrunched up. "Don't tell me"—he shook his finger at her—"that happened yesterday?"

Relief swamped through her. *Yes. Finally, someone to share memories with*. And there was no one she'd rather share them with than Braden.

He pulled his lunch bag and water bottle from the refrigerator and joined her at the table. "You know, it's true." He shook his head. "Certain details are coming back to me, but they're still really fuzzy."

Annie took a bite of her sandwich, enjoying its crunchy peanut butter goodness. "It's not just with you. Seems my neighbors are remembering things too."

"Oh yeah?" He paused in unwrapping his sub. "Like who?"

"There's this one mom downstairs, Jane."

Braden nodded. "Daughter's Caridad, right?"

Annie gasped. "Yes!" She widened her eyes at Braden. "But Jane calls her Cari."

"So, what did she say—this downstairs mom, Jane?" Braden began eating his sub, resting his elbows on the table.

Annie couldn't wait to tell him. "She mentioned feeling like she'd met me before—almost like she and I are meant to be friends, and I believe that too."

"Like the two of us?" His blue eyes shimmered, and she caught her breath. Definitely *not* like the two of them. With Braden, things were different, romantically tinged. In her dreams anyway. She couldn't outright admit that though. Embarrassing to publicly announce her crush. So instead, she just said, "Yeah." Annie stood to fix herself a coffee but kept talking. "Similar things have happened with Bea too."

Braden uncapped his water bottle. "The lady upstairs," he said. "The one who used to be a vet tech."

Annie's hopes rose. Was he really remembering? "Go on," she said, sitting down at the table with her full mug. "Who else do you know about?"

Braden shrugged. "The gentleman downstairs, Harrington, and the grad student."

Annie nodded eagerly. "That's Eric." She gaped at Braden. This was an enormous breakthrough! "I can't believe you—"

"Annie," he said, cutting her off. "I didn't actually recall all that." He winced. "Truth is, I kind of took notes."

"Notes? When?"

"Last night, after the Blue Dot, I typed it all in on my phone when I got home. I looked everything over this morning."

"Oh, wow."

"But I do think you're on to something," he said. "The fact that I've got certain vague memories surfacing must mean this time loop is weakening, losing its grip. I mean, can it really be a time loop if we're aware of it?"

"I've been aware," she said seriously, "and it's kept on happening for me."

"True." He crossed his arms. "But it's been happening differently, with lots of little changes every day."

"Some have been bigger." *Like my heart-pounding attraction to you.*

"Okay, yeah," he said. "We've changed up your window, and you and I have gone for coffee." He stared at her. "How many times now?"

"Let's see." She counted in her head. The first time she'd said no, but she did go the second day. This was her eighth Christmas Eve, so she'd been out with Braden—"Six times."

"Man." He chuckled. "We're practically exclusive."

I wish.

He misread her embarrassed flush. "Oh sorry, Annie. I didn't mean anything offensive. I was just joking around."

She waved her hand. "Of course."

"But I do think your situation with your neighbors is important. How close were you with them before?"

Annie frowned. "Not close at all, truthfully. I hadn't even met most of them. I still don't know one. That person really keeps to themself, I guess."

Braden unwrapped his cookie and broke it in two. He smiled and handed her half.

"Thank you." She set it on a napkin by her coffee.

He chuckled. "I had a hunch you were going to ask."

Annie grinned. "You really are the nicest guy."

His neck reddened above his collar. "Thanks, Annie. You're pretty amazing yourself."

Annie's heart fluttered. She'd never been amazing to anyone. Not even to Roy. And being amazing to Braden felt extra special.

"I mean, look at you," he said. "Look at all the care you've taken with your neighbors. Maybe you didn't know them before, but you do now, and in this little bit of time. Only a week, yeah?"

She nodded.

"In only one week," he continued, "you've made some kind of difference in their lives."

"Not a huge difference, probably," she said modestly.

"Maybe not huge, no." He glanced at the door. "But big enough to leave an impression. How else would they be remembering you?" He studied the ceiling and said, "It's kind of like that furniture thing, you know?" No. He'd completely lost her. "When furniture sits in place long enough," Braden explained. "Say, for instance, on a carpet, when you go to move it, small indentions are left where it stood."

His logic made an odd sort of sense. "But I haven't been in my neighbors' lives for very long at all."

"Maybe not," he said, "but still, something about you is sticking. Just like it is with me. I can't say how, or why, but I feel it in here"—he placed a hand on his heart—"and sense it up here"—he tapped his temple—"and coming from me, that says a lot. I mean, I've always been a very rational guy, which is why there has to be a rational explanation for all of this." He pushed back his chair, and Santa strolled down the hall.

"Afternoon, you two!" he said, peering into the room as he passed by.

Annie eyes widened.

"Not real magic though," Braden whispered.

Annie leaned toward him. "Oh right, then what is a time loop, exactly?"

"Physics?" Braden turned up his hands. "Some kind of wormhole, black hole, a causal loop? Annie, I don't know, but I'm pretty sure of one thing. This has got nothing to do with Lawson's store Santa."

She crossed her arms. "If you say so."

Braden glanced at his watch, developing a plan. "Do you think we can stop those boys tonight? Dillon and Marcus?" he asked her.

"I doubt it," she said. "I've tried before."

"Yes, but"—he grinned—"not with me there to help you."

"You *were* there," she said. "*Are.* Every single time."

"One important exception," he said. "This time, I'm better prepared."

"And if we stop those boys from trashing the window?" she asked him.

"We'll have more time to fix things the way you suggested. If we can pull off that window, showing the arrival of Christmas Day, maybe Christmas Day will finally get here? For you. For me." He picked up his phone. "Maybe you'll even finally give me your number?"

She smirked playfully. "I did give you my number. That's how we texted this morning."

"Oh yeah, right." He set his chin in one hand, his elbow on the table. "In that case"—his voice went a little husky—"maybe I'll finally ask you on a date?"

Annie held back a big grin. "You did that too."

"Oh yeah?" He cocked his head. "How did that go?"

"I, um." Her heart thumped when he took her hand. "I said yes." Annie fell into his eyes, instantly at home there. Welcomed, as if she'd been allowed through his private door and into the depths of his caring soul. Braden made her feel accepted and appreciated. She yearned to be there for him in the same way.

"Annie?" Patrice pushed open the door. She looked at Annie and Braden, and they immediately broke contact, pulling back their hands and picking up their drinks. "Do you have a moment, when you're done here?"

Braden approached Louise in the security office. She stood to stretch her legs after her stint manning the security cameras. "Hey, Lou," he said, "I've got a favor to ask." He glanced at Mike, who looked up from his paperwork at a nearby desk. "If it's okay with the boss."

Lou set her hands on her hips. "What's up?"

"Would you mind watching the door for me? I'd like to do some rounds in the store."

"We've got Tony and Randal on patrol," Mike told him.

"Yes, but." Braden pursed his lips. "I have a feeling about some rascally kids I saw racing around earlier, and I want to keep my eye on them."

"You personally?" Mike crossed his arms.

"If that's all right?"

Mike stewed on this and nodded at Louise. "You okay on the door?"

"Yeah, fine." She cracked her back. "Wouldn't mind standing for a bit."

Mike radioed Charlie, who'd been filling in for Braden during his lunch hour. "Lou's coming to relieve you," he said. "Braden will take over shortly."

Charlie's voice crackled through Mike's radio speaker. "That's a ten-four."

That settled, Braden went to make his rounds. He spotted Annie chatting with Kira in Juniors. She held a jumbo package of Christmas tree lights. Annie met his eyes as he passed them, and he shot her a wink. He was *not* going to let those boys trash her display. Not since he knew what was coming and when. Annie had been very specific about the time. He checked his watch, scanning the area as he passed the toy section. Santa was busy working his magic at the pretend North Pole. He beckoned another child forward and she eagerly approached, dragging her dad with her by the hand.

"No, Dylan! Let me!"

"Nuh-uh, Marcus! Me first!"

Braden whipped his head around to see two boys racing through the crowd. Their mom trailed close behind them. "Boys! Stop running!"

Braden's heart pounded, and he picked up his pace, determined to get to them first.

"Whoa!" Annie sprang back when Quinn stepped out in front of her. He lifted his fancy jewelry bag in the air. "Sorry!"

The boys barreled toward the front window, and Braden's senses went on high alert. "Hey!" he shouted. "You two! Slow down!" How had they dashed out ahead of him? Fast little buggers. He started running, determined to blockade the retractable belt shielding the window. He darted in front of the oncoming duo and stretched out his arms. "Now—"

"*Stop!*" their mom hollered, her voice high and tight. She caught the hood of Marcus's coat as he tried to evade Braden standing in front of him, squirming to the left and to the right. Braden scuttled from side to side with his hands outstretched, but Dylan pushed into Marcus, and the pair tumbled forward below Braden's raised arm.

You're kidding me.

Down went the retractable belt and its pole—slamming into the Christmas tree.

Annie dropped her package and broke into a sprint.

Braden scrambled over the lip of the window, but the tree crashed down, sweeping the items off the mantel and tugging down a row of icicle lights.

Annie gasped. "What a disaster."

Braden turned to see her hands pressed to her mouth.

This was what she'd been living through day after day? No wonder she'd gone pale.

"What happened here?" Veronica Lawson questioned.

Annie heaved a defeated breath. "It was an accident." She

rolled her eyes toward the boys, who were speaking with Santa while their mom frowned, dashing off a text.

"What a shame." Veronica shook her head. "Glad no one was hurt."

"Ronnie? What are you doing in that window?" Quinn arrived and tugged her out of the fake snow. She smoothed down her dress.

"Just hanging those stockings back on the mantel."

Wait. Braden got it now. There were two stockings in place, but the display had originally had only one, he was sure of it. He eyed the downed Christmas tree with its shiny strands of tinsel, staring at Santa's partially eaten oatmeal cookie on the ground and the nutcracker pair piled on top of the fallen angels. He squatted low to grab the upended train engine at his feet, shutting it off. Braden pressed the button on his mic.

"Mike, we've got a—"

"Saw it all on CCTV. Sending Charlie to assist."

Lou set her hands on her hips by the door, shaking her head at Braden. She knew he'd tried his best and was just as stunned as the rest of them about the mess.

Quinn turned to Annie. "Hello? Have we met."

She smiled. "I'm Annie Jones, Lawson's Assistant Visual Artist."

"Ah yes." He nodded. "Quinn Kelly."

Veronica tugged on his arm. "What are you doing at Lawson's?" She tried to peer behind his back, but he hid his bag. "A little Christmas shopping?" Her voice held a hopeful lilt, and he gave her a swift peck on the lips.

"Maybe," he said with a mysterious edge. "Not saying a word more!"

Annie walked over to Braden, and he held up the train. "I'm really sorry, Annie."

She set her chin. "None of this is your fault."

He peered into her big, dark eyes. "Yours either."

Her shoulders dropped. "It kind of feels like it is though." She leaned toward him and whispered, "It keeps happening again and again, and—for the life of me—I can't prevent it."

He considered the mess. "The display's changed though. You were right about that."

She stepped a little closer, and her springtime scent rushed toward him, making him think of meadows and flowers and picnicking with a very lovely lady with a penchant for holly wreath pins and snowman-patterned turtlenecks. "Are you saying that because you actually remember?" she asked. "Or based on what I told you earlier?"

"I do remember some of it," he said in hushed tones. "Enough to notice the things that are here now—that originally weren't."

She wrinkled her nose, the picture of cuteness. "But how?"

"I pay attention to things, Annie." Lately, he'd been paying loads of attention to her. The way her pretty eyes shone when she smiled, her sweet-and-sassy laugh. The good-hearted way she looked after her neighbors, and the kindly way she was with him. He never would have told her about Harper and Iraq unless he'd believed she was very special. He definitely sensed that about her. Regardless of what he did—and couldn't—recall about these past several days.

"I like that about you." Her words went wispy like dandelion petals scattering on the wind.

"Everything under control over here?"

Braden turned toward Charlie as Charlie shooed some curious onlookers away.

"Yes, thanks." Braden replied in an official manner. "Annie and I are on it."

Charlie nodded and corralled back the dwindling crowd as the young mom towed off her sons, and Santa returned to his workshop. Lou wished Veronica and Quinn a merry Christmas and a good night as the couple waltzed out the door. Quinn popped open a large umbrella, shielding them from the snow, and they traipsed past Lawson's front window, laughing and chatting merrily and looking very much like a couple in love.

"So those two?" Braden said to Annie.

She smiled sunnily. "Yeah. Think so."

Braden shook his head at the window display. "At least someone's getting good news tonight."

"Yeah." Annie picked up her package of Christmas tree lights. "So, what do you say? Want to start over?"

"Any time, Annie, with you."

"Are you flirting with me, Braden Tate?"

He pursed his lips. "Might be."

An image flashed through his mind of a falling cardboard box. He caught it as the same time as Annie, and their fingers overlaced. He got a snippet of a memory. A very welcome one. "Also, might be buttering you up to invite you to coffee." He bent down low to hoist up the Christmas tree and she walked over to help him. "Seeing as how you're single, and everything."

"Oh? So you remember that part, do you?" Her face glowed,

and other images came back to him, like flipping through the pages of an illustrated book. Annie stumbling on the ladder—and him catching her. The two of them holding hands at the café. So that's why having his fingers wrapped around hers had felt so familiar—and right—today in the break room when Patrice had surprised them.

"I am remembering things," he confided. "And all of them are good."

"I had a thought about your window!" Santa spoke to Annie with a raised gloved hand, and she winked at Braden. This was yet another thing she'd told him was coming.

"Oh yeah?" She folded her arms. "Do tell."

Santa stroked his snowy beard. "I was envisioning shiny baubles."

Shiny baubles? Right. Hadn't Annie said Santa might suggest just that? "What sort of shiny baubles?" Annie asked Santa.

"You can probably use your imagination," Santa said. "You might find one or two in back."

Annie squinted at Braden. "I think I have a set of miniature golden sleighs somewhere." She turned to Santa. "Something like that?"

"Excellent!" He nodded. "You get everything just right."

"Not everything," she groused under her breath to Braden. "Obviously."

"Come on, let's not lose hope. We can try again tomorrow, or is that"—he was still wrapping his mind around it—"really today?"

She nudged his arm with her elbow. "Now you're getting

it." He stared into her eyes, and suddenly he was swept away. Yeah, he was getting lots of things, including getting hung up on Annie. But he wanted Christmas Day to get here just as much as she did. His mom's day today was sure to be long and grueling in the ER. He couldn't see wanting her to repeat that again and again. Hopefully, him being stuck in this time loop wouldn't affect her. Merely two weeks ago, he'd asked her what she wanted for Christmas, and she'd given him a clear answer.

Braden's mom sat across from him at the deli. She didn't eat out on her own often, so he took the opportunity to invite her when he could.

"So, tell me, Ma," Braden said, enjoying his Philly cheesesteak sandwich. "What do you want for Christmas this year?" He surveyed her frayed coat, thinking she could probably use a new one, given the harshness of the winters here and the hours she worked on her job.

"I don't really need anything in particular." She smiled, and lines formed around her mouth and her deep-blue eyes. Her wavy hair had gone from nearly black to almost gray. "Other than to spend the day with my favorite son."

He laughed. "I'm your only son, Ma."

She sipped from her coffee. "Yeah, and also the only child I've got in the city." She was going to visit his sisters and their families after the start of the New Year, once things at the hospital slowed down.

"It's really good of you to work Christmas Eve and also New Year's Day." He knew she'd volunteered because so many of the other staff took vacation time during the holidays.

She shrugged and said, "It's nice being needed."

"Yeah," Braden answered, silently acknowledging the gap in his own life. He didn't need a woman to complete him, but he had a lot of love to give in his heart. Someday it would be nice to find someone with whom he could share it.

His mom finished her BLT. "Weather's supposed to get dicey," she said, "right around Christmas. They're calling for a major storm. So—"

"No worries, Ma. I'll be there." He grinned. "Rain or shine."

She viewed him tenderly. "I'm really sorry about why it happened, but—selfishly—I'm glad you got out of the army and settled here."

He splayed his hands out on the table and shrugged. "What's not to love about New York?"

"Braden?" He looked up to see Annie handing him another section of her strand of lights. "Ah yeah, right." He cleared his throat. "Sorry about that." He took the string and threaded it through the tree's branches.

"Are you all right?" she peeked around the tree from the other side. "You seemed far away."

"Just thinking about Christmas."

"I've been thinking about Christmas too." Her brown eyes shimmered. "I've got some more ideas."

"Yeah? That's terrific. How about we war-game this at the Blue Dot, you know, jot everything down."

"Are you sure the list will be there tomorrow when we need it?"

He wasn't one hundred percent on that, but he was hopeful. "When I used my notes app yesterday, it seemed to work okay."

Her face lit up. "And your cell number stayed in my contacts."

"Ditto."

"Okay," she said. "Let's try it."

TWENTY-FIVE

On the ninth Christmas Eve

FA-LA-LA—!

Annie nabbed her cell phone, her heart pounding. She checked her contacts first. *Yes*. Braden Tate. *Thank goodness*. She opened her notes app and there it was, as plain as day, their "Make it to Christmas" plan. Nice. Today, they were going to put it into action.

Annie climbed out of bed, and Leo dropped down onto the floor. This time, he was *not* making a mess of his breakfast—or stealing her name tag. There was no time for fun and games this morning, or for coffee with Jane either, regrettably. She'd have her second cup at Lawson's.

Annie entered the break room, unwinding her scarf. Braden turned from the coffee machine holding his full mug. They were alone. Good. They'd have a moment to talk.

"Oh, hey!" He squinted at her and read her name tag. "Annie."

Oh, no, no, no, no, and no. She undid a few coat buttons. "Braden?"

He snapped his fingers. "Oh *yeah*. You're the lady who does the windows."

Annie's heart landed at her feet. But soon his lips crept into a grin. He looked like a mischievous kid, bursting with a secret. "Sorry." He chuckled and shook his head. "Just playing."

"That was so *not* funny." She lightly shoved his arm, and coffee splattered out of his mug—spraying against his shirt. "Oh no!"

He dabbed at the stain with some napkins. "Guess I kind of deserved that, huh?"

"That was very naughty," she teased.

"Aw, come on, Annie. You know I'm mostly nice."

"So you *do* remember?" she whispered.

"Yeah," he returned in low tones. "This time, totally. I also recall our plan." They'd agreed at the Blue Dot that there had to be a way to stop those boys. They just needed to be more authoritative. He tossed the soiled napkins in a waste can. "Lunchtime in the first-floor stockroom?" He glanced toward the open door as Santa passed by in the hall. Kira and Patrice followed him, chatting lightly.

"I'll be there," she said, so relieved he'd only been joking about his memory lapse. Also slightly miffed.

"Great," he said. "So will I." He winked, and *all* was forgiven. Not forgotten though. Her skin still tingled all over from his sexy smile.

By the time Braden found Annie at a back table in the stockroom, she'd already wrapped three pretend gifts, meant for placing under the tree. She'd borrowed boxes and wrapping paper from her coworkers at the gift-wrapping station, along with some colorful bows. Annie owned tons of tape and scissors of all kinds. She cut another long swath of wrapping paper meant for an empty shirt box as Braden joined her at the table.

He set his lunch bag at his elbow. "How can I help?"

She nodded toward the end of the table. "Maybe stuff those stockings?"

"What. Now?"

Annie giggled at his confused look. "Those aren't the ones currently hanging in the display. They're replacements. Instead of stuffing those others last-minute, we'll just exchange them for this loaded pair. We'll have all the changes ready to go for our Christmas Morning display and, after preventing that window disaster, we'll swap everything out."

Braden tapped his temple. "Good thinking." He spotted the open container of packing material Annie had set on a stool beside them. "Want me to fill the bottoms first?"

"That would be great," she said. "Maybe you can add a few small gifts and fake candies on top."

He stared around the room. "Where do I find those?"

Annie pointed behind him. "In those blue bins on the middle shelf."

"Got it." He loaded both stockings with packing material, and she laid the shirt box on the long piece of wrapping paper she'd cut. This particular gift wrap was made of foil and apparently had a mind of its own. Each time she brought the two flaps together to tape them, one of them sprang back before she could get the tape in place. "Argh." She lunged for the paper again, and Braden reached forward.

"Here," he said, grabbing a roll of tape. "Why don't you hold that down and I'll tape it?"

"Thanks, Braden." She pressed the edges of the wrapping paper together so one side slightly overlapped the other, and he leaned closer, laying a piece of tape across the fold. Suddenly, they were very close, his handsome face so near hers. All thoughts of Santa and those rascally boys went out the window, and all she could focus on was Braden and his dreamy smile.

"No problem," he said, but he appeared just as lost in her eyes as she was in his. "Annie," he said huskily, "we *are* going to get to Christmas."

"Hope so," she said, hoping so many things. Like that—when they got out of this time loop—Braden would look at her half as longingly as he did now.

"Let's think positive, hmm?"

"That's a negative, Mike," Braden said through his two-way radio, when his boss asked about sending reinforcements to the salesfloor. "We've got this covered." Dylan and Marcus were young kids, and there were only two of them. He and Annie didn't need an army to thwart their dastardly deed, just a good game plan, and they had one.

Also, he and Annie were slightly worried about involving others in their efforts. The onus for getting out of this time loop seemed to be on them. If they couldn't fix things on their own, even their best-laid plans might not work. Braden had asked Mike about Lou manning the door because he suspected trouble, but he couldn't seriously tell him about the time loop. Braden couldn't risk getting fired. He needed his job as much as Annie needed hers. Braden balled his fist around his security whistle, and Annie stood beside him.

"That whistle should get their attention," she said. "Hopefully."

Braden held his whistle near his mouth. "Fingers crossed."

"No, Marcus! Let me!"

"Here comes trouble," Braden whispered to Annie.

"I want my Robo-bot!" Marcus yelled.

"I want my rocket drone!" Dylan said, darting past him.

Their mom followed, wearing a horrified frown. "Dylan! Marcus!"

Braden blew two short blasts on his whistle, startling several shoppers. He addressed the kids. "You two! Slow down! No running in the store."

"Yoo-hoo, boys!" Annie bounced up and down on her heels, waving her arms above her head. "Walk, please!"

But it was like the kids didn't even hear them. Dylan scowled at Marcus when he latched on to his coat. "Let me go, Marcus!" he cried, wiggling out of his brother's hold and dashing forward.

"Me first!" Marcus hollered, chasing after Dylan.

"Unbelievable," Braden groused as they advanced at full steam. He shot to the left and the right, cupping his palms toward the zigzagging minions.

"You won't get *anything*," their mom shouted, "if you don't—"

"*Stop!*" Braden and Annie yelped. Ugh. Marcus slammed into Dylan, who ducked beneath Branden's arm. Braden reached for Dylan's coat—and Marcus's—but they slid from his grasp like slippery eels.

On the tenth Christmas Eve

Fa-la—!

Annie hurried into the elevator at Lawson's, after—naturally—arriving late for work. Several sales associates crammed into the elevator with her, but she was the only one still wearing a coat. So they'd clearly gotten in earlier.

"Hey, Annie!" *Braden.*

She ripped off her too-hot hat. "Oh hi." She craned her neck, peeking around the few people who stood in between them. "Didn't see you there."

"Ah, but I saw you." *Plus, he remembers! Clearly. Yay.* The shimmer in his eyes gave it away.

"We, uh"—she licked her lips—"should probably talk."

"Right." He nodded. "Upstairs."

The others on the elevator pretended not to notice their conversation, but it was evident they were listening.

"I've got an idea!" Annie said. She removed her scarf and tucked it in her bag.

"Great," Braden said. "Me too."

Though they'd spent time at the Blue Dot war-gaming the scenario with Dylan and Marcus, neither had arrived at a satisfactory solution for preventing the window disaster. They'd parted agreeing to sleep on it, and Annie had woken up with an idea. Apparently, so had he.

The older man in front of Annie pivoted her way. "Would you like to—" He motioned toward Braden.

"Oh, no," she said, noting the elevator was nearly to the third floor. "But thanks!" Good thing she was standing far away from Braden too and not ogling his duty belt. It helped that they were surrounded by a crowd. No chance of overly intimate innuendos in here! Still. She remembered landing on top of him and his rock-hard—everything. She scurried out of the elevator before she could think too much about that.

"Annie," Braden said, sidling up beside her. "I've got bad news."

"What?" Panic gripped her. What could be worse than being stuck in Christmas Eve again?

"All that work we did yesterday at lunch?" He frowned as they walked toward the break room. "It's been undone. I checked the stockroom first thing."

Well, what did she expect? Miracles?

"It's all right," he assured her. "We can redo everything today."

They entered the break room together and she whispered, "Which would be great if we could actually change out that window." Yesterday, there hadn't been time. She and Braden had decided there was no going halfway with the swap to Christmas Morning. Besides adding loaded stockings and wrapped presents, there were other augmentations they intended to make to pull the new display together, and it was all or nothing. Their "Christmas

Morning" window had to be complete, and positively perfect, if it was the key to breaking out of this time loop, and both of them thought it was.

Braden gestured toward the coffee machine, and she made herself a cup. "You know what I think?" he said. "I think we should seal off that section of the store entirely."

Annie finished making her coffee and took a sip. "Yeah, I've been thinking about that too. But only for a short time. It *is* Christmas Eve. We can't block customers' access to merchandise."

Braden fixed a coffee for himself. "We don't really have to block any merchandise, maybe just the aisle fronting the window?"

"Yes." Annie smiled at their instant mind meld. "And I know exactly how."

At a little past two, Braden set up the bright-yellow warning cones while Annie quickly swabbed the aisle in front of her window with the mop and rolling bucket she'd gotten from the janitor's closet. Signs stating "Danger, Wet Floor" in both English and Spanish adhered to each cone. She dumped the mop in the bucket, and it plunged down to the bottom. "There," she said, resting on its handle. "Done."

Braden took the bucket and mop from her. "I'll put these away." He glanced toward the escalators. "You go grab those Christmas tree lights."

She frowned at the tree in the window. Its lights had—of course—gone out once again, even though she and Braden had replaced them *so many* times. "You're right. We'll have to contend with re-dressing the tree at least." If they were lucky, that would be the only fix they'd have to tackle, so they could get right on creating their Christmas Morning display.

Annie emerged from the second-floor stockroom holding her package of lights, and Patrice stopped her in Juniors. "Annie," she said, "we need to meet."

"I know, Patrice," Annie said, walking toward the escalators. "I really do!"

"Hey!" Kira shouted when Annie breezed past her, setting her mannequin off balance. Kira steadied the mannequin torso in her hands. "Where's the blaze?"

"I'm trying to douse those flames!" Annie cried, hurrying away.

But noooo! She was too late.

Dylan and Marcus bolted toward her window display.

"Boys!" their mom called. "Get back here! That sign says wet—flooorrrr!"

"Santa, Santa!" Dylan yelped, scooting past his brother. "Wait for me!" Santa turned by his workshop just in time to see the whole grisly scene unfold. Same time as Annie.

"You won't get anything," the panicked mom wailed, "if you don't—"

"*Stop!*" Braden shouted, racing toward them. He skidded on the slick floor, holding out his hands. Dylan slipped too, but Marcus fell first, stumbling forward into Dylan as their mom reached for Marcus's hood. Both boys burst through the retractable belt, and everything went *down, down, down*.

On the eleventh Christmas Eve

Fa!

"Annie," Braden told her in the stockroom, "tonight's going to be the night we break through. I can feel it. I mean, the third time's the charm, right?" They'd already wrapped all the packages, and Braden had stuffed the stockings. Next, they had to ready the fake snow they aimed to fashion into Santa's footprints.

Annie took a bite of her peanut butter sandwich and set it down. "That would be phenomenal." If only she could believe it—in her heart. This seemingly endless rat-wheel of a day just kept turning around and around. At least she had the joy of getting to know her neighbors and experiencing Braden's sweet support. But how long could she count on that to continue? The man wasn't made of steel, nor was he any saint. He was human just like she was, and capable of cracking under pressure. She just hoped they'd break out of this time loop before it came to that.

"You know what I think?" Braden asked her. "I think maybe we haven't taken the right tack. Maybe we should be catching flies with honey instead of vinegar."

"What?"

He shrugged. "Maybe if we give Dylan and Marcus the benefit of the doubt, they'll live *up to* our expectations—instead of bringing everything *down, down, down*?"

"By talking to them, you mean, before two thirty?"

Braden nodded. "And their mom."

"Well." Annie heaved a sigh. "We can try it? But Braden?"

He met her eyes. "Hmm?"

"I'd feel a whole lot better if we had a backup plan. Maybe like the one we came up with last night at the Blue Dot?"

"Agreed." He set his elbows on the table and leaned forward. "So, here's what I think we should do."

When Dylan and Marcus entered the store with their mom, Annie and Braden were ready to great them. "Good afternoon," Braden said brightly, walking toward the family. He cast an eye at Lou dutifully watching the door. "Bet you're here to do a little shopping?"

"We are." The kids' mom smiled. "I have to pick up a few things, then I'm taking my boys to see Santa."

"How fun!" Annie said from beside Braden. "Santa loves chatting with *nice* little boys."

The mom riffled her kids' heads. "That would be these two."

Okay. Deep breaths, Annie. Honey. Not vinegar.

Dylan beamed up at Annie in a deceptively angelic way. "We're always good." He glanced at his brother. "Aren't we, Marcus?"

Marcus concurred with a toothy grin. "Uh-huh!"

Annie's smile pinched. "That's great to hear."

Let's hope that holds.

Braden winked at the kids. "Santa's going to count on that."

Yeah, so are we.

But unfortunately...

"I want my Robo-bot!" Marcus shouted.

"Santa! Santa!" Dylan cried. "Wait for me!"

"Wait!" Annie shouted, jumping in front of Dylan. She and Braden had barricaded the front window with mounds of linen sets. Each soft package contained a big, fluffy comforter and bedsheets, and they'd used several of these stacked like building blocks to form a protective wall sealing off the window.

Braden squatted low, trying to catch Marcus. But the kids slipped past them, bumbling into the linen packages and knocking them over, scattering them across the aisle. Several fell into the fake snow as the boys crashed down on the retractable belt, and *down* went the Christmas tree, shiny baubles and all.

Braden fumed under his breath, "Three strikes and *I'm out*." So, this was it. This *time loop with loopholes* had finally taken its toll.

She turned to him, her heart hammering. "Wh-what did you say?" Ooh, her soul ached. Was he really given up on them now? In the stockroom earlier, he'd seem so upbeat, so positive. But that was before this most recent very negative turn.

"Three strikes, Annie." He picked up the toy train engine and switched it off. "I couldn't help you get it right the first time, or the second, or the third." He handed her the train engine, and she took it. "It's three days now we've been trying to start our 'Make it to Christmas' plan, and no dice. No matter what we do, we can't seem to stop those boys. How long will this go on?" He raked a hand through his hair. "Forever?" As much as he seemed to like being around her, this was obviously getting to be too much. Annie had to put an end to this excruciating quandary. Heat welled in her eyes. If only she knew how.

The young mom took out her purse—*again*. "I'm so, so sorry," she said, appearing precisely as chagrined as last time. "Look, whatever it costs—"

"Oh no"—Annie held up her free hand—"that's not necessary.

Lawson's will cover the damage." She eyed Braden, fretting over the damage this was doing to him. Maybe she'd been selfish to drag him into this whole thing. Would he have been better off living day after day in ignorant bliss?

Santa chatted with the boys, and Veronica Lawson came and went on Quinn's arm, after hanging the two Christmas stockings back on the mantel. Veronica whispered to Quinn, "There's something different about that window, isn't there?" *Yes! She noticed!*

"Yeah," Quinn retorted, "it's trashed."

Annie's heart sank, but Veronica continued. "No, it's not that." She glanced over her shoulder. "It's something else." She scanned the fallen tree. "Were there candy canes on the tree before?"

"Not sure." Quinn shrugged. "Those look like fake ones."

Annie waited until Santa and the family left. "Maybe we should just do it," she said, placing the wooden angels back on the mantel. "Go ahead and create that Christmas Morning display? Nothing else has worked, so why not go full throttle?"

He picked up the nutcracker pair and placed them beside the angels. "What? Tonight?" Braden checked his watch.

"No, I don't think we have time, even if we skip the Blue Dot. Tomorrow though?" She gestured toward the toppled Christmas tree, and they went over to it. "Maybe there's a way to get a jump on things. You know"—she shrugged—"get an even earlier start?"

"You mean *sooner than* at lunchtime?"

"Much sooner, yeah." They lifted the Christmas tree into place, and several plastic Christmas tree balls fell from it, bouncing across the floor. Braden scooped some up while Annie corralled another runaway group. "Maybe we've been too slow on this, Braden."

"How so?" He set his collection of colorful Christmas tree balls down in the cushiony chair, and Annie did the same.

"There we were talking about being proactive rather than reactive," she said, "and yet—we've still been responding to Dylan and Marcus wreaking havoc with this window day after day." Braden picked up Santa's partially eaten cookie, along with the shatterproof plate, and the rest of the cookies and the fake glass of milk. He set them on the side table Annie righted. "What if we change things up?" she asked him. "Get to Lawson's *before nine o'clock* so we can make all the tweaks before the day begins?"

She began removing the other ornaments from the tree so they could replace the faulty lights, and Braden helped her. "I get what you're saying." He paused, holding two shiny golden sleighs in his hands. "Maybe—*just maybe*, if the display *starts out* perfect, those boys won't get a chance to wreck it, because karma will be on our side."

She removed a small clutch of candy canes from the tree. "Didn't know you believed in karma?" she asked with a hint of sass.

"Didn't know I believed in time loops either." He grinned, and her heart danced.

"Fair point. There's just one problem." She winced. "Getting in early seems to be an issue for me. In fact, I always run late." He opened the ladder, stationing it by the tree, and Annie climbed up high to grab the last of the ornaments off its branches.

"Don't worry," he said as she passed him one trinket after

another, and he deposited them in the chair and on the table. "I'll spot you." He backed up a step as Annie descended the ladder.

"Oh!" Her foot slipped, and he caught her by the waist.

"Steady there!"

Annie flushed. "*Sorry* that keeps happening," she said, although she really wasn't.

Braden looked cutely caught out himself. "No problem." He quickly let her go and cleared his throat. "So about tomorrow," he continued when she reached the floor. "Now that I know what to do, I can get started holding down the fort until you come in."

"Great. Sounds like a plan." Her mind buzzed with thoughts of her many tasks ahead. "Maybe we should skip the Blue Dot tonight?" She darted a glance at the snowy evening. "I want to do some extra grocery shopping and plan out my tomorrow to the letter."

"If you think that's best. But, Annie"—he met her eyes—"can I still walk you to the subway?" She was touched that he still cared in spite of all she'd dragged him through. She didn't know how much longer she could count on his goodwill to continue, realistically. He'd appeared very put out earlier. Now that he was in it with her though, it was hard to see how he could get out. There was only one answer. They had to push forward.

"I'd like that," she said.

Once they'd fully restored the window, Santa paused on his way out the door. "Looking good, you two!" He adjusted his hat. "Just needs a little something."

Annie wanted to make sure they got this right. "Can you give us another little hint?"

"Or a big one?" Braden added. "One that will help us complete this display?"

Santa smiled, and Annie thought she heard sleigh bells. "The answer," he said, "is in your heart."

Braden placed a hand on his chest. "My heart?"

"Not yours." Santa shook his head and pointed to Annie. "In hers."

TWENTY-SIX

ANNIE HURRIED DOWN THE SIDEWALK, dodging the icy spots and hanging on to her bulging grocery bags. *The whole fate of Christmas rests with me. Awesome. Kira can't get sacked, she needs to get promoted, and Braden has to spend the day with his mom. My sweet neighbors all deserve a happy Christmas, or as happy a one as possible in the face of the giant storm. Plus, I can't lose my job and wind up penniless, homeless—and kitty-less. Poor Leo.*

Her heart wrenched.

No pressure.

What about Tina? OMG! During the drama of the past few days and working together with Braden to prevent her front-window fiasco, she'd totally lost track of delivering her apology to Tina. Maybe she didn't even deserve Tina's friendship? No, wait. Yes, she did. But she was going to need to do a bit of groveling first. Okay, a lot of groveling. *Major mea culpas coming Tina's way.*

Nerves churned through her, causing a mild bout of nausea. She'd secretly felt responsible for this time loop all along, and it apparently *was* her fault. It had something to do with what happened that very first day when she'd had her surprise run-in with Santa. Her already bad day had taken a nosedive from there. Now, Santa had hinted that *she* held the key to escaping this time loop. The major issue was, she had *absolutely no clue* where to look. *My heart? What's that mean?*

She'd put her heart into every repeat Christmas Eve so far. As soon as she'd realized she was stuck, she'd made efforts to do better. Not just at Lawson's Finest, but on the home front, as well. At least Braden was fully aware of the situation and trying to help her, but she needed to help him too by getting this time loop to end. What she'd once seen as an opportunity to improve each day was starting to feel like an odd sort of purgatory. A suffocating state of in-betweenness that would be unbearable to endure forever.

In the grand scheme, her window at Lawson's Finest seemed inconsequential. Maybe she'd been focusing on the wrong objective. Yes, she needed to get her display right. But there were other things she needed to get right too. She'd been nervous about taking that next step with her neighbors, crossing that thin line dividing cordial and committed. Friendly chats were easy. An invitation to a holiday meal meant welcoming them into her home—and into her heart. She could do that—reach out. The worst anybody could say was no.

"Harrington! Watch out!" Annie dropped her heavy grocery sacks and raced toward him, catching him around his middle just in time.

He glanced back over his shoulder. "Where on earth did

you come from?" His shaky breath clouded the air, and snowflakes covered his coat lapels and hair. He steadied himself on his walker handle when she tipped it toward him. "And how do you know—?" He blinked and shook his finger. "Why, yes, of course. You're Annie, aren't you? The young lady who lives upstairs?"

Her heart grew full.

He remembers.

But, how much?

Annie held Harrington's elbow and helped him toward the door. "That's right." She glanced at him and smiled. "I'm in apartment 3-A." She unlocked the front door and shoved it open, and Harrington scuttled into the foyer using his walker.

"Funny thing." He patted the breast pocket on his coat. "I found your phone number on a piece of paper." Lines etched into his forehead. "Can't say how I came by it."

"I—must have given it to you before your trip."

He glanced at the sidewalk and laughed. "Guess the suitcase gave me away."

Eric jogged toward them. "Hey, Annie!"

Her pulse raced. He remembered her too?

This is phenomenal.

Eric pointed to her groceries and Harrington's suitcase. "Need a hand?"

"That would be great." She hurried down the steps to help him. Two hugely filled grocery bags on top of Harrington's luggage was too much for one person. She picked up one grocery bag and Eric got the other. He grabbed the suitcase handle, hoisting it off the ground. Eric reached the foyer and passed Annie the other grocery bag before sliding Harrington's suitcase across his threshold. Winds howled, blowing snow into the building, and Annie shoved shut the front door.

"Coming home for Christmas?" Eric asked the older man.

Harrington braced himself against his walker. "Yep. This is home." He glanced into his apartment. "Thanks for bringing up my suitcase." He studied the younger man's face. "Have we spoken before?"

"Yes, sir. I believe so." He held out his hand and shook Harrington's. "Eric Park."

Harrington squeezed Eric's strong grip and grinned. "I must have seen you coming and going."

Eric nodded. "Same." The two men turned to Annie.

Eric scanned Annie's eyes. "You and I, though." He tugged down his stocking cap. "We must have chatted a bit."

"We did!" Annie said. "You're in grad school at NYU studying literature."

"And you...?" Eric looked like he was reaching.

"I work at Lawson's Finest," she volunteered.

Eric's face lit up. "Sure. You do the windows."

Annie's heart pounded in her throat. "Yes, that's right."

Eric shook his head. "I just had the weirdest feeling."

Harrington leaned forward on his walker. "Odd, so did I."

Eric chuckled with incredulity. "It's almost like we've had this conversation before."

Harrington squinted at Annie. "That probably sounds loopy to you."

"Oh no, not at all." The shopping bags grew heavy, and her

arms sagged. "I'll be doing some cooking later, and I'll probably have an excess."

Harrington noted the weight in her hold and joked, "Cooking for a crowd?"

"In a way"—she smiled at Harrington and Eric—"yes."

"What you making?" Eric asked her.

"A pot of chili first, and later"—she smiled at Eric temptingly—"some cinnamon rolls."

Eric grinned. "Those are a Christmas favorite."

Annie shifted the groceries in her arms. "I'll bring you some!" She stared at Harrington. "But I'm planning to bring you chili first."

Harrington smiled. "My, my, my. You must be some kind of...angel." He slowly turned back toward Annie. "Now that was definitely a blast of déjà vu."

"Was it?" Annie asked, so hopeful. Whatever was happening, it had to be good.

"Yeah." Eric slid his backpack off his shoulder. "For me too."

They both stared at her questioningly.

Annie shrugged. "Sometimes those déjà vu feelings are not so much about the actual events, but rather the feelings they inspire."

"All this talk about cooking is inspiring me to be hungry," Harrington teased her.

"Me too," Eric said, and everyone laughed.

Annie turned toward the stairs. "Then I'd better get busy."

Eric called after her. "Can I help you carry those upstairs?"

"No thanks," she said. "I've got it."

I do have this. I do.

Annie spun back around and smiled. "The weather's not expected to get any better. In fact, it's predicted to get worse. And, if it does, nobody will be getting out much of anywhere tomorrow. So." She blew out a breath, gathering her courage. "I was thinking I might ask the folks in the building to dinner."

Harrington blinked. "Christmas dinner?" He looked inordinately pleased.

"That's really nice of you Annie," Eric said.

Harrington glowered at his walker. "I'm not sure how—"

"We'll help you!" Annie leapt in.

Eric picked up on her idea immediately. "Of course we will, Annie and I."

"Well, in that case"—Harrington grinned from ear to ear—"I'll have to accept."

"What can I bring?" Eric asked her.

"What have you got?"

Eric smiled. "Wine?"

Annie nodded. "Wine's good."

Harrington pursed his lips. "Since I've been away, I'm afraid I don't… Oh, wait!" His expression brightened. "I might have a box of chocolates. The MTA sends a big one over each Christmas, and I haven't even touched it."

"You're not a chocolate eater?"

Harrington set his chin. "I stay very loyal to one kind."

This intrigued her. "Yeah? What kind?"

"Peppermint bark." He patted his chest. "My favorite."

Annie decided to remember that. "Your box of chocolates sounds perfect, thanks. We'll break it out during dessert." They said their goodbyes and she climbed up the stairs, vowing to see them again soon.

This time, when their apartment doors closed, the echoes in the hall were far from lonely. A certain happiness permeated the building. When she saw Bea tonight, she'd invite her to Christmas dinner too. She'd asked Jane and Cari over tomorrow, and leave a note for whoever lived in apartment 2-B.

Annie reached the third floor and stopped short. She hadn't bought nearly enough groceries to feed all those folks, but maybe if Bea brought her casserole and Annie scrounged other things together... Wait. She still needed to meet Braden at Lawson's to work on her window display. Plus, she wanted to connect with Tina.

Okay. Things were falling into place. Tonight, she'd do her cooking as planned. Then, if tomorrow was Christmas Eve all over again, she'd make it the most perfect Christmas Eve ever, and when she stopped by the store after work, she'd buy gobs of groceries. She might even pick up one of those collapsible, rolling grocery carts that they sold at the hardware store next to the grocers, so she'd be able to get it all home.

Annie shifted her grocery bags in her arms and jostled open her apartment door.

Leo sat up on his haunches and mewed.

"Hey, big boy," she said with a happy song in her heart. "Miss me?" She quickly surveyed the living room and hall, spying no signs of kitty mischief. She hadn't really given him a chance. Annie had learned her lesson about that toilet paper. Her name tag too. Not to mention Leo's breakfast.

He stood and plodded toward her. "Of course you did," Annie said. "I bet you're also hungry." She felt ravenous too. She couldn't wait to make that tasty chili and sample a gooey pinch of those yummy cinnamon rolls.

She shut her apartment door behind her using one of her worn-out boots and carried her groceries into the kitchen as Leo darted ahead of her. Her little Christmas tree stood in the corner, and behind it in the shadows, her dad's painting of the snow globe showcased a mirror image of the keepsake glinting in the dim light. Annie left her groceries in the kitchen and came back to plug in the tree. She picked up her snow globe and shook it, and baby snowflakes flitted all around inside. *Believe.*

Annie pressed the snow globe to her heart through her heavy winter coat, and everything in her world felt good, and right. No, she didn't have her parents. But she had Leo, and Braden, and Harrington. Eric and Bea, and Jane. Plus, she'd soon meet Cari and whoever lived in Apartment 2-B. She was going to get promoted and not fired, and Kira would take her place as Assistant Visual Artist. She was texting Tina tomorrow, and—this time—she really meant it. And maybe—for once—her Lawson's Finest window display would be *so very perfect* that no one would trash it. Veronica Lawson might even lend her praise.

Santa would say good night and merry Christmas, then he'd be off on his supposed sleigh to deliver toys to eagerly awaiting kids everywhere. Wait. Annie opened her eyes, and she stared at her snow globe. There was one last thing she could do that she hadn't.

Of course.

Someone knocked at the door. It was Bea, a little early.

"I'm sorry to bother you." She noted Annie's coat. "Looks like you've just gotten home. But I've started baking for tomorrow, and just now realized I'm running low on sugar."

Annie took Bea's empty measuring cup. "I'm happy to loan you some. In fact"—she smiled at Bea—"what are you doing for supper?"

Bea patted down her hair clips. "What? Tonight?"

Annie nodded. "I was about to make a pot of chili, and I have a hunch I'll have plenty."

Leo bounded into the room, interested in the new arrival. Bea stepped into the apartment and pulled shut the door so he wouldn't get out. "Who do we have here?" she asked, bending down to stroke the cat.

"His name's Leo."

"Leo?" Bea patted his head and looked up. "I feel like I've met this kitty before."

"It's possible you have."

Bea straightened with a chuckle. "No. Don't think so. That would mean…" She smiled at Annie's Christmas tree. "What a sweet little tree." She blinked. "Hang on. Didn't you have me over for cocoa?" She gasped. "That's right. Must have been last year. Soon after I lost my Harry."

Annie frowned. "I'm very sorry for your loss."

"Thanks, dear. I guess I was in some kind of fog, because I don't remember too much about our talk, just that I was"—she stared around Annie's apartment—"here, and that you were really kind."

Annie's shoulders dropped. "I'm sorry that we haven't talked more."

"I guess it has been a while," Bea said. "But in some ways"—she turned to look at Annie—"it seems like only yesterday."

That's because it was.

"What are you doing tomorrow?" Annie asked carefully, even though she already knew.

"I'm going to my daughter, Caroline's, place in Queens."

Annie nodded. "If the bad weather holds, you're welcome to come here. I'm inviting anyone in the building who doesn't have other plans to join me for Christmas dinner."

"What a nice invitation. I'll keep it in mind—in case."

"In the meantime," Annie said, "I'm still offering chili."

"What are you?" Bea chuckled. "Our building's food elf?"

Annie shrugged. "Something like that."

"Okay," Bea said. "But I can't stay long. I've got a sweet potato casserole to bake."

"Why don't you work on that while I put together my chili?"

"Stellar idea." She surveyed her bathrobe. "I'll put on some more suitable clothing too."

"Oh no, don't bother!" Annie grinned. "I'll change into my pj's, and we can both be comfy. Maybe I'll even make us some cocoa after, if you'd like to stay and watch a movie."

Bea smiled softly. "You're a very sweet girl. I know you make your mother happy. No doubt your father too."

Annie's heart clenched momentarily, but then her tensions eased. She smiled softly at Bea. "Yeah, hope so." She spied her dad's snow globe painting and sensed her parents' presence. They *were* happy, wherever they were—and they were also happy with her.

Annie was happy too.

TWENTY-SEVEN

On the twelfth Christmas Eve

FA—!

Annie snatched her phone off the nightstand and sat up in bed.

Leo raised his head, blinking in the gray light.

"Okay," Annie told him. "This is it. The day we change everything."

I hope.

Leo stood and stretched, trudging toward her across the rumpled blankets. The minute she petted him, he began purring, pressing the top of his head into her palm. "Merry Christmas Eve, boy." Annie ran a hand down his back. She *was* going to adopt him, and she was *not* losing her job. She was also getting out of this time loop.

Annie checked the time on her phone. It was just after seven. Ugh. She'd set her alarm to wake her an hour early since she was meeting Braden, but of course. The time she woke up never changed. What did change were the nuances of the day that occurred after that.

Annie pushed back the covers, gently nudging Leo aside, and he hopped down on the floor. Annie picked up and placed his wand toy on her nightstand next to her phone. A text alert popped up on the screen.

Braden

We still on for 8:30?

Eight thirty. Right.

Annie's heart pounded. She was going to do her best. She was also so grateful she hadn't imagined Braden being aware of her whole sorry predicament. It was his predicament now too.

Annie

Yes. See you soon!

Annie rushed through her morning routine of feeding Leo, showering, and grabbing a quick bite. She slurped her coffee and munched on her toast while getting dressed—in record time. Annie tugged on her snowman-patterned turtleneck and slipped into her black vest, attaching her name tag and holly wreath pin.

I'm going to burn this outfit once this day's finally over.

How many times had she worn it now? Right. This was day twelve. Wait. There were twelve days of Christmas, according to the song, and certain cultures celebrated it that way with the twelfth day occurring on the Epiphany. Maybe this was *her* epiphany.

She knew what she had to do. Get to Lawson's and finish her window. Text Tina. Kiss Braden. What? The notion had come out of nowhere, but still. She'd been seriously dying to before.

She suspected he had too. But she couldn't do that at work, no. Maybe after coffee, at the subway? In thanks? Heat swamped through her, and then she heard Tina's voice in her head. *Come on, Annie. Be brave.* She wasn't sure if she had the nerve, but she'd just have to see about that. She for sure had shopping to do, and cooking too. Lots and lots of that. She hurried into the living room and rummaged through her work bag. Shoes, check. Purse, check. Lunch, check. She glanced at her dad's painting and her snow globe gleaming beneath her tree. *Believe*, yes. She did. She was getting out of this day one way or another, and making it to Christmas.

When the intercom buzzed, she was dressed in her boots, hat and coat, and ready to head to work. "On my way down," she said to the delivery guy. "Thanks!" She scooped Leo into her arms and kissed him goodbye. "Be a good boy today. I'll be back soon."

Annie picked up Jane's package and the big snowball dump whizzed by—splatting out in a mound near her feet. Annie held the package against her coat and hurried back inside, taking the steps two at a time to reach the second floor. No time for coffee today.

Jane opened her apartment door as Annie approached. "Oh hi." Jane's eyes widened. "I thought I heard someone out here."

Annie huffed out a breath, winded from her dash up the stairs. "This came for you. Delivery guy buzzed me by mistake."

Jane accepted the package, scanning its label. "*Yes.* I've been waiting for this. Thanks for bringing it up"—she met Annie's eyes—"Annie, right?"

Yes! So, Jane remembers too.

"Yeah, that's right." She smiled at Jane and motioned with her thumb. "I'm in 3-A upstairs."

Jane nodded. "Sure. I've seen you around. We've probably even"—she searched the ceiling with her eyes—"spoken once or twice?"

Annie beamed brightly. "Yeah, and you're Jane. Your kid's name is Cari."

Jane lifted the box in her hands. "Did I mention Amazing Agatha?"

"You *did*," Annie answered.

"The woman's got everything," she said, speaking of the doll. "The job, the man, the wardrobe." Jane's expression saddened. "If only I'd been able to get Cari that." She shrugged and looked at Annie. "But this is close enough." She set the package down inside her door.

Annie shrugged happily. "Maybe Santa will surprise you?"

"Santa?" Jane tsked. "Sure." She peered at Annie. "Where did you say you worked again?"

"At Lawson's Finest." Annie steadied the strap of her canvas bag on her shoulder. "I wish I could stay and have coffee, or something."

"Coffee?" Jane's coffee maker's beeper went off and she scratched her head. "Ah, yeah. Coffee would be great. We should do that sometime. I don't really know anyone else in the building."

Annie stopped walking and turned. "This winter storm is supposed to get bad. If you and Cari aren't doing anything for Christmas dinner tomorrow, I thought I might have a few people over. Some of our neighbors."

"Oh, nice. Thanks. We're supposed to go to my brother's in Flatbush. But, if we can't get out—then, sure. That'd be great."

Annie remembered the note in her bag. She dug it out with her fingers and hurried to apartment 2-B, sliding it under the door. "Do you know who lives here?" she asked Jane.

"Not sure," she said. "I think we keep different hours. I might have seen a guy go in, once or twice. Uniform, but not police."

Annie immediately thought of Braden. But no, he lived in Sunset Park. "Huh. Well, okay, thanks! Maybe we'll get a chance to meet them soon enough."

"That would be cool." Jane backed into her apartment. "Thanks for the invite, and thanks again for bringing up the package."

Annie slid on her mittens. "No problem."

"Merry Christmas Eve!"

"To you too."

Jane partially shut her door, then yanked it back open. "What time tomorrow, and what can I bring?" Her grin broadened. "Assuming we're all stuck."

That's precisely what Annie was trying to do. Get them *unstuck*. She smiled at Jane. "Two o'clock. And just bring Cari."

Seconds later, she was out on the sidewalk, hustling through the snow. The crisp scent of winter clung to the air, filling Annie's lungs with sharp bursts of cold. Icy pinpricks stung her eyes and nose, as people raced toward their rides, darting for cabs and Ubers, their chins tucked in. A woman in a puffy black coat collapsed her red umbrella and ducked into a taxi, shutting its door.

Annie bolted down the subway stairs, sliding her bright-red

mitten along the railing, flying through the turnstile and down another set of concrete steps, only to be greeted by a sea of commuters. The entire platform was flooded. Waylaid passengers held purses, bags, and satchels, with straps slung over their shoulders. All wore heavy coats, and many donned hats and gloves. Several were also wrapped up in scarves, like Annie. She turned to the middle-aged man beside her. "What's going on?"

The man's brow furrowed. "Mechanical difficulties. Train's stuck in a tunnel."

"What?" *Nooo.* Annie checked her watch. Trying to catch a car in this mess would be impossible. Plus, that would likely take even longer than simply waiting here. "Did they say when they'd get things cleared?"

The man shrugged. "Fifteen? Maybe twenty minutes?"

Annie took out her phone to text Braden.

Annie

Ugh. Train delay.

Braden

No worries. I'll get started.

Annie

Great, thanks!

But it didn't take twenty minutes.

It took thirty-five.

The train pulled into the station, and Annie clamored toward it, along with the slow-moving stampede. She was lucky to find a spot just inside the doors before they shut at her back. One more passenger squeezed in behind her, accidently bumping her elbow.

"Oh! Sorry!" She knew that voice.

Annie spun toward Quinn, and he smiled. "Mad day for us Brooklynites." He squirmed sideways, making a sliver of additional space between them.

She made a stab at conversation, wondering if he'd remember her, like her neighbors had. "But you're not from Brooklyn originally?"

"Good call." He dipped his chin. "London." He narrowed his eyes. "Say, do you work in the financial district, by chance?"

She shook her head. "Midtown."

"Ahh."

"At Lawson's Finest."

He nodded. "I know Lawson's. Veronica Lawson, most particularly." The train picked up speed, and he latched on to a pole. So did Annie. "Maybe I've seen you there?"

"Could be!"

"What is it you do there, if I might ask?"

"I do the windows." She laughed. "Design them. I'm their Assistant Visual Artist." Annie held her breath. "Hoping to get promoted soon."

He grinned, and his dark eyes shone. "An excellent plan for Christmas."

Annie scurried into Lawson's finest, clocking in on her phone at 9:08 a.m. *Why am I not surprised?* She hustled across the salesfloor, nearly colliding with Santa.

"Oh!" She jumped back by the jewelry counter.

"Hello—Annie." His baby-blue eyes twinkled, and Annie was taken back—but not to that Christmas when she was nine. Back to the evening her parents left for the show in Manhattan. Eleven days after Christmas. *Christmas's twelfth day*. An image of her dad's painting flashed through her mind, and she thought of her snow globe. So much had changed during these past twelve days, even though a lot of things hadn't. She'd made connections with her neighbors and gotten to know Braden. *Where is he anyway?*

She glanced around the store, and Santa thumbed over his shoulder. "He's been as busy as a bee this morning," Santa said delightedly. "Or should I say an elf? A Christmas elf?"

Annie spotted movement in the front window. Braden stood by the mantel, hanging up the two stuffed stockings. "Yes, we're working on something special."

"The two of you together?" Santa chuckled. "How nice."

"Santa"—she met his eyes—"whatever's been going on here, thank you."

He patted his barrel chest. "Thank me?"

"Yes." Annie set her chin, her confidence building. "I think I know what I need to do now to make this day right."

"Don't let me hold you up." Santa gestured ahead of him. "Get to it."

Annie huffed out a breath. "O-kay!"

Braden saw her approaching, and she unwound her scarf. "I'm really sorry—"

Braden held up his hand. "Don't be. It's fine."

Annie glanced at the prettily decorated Christmas tree, which now had fake candy canes on it, along with shiny golden sleighs, tinsel, and extra sparkly lights.

Braden walked toward her through the fake snow. "The lights seemed in good order," he said. "I checked all their connections, so fingers crossed we don't have to start over with that today."

Annie held up her crossed fingers. "Fingers crossed." She noted a bunch of pretty packages under the tree. "Did you wrap all those yourself?"

"I did." He chuckled proudly. "I'm getting pretty good at it too. You might call me a gift-wrapping pro."

She laughed, spotting the two nutcrackers on the mantel beside the three singing angels. Santa's partially eaten cookie sat on a plate next to the pretend glass of milk. Annie stared down the aisle at the glitzy display for Amazing Agatha. Yeah, that was on her list, but first things first. "Thanks for all you've done here."

"We still need the note *from* Santa," Braden said. "And a few other things."

"You've given us quite a head start. Thank you."

He grinned, and her pulse fluttered. "My pleasure."

She unbuttoned her coat and removed it, passing him her bag to hold. He gave the bag back to her and a high-heeled white shoe dropped out of it, nose-diving for the floor. Braden picked it up, handing it to her. "Looks like you dropped something."

She held out her hand. "*Again.*"

He narrowed his eyes when she grabbed the toe of the shoe.

He held the heel.

A blast of current shot through her.

Braden blinked. "Whoa. Feel that?"

Snowflakes flitted around her, and the whole world went snowy white. She heard sleigh bells, but they were all alone, she and Braden, caught up in some magical place like their own special snow globe. Hope and wonder bloomed in his eyes. Attraction as well. The same deep yearning Annie felt in her soul.

He slowly released the shoe, and she took it. "What's happening, Annie?"

"Christmas magic?" She'd gone a little breathy. Could this really be happening to her—and to him? Were they falling for each other in this alternate reality? The revealing sparkle in his eyes said that they were, and that he knew it too.

"Don't tell me you still believe…? Wait." He stopped and stared at her. "We've been here and done this before, haven't we?"

"Yes," she said firmly. "That's how it all got started, but—today—we're going to finish." *So I can save my job and we can get to Christmas. You can see your mom, and—ooh, how I want this to happen—you and I can go out for more than coffee.*

"Okay." He set his hands on his duty belt, appraising the window. "Let's wrap this up."

TWENTY-EIGHT

PATRICE APPEARED BESIDE ANNIE AT her locker. "Where have you been all morning?" Patrice held up her phone. "Saw you clocked in at 9:08 a.m."

"I was tweaking my window display."

Patrice pushed back her glasses. "Tweaking?"

Annie nodded. "Wanted to enhance it a little. Make it, you know"—she shrugged—"groundbreaking, fresh!"

Patrice aligned her jacket. "Funny. I was just going to suggest—"

"That we have a little chat?"

Patrice blanched. "How did you know that?"

"Don't worry, Patrice." Annie shut her locker. "I've got this covered."

"What's this?"

She met her boss's eyes. "This day, my job, my window."

Patrice stared at her long and hard. "Annie, we need to talk."

"I know," Annie said. Her spirits rose. "About my promotion." Her window had turned out spectacularly. It was now whimsical and fun! No longer about waiting on Santa, and more about providing evidence that he'd come.

Patrice grimaced. "Ahh, about that—"

Annie persisted cheerfully. "Can't wait!" She frowned at Patrice. "But I'm afraid I'll have to. Today's a really busy day."

"Annie!" Patrice called as she hurried away. "I heard from Ms. Lawson!"

Annie spun on her heel. "Don't worry, Patrice. Keep the faith."

Patrice stared at her, dumbfounded. "Two o'clock!" she shouted. "Conference room!"

Annie scooted down the escalator to the first-floor salesfloor. She passed Kira on the way. Kira was riding up and Annie was riding down.

"Morning!" Kira grinned. "Big day."

"Yep." Annie shot her a thumbs-up. "Hope it's a great one for everybody."

There were several merchandise displays she had to check, and she'd have to pinch-hit on some registers, but she needed to complete an important purchase first. Annie reached the toy section and hoisted the box for Amazing Agatha into her hands. She set it down on a checkout counter and the sales associate, Barry, grinned at the package. "Doing some last-minute Christmas shopping?" The older man had spent his entire career at Lawson's Finest. He normally worked in the Men's Clothing Department, but they had extra staff on the registers down here today.

Annie smiled at Barry. "Better late than never."

He nodded and rang up her purchase. "Guess that's true."

She paid with her personal credit card, and Barry passed

her the receipt. He stuffed the box into a large Lawson's Finest bag with handles and gave her the package. "You can get it gift-wrapped for free in Homewares."

"That's a great idea, Barry. Thanks!"

"Neat display." He motioned toward her newly tweaked front window. "You've got them lining up outside."

"What?" Annie stared toward the street. A small group of shoppers gathered on the sidewalk facing her window. They pointed out items in her display, chatting merrily amongst themselves as snowflakes rained down from the heavens, coating them all in white. Annie dropped her package off at the gift-wrapping station and walked up to Braden as he unlocked the front door. He nodded toward the street. "Get a load of that crowd."

Happiness welled up inside her. "I know. I can't believe it." Ten o'clock a.m. and Lawson's was open for business. Christmas Eve business. She had work to do, but that could wait for the few minutes it would take for her present to get gift-wrapped. Annie moved aside as the first customers entered.

"Fun window!" a lady said to Braden as he stood at his post.

Braden nodded with Annie beside him. "Our visual artist team does great work."

"Boy do they ever," another guy said, walking in. He shook his head, clearing the snowflakes off with his glove. *Wait. That's Quinn.*

He stared at Annie. "Hello, you! You're the gal who's going to get promoted, yeah?"

Annie's nerves skittered because she wanted this so badly. "If all goes well."

Quinn strolled toward the jewelry counter, and a young mom entered with two kids. Hang on. Dylan and Marcus? No way. Braden cut Annie a look. "You're getting an early start," he told the family.

The mom smiled and hunted around the salesfloor, locating Santa's workshop. "My boys couldn't wait to come see Santa." Annie just hoped those boys wouldn't break loose like wild banshees again and bulldoze her front window. Oddly though, they seemed exceptionally well behaved, sticking close by their mom. "Remember what I told you," the mom said. "Mind your manners."

They slurped up every word with big, dark eyes.

"We'll be good," Dylan promised.

Marcus nodded. "And say thank you."

The mom ruffled Dylan's hair and gently squeezed Marcus's shoulder. "I know you will," she said in caring tones. "Look!" She glanced toward Santa's workshop and smiled. "We'll be first in line." Santa motioned them forward with his gloves, and Annie's mouth fell open.

"What's going on?" she whispered to Braden.

"Something's working." He peeked at Santa's workshop, and Santa waved. "Very, very well."

More folks clamored around Annie's window and flooded into the store.

"*What happened here?*" Annie blinked at Veronica Lawson. She'd missed the signature green velvet hat and animal-print coat amid the large group of people streaming in the door. Veronica clasped her gloved hands together, gawking at the Christmas Day display.

Annie held her breath, her heart pounding.

Please think it's awesome.

Please, please, please, please, please.

"This window," Veronica declared on a gasp. "It's excellent!"

The air whooshed from Annie's lungs. *At last.*

Veronica waded through the crowd and toward Braden. "Do you know the visual artist responsible for this?"

"Yes, ma'am," he said proudly. Braden beamed at Annie. "She's standing right here."

Veronica Lawson held out her hand, and Annie shook it as they exchanged introductions. "You should hear the buzz on the street," Veronica said. Annie noted more people huddled around her window. Many of them consulted with one another, opting to venture inside.

Veronica scanned the display again, addressing Annie, "Your Christmas Morning scene has so many special touches. Love the little sleeping mouse with that tiny stuffed stocking and the small, gift-wrapped packages stacked at the end of his bed. And, oh! The other filled stockings hanging from the mantel, *not to mention* all the pretty presents under the tree, *and* the note *from* Santa. Ha-ha! He even took a bite out of a cookie!" She covered her mouth and giggled. "Naughty elf."

Veronica stepped closer to the window's border and stood by the retractable belt. "Aww, *sweet*," she said, pointing with her thin leather glove. "The toy train circling around the tree has its boxcars filled with peppermint candies! And gracious!" She covered her mouth with her hand and laughed. "How much tinsel can you seriously get on a tree? It's so, so"—her eyes grew huge—"silvery!" She glanced at Annie and whispered, "Though honestly, I love it."

She examined the scene further. "Ooh! Are those snowy footprints left from Saint Nick?" she asked, noting the blotches of fake snow that Annie and Braden had strategically arranged across the rug to look like they'd emerged from the fake hearth. "And wait!" She covered her mouth. "Were those carrots on the mantel meant for Santa's reindeer? Looks like he took a few."

Annie nodded, and Veronica beamed happily. "Why, it's groundbreaking! Fresh! It not only looks like Christmas Day is here, I can practically feel it too." She peered out the window at the gathering crowd and announced delightedly, "*So can they*."

Yes, yes, and yes! Braden's blue eyes sparkled, and Annie's heart did cartwheels. Outwardly though, she remained composed. She squared her shoulders and smiled professionally at Veronica. "All in a day's work."

Veronica took out her phone, double-checking Annie's name tag against an app she'd opened. "One day? I don't think so. My goodness! How is that even possible?" Her mouth fell open. "Have you been working around the clock? For the past ten—No. Eleven. Twelve?" She squinted at her phone. "This app must be buggy," she said, looking up. "I'll have the tech team investigate. In any case, congratulations." She tipped her enormous hat at Annie. "I have to say, I'm impressed."

"Ronnie? Fancy meeting you here." Quinn strolled up to Veronica with a gift bag stashed behind him.

Her mouth pulled into a grin. "Quinn! What a fun surprise.

What are you doing in the store?" She tried to peer behind his back, but he stepped sideways as shoppers bustled past him.

"I was actually looking for you."

"Sweet." She cocked her head. "But why?"

"I wanted to ask you to lunch."

"Lunch?" She scanned his eyes. "I thought we had a dinner date?"

Quinn smiled. "That too."

"I can't do lunch, I'm afraid." Veronica glanced at the elevators. "I've got something to take care of here."

Quinn frowned playfully. "Can't it wait?"

Veronica peeked at Annie before answering, "I'm afraid it can't, really."

Quinn lowered his voice. "Why's that?"

Veronica leaned toward him and murmured, "I think I've made a mistake." She gave Quinn a swift peck on the lips and patted his cheek. "See you later?"

He shared a lovesick grin. "Pick you up at seven?"

Veronica smiled. "See you then."

She walked away, and Quinn exited the store. He held up his gift bag as he passed Braden and Annie. "Happy Christmas!"

Annie held up crossed fingers. "Good wishes for them."

"Good wishes for *all of us* today," Braden replied.

She was so, so tempted to kiss him. But not now, and definitely not here.

She spied Dylan and Marcus talking with Santa. Both boys nodded seriously, sitting at rapt attention on Santa's knees. They evidently were good kids at heart. Santa patted their backs, and they hopped off his lap, cheerfully approaching the exit. They grinned broadly and waved their mittens at Annie when their mom ushered them out the door. Annie smiled and waved goodbye, seeing them in *such* a better light.

"Not doing any shopping today?" Braden asked their mom.

"They're off to their sitter's now." The mom spoke from behind the back of her hand, with her kids walking in front of her. "I'll be back on my own later to pick up a few things."

Annie whispered to Braden when the family left. "I think we can guess what those are."

"A Robo-bot and a rocket drone?" His knowing expression was so adorable, Annie ached to hug him. But that would have to wait too.

The gift-wrap associate held up Annie's finished present, indicating it was ready. Now, all Annie had to do was set up the package delivery and make sure it got there today. She grinned at Braden. "Thanks for your help with, well—everything."

"See you at lunch?"

Her heart thumped happily. "I'll be there."

Annie rode the escalator to the second floor around noontime. Kira was in the process of dressing a headless mannequin in a sequined red top and jeans in Juniors. "Patrice wants to see me at two fifteen," Kira confided in low tones. She squealed softly. "This is it! I think I'm getting promoted." She grinned. "Which means you are too."

"That would be so great," Annie whispered back. "I hope you're right."

"This day has been like a dream," Kira confessed, pulling the sparkly top onto the mannequin's torso. "Every stinking thing has gone perfectly. Avery and I found *the best* apartment listed online, I got a text that my kid brother's getting married, not a single customer's messed up my tables—and now this." Kira tugged at the glittery red fabric, covering the mannequin's chest. The top was a sexy midriff, exposing the mannequin's white plastic belly above the waistband of her tucked-under jeans. The mannequin's legs ended mid-thigh.

Kira confided in hushed tones, "Almost makes me worry about when the other shoe's going to drop."

Annie's breath hitched. Maybe this day *had been* too perfect. Apart from her early-morning train delay, everything else had played out seamlessly. It was almost too good to be true. "I know what you mean." If she *did* move forward tomorrow, how would things change? She trusted her relationships would be better with her neighbors, and had always thought that was a given with Braden, but she couldn't know that for sure. She didn't even know one hundred percent that she and Braden were meant to be together.

Who have I been kidding with this?

Oh yeah, me.

When she and Braden broke out of this time loop, would their paths diverge? The only thing she felt certain about was what a good guy he was. Kind, generous, and trusting. Plus, he'd genuinely trusted her. It had been a huge stretch for him to buy into her time loop story, and yet he'd done it. That was one thing that made him so appealing. He saw the good in Annie and didn't judge her the way Roy had.

Roy had never trusted Annie's judgment about anything,

much less about how to run her personal life. He'd tried to tell her when she should and shouldn't text Tina or call her. In retrospect, he might have been trying to drive a wedge between them. Congrats to Roy! He'd succeeded. Shame washed through Annie. She'd played a major part in that too, but she was going to make things right.

The morning whizzed by in a pleasant blur for Braden. The retail pace was brisk at Lawson's, with the store having announced an early closing. Since Marcus and Dylan were no longer an issue, Braden and Annie would save tons of time at the end of their workday. More time for the two of them to get coffee, and for him to learn more about her. She'd filled him in on her past and her parents, and he'd shared many personal details too. Though he looked forward to taking her to the Blue Dot, spotted Formica tabletops were no longer enough.

He wanted red-checkered tablecloths and candlelight. A good bottle of Chianti, a romantic spot by the window, and the best Italian food the city had to offer. Braden was primed to ask Annie on a real date, and he would do so this evening. As hard as she'd worked, and as special as she was, he wanted to take her out and treat her right. Maybe they'd be celebrating her promotion? That would be amazing for Annie, and so well earned.

Braden studied the window display in front of him. Annie had turned a great window display into a wonderful one, making it seemingly magical. He'd helped her, sure. But the creative ideas had all been hers. It made his heart light to see her getting recognized for her talents. He sure appreciated them and had all along. What was new here was how greatly he was appreciating *her*.

TWENTY-NINE

ANNIE ENTERED THE BREAK ROOM and pulled her lunch bag from the fridge. She sat and stared at her phone. She could do this, of course she could, and she needed to—for Tina. She opened her text app before she lost her nerve.

Annie

I'm so sorry for everything. For doubting you and trusting Roy. I've been the worst friend on earth, but I want to make it up to you, Tina.

Annie's thumbs shook.

I'd love to see you sometime and talk.

Tears dripped down onto her knuckles.

But only if you want that.

She hit Send and grabbed a paper napkin, dabbing her eyes.

Maybe she'd hear back, and maybe she wouldn't. Either way, she'd made an effort at last, and now the ball was in Tina's court. She'd really let Tina down and would understand if Tina wanted nothing more to do with her. The walls closed in around Annie, making it harder for her to breathe.

She surveyed her peanut butter sandwich, but she'd lost her appetite. She'd eat it in a bit, after she'd hopefully heard back from Tina. The walls closed in further, and Annie thought about losing her parents. While her Grandma Mable had been loving to her, some of the kids at school had been downright hurtful. She'd never really had a friend she could count on until Tina, and now she'd lost Tina. Grandma Mable had now passed too. Because, of course. Anyone who cared for Annie ultimately left her. The room seemed to be shrinking smaller, sucking Annie into a vortex of sadness and regret.

Her life had taken a downward spiral after her breakup with Roy. She'd sunk so low, Annie hadn't fully realized how closed off from others she'd become. Then this Christmas Eve had come along and changed everything. When she broke out of this time loop, would her life return to its previous depressing state? Or possibly turn out even worse than before? No. She'd still have her job, hopefully, and Leo. Braden was a toss-up. Unless he wanted what she wanted—and just as badly—they might not connect on the other side of today.

Annie sighed and picked up her phone, staring at the text she'd sent Tina. She shut her eyes and thought of her parents, and Lawson's enigmatic new store Santa, wanting so desperately to *believe*. She willed—with all her might—for Tina's reply to materialize on her phone. But sadly, it didn't.

Annie heard Braden's voice in the hall and got to her feet, pulling the door open. He stood near the elevators talking on his phone, his back to her.

"Yeah, Ma, I promise. I'll be there tomorrow, rain or shine." There was a pause and then he said, "Love you too." Braden stared at the ceiling, clutching his phone. "I can't wait to get out of this time loop," he groused, "and on with my life."

Annie took a sucker punch to her gut.

He no doubt blamed Annie for him being stuck here, and maybe it *was* her fault. He hung his head, looking miserable, and Annie wanted to weep. She didn't know why this was happening to her, but—because she'd enlightened Braden to her dilemma—he was now painfully aware of her twisted circumstances, and all caught up in them too.

He probably thought he would have been better off never having known her, and Annie could see why. She ducked back into the lounge and took her seat at the table, shaken by this new truth. Braden couldn't wait to escape this time loop, and more than likely get far, far away from the person who'd embroiled him in it in the first place: her.

The door opened, and Annie looked up from her phone.

"Everything all right?" Braden asked, walking toward the refrigerator.

She smiled wanly and met his eyes. "Yeah." Her peanut butter sandwich was in front of her, but she hadn't taken a bite.

Braden placed his lunch and his cell phone on the table. "Lots of good things happening today," he said, sitting across from her. "Veronica Lawson's visit being a case in point."

"Yeah, that timing, fortunately, worked out." She flipped over her phone, staring at the screen. Still nothing from Tina.

"Annie," he said. "About Tina—"

Annie stared up at him. "What about her?"

"I don't want you to give up, that's all."

"Give up? What, me?" He'd inadvertently hit a nerve, but she knew he hadn't meant to.

Braden raised his hands. "Hey. If anyone knows about your persistence, it's this guy." He thumbed his chest. "I'm just saying that whenever you decide to text her—"

"Braden," she said flatly. "I already have." Disappointment coursed through her.

"Ahh," he acknowledged softly. "But you haven't heard back?"

Heat prickled the backs of her eyes. "Not yet."

Braden turned up his hands. "So. Maybe give it time?"

"Time is all I seem to have these days, isn't it?" She didn't mean to sound bitter, but she had. "Sorry." What was wrong with her? She couldn't blame him for being frustrated about their circumstances. She was too. Hurt bubbled up inside her at the thought they might not last. Might not even really get started to begin with. What if they never made it out of this time loop? Or, what if they did, and he forgot all about her? It had been easy enough for him to do that previously. He'd completely forgotten her day after day.

"I know this day has been rough on you," he said gently, "but there've been bright spots too, right? You've shared several of those with me."

"You've been one of the brightest." She spoke in choking sobs and cupped a hand over her mouth. She wiped her tears. *Stop it, Annie.* She sniffed and dabbed her eyes with a napkin.

"You've been a bright spot for me too," he said hoarsely. "The brightest." He smiled and tried to take her hand, but she pulled back. He was stuck in this time loop because of her, and he hated it. No number of bright spots could outweigh that cloud of doom.

"Really?" Her lower lip trembled. "So where will you be tomorrow?" As much it pained her to ask the question, she needed his answer. Did he care about her like she did him? If he did, maybe she could stand this, because they'd stay in it together, both here and afterward—on the other side of Christmas Eve.

"I don't—know." He raked a hand through his hair. "Hopefully, not here." That stung, and she flinched. But what did she expect, really? Nobody wants to stay in a time loop indefinitely. His earlier groan came back to her, *Three strikes and I'm out*, as well as his recent grumble in the hall...*can't wait to get out of this time loop...get on with my life.*

She fiddled with her holly wreath pin, avoiding his eyes. "Not here with me, you mean."

"Not here *on Christmas Eve*, Annie." He exhaled sharply, and she looked up. "You've got to know I want to make it to Christmas Day just as much as you do. The future's on the other side of tonight—on tomorrow's horizon."

"Your future," she said, reading between the lines.

He met her eyes, evidently not understanding. "Yours too."

"And our future together?" *There. She'd said it plainly.* Every ounce of her ached as she waited on his response. Until now, she hadn't seen the deepness of this abyss. How lonely she'd been, and how desperately she wanted to be wanted, but she was asking too much, and she knew it. Still. Her heart wept and bled. She couldn't have imagined everything. His kindness, his caring. His tender touch.

Braden pushed back from the table. "Time will tell with that too, won't it?" He shook his head. "Listen, this day isn't brand new to *you*, I get it. But—in lots of ways—it still is to me. Do I sense something between us? Yes. Yes, I do. Am I willing to explore it? Absolutely. But, Annie," he said, "I can't make promises that I'm not positive I can keep." His words were raw with emotion, and so were hers.

"I don't want you to make promises." Her breath shuddered, and she hugged her arms. Shivers raced through her like her world was falling apart, and the pain in his eyes said it was.

"Then what?" he rasped, and she felt him slipping away, like ocean waves rolling out to sea. Still. She tried to hang on, even knowing he was going.

"I want you to *believe*"—her voice cracked on a high note—"in us."

Patrice knocked on the door and pushed it open. "I'm sorry if I'm interrupting."

Annie smoothed back her hair, hoping her eyes weren't as red as they felt. "Did you need something, Patrice?"

"Actually," Patrice said, peering into the room. "I was looking for Braden."

He glanced at her. "I'll, uh—be right there."

Patrice ducked out of the room, and Braden stood. "I'm

sorry, Annie," he said, and her heart broke in two because she knew he was.

Braden departed, leaving Annie alone with her thoughts. She'd been wrong to put him on the spot, and she knew it. Of course they viewed their time together differently. She'd banked all the memories of their precious times together, whereas his recollections were largely limited to the past few days. Braden probably would have been better off not knowing about this time loop to begin with. Maybe—in his universe—he would have been beyond Christmas Day by now, instead of still stuck here on Christmas Eve with her.

She'd been selfish to share her burdens with him, and he'd been incredibly kind to try to help her clean up her very big messes. He'd fixed her window time after time and lent her moral support—amazingly. He'd also tried to help her break out of this time loop, to no avail. An uncomfortable truth gripped her. She'd weighed him down long enough. If today didn't end Christmas Eve for Annie, she wanted to find a way to end it for Braden, at least. To let him go, set him free. Wasn't there some saying about that?

When you love something, let it go...

If it comes back to you, it was yours.

If it doesn't, it never was.

Hurt seared through her chest. She needed to let Braden go. Give him a fighting chance to get to the other side of this time loop, and maybe his best shot was without her. Braden's cell phone lay on the table in front of her. He'd taken notes on his phone to remind him of their previous days together, and of all the things she'd told him. She'd been added as one of his contacts as well. But what if those things could be undone? Completely erased?

Annie's holiday ringtone jazzed up the room, and she grabbed for her phone. "Tina?" she asked, breathless. "Is that you?"

"Annie, *hi.*"

Annie's heard pounded.

"I'm sorry for the delay," Tina said. "My phone was still in airplane mode."

"It's, um"—Annie licked her too-dry lips—"really okay."

"*I've missed you.*" Tina sounded so caring, so sincere, like she hadn't changed one bit.

Annie's eyes grew hot. "I've missed you too."

"So, yeah!" Tina's tone brightened. "I think we should talk!"

"That, that would be great."

"We're out of town for the holidays," Tina explained, "but I'll be back on the second. Will you be around?"

She really hoped so. "Sure."

"Maybe we can grab a drink one evening after work?"

"I'd like that, Tina. A lot."

"Great, Annie. I'd like that too." She paused and then asked, "Doing anything special for Christmas?"

"I've—made some plans."

"Nice. Can't wait to hear about those when we catch up." Annie heard Tina's husband in the background, saying they needed to get going. "Ugh, sorry. Lloyd's family has roped us into this annual caroling thing."

Annie laughed, recalling Tina telling her about it before.

Apparently, none of Lloyd's family could carry a tune, but that didn't rob the joy from their singing. "Hope you have a great time."

"Thanks, Annie. You too. Merry Christmas."

"Merry Christmas."

Annie ended her call and stared at Braden's phone. He probably had it password protected. He was a security guard after all. She glanced at the door and moved quickly, snatching Braden's phone off the table. She typed on its keypad, but—ugh—it was locked. The door swung open, and she nearly dropped the phone in her haste to set it down.

"Afternoon, Annie." Santa entered the break room wearing a cheery grin. "How's your day going so far?"

"It's, er...going—better, for the most part."

He nodded and fixed himself a coffee. "You really rocked that new window display."

Annie sat up straighter in her chair. "Thanks for all your tips."

Santa lifted his mug and took a sip of coffee. "I'd say it's just about perfect."

She blinked, so relieved. "Really?"

"You've put your heart into it," Santa said approvingly. "Anyone can see that."

"So then..." She braved it. "This time loop will—?"

He tugged on his hat. "What time loop is that?"

"Ha-*ha*." She rolled her eyes. "The one that we're in, Santa."

"I'm not in any time loop." He set his mug on the counter. "Heavens! What a catastrophe that would be for all those little kiddos out there."

Annie thought on this. "Hmm. Yes."

"Including Dylan and Marcus." He strode over and picked up Braden's phone. "Oh dear, looks like someone's forgotten something." He tapped on the keypad and chortled, "Oh, ho! This belongs to Braden." He stared at the screen. "Isn't that sweet?" Santa flipped around the phone, revealing a photo of Braden with an older woman with his same eyes and smile. "This looks like a pic of him with his mom."

Annie leaned toward him. "Wait. How did you—?"

"Must be his screensaver." Santa handed the phone to Annie. "You'll get this back to him, won't you?"

Annie took the phone from Santa. "Sure." She glanced at the screen, seeing Braden's contact list open. Her name was front and center. Had Santa done that on purpose?

"Here's the funny thing about faith." Santa's light eyes glimmered. "You can't really force it on others. Everyone has to come to their beliefs of their own accord." He surveyed Annie carefully. "Don't you agree?"

Her grasp tightened around Braden's phone. "Yes, yes. I do."

"That's why your new window display is so great," Santa told her. "Gives folks a nudge in the right direction"—he winked—"without pushing."

But Annie hadn't been *pushing*, had she?

"If you love something, Annie," Santa said.

Annie blinked. "I don't lo-love Braden."

Santa placed his finger beside his chubby nose. "Maybe not yet."

He shut the door behind him with a click, and Annie inhaled deeply.

Maybe she *had been* pushing Braden without meaning to.

Braden was right. Time would tell about so many things, and if she and he were meant to be together, it couldn't be on account of any time loop—or magic. It had to be because of the two of them were the ideal fit.

She lifted Braden's phone and opened her contact icon. This felt a tiny bit stalkerish, but Santa had essentially given her his blessing. So. She stealthily scanned the room, deleting her phone number. Done! *Notes, notes, notes…* There! She found the app and highlighted Braden's entries over the past several days, making sure they only had to do with her. She stopped at the bottom of the entry he'd logged yesterday, and her heart caught in her throat.

I think I'm falling for Annie.

Every inch of her ached. She was falling for him too, so, so hard. Which was why she had to do this: give him wings, not clip them by keeping him tethered to her.

She hit Delete.

She scooped up her phone next and deleted Braden's contact information as well.

The door popped open when Annie was halfway to it. Braden! She held out his phone. "You left this on the table."

He took it and slipped it in his pocket. "Oh, thanks."

"Is everything okay with Patrice?"

"Yeah. She, uh…"—he shifted on his feet—"said a 'little bird' had told her I helped you with your window, and she wanted to thank me, said she'd mention it to Mike too."

"Sweet. Was that little bird Santa?"

"Not sure. Maybe Veronica? Hey, Annie." He met her eyes with a sorrowful frown. "About our talk earlier. I didn't mean things to end badly."

"They didn't," she said. *And they're not over yet. Don't give up hope, Annie. Be brave.* "I'm sorry if I pressured you."

His eyes glinted sadly. "I would promise if I could."

"I know." He started to turn, but she stopped him. "And Braden?"

He turned back around. "Yeah?"

"I heard from Tina." She wanted to share some good news and not end on a down note.

He grinned from ear to ear. "Wow, Annie. That's great."

She smiled at his fast assumption everything had gone well. "It was great. We're going to meet up after the holidays."

"So, you see there," he said. "Good things do happen at Christmas."

"Yeah, they do." She studied him longingly, guessing he wouldn't remember any of this tomorrow, but that was okay. He'd hopefully be out of this time loop by then, and maybe so would she.

"Annie?" Patrice stopped her in the hall. "Do you have time for a little chat?"

"Of course." Maybe this would finally be the talk she'd waited for.

Annie followed Patrice into the conference room, and Patrice sat at the table, motioning for her to do the same. "Annie," she said, "I have great news." She removed her glasses and folded them in her hands. Her stern look morphed into a grin. "You're getting *promoted* to Lead Visual Artist!"

"Really?"

Patrice nodded. "At the start of the new year."

Annie lunged forward and hugged her. "Oh, Patrice, that's awesome!"

Patrice stiffly patted Annie's back. "You've earned it."

Annie sat back in her chair. "What about Kira?"

Patrice's dark eyes shone. "You can have your pick when it comes to your assistant."

Annie spoke without hesitation. "In that case, I choose Kira."

"I had a hunch that you might say that," Patrice said knowingly. "I've scheduled a meeting with her next."

Annie gasped, but it was all in fun. "Patrice! What if I'd named somebody else?"

Patrice playfully shook her folded glasses. "But you wouldn't have, would you?"

Annie hugged her again. "You're right."

THIRTY

BRADEN WAS AT THE MAIN entrance when Dylan and Marcus's mom walked in. Snowflakes covered her coat and hat. "Good afternoon," he said.

She smiled at him. "Hi, again!"

Braden nodded politely. "Just so you're aware, Lawson's is closing at four today."

"Four?" She stared around the store. "Oh. That's early."

"Yes, ma'am." Braden glanced toward the street. "On account of the weather."

She pulled off her gloves, sticking them in her coat pockets. "Thanks. I'd better hurry along." She strode through the busy crowd, heading to the toy section.

Braden checked his watch. Yesterday, at this time, he'd noted that the lights on Annie's Christmas tree had gone off. Then he'd seen her traipsing toward her window with a huge box of lights in tow. Memories of that day were crystal clear. He also fairly well recalled the rewind days *after* he'd found that napkin in his jacket pocket, but the part of the time loop before that was largely a blur. Good thing he had his notes app on his phone to keep straight everything Annie had told him about. Otherwise, he might start to doubt this was actually happening.

If things went well, it wouldn't be happening any longer tomorrow. He frowned, recalling Annie's disappointed expression in the break room after she'd asked him about their future. She was right to worry about how things would wind up between the two of them after Christmas Eve. He had his questions about that too. How could he know how they'd both feel, or what they'd each remember after all this zaniness ended? Only one thing was certain: Braden was done making promises he couldn't keep. He'd promised his soldiers he'd get them through. He hadn't. He'd promised his mom he'd make Fred's funeral, but the hospital had held him back.

Santa paused in front of Braden. "Sometimes it's good not to dwell on the past," he said.

Braden blinked. "I wasn't—dwelling," he lied.

Santa gave him a knowing look. "You did your best in each case, given what was laid on you. Now it's time to move on."

Right. If only I could move on to Christmas.

Annie approached Braden at his post wearing a grin. "Guess what?" she asked Braden and Santa, but her joyful expression gave it away.

Braden's heart pounded. "You got the promotion?"

She nodded proudly. "I did."

"Annie!" Braden stepped forward and embraced her. "That's great." Seconds later, he realized his arms were wrapped around his coworker at Lawson's Finest and that they were blocking the entrance. *Unprofessional.* He released her, his face burning hot.

Pink spots formed on Annie's cheeks. "Thanks, Braden."

Santa held out his hand. "Congratulations on a job well done."

Annie shook his hand and laid a finger aside her nose. "All in a day's work," she said teasingly to Santa. Braden had never seen her appear so accomplished, or beautiful.

"Ho, ho, ho!" He hugged his big belly. "You make a very fine elf." He peeked at his workshop and the line that had formed during his short break. "Looks like I'd better get back to work."

He shuffled away, and Annie perused her window. "I guess there's nothing left to do here." She shrugged happily.

"No need to start over," Braden agreed.

She beamed at him. "The Christmas tree lights seem to be working fine."

"Everything looks great, Annie. Really."

She ducked her chin. "I couldn't have done it without you."

"Oh yes, you could have." Braden set his hands on his duty belt. "But I'm happy you didn't have to. I was more than glad to help."

Kira hurried toward Annie and braced her arms in her strong grip. "Say hello to your new Assistant Visual Artist." She grinned broadly.

"Yay, Kira!" Annie whooped. "That's awesome."

"Congrats," Braden said from beside them.

"Thanks"—Kira read his name tag—"Braden." She stared at Annie and then at him. "Hey, are you two—"

Annie stepped back. "No, no."

"Not us," Braden added quickly. He avoided Annie's eyes and greeted another group of customers scurrying in the door. "Store's closing shortly, folks."

"Don't worry," one lady said, tugging along her companion. "We'll shop fast."

Kira walked away, talking to Annie. "I can't wait to let Avery know. What a great Christmas."

Braden turned to Annie and nodded toward her window. "Seeing as how everything's good here, looks like we'll be leaving at closing today. So." He held his breath, hoping. "Maybe there's time for coffee?"

"I've got tons of shopping to do." Annie grimaced. "Cooking too."

"As long as you're home in time for Harrington though."

"I intend to get there *before* I'm needed to help him," she said. "Otherwise, I might not be able to get it all done."

"Gotcha." Braden's heart sank. What did he expect? She'd asked him about their future together, and he'd basically blown her off.

Santa approached, wearing his heavy overcoat. "Have a very merry Christmas, you two." He smiled at Annie and Braden. "I hope it's your best one yet."

"Merry Christmas," Annie said. She grinned at the older man. "And thanks."

"Ho ho ho." He laid a finger beside his nose. "All in a day's work." He winked at Annie. "Now, I'll have a busy night."

Braden waved. "Fly safely!"

Annie watched Santa stroll out the door. "I wish"—she turned to Braden—"I knew what he was really doing tonight. Do you think he'll be okay?"

Santa paused on the street, cinching his overcoat around his thick middle. "He seems like the sort to land on his feet."

Annie turned her questioning eyes on Braden. "What if we've missed something?"

He looked concerned. "Like what?"

"Not you so much," she said. "Me. About Santa? Here I've been reaching out to my neighbors while forgetting all about him. He's an old man, Braden. Maybe he's lonely? Maybe he lives in a shelter?" She gasped and covered her mouth. "What if he's homeless?"

"Annie," he said kindly. "He had to have given an address when he got hired by the employment agency."

"I know." She bounced on her heels, and her whole face lit up. "I'll invite him to Christmas dinner!"

"He'll have plans!" Braden shouted after her as she raced for the door.

She grinned over her shoulder. "I'll ask!"

"Annie! It's freezing—"

She dashed out into the snow and stood on the sidewalk, staring in both directions. She looked up, shielding her eyes with her hands.

Braden hurried through the entrance, pushing open the door. "Come back inside!" he cried. "You'll catch your death."

Snowflakes dotted her hair and clothing. "Look!" She pointed to the sky. "There!"

But all Braden saw was a big slosh of snow hitting him in the face. He blinked and rubbed his eyes. "Come on, Annie." He stepped toward her and gently took her elbow. "Let's go back inside."

She stared into his eyes and—for an instant—he was floating. Drifting away to some special place. Snowflakes flitted around them, dusting their hair and eyelashes. Annie's cheeks were pink from the cold, her pretty lips so inviting. Somewhere high above them—and beyond the gloomy clouds—Braden thought he heard sleigh bells. No. Impossible.

Annie grinned. "Did you hear that?"

He shook his head. "We must have imagined it."

"What? The two of us, together?"

"Annie."

"Braden Tate!" She playfully shoved his chest. "When are you ever going to believe?"

He laughed at her antics. "The jury's still out," he said. "Now, come on." He nodded toward the store, and she finally came along. Heat enveloped them the moment they stepped indoors. They dusted the snow from their clothing and hair as others walked past them, exiting Lawson's Finest.

"Some Christmas Eve, huh?" he asked her.

"Some Christmas Eve," she agreed on a wispy breath.

Her gorgeous eyes glimmered, and he was desperate to hold her. He'd experienced that sensation over and over, and not just on account of the revolving day. It was all because of Annie and how she looked at him. The way she made him feel. Like someone who could be special in her life. True, he couldn't promise, but he could hope.

He gathered his nerve, knowing she could easily say no, but

somehow saying goodbye at Lawson's didn't seem right. "Look," he said. "I totally understand about not having coffee, but..." He faltered and pressed ahead. "Can I at least walk you to the subway?"

She smiled, and his heart soared. "That would be nice."

Annie strolled along beside Braden, stewing over how to get that napkin. It was the only shred of evidence he still had about the time loop. Without it, he might totally lose his memories of being here—Annie's heart ached—and becoming close to her.

"I love this time of year," he said as snow cascaded around them. "Everything just seems so, you know." He shrugged, and snowflakes fell from the shoulders of his jacket. "Christmassy."

She smiled despite her inner melancholy. She'd done the right thing in deleting her information from his phone, but she didn't feel great about having invaded his personal device. "I love the holidays too."

"Glad this one's worked out for you, finally." He lightly nudged her elbow, and she went all fluttery inside. "With Tina, and your job and that promotion. Patrice hinted I might be getting one too."

"What?"

He shared a handsome grin. "Said Mike was looking for a new daytime supervisor. I knew that, only I thought he'd pegged Lou for the job."

"But no?"

He shook his head. "Lou's retiring in February. She hadn't let on to the rest of us."

Annie was so happy for him and also for herself. He'd be working different hours in that case, so they'd have potential to see more of each other. Hope bloomed in her heart like the faintest candle flame. Maybe it wasn't too much to wish for a romantic relationship with Braden—even if he *didn't* remember all of his Christmas Eves with her.

They passed a storefront selling cell phones. Each device in the window wore a small Santa hat, and Annie thought of Lawson's Santa. Where would he go after tonight? There weren't too many Santa gigs beyond the holiday season. She hoped he'd be all right. Annie glanced at Braden. "Guess we'll both be a little richer going into the new year."

He nodded. "Always a good thing in New York."

She was curious. "Any big plans for the money?"

He laughed. "I'm not sure it'll be that big a raise, but any little extra I get I intend to tuck away in the cookie jar, figuratively speaking. In reality, I'll put it in the bank. I've started a small investment account."

"Oh yeah?" This intrigued her. "For what?"

His eyes took on a dreamy cast. "A sweet little cottage in New Jersey."

She gasped. "For real?"

"Hope so. That's the dream."

The wind blustered around them, and she held her shoulder bag tighter.

"You know," he said. "A home, someday a family."

Annie's pulse hummed. She couldn't let herself think that far ahead. Still, she could almost see it. Braden in the yard of a cute little house chasing around a kid, maybe two. Her heart soared, but then she did a reality check. He wasn't talking about buying a place with her.

"What about you?" he asked her. "Any big plans for your newfound wealth?"

"Not sure it will be that big a raise either, but it should hopefully be enough."

"For?"

She grinned so big it hurt. "I'm planning to adopt Leo."

"He's not yours?"

"I've only been fostering him so far."

"What a lucky guy."

Braden stopped walking, and Annie saw they'd reached her subway stop. Part of her badly regretted declining Braden's offer for coffee. She didn't want her time with him to end. But her more rational side knew it had to. She had lots to do, and she wanted Braden to wake up tomorrow at Christmas. If she was lucky, she would too.

"Looks like this is my stop," she said, glancing at the entrance that led underground.

"Yeah." He shoved his hands in his jacket pockets. "Looks like."

The snow came down harder, coating his hat and hair in white, and she could see him as an old man. Even a grandpa. He'd make a great one, and probably a super dad.

Stop it, Annie. Don't hope.

But a lilting voice in her head said *believe*.

Commuters jostled around them, hurrying for the subway stairs, and Braden stepped closer. He raised his hand and lightly stroked her cheek. "I hope you get everything you want for Christmas." Warm tingles ran through her from her head down to her toes.

"You too." Her words were mere wisps in the wind because his mouth was so near—inches away, hovering over hers.

"It's funny," he said. "I have a feeling I'm going to miss you." He traced her lips with his thumb, and Annie's breath hitched.

"Braden," she murmured. "I'm going to miss you too."

"Yeah?" He slid his arms around her, holding her close.

Her pulse fluttered. "Yeah." She didn't know where she'd wind up tomorrow, but one way or another, she hoped she'd find her way back to Braden. That's when Annie realized what she wanted for Christmas. She wanted time. More time with the people she cared for, including Braden. It was hard to know what he was thinking, but from the look in his eyes, he was considering similar things about her.

"This probably is wrong," he said, "but I'm dying to kiss you."

Annie met his eyes and whispered, "It's not wrong."

His gaze poured over her, all liquid heat in the falling snow, and then his lips met hers, so satiny soft at first, until he increased his pressure, his mouth full on hers. Annie slid her mittens around his neck, and his kisses deepened, sending her spirit sailing through the heavens like Santa's sleigh on a snowy evening. "Annie." He held her tighter. "I've got to see you again. Please say yes."

She murmured between kisses. "Yes." Annie thought she heard sleigh bells.

She and Braden broke apart, staring at the corner. He nodded over his shoulder, still holding her in his arms, and she laughed. A volunteer collecting charitable donations chimed a bell with several quick flips of her wrist. She was dressed like Santa.

"For a moment—" She giggled.

"Yeah." He smiled. "Me too."

She suddenly remembered. "Braden, about that napkin? The one from the Blue Dot."

"I'm keeping that forever," he said huskily, nuzzling her nose with his.

"No!"

"No?"

"It's, ah." She licked her lips. "I was wondering if I could hang on to it."

He eyed her suspiciously, but then he grinned. "What for?"

She shrugged in his embrace. "As a keepsake maybe?"

He shook his head. "Nothing doing, Annie Jones." He patted his jacket. "This one's mine. I want it to help me remember."

"But, I"—her chin trembled—"think you should give it to me."

"All righty. I will. Eventually." He kissed her firmly on the lips. "You did say you'd go out with me?"

"Yes," she breathed happily. *A million times yes.*

Braden beamed from ear to ear. "Great." He glanced at the subway stairs. "You should probably get going, if you're going to make all that food, *and* rescue Harrington." His eyes shone brightly. "*And* save the day."

"Ha." Annie gripped her bag handle with her mitten. "Yeah, I'd better go." She kissed him goodbye and turned.

He called after her. "See you soon!" She spun on her heel, and Braden held up his phone. "I'll text ya!"

She waved cheerfully, but deep inside, her heart broke in two. "Great!" *What* had she done erasing everything on his phone? Tina's mantra rang out in her head. *Come on, Annie. Be brave.* Right. She had to solider on.

Now was not the time to give up.

Not on Braden, or on Christmas.

THIRTY-ONE

ANNIE PUSHED HER ROLLING SHOPPING basket through the cascading snow, her heart happy and her spirits light. The collapsible carrier sat low to the ground, with high wire basket sides and a handle. She'd filled it with three heavy grocery bags and purchased a bouquet of fresh flowers for her table. Their petals accumulated the rapidly pelting snow, but she'd have them indoors and in a vase soon enough.

She reached her building an hour before she knew Harrington would be there. That would give her plenty of time to stash her groceries away and get started on that chili before dashing downstairs to watch for Harrington's arrival. Annie hurried inside, carting her things into the foyer, collapsing the folding cart and dragging that into the hall last. Leo greeted her when she nudged open her apartment door, her arms weighted down with heavy groceries and her work bag slung over her shoulder. "Hello, Leo."

He pressed up against her pants leg and purred. "Yes, yes." She stepped past him to deposit her things in the kitchen. "I'll feed you in a minute." He followed close on her heels, sitting to watch her remove her hat and mittens and lay them on the radiator.

Annie unbuttoned her coat and leaned toward him, stroking the top of his head. "Mom's had good news today." She gathered him up in a hug. "I got promoted," she whispered, her face very close to his. He stared at her with his big eyes. "Which means"—she firmly kissed his head—"you're getting adopted!"

He squirmed in her hold, evidently more interested in food than celebrating. Annie smiled and set him down. "All right," she said. "You can have your dinner. But then, I have to get to work." Memories of Braden standing in the snow flooded her, and her heart fluttered. He'd been so incredibly handsome, she hadn't been able to resist him, or his sexy kisses. She hoped she'd get more of those someday. She looked up and begged the heavens. *Please, please, please. Please.*

She also really wanted to go out on that date. If she woke up in the morning to yet another Christmas Eve, she wasn't sure what she'd do. At least she'd get to see Braden again, or would she? Annie frowned. Going through that do-over day without him would be incredibly sad. But she wasn't going to think about that now.

Annie removed her coat, hanging it over the back of a kitchen chair. She draped her scarf across the radiator and held up her finger to Leo. "I've got to grab the rest of my things from downstairs, then you'll get to eat." The cat complained with a loud mew.

"Spoily!" Annie laughed and shook her head. "You can wait two more minutes." Come to think of it, she felt hungry too. Maybe she'd munch on a snack while she was cooking and make a couple extra cinnamon rolls to share with Bea when she came by. Even though it was smallish, she'd bought a whole fresh turkey this time, and creamed corn to make corn pudding like her mom used to make. Frozen green beans for a green bean casserole too.

Harrington was bringing chocolates for dessert, but she'd still purchased ingredients for a simple pumpkin pie and she intended to make one, assuming tomorrow actually was Christmas Day. Otherwise, none of these expensive groceries would be here when she woke up tomorrow anyway. Annie retrieved the rest of her stuff from the foyer and hauled it up the stairs, grabbing a vase from beneath her kitchen sink for the flowers. She arranged them in the vase and glanced at her kitchen table. It came with an extra leaf that she kept in the coat closet, and she could add that tomorrow to accommodate everybody. Having the others in her building over for Christmas dinner would be so amazing.

Her heart caught in her throat.

Assuming she didn't mess something up.

And assuming Christmas Day actually came.

Annie set the vase on the table. She didn't have nearly enough chairs. Only three here, plus the one at her desk in the bedroom, but that only made four. Her sofa and living room armchair were bulky and not budging. Maybe she could ask some of the neighbors to help out.

Annie strapped on her apron and opened her cookbook binder. She'd already made several notations on the side of the index card about her minor modifications. Tonight's chili was going to be better than ever. She heard her dad's voice in her head, *world class*.

Annie's phone alarm went off forty minutes later. Thank

goodness! She'd become so involved in her cooking, she might have otherwise neglected to think of Harrington. She opened the building's front door as he exited his cab. The driver deposited his suitcase beside him on the sidewalk. "Need help with your bag?" the driver asked, viewing the icy steps.

"I'm fine," Harrington grumbled. "Perfectly capable of doing this on my own."

"Maybe so!" Annie marched down the steps in her snow boots and coat as the cab driver took off. "But there's really no need with me here to help you."

Harrington leaned into his walker and stared at her while snow swirled around them. "And you are?"

She smiled and picked up his suitcase. "Annie."

He shook his finger. "My guardian angel, yes."

Annie blinked. "What?"

"You helped me another time, didn't you?" He scratched his head. "Can't precisely say when, but I do know you were there."

"I—want to be here more often too." He didn't argue with her about the suitcase, merely followed her along. They paused at the base of the steps.

"What's that mean?" Harrington asked her.

Annie grinned. "I'm inviting you to Christmas dinner."

"Oh?" He looked surprised but secretly pleased. "What makes you think I'll accept?"

"I have a hunch you like peppermint bark," she said slyly, "and I've got some."

Harrington patted the front of his coat. "A woman after my own heart." He started to climb the stairs using his walker, and she waited behind him, intending to go up second in case he slipped. She'd bring the suitcase up after that.

"Hold on," he said, peering over his shoulder. "Don't you live on the third floor?"

"I do," she said, "but we'll help you."

"We?"

Eric appeared right on cue. "You guys need any help?" He eyed Harrington's suitcase and viewed Annie, noting her careful attention on Harrington as he struggled up the stairs.

"Uh, sure," Annie said. "Could you grab the luggage? Thanks."

They all made it into the foyer, and Eric shut the door. "You're Annie, right?"

She nodded and Harrington held out his hand, intending to shake Eric's. "My name's Harrington."

"Yes, sir." Eric nodded. "I believe we've met."

Harrington narrowed his eyes at Eric. "That's right. You're in school somewhere."

"NYU, sir."

Harrington's tone grew wistful in a put-on way. "Studying poetry."

Eric chuckled. "Literature. Yes, sir."

Harrington unlocked his door, and Eric carried his suitcase over the threshold. Harrington thanked him and said, "Wicked storm out there. Runways shut down at LaGuardia."

"Tomorrow's supposed to be bad too," Annie commented to both of them. She glanced at Eric. "I'm making a pretty simple Christmas dinner for people in the building, and you're invited too."

Eric shifted the backpack on his shoulder. "That'd be great. I accept."

"It's a mess out there," Harrington said, shaking the snowflakes from his coat.

"But a great night for chili." Annie grinned at the older man. "I'm bringing you some in a bit."

Harrington placed a hand over his heart. "You really are some sort of angel, aren't you?"

"No. Just a neighbor." *And maybe a friend.* She stared at Eric. "And you can be on the lookout for some fresh cinnamon rolls."

Eric grinned. "Now I know I'm dreaming."

Harrington's nose scrunched up. "Maybe we all are?"

No, no, no, no, no and no.

"What a merry Christmas Eve," Harrington said in parting as Annie climbed up the stairs.

"Sure is," Eric said before he shut his door.

Harrington closed his door as well, and the resulting echoes were in tune. Though she'd only been getting to know them a short while, Annie's connections with her neighbors already felt heartwarmingly strong. She had the very keen sense that she was doing what she was supposed to do, and that she was where she was meant to be. She only hoped she wouldn't be here forever.

A short time later, Annie led Bea into the kitchen where she filled her sugar cup. Bea stared around the room at Annie's works in progress: the cinnamon rolls, the pumpkin pie, and the green bean casserole. Her world-class chili simmered on a back burner on the stove.

"My," Bea said. "Someone's been busy."

"I've invited a few of the neighbors over tomorrow for a holiday meal. You're welcome to join us."

"Oh, thanks! That's very kind, but I'm expected at my daughter's place in Queens."

Wind slammed against the window, and Annie glanced at the snowy streaks leaving trails down the glass. "Weather's looking bad though. So, if for any reason you can't make it..." Annie passed Bea the cup of sugar, and she took it.

"Thanks, Annie. That's very nice."

Annie delivered the chili to Harrington and set it on his stove.

"Thanks for the supper," he said, leaning into his walker.

"No problem. I hope you enjoy it." Annie paused on the threshold on her way out. "Don't forget about Christmas dinner. Eric and I will come to get you a little before two."

"I look forward to it." He bowed his head. "Thank you."

Eric was next, and she knocked on his door, holding the cinnamon rolls. They were fresh from the oven, and their sweet aroma filled the foyer. Eric pulled open his door and grinned. "You're awesome." He accepted the covered platter she handed him. "And these smell incredible." He set the plate down on a table by the door. "Thanks."

"You won't forget about dinner?"

Eric pulled his cell phone from his jeans pocket. "Got it on my calendar."

"Excellent. See you tomorrow." She snatched a quick look at Harrington's apartment. "Would you mind helping me get Harrington up the stairs?"

"Absolutely," Eric said. "No problem."

"You wouldn't happen to have any folding chairs?"

"That's all I've got!" he said. "I've got a card table too. That's what I use in the kitchen. Want to borrow them?"

"Just the chairs would be great," she said. "How many have you got?"

"The four that came with the table."

"We could probably use them all."

Eric nodded. "I'll bring them up a little early. What? Around one thirty?"

"One thirty's good." Annie grinned. "Thanks! See you tomorrow."

Eric waved. "I won't forget the wine."

Annie set two empty hot cocoa mugs in her sink later. She'd had a good chat with Bea over chili, and they'd watched a rom-com together, with Bea popping out across the hall every so often to check on her casserole. For her part, Annie had almost everything ready for tomorrow. All she had left to do was stuff the turkey and get it in the oven, then make the gravy. She couldn't say how long it had been since she'd had a big Christmas dinner. It was probably when she'd been invited to Tina's parents' holiday meal when she was still dating Roy.

"Okay, kitty." She spoke to Leo when she entered the living room. "It's time for one big boy I know to hit the hay." He raised his head from his snuggly spot in the sofa blankets. "Santa comes tonight." *I hope.*

He sluggishly hopped off the sofa and plodded into the bedroom, dutifully claiming his place at the foot of her bed on the soft duvet. Annie reached into her bedroom closet and grabbed the shopping bag of kitty stocking stuffers she'd purchased from the high shelf. "You stay put," she told the cat. "I'll be right back."

She went to work stuffing his stocking and filling it to the brim with new toys and treats. She hung it back on the small nail she'd driven into the window frame by the living room radiator. She patted the stocking once she'd set it in place. "You stay put too, and don't go emptying yourself on me."

Annie strode to her small Christmas tree and reached down to unplug its lights.

She stopped suddenly, picking up her snow globe instead. She shook it heartily, observing her dad's sweet painting propped up behind the tree. *I do believe, I do.* Annie shut her eyes and pressed the snow globe to her chest. *In friendships, and miracles, and Christmas. Maybe in finding my place in the world. In my own little snow globe, here in this very vast universe.* She'd been so isolated before, but she didn't feel that way anymore. She felt connected and hopeful about the future. Maybe even a future with Braden, whether he remembered her or not. They could always start fresh. She'd done that with him already—so many times. And, if time finally moved forward, maybe their relationship would progress.

And if it didn't?

Annie experienced a fleeting moment of fear, and she released a deep breath.

If it didn't, she would handle that too.

She'd have her job and Tina, friends at work and in her building. She'd create a solid and satisfying existence for herself and

Leo. Then, if the stars aligned, she might someday find her fated match, like one of the heroines in her favorite rom-coms. But for now, she was good. Good with who she was and the person she'd become. Someone stronger in herself and with a keener appreciation for others, folks who were feeling like family. The family she didn't have.

Her mom's voice lilted through the air. *We're here, Annie.*

No. Not the family she didn't have. But rather, the birth family she'd always have and hold dear in her heart, along with her new "found family" of special people. She wanted to give as many of them as possible a really happy holiday in the small ways that she could. She wished she'd learned more about that department-store Santa. She hoped that he was safe and happy and enjoying his Christmas to the fullest, wherever he was.

Annie opened her eyes and kissed the top of the snow globe for luck before setting it down. "Here's hoping tomorrow's Christmas."

She reached beneath the tree and unplugged its lights.

THIRTY-TWO

On Christmas Day

BRADEN STRETCHED OUT HIS ARMS, folding them behind his head on his pillow. Christmas Day, great! He had the whole day off and had somewhere important to be: with his mom. He'd slept in his undershirt and sweatpants. All comfy-cozy for a cold winter's night, during which it had been snowing buckets.

He sat up, feeling groggier than he should be. He'd only had two beers last night. It wasn't like he'd been on a bender. Not that Braden did "benders." He didn't. He prided himself on remaining in charge of himself and his situations—except for on those rare occasions when the fates blew him sideways.

His duty belt lay on his dresser, and his holster was empty. He recalled locking his firearm and mag pouches away in his personal safe. Good. He'd obviously been thinking clearly when he'd turned in. It was the entire day beforehand that grew fuzzy. Faint light crept into the room, stealing in through beneath the lowered shade. An image of him helping a pretty brunette fix her window display flitted back to him. Annie? Right. Annie Jones. The Assistant Visual Artist at Lawson's Finest. He'd helped her pick up when those kids trashed her window.

A boy's cries echoed in his ears. *No, Dylan! Let me!* Braden massaged his tight temples, recalling the bad scene those kids had caused. The store Santa had seemed to take it in stride and had issued them a gentle warning. Braden ran a hand through his mussed-up hair. He couldn't say exactly *how* that Santa was different. He just was.

So was Annie Jones. She seemed sparkly and effervescent, like the brightest, bubbly prosecco. Special in her own unique way. Still. Braden frowned. When he'd asked her out for coffee, she'd summarily shot him down. So that, as they say, was that. No matter what he'd thought about their flirty "do you believe in Santa" exchange, she clearly wasn't interested in him romantically. She probably had a boyfriend anyway. The name Leo tugged at the recesses of his brain. Yeah, likely him.

Who calls their kid Leo these days?

Maybe somebody Italian. A couple of famous Leonardos came to mind, and Braden sighed. Annie was so out of his league. Why had he even tried? His gut tightened as the bomb blast went off in his head. Braden pressed his palms to his temples, breathing hard. No, those were his demons talking. He was *totally worthy* of Annie. No fault of his that she was already taken, or he simply wasn't her type.

Braden got out of bed and strode to the window, rolling up the shade. Snow slashed against the window, and the wind howled wildly. Whoa. He couldn't even make out the steps on the fire escape. They were buried in snow, and the visibility was nearly zero. His mind flashed to the sandstorm in Iraq. Blinding gusts of sand whirled around him, stinging his face and arms. Even through his goggles, he'd been unable to see a thing. But no, this was different. He needed to leave what was in the past behind him. Someone really wise had recently told him that, he just couldn't say who.

Braden checked his watch when his phone rang later that morning. Nine o'clock. It was his mom. "Hey, Ma. Merry Christmas!" He sat at his kitchen table nursing his morning coffee. His apartment was pretty bare-bones and not decorated much. Although he had hung a plastic Christmas wreath on his front door, mostly because his mom had given it to him as a present.

"Merry Christmas, hon." She paused. "I suppose you've heard about the subway. It's probably for the best that everything's shut down. Safety first."

"Yeah." He glanced at his ballistic vest hanging over the back of a kitchen chair. He'd left it there last night after he'd removed his uniform shirt, stripping down to his undershirt and trousers. That was weird. It looked like it had a coffee stain on it. Wait. Two coffee stains? When did those happen? He didn't recall any mishaps like that. Luckily, while the body armor was regulation, he'd never had an occasion to need it at Lawson's. Braden set down his mug, returning to his conversation with his mom about the weather. "Doesn't mean I won't be there though."

"What? No, Braden. I don't want you to—"

"But I want to. Besides"—he put on a teasing lilt—"Santa left you a present over here that I said I'd deliver."

"That's very sweet, but there's no way for you to get here."

He scoffed teasingly. "What's wrong with my two feet?"

"Braden."

"I've got lots of cold-weather gear, Ma. I'm sure I can make it. It just might take me a little longer to get there."

"You'll get frostbite!"

"No, I won't."

"Or get sick!"

He stretched his legs out under the table. "That's a negative."

"How do you know?"

"I'm hardy," he joked. "My mama raised me tough."

She laughed. "Your mama raised you stubborn."

He took a swig of coffee. "That too."

He could almost see her shaking her head. "I can tell you're set on this."

Braden put down his coffee. "I am."

She clicked her tongue. "Fine. Be careful then."

"Ten-four, chief."

She chuckled and asked him, "Have you heard from your sisters?"

"I have." He smiled fondly. "You?"

"Very early. The grandkids got everyone up. So excited. I can't wait to see them all shortly, when I visit after Christmas." She paused a beat. "I wish you could come too."

"I know, but"—he shrugged—"work."

"You work too hard."

He laughed. "I could say the same of you."

"Fair. What time will you be over tomorrow?"

"What time's dinner?"

"Whenever you get here."

Braden ended the call and placed his phone on the table, but then he picked it back up, scanning through his contacts. Weird. *Now why would I think I had Annie's number in there?* Braden shook his head. If she'd declined his offer of coffee, she definitely wouldn't have given him her number. Maybe he'd dreamed it.

He stared at his ballistic vest and the uniform shirt draping over it on the back of a kitchen chair. He needed to tidy up a bit and get ready to head over to his mom's. He stood and washed out his coffee mug, leaving it in the drying rack by the sink before strolling into the living room and nabbing his uniform jacket off the desk chair positioned near the radiator. He patted down the jacket, noting it had dried nicely overnight. He shook it out to hang in his closet, and something slipped from an inside pocket, fluttering to the floor. It looked like a paper napkin. He picked it up and flipped it over to the writing on the other side.

Handwriting. *My handwriting.* Braden's heart hammered. "Believe Annie?" *What on earth does that mean?* The only Annie he knew was Annie Jones at Lawson's Finest. For the life of him, he couldn't remember writing that down, and why on a napkin? *Believe Annie*—about what? He had no idea.

They'd met when she'd dropped her lip gloss, then he'd seen her later the salesfloor, right before those rascally kids trashed her window. He'd helped her pick up, and they'd added tinsel to the tree—at the store Santa's suggestion. She'd had a brainstorm about including all this other Christmassy stuff. Somewhere in the middle of all that action, Veronica Lawson dropped by to disapprove of—*No, wait. Compliment?*—Annie's window. These conflicting images made no sense.

He did have a sense about Annie though, a sense that she was a really special person. He stared at the napkin in his hand. But this napkin thing was bizarre. Something must have happened. Some tiny detail he didn't recall, but that wasn't like him to miss things. If he thought on it hard enough, maybe it would come back to him.

Annie opened her eyes, greeted by an eerie calm and the faint sound of the wind whistling outside. She snatched her cell phone off her nightstand, holding it up above her head.

Dec 25

Winter Storm Warning

Yes, yes, and yes! Annie squealed and kicked her heels under the covers, disturbing Leo. He spilled onto the floor with a sleepy yawn. "Oh! Sorry, Leo."

A weather advisory flashed across the screen. Steady accumulation and high winds expected. Public transportation had shut down. No one was going anywhere today. She set her cell phone on her nightstand and tossed back the covers, peering down at the floor, but Leo's wand toy was on her dresser where she'd placed it yesterday. Her heart thumped. Was this really happening? Had she broken through to Christmas Day?

Annie raced to her window and yanked up the blinds.

Woo-hoo!

The world was a winter wonderland, the rungs of her fire

escape buried deep. Snow pummeled the metal platform, sending big bursts of flurries up against the glass. "Leo," she gasped as he wandered over to circle her ankles, "we made it." He peered up at her, and she scooped him into her arms, cradling him like a baby. "Yes, yes. I know you're hungry." She nuzzled her nose against his. "And, you know what? So am I." If this was really Christmas, she couldn't wait to sink her teeth into one of those cinnamon rolls she'd saved for this morning.

Annie carried Leo toward the hall and shut her eyes, almost afraid to peek at the living room. But finally, she did. Leo's kitty stocking was full! "Oh my gosh!" She scuttled over to it, holding Leo. She turned him to face his stocking. "Look what Santa brought you, boy." He appeared unimpressed, meowing and squirming instead.

She set him down on the floor. "Yeah, yeah," she said sweetly. "Breakfast first."

Annie plugged in her Christmas tree lights, and they cast a colorful sheen on her pretty snow globe. She picked it up and held it against her heart. She stared at the ceiling and beyond that up to the heavens. "Thank you." She lifted the snow globe and smiled at the tiny Santa inside with his reindeer team. "And thanks to you too, Santa," she said lightly. She returned the snow globe to its spot beneath the tree. *Believe.* Yes, right. What she wanted to believe was that all the cooking she'd done last night hadn't been in vain. She stared at the candy canes on her tree and counted. Only ten. Woot! That had to mean she'd invited Bea in for cocoa and had given her one. There'd been no morning coffee with Jane yesterday.

Annie dashed into the kitchen with Leo following her. The countertop was loaded with goodies. A covered tray of cinnamon rolls, a fresh pumpkin pie, canned cranberry sauce, a few bags of stuffing. Annie's pulse raced as she darted to the refrigerator, yanking the door open. A fresh ten-pound turkey sat on the top shelf. "Yes!" she shouted out loud. "Woo-hoo!" There were other items in her fridge too, like the green bean casserole she'd prepared along with the corn pudding, and a small container of chili she'd reserved for herself after taking a pot of it to Harrington and having Bea to dinner. Annie shut the refrigerator door, smiling at the photo of Tina. "I have sooo much to tell you. You'll never believe it."

Leo mewed at her heels.

"All right," she said. "I'll feed you."

That was awfully familiar. Panic gripped her. But no, she said that every day. Annie spied her open laptop on the kitchen table beside a pretty vase of grocery store flowers, and—*yes*—two empty hot cocoa mugs rested in her sink, the telltale red smudges from melted candy canes marring their insides. She prepared Leo's cat food on the counter, gingerly placing his dish on the floor. He dug into his food as the sweet scent of cinnamon rolls filled the air. She was definitely having one. Possibly two, if she felt like it. It was Christmas, hey! *At last.*

She fixed her pour-over coffee and grinned at Leo, still devouring his food. "Guess who got promoted?" Had that really happened? She hoped so. She carried her coffee to her kitchen table and sat, turning her laptop toward her to check her email. There it was—in her inbox! A new message from Patrice Winston, Promotion Memo. Annie scanned the brief note.

Due to your exemplary contributions at Lawson's Finest, we are pleased to promote you to Lead Visual Artist with an effective start date of January 1. Please report to HR when the store reopens after Christmas to complete any necessary paperwork. Congratulations on a job well done. We look forward to your continued service at Lawson's.

All best,
Patrice

Annie fist-pumped in the air. *Yes!*

She stared at her intercom and waited, her heart pounding so loud she could almost count the beats. But the buzzer remained silent. Naturally. The roads were pretty much impassible today, so there'd probably be no deliveries. Annie glanced down at her slippers and smirked. "So much for those new snow boots." Ah, well. Maybe they'd come after Christmas, once the storm had cleared.

She leaned back in her chair and sipped her coffee, her heart happy. She was hosting Christmas dinner today for everyone in her building. She hoped Lawson's store Santa was okay and settled in someplace safe out of the elements. But what about Braden? Would he make it to his mom's? That would be a challenge in this storm, but she knew he'd try. He was a good man, and a caring person. After a while, she'd begun to believe he'd started caring for her. Then the note she'd found on his phone had confirmed it.

She shouldn't have become upset with him about not being able to make promises. He'd been just as stymied by the time loop as she had, and uncertain about how they'd wind up. And still.

He'd been so tender and caring, supporting her through each do-over day. Her pulse hummed at the memory of his goodbye kiss. Did he recall that at all? She frowned. Doubtful.

But maybe he remembered something—at least their first Christmas Eve together. They'd gotten along really well then, and he'd invited her out for coffee. Even though she'd said no at first, that gesture gave her something to work with—and hopefully build on. Time would tell. And now time was moving forward. Thank goodness. She peered at the time on her laptop: 9:07 a.m. She'd slept in, just like she'd wanted, and now she needed to get busy preparing her turkey to pop in the oven.

Annie took another quick sip of coffee and set down her mug. "What do you say, Leo?" He sat back on his haunches and licked his chops, having thoroughly enjoyed his meal. "Ready to see what Santa brought you?" She'd give him a few toys to keep him busy so she could get to work stuffing that bird. But first! She was serving herself a cinnamon roll to take with her into the living room. Yum.

Once she'd put the bird in the oven, Annie showered and dressed. She browsed through the offerings in her closet, noting the snowman-patterned turtleneck and her winter white stretch pants in her hamper. *Thank God.* She blew out a breath and began whistling brightly. It was a Christmas tune, the same one her snow globe played. "It's Beginning to Look a Lot Like Christmas." Annie grinned to herself. *Yeah, it is.*

Ah-ha! She found the item she was looking for: a pretty red cowl-neck sweater. She'd pair it with black leggings and black flats. She felt so festive, she wanted to dress up a bit for the holiday. No holly wreath pin today though. That might damage her sweater. But she did have some fun reindeer earrings she could wear.

She twisted her hair into a French knot and held it up behind her, peering at her reflection in her dresser mirror. Maybe for a change, she'd wear her hair up. She considered her many interactions with Braden, wondering what he would think of the look. Also wondering what he was doing at the moment, and whether he was thinking about her. Hoping he remembered her somewhat and hadn't totally wiped all memories of her just as cleanly as she'd erased her contact information from his phone. Darn it.

But no. Maybe that act was part of what helped her get here to the other side of Christmas Eve. *If you love something, let it go...* But she didn't love Braden, she really didn't. Santa's words came back to her. *Not yet.* Annie sighed, but soon happiness filled her heart. It was finally Christmas, and she had plenty to be grateful for.

THIRTY-THREE

"HELLO!" ANNIE SAID, WELCOMING BEA into her apartment. "Merry Christmas."

"Merry Christmas, everyone. Ooh, something smells divine in here." Bea came inside, using oven mitts to carry her sweet potato casserole. She wore dark slacks and a festive Christmas sweater featuring gingerbread men and candy canes. "I'll just set this on your stove." She nodded at Harrington and Eric, who were already in the living room. Both held glasses of wine, and Harrington's walker was beside his spot on the couch. Eric sat in one of the folding card table chairs he'd brought over. "Hi there. I'm Bea Holly from across the way."

Eric stood and shut the door behind Bea before Leo escaped. "I'm Eric Park. Good to know you." He'd dressed nicely in khakis and a green sweater. Harrington had worn a button-down shirt under his brown cardigan and had even put on a crimson-colored tie covered with green and white letters spelling *Ho ho ho*.

Harrington lifted his wineglass. "Harrington Bryte from 1-A downstairs."

Annie tilted her head toward Eric. "He's in apartment 1-B."

"Ah-ha! Nice to finally meet my neighbors." Bea laughed. "I've only lived here ten years."

"Ten? My," Harrington said. "I've been here fifteen."

Bea deposited her casserole in the kitchen and returned. "Yes. I think I've seen you around."

Harrington nodded. "We've passed each other down at the mailboxes, of course."

Bea turned to Annie. "It was so nice of you to do this."

"I know," Eric said. "And you barely know us at all."

Annie wiped her hands on her apron she'd inherited from her mom. "I'm glad you all could come."

Someone knocked on the door. Annie addressed Bea. "Please, have a seat. Eric?" She caught his attention. "Can you pour Bea some wine if she wants it?"

"Sure thing." Eric glanced at Bea, and she grinned.

"Yes, please!"

Annie opened the door, and Jane stood there with the cutest little girl in pigtails. She wore stretch pants, high-top sneakers, and a snowman sweater. "Hi!" the child announced. "I'm Cari!" She waved around the room. "I'm eight!"

"Welcome, Cari!" Annie bent down to look her in the eye and whispered, "Eight's a great age to be."

The kid glanced adoringly up at Jane. "That's what Mommy says too."

Another adult was with them, a stocky woman with short blond hair. She had on a red tartan plaid vest over a black turtleneck and jeans and held a small shopping bag. Jane wore a green dress and flat-heeled brown boots. She had a wine bottle in her hand. It was the first time Annie had seen Jane with her thick, wavy hair down, and she looked great. "I hope it's okay that I brought Sam?" Jane asked. She shot a glance at her companion and grinned. "She kind of surprised us."

"Of course!" Annie said. "Please come on in and let me introduce you." She glanced at the others. "Jane and Cari are in 2-A."

Jane handed Annie the bottle of wine. "Thought you could use another."

"Thanks!" Annie said. "Good call."

Sam opened her shopping bag. "We weren't sure if you needed bread." She extracted two baguettes in paper sleeves from her bag.

Bread. She'd totally forgotten. "Thanks," Annie said. "That's fantastic." She shut the door behind them and remarked to Sam, "How lucky that you got in with the storm—all the way from Ohio."

Jane blinked. "Wait. What? How did you—?"

"Ooh, my ears are burning," Sam teased. "You must have told her about me." Sam rolled her eyes, playfully nudging Jane. "It's nice to be talked about—in a good way," she added, and everyone laughed. "So yeah," she told the group, "I came in by train late last night. Glad I didn't wait until today. Might not have made it."

The wind roared against the windows, accentuating her point.

"Not a fit day out," Harrington quipped, "for man nor beast."

Braden raised his forearm in front of him, shielding his eyes from the wind, when his face went tingly numb. A large Lawson's shopping bag draped from the crook of his arm by its handle. It held the wrapped package containing his mom's new coat. He gripped the poinsettia pot against his jacket, pressing ahead through the blustery winds, the plant's red petals doused in snow.

He wasn't leaving his mom alone this Christmas. He'd get there soon enough. Braden trudged along the sidewalk, watching his step as snow piled up higher. He wore ski pants over his jeans, and sturdy waterproof boots.

He plowed ahead down the desolate street, interior lights from the brownstones around him glowing. Several bay windows framed Christmas trees. Others, menorahs or fake candles. Many were crowned by colorful holiday lights. He saw families gathered inside, lounging around in groups, animatedly waving their hands and holding glasses of eggnog or wine.

Most folks were smart enough to stay indoors today. He might have done that too, were it not for the promise he'd made. Guilt swamped him, but he couldn't say why. In keeping this promise to his mom, he couldn't shake the feeling that he was somehow breaking another. Did it have to do with what was written on that napkin?

He'd tucked it in his jeans pocket and brought it along, still puzzling through its meaning. *Believe Annie.* His mind raked back over their conversations yesterday, but they'd only engaged in surface chitchat. It wasn't like she'd shared some enormous state secrets or had predicted the world would end. His heart stuttered. No, absurd.

Then why did today feel so much like a new beginning?

Braden passed Greenwood Cemetery, its high iron gates coated in snow. Its tombstones were covered too, appearing like white-capped waves in an ocean blanketed in foam. There wasn't an inch of grass in sight. The wind whipped up, and a chill seeped through his veins. Despite his gloves and double layer of socks, he was losing feeling in his fingers and toes. But he kept going, focused on his goal. One hour from now he'd be sitting down at the table with his mom to a hot Christmas dinner.

A while later, Braden studied his surroundings, seeing he'd completed most of his journey. He paused at a crosswalk, out of habit more than anything. There was no one on the roads today. Winds howled as he stepped into the street and a car horn blared. Then suddenly, he was snow blinded.

"I have a Santa joke!" Cari crowed. They'd been swapping goofy puns for the last ten minutes while enjoying their meal. Annie had added the extra leaf to her table, and they now had eight seats crammed in around it, including one vacant place for the neighbor in 2-B in case they decided to show up.

Jane leaned toward her daughter. "Go ahead and share."

Cari glanced around the table. "What's Santa's favorite kind of music?" she asked with big, dark eyes. The others watched and waited, while Harrington quietly snickered.

Cari sat up straighter in her chair. "Wrap!" she proclaimed, beaming.

Laughter rang out, filling the small kitchen.

"That's a good one," Harrington said. "Plus, it reminds me." He dug into his shirt pocket under his cardigan sweater and passed something to Annie. "I meant to give you this. I found it packed away with some of my Christmas decorations. I thought someone as young and pretty as you could use it," he said, flirting a bit.

Annie stared down at the shiny plastic green leaves and round white berries. "Mistletoe?" she asked, looking up. She chuckled lightly. "I'm not sure I'll have much need for this."

"Nonsense!" Bea said. "It's the holidays. You never know."

Jane smiled at Annie. "True."

"What about you, Eric?" Harrington asked. "Seeing anyone?"

Annie gasped and pushed his arm. "Harrington!"

"Just kidding." He winked at Eric. "I have an eye on her myself."

Annie squared her shoulders. "I do like older men." Not forty years older, but still. Three or four years sounded good. Ooh, how she wished she knew how Braden was doing.

"Please pass the salt and pepper, Annie," Harrington said, snapping her back to attention. Harrington took another forkful of corn pudding. "Everything's delicious."

Even though Harrington had clearly been teasing about Eric possibly being available for Annie, Eric still looked a little embarrassed by the insinuation, given that they were the only two younger—and apparently single—folks in the room. "I do have a girlfriend," he admitted sheepishly. "She's back in LA."

"How sweet!" Bea said, ever the romantic. "What's her name?"

"Jasmine."

"Like the flower." Harrington glanced at Eric. "You two been together long?"

"Just over a year," Eric answered. "She's in film school there."

"Well, good for you!" Jane told him.

Harrington toasted him with his wineglass. "When it's right, it's right."

Jane winked at Eric, rolling her eyes toward Sam. "We know a thing or two about long-distance."

"Boy, do we ever." Sam took Jane's hand and squeezed it.

Annie recalled Braden taking her hand, and her heart sighed. Would he remember that too, or anything about her? She trusted that—at the very least—he'd broken out of the time loop, same as she had. She hoped he was okay and enjoying Christmas with his mom by now.

Eric reached over and refilled the empty wineglasses from his seat beside Harrington. "Can't say when I remember tasting stuffing this good."

The others concurred.

Sam rested her knife on the side of her plate. "Everything *is* super tasty."

Annie smiled around the table, glad her food had turned out all right. "Thanks, everyone." She turned to Bea. "Your sweet potato casserole's to die for. I want the recipe."

Jane nodded, chowing down. "Same!" She dabbed her mouth with her napkin and leaned toward Annie, lowering her voice. "I wanted to thank you, by the by"—she glanced at Cari, who was engaged in conversation with Sam and Bea—"for the little surprise you sent our way. The kid was *super happy*. Over the moon."

Annie angled toward her and whispered, "It wasn't me." She darted a look at Cari. "It was Santa." When the store Santa had seen her looking at the box, he'd asked if she was buying it for anybody special. That had given her the idea to do something special for Jane—and Cari.

"Santa? Yeah, right." Jane nudged Annie's shoulder with hers. "In any case, thank you, but that was too big a gift. I aim to pay you back."

"Oh no, you don't have—"

"In cups of coffee," Jane finished, smiling, and Annie laughed.

"In that case," Annie replied. "Maybe I'll let you."

Jane nodded. "Good."

Having coffee with Jane sounded fine. She hoped they could become real friends someday. She was liking everyone here so much, all these awesome folks in her building. She was glad she'd had the inspiration to invite them over, and that they'd all said yes.

Bea gestured to the empty chair. "Shame that whoever's in 2-B couldn't join us. Does anyone know them?"

THIRTY-FOUR

BRADEN JUMPED BACK JUST IN time, the heel of his boot hitting the curb and sending him tumbling backward. He careened to the sidewalk, landing on his back, and the poinsettia burst out of his hold, its pot smashing apart on the icy road. It was a miracle he hadn't been hit.

A vehicle whizzed past him and screeched to a halt, turning on its flashing emergency lights. "Hey, sir!" A youngish man stepped from the SUV. "Are you all right?" Through the blinding snow, Braden spied a woman in the passenger seat wearing a heavy coat, her hands wrapped around her middle. The man jogged toward Braden. He looked to be in his thirties. "I'm so sorry." His labored breath clouded the air. "I didn't see you, I—"

Braden clambered to his feet and grabbed the shopping bag handle. "I'm fine," he said, a little shaken. That had been a very close call. Too close for comfort. "You really shouldn't be on the road. Not today in this storm."

"I know." The man said, panting. He placed his hands on his hips and hung his head. "It's my wife." He looked up. "She's in labor."

"You didn't call 9-1-1?"

"This is our third," the man explained. "The doctor told us not to wait."

"David!" the woman called in a panic through the open driver's side door.

"I'm sorry," the man said. "I wish I could give you a lift." His eyes watered as he surveyed Braden. "Can I take you to the hospital maybe?"

Braden dusted the splattered soil from the broken poinsettia pot off his ski pants and jacket. "No, no. Seriously. I'm good." He stared down the street, spotting his mom's apartment building. "I'm almost to my destination anyway."

David eyed the destroyed plant and reached for his wallet. "Can I give you something for that?"

Braden picked up the broken pieces of the poinsettia pot and deposited them in a public waste can. "No worries. It's fine."

David's wife moaned in the car, and he hurried along. "Okay," David said to Braden. "Stay safe."

"Yeah," Braden said, "you too."

Braden climbed the front steps to his mom's building and took out the spare key she'd given him. The key jammed in the lock, but he jimmied it open. He glanced down at the torn gift bag from Lawson's hanging from his arm. At least the gift-wrapped package inside it was pretty much untouched. He'd covered the top of it in plastic to keep it from getting wet. That poinsettia though—he stared back at the snowy street—was a total loss.

He entered the foyer, and the heat of the building enveloped him, taking the bite out of the cold. He shut the door behind him and shook the snow from his jacket, dusting off his hat with his gloves before heading up to the second floor and knocking on his mom's door.

"Braden, you made it!" She held out her arms to hug him but cast an eye at his damp clothing—pulling back. "Come on, let's get you inside."

"Something smells great."

"I made a standing rib roast," she said. "It's probably a lot for the two of us." She shrugged. "But I wanted to do something special."

"Thanks, Ma." He handed her the gift. "This is for you."

"How sweet." She smoothed back her hair. "You didn't have to."

"I know that." He smiled. "I wanted to."

She pulled the present from the gift bag, removing the plastic shopping bags Braden had used to cover it . "Smart of you to keep this dry," she said. "Whoa, what a big box! I'll tuck it under the tree." She glanced at the four-foot Fraser fir that she'd decorated. "Santa left something there for you too."

Braden smiled at his mom. "Can't wait." He unzipped his jacket and removed it, bending down to strip off his boots. The corner of an envelope caught his eye. It was mostly covered by his mom's entryway doormat. "What's this?" he asked, pulling it out from under the mat.

"Looks like a piece of mail?" She walked toward him. "Maybe it landed in the wrong post box and one of the neighbors—" She took it from Braden, seeing it was hand addressed:

To my neighbor in 2-B

"That's funny," his mom said. "Let's hope it's not someone complaining about my TV being on at odd hours." She broke the seal on the small envelope and removed a note card.

You are cordially invited to Christmas dinner with your neighbors!

Christmas Day at Two O'clock, Apartment 3-A

His mom frowned. "Oh my, I didn't see this. I wonder when it came?"

"No date?" Braden asked.

She shook her head. "Just a signature."

"You think it's on the level?" Something in his head urged caution. This note had totally come out of the blue.

"I assume so." His mom's shrugged. "I haven't met any of my new neighbors." She'd only lived there since losing his stepdad. She'd moved to this smaller place then. "And I certainly don't know this one." She handed him the card, and his heart thumped. The note was signed, *Annie*.

Not *the* Annie. Not Annie Jones? She'd said she lived in Brooklyn, but near the museum. Although that actually wasn't very far away, in his view, the library was closer.

"What a kind thought," his mom said. She stared at the wintry scene through the window. "No one's ever gotten all the neighbors together before, as far as I know. That's really nice."

Who does that? *Annie Jones, that's who.* Braden searched his mind, not sure how he knew that. He and she hadn't spoken that extensively yesterday. "Yeah," he agreed. "What a gesture." He took off his ski pants and hung his wet things over the towel bar in his mom's bathroom, returning to the living room where she still puzzled over the note card. "What do you want to do?" he asked her.

"We're running a little late," she said. "But not that late." She smiled decisively. "I think we should go."

"And your roast?"

"We can bring it to the party!" She stared at the blustery weather. "I hate to say this, but you're probably stuck here overnight. Maybe two nights."

Yeah, he wasn't looking forward to doing that trek again today. It was also doubtful that Lawson's would be open tomorrow, given the storm. Braden pulled the napkin from his pocket and stared at it. He'd asked Annie out for coffee, but she definitely hadn't gone. He would have remembered that. He saw a flash of two jelly donuts inside a paper bag. What silliness. No.

"What's that?" his mom asked, stepping nearer.

He handed her the napkin. "Believe Annie?" she asked. "About what?"

Braden shook his head. "I honestly don't know."

Her fingers traced over the napkin. "That looks like your handwriting though."

Distant memories flitted through him like small snowflakes in a snow globe, but none of them were clear. It was like trying to grasp at sand that kept sifting through your fingers. His mom scanned his eyes. "Do you know this Annie? The one in my building?"

"If her last name is Jones, I might."

Harrington hobbled back to the table using his walker and picked up the mistletoe he'd given Annie earlier. "Say, Eric?"

Eric deposited a few dishes in the sink and turned. "Yeah?"

Harrington held the mistletoe toward him. "Hang this up for me, why don't you?"

Eric glanced at Annie, and she laughed. "Sure. Why not?" she said. "There's some masking tape in the top drawer to the left of the refrigerator."

Eric retrieved the tape and stared up at the ceiling in the kitchen. "Not sure where—?"

"On the doorframe leading into the back hall," Annie decided. The short hallway led to bathroom at the end of it. Her bedroom was on the right and the coat closet on the left.

Cari tugged at Jane's arm as the adults cleared the dishes. "Mommy?" she asked, "can I play with the kitty?"

Jane glanced at Annie while holding the bread basket.

"Oh, sure," Annie said. "It's fine. Leo's one big fluffy marshmallow."

"Gently," Jane urged the little girl.

Cari squatted low in the living room and held out her hand. Leo bounded toward her from his place by the front door. He'd been guarding it, seemingly waiting on their final arrival: the person in 2-B, who at this point was unlikely to come. Annie checked her watch and saw that it was after three.

Jane reached for some unused silverware on the table. Annie

had borrowed extra cutlery and dinner plates from Bea. Otherwise, she wouldn't have had enough.

"Why don't we leave those for dessert?" Annie suggested. "Our water glasses too."

Harrington moseyed into the living room, pausing to examine Eric's progress with the mistletoe. "Looks good."

Eric hopped off the sturdy chair he'd pulled over and returned it to the kitchen table. "Yeah, thanks."

Bea smiled at the decoration. "That does lend a festive air!"

"Yes, but the only one who's getting kissed under it," Annie said jokingly to Harrington, "is Leo."

Harrington snapped his fingers and play frowned. "Darn." He sat on the sofa to watch Cari and Leo's cozy interactions. The cat purred as Cari squatted down to stroke his head.

"I think that kitty likes you," Harrington told the child.

"I like Leo!" She hoisted the heavy animal into her arms and cradled him, grinning at Harrington. "He's sweet."

Leo purred louder, and Cari kissed the top of his head.

He blinked at her with doting kitty eyes.

Annie smiled as she observed the scene. She'd badly wanted a pet while she was growing up but had never had one since her dad was allergic. Her Grandma Mable too. Maybe if she'd had a neighbor's pet to cozy up to that would have sufficed.

Bea glanced at Annie and over at the kitchen. "Can I help you wash up?"

"Thanks, Bea, we'll get the rest of it." She stole a peek at Harrington and whispered, "Why don't you go keep Harrington company?"

Bea went and took a seat in the armchair near Harrington, still holding her wineglass.

Sam held two items in her hands. "Jam and butter?" she asked Annie.

"Those can go in the fridge," Annie answered. "Thanks, Sam!"

Leo squirmed in Cari's hold, and she carefully put him down. Annie watched the action from the kitchen as she transported things to the counter. Everyone was getting along so beautifully. What a wonderful Christmas.

Cari pranced over to Annie's little Christmas tree. "Ooh, look Mommy," she cooed as Jane brought a wine bottle into the living room. "A snow globe!" she said, picking it up.

"Ahh." Jane grimaced at her child, topping off Bea's wine-glass. "Careful, Cari."

"I am!" She grinned and hugged the snow globe against her sweater. Annie walked over to her, not minding Cari's interest, but she felt very protective of this memento.

Cari held it out in front of her and shook it vigorously.

Annie's heart raced. "Here," she said gently, extending her hands. "Let's set it back down."

Jane apologized to Annie, adding a splash of wine to Harrington's raised glass. "I'm really sorry." She lightly admon-ished her kid. "You should have asked."

"Sorry, Miss Annie," Cari said with sad, dark eyes.

"It's all right." Annie tousled the top of her head and said, "It's just a very special snow globe to me."

Cari nodded, mesmerized by the cascading miniature snow-flakes. They twirled around Santa's sleigh and his reindeer team, landing on the candy-cane-striped North Pole and the sign in the snowy white yard that said: *Believe*.

Annie was transported too—all the way back to that long-ago Christmas when she was nine. Then, she was catapulted into Lawson's Finest on Christmas Eve and her abrupt run-in with that department-store Santa. Afterward, she'd met Braden Tate, and—later—he'd helped her pick up. Her heart sighed. He was such a nice guy. She hoped she'd get to see him again at Lawson's. Above all, she hoped he'd remember knowing her.

"It's so pretty," Cari said, in awe of the snow globe.

"It plays music," Annie told the child. "Want to hear?"

Cari nodded eagerly, and Annie turned over the snow globe, cranking its key. The tune for "It's Beginning to Look a Lot Like Christmas" flitted through the air like fairy dust falling around them, all sparkly and joyful. Cari covered her mouth and giggled. "It sounds like magic."

"Yeah," Annie said. "It does." She placed the snow globe back under the tree, suddenly filled with comfort and joy. Something else too. *Hope*. And a sense of miracles past, and those that might happen.

"Where did you get it?" Cari asked as the dainty music filled the air.

"From Santa." Annie smiled at the girl. "When I was just about your age."

"Did you do the painting?" Harrington asked her. "It's very good."

"No, that was my dad."

Harrington nodded. "Talented man, your father."

"Yeah," Annie said wistfully. "He was."

Someone knocked on the door, and all heads turned in that direction.

Bea grinned in her chair. "That must be 2-B!"

THIRTY-FIVE

JANE SET DOWN THE WINE bottle. “I’ll get it.”

She opened the door, and a woman’s voice said, “Hi. You must be Annie.”

“Oh no. I’m Jane from 2-A.” Jane nodded over her shoulder. “That’s Annie.”

Jane moved aside, and Annie’s heart leapt. A heavyset woman with salt-and-pepper gray hair stood in the hall in a black turtleneck sweater, blue jeans, and boots. She wore a decorative scarf and held a covered glass dish. And, beside her, stood *Braden*. Looking more handsome than ever in a navy-blue crewneck sweater and jeans. The large roasting pan in his hands was tented with tinfoil. Annie detected the savory smell of roasted beef, and herbs and garlic.

“Annie?” His eyes glinted in wonder.

She couldn’t believe it either. Maybe she was dreaming? In that case, this was her dream. She was owning it. *Oooh. That felt freakily déjà vu–like.* In the very best possible way. “Braden?” she managed, although her tongue felt glued to the roof of her mouth. She walked forward in a daze. “And, um”—she smiled at the woman—“this must be your mom?”

“This *is* my mom,” Braden said in an apparent stupor. “Her

name's…uh." He stood there, staring at Annie like she was the most amazing creature on earth. Someone fascinating and beautiful. Ethereal, even.

His mom nudged him with her elbow. "My name's Isadora, Braden," she said with an amused air. She smiled at the others. "But everyone calls me Dora."

Annie blinked, addressing Dora. "Oh, hi. I'm Annie." She peeked at Braden again, melting into another existence, someplace so happy. *Nice.*

"Why don't you folks come inside?" Jane asked, intervening.

"Yes, please, of course! Come on in," Annie said, remembering her manners. She turned to Dora. "I'm really glad you could make it."

"I'm sorry we're late," Dora said. "I'm afraid I didn't even find your invite until today." She chuckled. "Rather, Braden found it. It got hidden under my doormat."

Annie smiled at Braden. "What a surprise." What did he remember? *Anything?* She tried not to get her hopes up, but it was hard not to wish.

"Annie and I work together at Lawson's," Braden explained to his mom and the others. "We only just met—yesterday." He squinted, like something wasn't adding up.

Bea laughed. "Yeah?" She glanced at Annie. "Us too!"

Jane nodded. "Us three."

Harrington leaned forward on the sofa, resting his elbows on his knees. "I think—same."

Eric glanced around the room. "Sounds like it was a very busy Christmas Eve for Annie."

No kidding. She was exhausted. Annie laughed. "I could have sworn I had twelve Christmas Eves." Wait. *The twelfth day of Christmas.* Annie's gaze flitted over her snow globe, and a white-hot arrow shot through her heart. Suddenly, she was a tender little girl again, full of loss and mourning, but then that girl grew up into someone strong and beautiful, a person so full of love—and who could share that love with others.

Dora passed the dish she was holding to Annie. It was chilled and covered with a lid. "I brought cannoli," she said. "I hope that's all right?"

"Better than all right." Annie grinned. "I hear your cannoli's—"

Dora's eyebrows arched at Braden.

Annie heaved a breath. "What I mean is, I'm sure it's delicious!"

"For a moment there, I thought my son had been singing my praises," Dora quipped.

"Always, Ma," he said, and people laughed. Jane approached Braden, taking the platter from him. "What else did you bring us?"

"Ma's famous rib roast."

"Ooh, yummy," Jane said, carrying it into the kitchen. Sam followed her cue by taking the cannoli from Annie and carting it toward the kitchen as well.

Sam chuckled. "Think we'll all be spoiled by good food by the time this day's over."

Dora frowned at the table, which had been obviously cleared. "It looks like we're too late though."

"Nonsense!" Annie said. "We can all squeeze in a little something more." She glanced at the group. "Can't we?" She wasn't sure how, but she didn't want to decline Dora's kind offering.

Harrington held up his hand. "I'll take a slice of roast for later. I bet it'll make delicious sandwiches." The others said what a great idea, they'd love to have some too.

"Of course!" Dora told them, smiling all around.

"Meanwhile, Ma," Brandon teased, "I might have to go ahead and have some now. It smells too temptingly delicious." Everyone laughed and agreed.

Eric shook hands with Dora and Braden. "Eric Park. Nice to meet you."

Harrington stood using his walker and nodded. "Merry Christmas." He introduced himself. Sam returned from the kitchen, exchanging hellos as well.

Cari skipped over to Dora and Braden. "I'm Cari." She lowered her little eyebrows and said seriously, "We're not supposed to touch the snow globe."

"Snow globe?" Braden scanned the room, spotting the precious piece situated beneath the Christmas tree. He walked over and observed it, his hands dutifully clasped behind his back. "Ahh, yeah. I can see that it's special." He looked up, and Annie was standing right front of him.

Her heart skipped a beat.

"You must have told me about this," he said.

"I—I'm not sure." She had told him lots of things though. Day after day while they'd been fixing her display and during their special trips to the Blue Dot.

Ooh, how she ached to tell him the truth about the time loop, but she was also terrified. She'd needed to let him go to get to the other side of Christmas Eve, and—now that they had—she didn't want to jinx things. Maybe he would remember on his own, and maybe he wouldn't? But that was okay. They could start over from scratch, of course they could. They'd already done that so many times. The last thing Annie wanted to do was risk throwing them back into the time loop again. That would be terrible for Braden—and for her.

"There's still plenty of food in the kitchen," Jane informed Dora and Braden. "You should come and serve yourselves a plate."

"Please do," Annie said kindly. "There really is plenty."

Harrington sat back down on the sofa. "That peppermint bark though," he teased, "is all for me."

"I like peppermint bark," Cari piped in.

Harrington smiled good-humoredly. "In that case, I'll share."

"Do you mind eating buffet style in the living room?" Annie asked Dora and Braden, "So we all can visit? I've got a few TV tables."

Eric spied the set of collapsible metal TV tables on a stand in the corner. "I can set those up."

Annie smiled. "Thanks, Eric."

Braden nearly knocked elbows with Annie when she handed him a plate in the kitchen. His mom stayed a few paces ahead of him, loading up her dish. "Oh, sweet potato casserole, and corn pudding!" she cried. "I haven't had these in ages."

Braden leaned toward Annie and whispered. "I hope this isn't inopportune, me showing up here like this."

"Inopportune?"

"You *did* shoot me down when I asked you to coffee," he joked, trying to disguise his hurt. "So, you know." He shrugged.

"That was *entirely* my mistake."

"Oh yeah?"

"Yeah." Annie grinned. "And next time, I'm going."

He liked the sound of that—a lot. "How 'bout the Blue Dot?" He froze with his empty plate in his hands. "Wait." He had a vision of the two of them seated in a booth. The tabletop was covered with little turquoise dots. But no, that didn't happen. Couldn't have happened. Right? "We've never—?"

"Been to the Blue Dot?" she whispered.

"Yeah." Somehow, he could picture her sitting across from him and holding a coffee. There were white-powdered donuts involved too. Jelly donuts, his favorite. Recollections tugged at him. Bright holiday lights on the sidewalk, a charity bell ringer. Lots of swirling snow. But all of them were fuzzy.

He pulled the "Believe Annie" napkin from his pocket and showed it to her. "Any idea how I got this?"

She stared into his eyes. "It's not my handwriting."

"That's just it," he whispered. "It's mine. Annie..." He tucked the napkin away and rasped quietly, "What on earth is going on?" Whatever it was, they were in it together. Bonded somehow. Over what though? Fantasies of a coffee date they'd never been on? That didn't make sense. He'd only met Annie yesterday by the elevators. No, wait. On the elevator? Escalator? Upstairs by the lockers? This was nuts. Had she dropped a shoe?

"Braden?" his mom said, turning. She caught Braden and Annie in an eye-lock. "Oh, sorry," she said coyly, stepping past them. "I'll just go find a seat in the living room."

His mom left and Annie nodded to the food, so he began serving. He added turkey and stuffing to his plate, coating them with gravy, and took a bit of roast and root vegetables too.

"There's a lot I can't explain," Annie whispered. "What I do know is that it was a very strange day from start to finish, and I can't shake this feeling that Lawson's department-store Santa had something to do with it."

He added sweet potatoes to his plate, and green beans. This was a sumptuous feast. "You're talking about the guy who filled in yesterday?"

She followed along beside him, and they both kept their voices down. "Yeah, him. He was *very good*. I mean, I know he was an actor and all, a paid employee. Still, I can't help but wonder if he's mixed up in this somehow? It was only *after* meeting him that things started going haywire."

He grabbed a piece of bread from the basket and laid it on his plate. A big *ho ho ho* rang out in his mind, and other snippets of conversation too, Santa repeatedly saying that Annie's window display wasn't quite right.

"Weird. I sense that too." He studied her. "I mean, me being here with you? It just seems—awfully coincidental. It feels like something else is at play. And that guy? Yeah. There was something *really different* about him. The way he charmed those kids—"

"Braden Tate," she teased. "You're not saying you believe in Santa?"

He laughed. "Santa, no. Still." He lowered his voice even further. "I've got this super-strange feeling that you and I have been through something similar before. Like we've talked or spent time together?" He shook his head. "For more than just a few hours on Christmas Eve." There had to be some way to explain their tantalizing connection. His intense attraction to Annie couldn't possibly have developed in only one day. Not without some kind of special intervention.

She passed him silverware and a napkin. "Maybe we should look into that Christmas Eve Santa? Learn where he came from?" she whispered. "Because it surely was *not* a toy workshop in the North Pole."

Braden laughed. "Right. I've got contacts in HR and can try to find out. I'll let you know what I learn."

They both turned toward the living room at once. "Whoa!" Braden steadied his plate between them. "Sorry about that."

"No problem." His heart thudded at the dreamy look in her eyes. "Braden?" she said, growing a little breathy.

"Yeah, Annie?"

"I'm just really glad you made it here for Christmas, that's all."

She grinned, and his heart took wings. "So am I."

THIRTY-SIX

ANNIE AND BRADEN ENTERED THE living room, and Harrington scooted over on the sofa. "Here," he said. "I can make room for two more."

Annie blushed and took her seat. "Thanks, Harrington."

Bea was in the armchair and the others sat on folding chairs. Cari sat cross-legged on the floor, tempting Leo with his new wand toy, which had a stuffed candy cane attached to its end.

"So, how long have you worked at Lawson's?" Dora asked Annie.

"About three years," Annie said at the same time as Braden. She jerked her wineglass away from her lips, and wine sloshed in the glass. She hadn't told him that on the first day. Only on the second day, when they were at the Blue Dot. Maybe he *was* remembering some things? She'd take even a little bit because those "little bits" might bring back more.

"I, um—" Braden set down his fork. His face screwed up as he stared at her. "You must have mentioned it?"

"Yeah, sure." Annie addressed the group. "A couple of kids running wild through the store bulldozed into my front-window display."

"Oh no!" Dora gasped.

"Yeah, really trashed it," Braden agreed.

Jane frowned at Annie. "What a rotten thing to have happen on Christmas Eve."

"It wasn't—great." Annie sipped from her wine. "But luckily, Braden helped me pick up." They'd augmented that window display—so many times. And now, it was perfect.

"Yeah," Braden said. "We got it done." He seemed to be searching for certain answers in her eyes. Annie had questions too. Especially about Lawson's new store Santa with his big, round belly and ho ho hos. He'd commented on her window, providing her and Braden with tons of tips. Braden was right about that guy being different. *Ultra convincing. But not that convincing. For goodness' sake, Annie! Everyone knows Santa isn't real.* Still. A sneaky, tiny doubt tugged at her soul. She was glad Braden was checking with HR about him.

Braden set his plate on the coffee table in front of him. "We finished up just in time too," he said about fixing her window. He folded his cloth napkin, resting it beside his plate.

"Before closing?" Harrington asked him.

"Before Veronica Lawson made her surprise appearance at the store," Braden answered.

"Oh *yeah*." Annie laughed. "What a stroke of luck!" *That last time*.

Braden chuckled. "Imagine if she'd come in earlier. *That* would have been a disaster."

"Ha! Yeah." Not long afterward, Patrice had told Annie about her promotion. Kira got promoted too. Even though her first Christmas Eve had started out badly, her twelfth Christmas Eve had turned into a stellar day. True, it took her long enough to get there, but she wasn't giving any of it back. Not one precious second.

Braden nodded. "The big boss was super pleased with Annie's window."

Harrington winked at Annie. "Sounds like that cloud had a silver lining."

Annie glanced at Braden and smiled. "Several, actually." Every time his sparkly blue eyes caught the light, her pulse hummed. But of course. He was a very attractive guy, and he'd so generously helped her. He'd supported her emotionally too. She'd always be grateful for his kindness and—*sigh*—his sexy grin.

"And you, Braden?" Bea asked him. "Have you worked at Lawson's long?"

He smiled at the older woman. "Not as long as Annie. Going on two years now."

The group made casual chitchat about this and that, with Annie and Braden stealing occasional glances at each other. Each time his eyes met hers she felt a *zing*—an incredible sense of connection. From the sparkle in his eyes, he sensed it too. She wanted so badly to hang on tight, but another part of her said, *Easy, Annie. Have faith in how things will unwind.*

Oh, how she hoped with all her heart that they'd end favorably.

Once Braden and Dora had finished eating and complimenting the chefs, Harrington surveyed their empty plates. "How about we break out my chocolates and that peppermint bark?" he said to Annie.

"Great idea." She grinned around the room. "Who wants pumpkin pie? *And* cannoli!" Snow fell beyond the windows, and the wind blew white streaks against the glass, but inside everyone was warm, comfy, and dry.

"This has been a very nice Christmas," Bea said as she stood by the doorway a while later. She held her empty casserole dish in her hands, and all the guests, besides Dora, carried small takeout containers of roast beef for making sandwiches later. "Thanks so much for thinking of it."

"Yeah," Jane said. Sam and Cari were beside her. "What a very nice treat."

Sam nodded at Annie. "Thanks for letting me crash your party."

Annie smiled at Sam. "Of course."

Harrington eased himself over the threshold using his walker. "Thank you, young lady. I was honored to be included."

Annie smiled fondly at the older gentleman. "It was an honor to include you. Thanks for coming."

Harrington eyed the steep stairs.

"I'll help you down," Eric offered, coming up alongside him.

Braden stepped toward them. "So will I." Annie's heart ached at him going away. Totally uncalled for and silly. It wasn't like they were involved—romantically.

Annie's heart beat harder, and sleigh bells sounded in her head.

Wait.

Dora grasped the covered platter holding her roast. She'd left the remaining cannoli with Annie for her to enjoy—thought there was honestly very little left. "Thanks for the generous invite. I'm so glad we found your note."

"Yeah," Annie answered, "me too." She observed Eric and Braden helping Harrington down the stairs. They'd left Harrington's walker on the landing, and the older man gripped the railing with his right hand, cautiously navigating his descent. Eric braced Harrington's left elbow, and Braden spotted him from in front, easing his way down each step.

Sam watched the action, speaking to Jane, "I can take the walker down for him and meet you and Cari back upstairs."

Jane smiled at her thoughtfulness. "Sounds good." She took Cari's hand and spoke to Annie. "Thanks again for everything." She darted a fond glance at her child. "And I do mean everything."

"My pleasure," Annie said. What a Christmas it had been, leaving her apartment and her heart so full. Sam picked up the walker, and she, Jane, and Cari waited patiently for the stairwell to clear.

Eric shot Annie a look over his shoulder. The small group was halfway down the stairs to the second floor. "Thanks for the great dinner, and also those amazing cinnamon rolls!"

Annie chuckled. "Glad you liked them."

Braden peered up at her, and her heart stilled. "Yeah," he said. "Thanks, Annie." But that somehow wasn't enough. She wanted more. More time with Braden. Just a chance for the two of them. She had let him go, and now the fates had brought him back to her. She wanted it all.

Bea disappeared into her apartment and waved. "Merry Christmas, everybody!"

"Merry Christmas!" the men called up the stairs.

"Happy holidays!" Jane said.

Annie shut her door, and Leo bounded over. She scooped him

up in her arms. "What do you say? Did you like meeting Cari?" He purred, and she snuggled him closer. "I bet you did." What an ideal Christmas. Only one thing could have made it better. Someone knocked on her door, and nerves flitted around in her belly.

Please let it be him. Please, please, please, please. Please.

She pulled open the door, and there he stood.

Braden.

He shared a lopsided grin. "I didn't really get to say goodbye."

"Oh." She stepped back, holding the cat. "Do you want to come in?"

"That's all right. Ma's waiting for me downstairs." He shifted on his feet. "This was kind of uncanny though, wasn't it?" His eyes twinkled. "I mean, the two of us?" He gestured between them. "Both at Lawson's and now here?"

"Yeah." Her pulse raced. "It's really something."

"I mean, I don't normally believe in fate." He held open his hands. "But sometimes, when the universe kicks you in the head, you've got to listen."

Annie's heart warmed. "I know exactly what you mean."

"So yeah, Annie. I was thinking." His neck colored slightly, and so did his ears. "Maybe I should get your number? You know, so I can text ya—about the Blue Dot. Or any other old thing." His face looked so hopeful she wanted to kiss him. Really, really, *really* wanted to kiss him, so hard. Like she had that one time that he seemed not to remember.

"All right." She put Leo down and stepped into the hall, closing the door behind her. She handed Braden her cell phone, and he gave her his, so they could enter their contact information.

"Great." Braden grinned and held up his phone. "I'll be in touch."

Annie smiled happily. "Okay."

She couldn't wait. From the look in his eyes, neither could he. The two of them were meant to fit, like two candy canes in a cup of cocoa, or a hand in a holiday mitten. And it wasn't because of any time loop with loopholes. It was because of who they were—both individually, and together.

Maybe she would get to use that mistletoe after all.

THIRTY-SEVEN

On the day after Christmas

ANNIE SNATCHED HER CELL PHONE off her nightstand and sat up in bed.

Okay. This is it.

The big moment she'd been waiting for.

Right. But why?

Her alarm hadn't gone off. She'd imagined it. Maybe it was like getting a song stuck in your head. She used that same ring tone every day during the holiday season, starting with the day after Thanksgiving and running until after New Year's. But today, she'd woken up naturally, roused by the sound of snow thudding against her window. There was no reason her phone should be intimating. Still. She viewed it askance. She drew in a deep breath and released it, daring to look at the date.

Dec 26

Winter Storm Warning

Relief crashed over her like a heavy ocean wave. *Yes*. Time was moving forward again. She'd gotten to—and through—Christmas

Day. Yeah, she had. She'd hosted an enormous Christmas dinner too, for all the folks in her building! Wow.

Leo raised his head and blinked, kneading the covers by extending and withdrawing his claws. "Morning, boy." He kept up his work, purring louder.

Braden's surprise arrival had been the biggest *wow* of all. Maybe the universe *had been* kicking them in the head, because him showing up here, after the days they'd had together at the store? That had to mean something. Her phone buzzed in her hand, and a text message popped up on the screen. *Braden.*

Braden

Got the official word. Lawson's is closed today.

Another day off! Maybe she could spend some of it with him? *Sigh.*

Braden

Feel like going for a walk?

Not saying no this time.

Annie

I'd love that.

Braden

How's noon?

Annie

Noon sounds good!

Braden

Great. See you then!

Time to get going. Annie threw back the covers and Leo plopped onto the floor, looking stunned. Annie laughed. "Sorry, Leo!" She started to set her sock-covered feet on the floor but yanked them back. *Why?* She peered over her bed, but the floor was clear, of course. A couple of Leo's new cat toys sat on her dresser, along with one of his older ones: the wand toy with the feather attached. She gingerly placed her toes on a floorboard and rocked back on her heels, standing up and holding her arms out at either side for balance. The floor didn't open up, nor did the room cave in. What had she expected? Not that. It was December 26, the day after Christmas! She'd really broken out of that time loop!

She surveyed the window and then Leo. He sat down by the open doorway and meowed. She smirked. "Fine, okay. I'll feed you." *But first! I'm checking the fire escape.* She briskly strode to the window and yanked up the blinds. Deep mounds of snow covered the fire escape's rungs and clung to its railings, as more white flakes cascaded from the sky. *Yes! Woo-hoo!* Not a great day for work, but a fine one for a wintry walk with a very special someone. *If only I had those new snow boots.*

A few hours later, Annie was dressed and enjoying a second cup of coffee at her kitchen table. She'd read through Patrice's email at least a dozen times, making sure it had really happened. She was getting promoted to Lead Visual Artist, and Kira was her new full-time assistant. Leo strutted into the kitchen, and she picked him up and hugged him. Now he'd be taken care of too.

The intercom buzzed, and a weird déjà vu hit her. The room seemed to spin, and the lights grew brighter. *Come on, stop it, Annie. Get a grip.* It was probably someone buzzing the wrong apartment. That happened all the time. She put Leo down and walked to the intercom speaker in the hall, pressing its button. "Hello?"

"Package delivery for you." Her heart soared. She'd know that voice anywhere. That was Braden. She checked her watch. A few minutes early, but she'd take him.

Annie laughed. "Well then, come on up."

He knocked on her door, and Annie opened it, greeted by his big, handsome grin. He wore a heavy coat and snow boots and held his hat and gloves. "Found this for you down in the foyer." He passed her the package, and she took it, letting him in and shutting the door.

"Yeah? What were you doing down there?"

"Checking my mom's mail and peeking at the weather. Still coming down pretty hard. We may not last long."

"I'm willing to risk it."

His blue eyes danced. "So am I." Leo pranced toward him, and he stooped to pet his head. "Good morning, Leo. Have you been a good boy?"

"He *has been* very good. Not like he was on Christmas Eve."

Braden straightened to his full height. "Yeah? What happened then?"

Annie shook her head. "He jumped up and hit my hand when I was feeding him breakfast. Made a nasty cat food mess all over the kitchen floor. He also hid my name tag before work—*and* went a little wild with some toilet paper while I was gone."

"Oh nooo." Braden chuckled and glanced at Leo's empty stocking. "But he still got Santa?"

"Of course." Annie squared her shoulders, feeling sassy. "Santa's always forgiving and kind." She carried her package into the kitchen and set it on the table, fishing through a drawer for her heavy-duty scissors. She hoped this was what she thought it was.

"Speaking of Old Saint Nick." Braden leaned his shoulder into the door jam. "I caught up with Jerry over text."

Annie located the kitchen shears and shut the drawer. "HR Jerry?"

"That's the one." Braden crossed his arms. "Funny thing about that department-store Santa. No one can find his records anywhere."

Annie's mouth dropped open. "How can that be?"

"He came from an agency, but they've got no paper trail. Said he must have been sent by the other staffing firm Lawson's uses, but they claim it was the other guys, not them."

Annie wrinkled up her nose. "He didn't just appear out of nowhere."

Braden rubbed the side of his neck. "No."

"Because, *obviously*, there is no Santa Claus."

"Right."

Braden laughed first, and then so did she.

"Santa Claus!" She shook her head. "Ha-ha-ha!"

He snorted. "I believe that's ho ho ho!"

The room fell silent, and they stared at each other.

Braden shook his head. "No."

"Of course not," Annie said. Because, seriously? There were no elves or reindeer. And there *most definitely* wasn't such thing as Santa. Outside of her snow globe, and many hopeful kids' imaginations.

Braden noted the kitchen scissors in her hand, poised over the package.

"What do you have there?" he asked, bringing her back down to earth and away from fanciful musings. *Santa Claus? Really, Annie.*

"New snow boots, I hope." She cut through the tape on the box and flipped open its lid. "Finally!" She pulled one shiny red snow boot out of the box and then the other. They were waterproof and fleece lined with sturdy nonskid soles.

Braden studied her boots. "I like the color. Very Christmassy."

She sat in a kitchen chair to try them on. "Yes, but Christmas is over."

His smile took her breath away. "Not in my mind, it's not."

Yeah, she got that part. She couldn't believe it was the day after Christmas, and she was spending it with Braden, the most handsome and charming guy she knew. Annie wiggled into her new pair of boots and stood, doing a small pirouette in the center of the kitchen. "So, what do you think?"

"They're perfect," he said. "They suit you."

"Let me get my coat."

He nodded and followed her into the back hallway. She grabbed her coat off a hanger in the closet and put it on. Her arm caught in one of the sleeves.

"Here, let me." He held the coat up for her.

"Thanks." Annie peered over her shoulder, and her heart fluttered. His face was so close, his blue eyes shining.

"You're welcome." Her pretty snow globe in the living room caught her eye, its shiny dome glistening beneath the colorful lights of her Christmas tree. She did *believe*, she did. Now more than ever. In so many things.

"Annie." He pointed above them, and she spied the mistletoe. "I think"—he gently held her waist and turned her toward him—"that's a sign." His heady scent washed over her, lemon and spice and *everything nice*.

Her face warmed. "Has to be."

He pulled her into a hug. "I had the weirdest dream about us."

"Did you? Oh?"

"It was like we'd done all these things together, and then? I woke up, and poof! It was gone. Annie, level with me." He scanned her eyes. "Did we spend more than one day together at Lawson's?"

"Er." She bit her lip. "Is that what you remember?"

"It's what I believe," he said. "And something in my soul says maybe that's what that napkin was about. *Believe Annie*. Funny thing." He cocked his head. "This morning, I did a little research on my phone. I was looking for information on our department-store Santa, but guess what popped up on my browser?" Annie's pulse stuttered. When she'd erased her contact information and his Christmas Eve notes from his phone, she'd forgotten all about his internet search history. It hadn't even occurred to her. "Tabs from my previous searches on time travel," he said. "Wormholes, black holes, causal loops. Any idea why I would have looked up those?"

"Braden." She swallowed hard. "Yes, actually."

He grinned and tugged her nearer. "That's what I thought."

"And you're—okay with that?" she asked.

"Maybe not *okay*, but I am okay with admitting there's a lot to unpack here." He smiled softly. "'There are more things in heaven and earth, Horatio—'"

"Shakespeare," she said, growing breathy.

"Yeah." He laid a palm on her cheek. "I'm still not clear on everything in the past, but I do have a sense about my future. I want you in it, Annie." His mouth drew nearer. "I mean," he added hoarsely, "if you'll have me?"

Yes, yes, and yes! "Boy, will I ever."

"That's good to hear." He kissed her full on the lips, and she went all melty inside.

After a lingering moment, he pulled back and nodded toward the door. "Now, how about that walk? Still want to brave it?"

She put on a sassy smirk. "I will, if you will."

"All right." His eyes glinted impishly. "Just watch out for flying snowballs."

"What?" She gasped at his challenge. "You wouldn't dare."

He held up his hands. "Just a friendly warning."

"Friendly? Ha!" She nudged his arm. "In that case, I'll warn you too."

Braden took her hand and kissed it. "Can't wait."

She couldn't wait for a lot of things with Braden. She peeked at her open bedroom door, but no. Not yet. If things kept going well though, time would tell.

They got all suited up and traipsed down the stairs, passing Harrington in the hallway. He stood by the line of mailboxes, retrieving his mail. "Hello, lovebirds."

Annie blushed hotly. "Harrington, hi."

He winked at her. "Can't put much past this old man." She didn't mind Harrington noting the happy glow on her face, and—more than likely—the stars in her eyes. A couple of weeks ago, she never would have imagined starting a relationship with a brand-new man. *A brand-new gorgeous and wonderful man.*

Braden latched on to Annie's hand, holding her mitten in his glove. "Come on, sweetness." He gave her hand a squeeze. "Let's go play in the snow."

Frigid gusts blustered through Annie's hair as they trod carefully down the outdoor steps in their snow boots, and her eyes burned from the cold. Braden cuddled Annie in his arms on the sidewalk where heavy snow pummeled them, coating their hats and eyelashes. "Maybe this was a bad idea?" he joked.

She traced his handsome jaw with her mitten. "I'm okay so far." Despite the icy winds, Annie wasn't cold. She felt blanketed in his warmth.

He tightened his embrace. "I have a feeling this is going to be fun." His smile lit up her soul. "And I'm not just talking about our snowball fight."

"Yeah." She grinned, her heart so happy and light. "Me too."

They kissed sweetly, and visions of their tomorrows flitted around them like tiny snowflakes in a snow globe, swirling and twirling through the air, and putting the challenges of the past behind them.

Soon, nothing was left but the present—and a very bright future.

Read on for more
Christmas romance from Ginny Baird in

the Holiday Mix-Up

ONE

One Week before Christmas

KATIE SMITH PAUSED WITH HER coffeepot held midair and stared at gorgeous Juan Martinez. "Wait. You want me to do what?" Her heart skipped a beat. She'd probably misheard him. He wore a starched white button-down shirt under a charcoal suit jacket with no tie. His slacks matched his jacket. Juan was always dressed to a T, and his sturdy build filled out his business clothes expertly.

"Pretend to be my girlfriend"—he shrugged sheepishly—"for Christmas dinner?" His eyebrows rose. "You said you don't have family plans, right?" He sat at the counter on his customary stool, eating a piece of gingerbread cheesecake. Beyond him, a Christmas wreath adorned the door, and swags of fake greenery dripped from the cracked plaster walls. It was slow season in wine country and a dead time of day at the diner. Only one other patron sat in a booth, waiting on his late lunch and reading his tablet. Tiny Castellana, California, did its fair share of tourist trade three fourths of the year. From December through March though, not so much.

Katie's mind whirled as she refilled Juan's coffee cup. She'd crushed on him for the past three months, which was approximately how long he'd been coming in for coffee. When he'd begun asking for her advice, she'd secretly hoped their quasi friendship would lead to something more. Like a real date, not a fake one. Although beggars couldn't be choosers. Not that she was begging, exactly. He was the one who seemed borderline desperate.

He dropped his voice to a whisper. "Remember when I told you about my Titi Mon coming from Puerto Rico for Christmas? Well." He winced. "She's already here, and my great-aunt takes her double role very seriously."

Katie returned the coffeepot to its warmer. "Double role?"

"She's also my godmother. And as my *madrina*, she feels a certain obligation to find me a 'nice Latin girl.'"

Katie didn't exactly fit that profile, what with her extremely Anglo roots, light brown hair, and basic brown eyes. At least she wasn't *that* pasty—when she wasn't wearing makeup. Only medium pale.

Juan leaned toward her and continued. "Last year was such a disaster. She had three poor women lined up. One for Christmas Day. Another for New Year's Eve. And a third for Three Kings' Day."

"Three Kings' Day?"

"The Spanish tradition of the wise men bringing gifts to Jesus. In our house, they brought presents to us kids, Mateo and me, when we were small. Last year, my Titi Mon invited her best friend's second cousin's grandniece to my parents' house for dinner to meet me. I don't think she was much interested in being there though, because she stayed glued to her phone."

Katie laughed when he pulled a face. "Oh no. But why would these women even agree in the first—" She looked at Juan and bit her tongue. Why wouldn't they? Nearly every living, breathing soul in Castellana wanted to go out with him once they'd seen his picture. Katie had to pinch herself to believe she might actually get a chance. She dropped her chin when she blushed. "Never mind."

"I can't figure out why they'd do it either," he confided huskily. "I think mostly as a favor to their moms or grandmothers or great-aunts." His eyes sparkled. "Or maybe their *madrinas*." He shook his head. "Seriously. If not that, then probably on account of my connection to the winery. I mean, come on. The place is beautiful. What's not to love?" He laughed self-effacingly. "I certainly don't think it's because of me."

She appreciated that he didn't have an ego. At least not as big a one as he rightly could own, with his deep brown eyes and his nearly black hair. Juan was very handsome and accomplished. He also had somewhat of a checkered dating history. Katie had read about that online. None of his relationships ever lasted very long, but that was likely because he kept dating flighty jet-setters. Maybe if he settled down with somebody stable and ordinary, things would go differently.

"Well, if you don't want her to fix you up—"

"Katie," he said smoothly, and her mouth went dry, because he looked so helpless, and ooh, how she wanted to rush to his rescue—with open arms. "There's no talking to my Titi Mon. She's trying to set me up this year with Adelita Busó."

"Who's Adelita Busó?"

He sighed. "Only her grandniece's second cousin's cousin—by marriage."

Katie winced. "That sounds complicated."

"It is complicated—by the fact that I don't even know her. She supposedly lived in Castellana years ago and has recently returned to town. So what if she's the CFO of some mega media company that she now works for remotely? Fact is, I'm not interested. But it's hard getting through to Titi Mon, especially with Abuelo on her side. The two of them are always going on *and on* about how I don't value my culture." Juan's family had owned Los Cielos Cellars for generations.

She hesitated and then asked, "Do you?"

"Sure I do." Juan took a sip of coffee. "I also value my independence. So I think I should be able to make up my own mind about who I do—and don't—see. Don't you agree?"

"Well, sure." That sounded reasonable enough.

His expression oozed sincerity. "Look. You're a nice woman. Kind. Genuine. Once my family sees me with someone like you, they'll finally back off."

"Back off how?"

"By letting me lead my own life." Juan squared his shoulders. "I'm thirty-two. A man and not a kid. Old enough to make my own choices."

Over the past few months, he'd told her about some of those. While the rest of his family lived at the vineyard, Juan owned a fancy modern condo in town. He also followed his industry and was keen on modernization. Always up on the latest trends.

Her heart beat harder when she imagined herself with him. Juan was active on social media, and pretty much every single woman in Castellana followed him. Maybe a few of the married ones too. What if fake led to forever and they actually coupled up?

She bit her lip, knowing that was a stretch, but still. A girl could dream.

Katie had never had a serious boyfriend. Well, not since Wes in high school. He'd been smart and ambitious and had gone on to do other things. He was an entertainment lawyer in Los Angeles now. He also had a girlfriend. Katie checked in on him once in a while on social media. Members of their old friend group too. It was hard to believe she'd once been one of them. But that was before her life had taken a different turn.

"I don't know, Juan." She frowned. "I mean, I get what you're saying—"

"Then please, say yes."

He pleaded with his eyes, and Katie found it impossible to resist him. Why would she turn down an opportunity like this? The diner was closed on Christmas Day, and all she had going on was her regular volunteer stint at the soup kitchen. Maybe she'd get to experience a real heartwarming holiday for the first time in forever. Plus, she'd get to meet Juan's family.

The family that wanted Juan to date someone *not like her*.

Her stomach clenched.

Maybe this was a bad idea.

But no, Juan would be there with her, holding her hand. Possibly even literally. *Yes*.

"Just for Christmas dinner?" she asked, acting like her cheeks weren't burning so, so hot.

He grinned, reading her expression, which must have looked goofily giddy.

Gah.

"So, what?" His face lit up. "You'll do it?"

Katie pursed her lips. It was only for a couple of hours, and maybe after doing him this favor, she'd stand a chance with him for real. Assuming she impressed him enough. She'd also have to win over his family. This last thought filled her with dread. She was a simple person, and the Martinezes were, well, the Martinezes, with their beautiful winery and all that land with so much history behind it. She'd never been there, but she'd seen Los Cielos Cellars written up in area wine magazines and online blogs. She'd bookmarked all the pages that had photos of Juan on them. Embarrassing.

"Okay, yes," she agreed. "I'll do it." She peeked at him shyly. "If it will help you out." And *helping* was a good thing. *The right thing*, especially to do at the holidays.

"Great!" His cell dinged and he took it from his pocket, scanning an incoming message. "Ugh, sorry. I've got to respond real quick." He texted back, engaged in a fast exchange, then set his phone down by his plate, grinning at her. "Thanks, Katie," he said. "You're awesome." He winked and her stomach fluttered. "I won't forget this. Just promise me one thing."

"Huh?"

He lowered his voice. "Don't breathe a word about this being fake to my family. This has got to be our secret." He glanced over his shoulder, but there was nothing behind him but the coatrack, holding the lone other customer's jacket. "None of them would understand."

Katie swallowed hard. "Okay. Sure."

Panic gripped her when she realized she had nothing to wear.

But that was fine. She had a whole week to think on it. It was a lot more time than she'd had to prepare for some of her last-minute dating-app meetups, none of which had ended well. Maybe she was being too picky, but she wanted someone she was comfortable with and whom she could talk to. Someone like Juan.

Although, technically, when Juan was here, he did most of the talking and rarely asked her about herself. Okay, not rarely. Never. But hey, that would change now. He'd have to get to know her at least a little better before bringing her home for Christmas dinner. If they wanted to convince his family they were really a couple, they'd need to put their heads together and plan. That could be fun.

Juan finished his gingerbread cheesecake and set down his fork. "This is delicious. Can I take a piece to go?"

Katie nodded and boxed up the slice, setting it beside Juan's coffee cup. This was going to be good. No. *Amazing*. She was going out to Los Cielos with Juan! She wiped her damp palms on her apron, and her cell phone jiggled in its pocket. Too bad she didn't have someone to text with her stellar news. Like Jane. Or Lizzie. But she'd lost touch with those girlfriends so long ago, it would be weird reaching out to them now, all of a sudden and over something like this.

"Order up!" The diner's cook, Mark Wang, spun from the griddle, setting a plate on the high metal shelf beside Katie. His dark eyes gleamed, offsetting his amber skin. "BLT with a side of fries." Mark was in his forties and married with two kids. He was also a secret romantic and forever ribbing Katie about her private crush on Juan, goading her to do something about it.

So there. Now, she was.

Mark sent her a sly look, rolling his eyes toward Juan, like he suspected something was up. Katie smugly set her chin, deciding she could tell him later. She wanted to tell Daisy first.

"Sorry." She glanced at Juan. "Duty calls."

"Sure." He stood and grabbed his overcoat from the stool beside his, sliding it on. He held his cell phone in one hand and lifted the pie box in the other. "Thanks for this." He smiled. "And thanks especially about Christmas."

She picked up the lunch order and delivered it to the other customer, who asked for more coffee. When she turned around, Juan was already at the register, and her boss, Daisy, was ringing him up. Before he left, Juan said to Katie, "We'll work out details tomorrow."

She couldn't wait. "Sounds good!"

As soon as he'd gone, Katie scuttled over to Daisy, dying to share.

"Juan's invited me to Christmas dinner," she said in an excited whisper. She had to stop herself from squealing.

Daisy's forehead rose, the creases in her dark complexion deepening. "Is that right? My, my." Daisha Santos had come to Castellana from Panama and still had a bit of an accent. Everyone knew her as Daisy, as that was the name she'd given her diner.

Katie nodded, beaming.

This was really happening. She was going out with Juan!

Sort of.

"Well, congratulations. I'm glad the boy has finally seen the light." Daisy shared a motherly smile, and Katie wanted to hug her, but she didn't. Daisy and Mark were the closest things to family she had, but they each had families of their own. So Katie kept her relationships with them friendly but distant, because distance was what she knew best.

She sighed, hoping that Daisy was right and that Juan really would come around. She didn't tell Daisy that her Christmas date was just pretend, because that part didn't matter so much. The important thing was that she'd been legit invited to Los Cielos.

By Juan.

Who knew what would happen from there?

Daisy's eyes twinkled. "You know, if Juan hadn't asked you to his parents' house, I would have invited you to Christmas dinner myself. You'll always have a place at our table."

Daisy was so kind. She'd invited Katie home for various holidays before, but Katie had never been able to let herself cross that line. Daisy already had five kids and a husband, plus multiple grandchildren. So Katie typically invented excuses, saying she'd made other plans. She never mentioned those plans involved eating sandwiches alone while working online crossword puzzles, because even to her, that sounded a little sad.

"Thanks, Daisy."

Daisy glanced at a spot in front of the register and frowned. "Oh no."

Katie saw what she was staring at. Juan's wallet.

"He set it down to check his phone," Daisy said. "It kept buzzing."

Who'd been texting him like crazy?

Maybe his mom or his Titi Mon?

Katie's pulse stuttered. What if he'd already told them about bringing her home for Christmas dinner? Maybe he had and they were going ballistic.

Stop being so negative and paranoid.

Or maybe he had, and they were super happy?

Sure, that could be it. Think positive!

It's Christmastime. Good things happen.

It was true they very rarely happened to her, but now she had a date for Christmas. So things were looking up.

Katie grabbed Juan's wallet and dashed for the door. "I'll catch him!"

Luckily, Juan hadn't gone far. He had paused at a crosswalk and stepped into the street, carrying his pie container in one hand. He held his cell phone in the other and was one-handed texting. If he wasn't answering his family, maybe he was caught up in some business deal.

"Juan! Wait!" she called, but he was so absorbed in his messaging, he didn't hear her.

Katie hurried toward the crosswalk, moving faster. "Juan Martinez!"

The lights changed and a large white van screeched around the corner, driving way too fast. Katie's heart lurched.

It was heading right for him.

"Juan!"

He startled and his eyebrows shot up.

Next, he saw the oncoming van.

But it was too late.

The van driver hit his brakes.

Tires squealed and the van slid sideways, a two-ton lightning bolt of metal streaking in Juan's direction. Katie shot into the street and shoved his arm with all her might, pushing him out of the way of the oncoming van, which slammed past them and into a lamppost with a thundering crash.

Juan tumbled backward toward the curb, and she tripped and fell.

People called out and a woman screamed.

Then everything went black.

ACKNOWLEDGMENTS

I have many people to thank for the publication of *Christmas Eve Love Story* beginning with my acquiring editor, Deb Werksman at Sourcebooks Casablanca, for her enthusiastic belief in this project and thoughtful editorial suggestions. Many thanks as well to my literary agent, Jill Marsal, for securing this deal and providing valuable input on the story, which I'm so happy to share with readers.

Kudos and appreciation to my entire Sourcebooks Casablanca team for their important roles in ushering *Christmas Eve Love Story* through production, publicity, and distribution, with special nods to: Shannon Barr, Susan Barnett, Susie Benton, Madeleine Brown, Cid Cardoz, Jessica Castle, Stephanie Gafron (for the delightful cover), Alyssa Garcia, Rosie Gaynor, India Hunter, Pamela Jaffee, and Jocelyn Travis. If I've neglected to name anyone, please forgive me and accept my thanks!

No acknowledgments would be complete without thanking my husband and family for their enduring support, and you, my readers, for generously selecting this story with which to fill your precious hours. To every reader, reviewer, bookseller, retailer, librarian, book club organizer, social media influencer, podcaster, or blogger who's placed this book on your literal or virtual shelves, and/or shared your impressions of *Christmas Eve Love Story* with others, thank you! I'm very grateful for your time.

I hope you found a big dose of holiday cheer within the pages of this book, along with hints at the many small wonders that make up our world. Though we may not get the chance to "do over" our days like Lawson's Annie Jones, here's to each of us making the most of the days we have. Merry Christmas!

ABOUT THE AUTHOR

New York Times and *USA Today* bestselling author Ginny Baird writes wholesome contemporary stories with a dash of humor and a lot of heart. She's fond of including family dynamics in her work and creating lovable and memorable characters in worlds where romance is a given and *happily-ever-afters* are guaranteed. She lives in North Carolina with her family.

Website: ginnybairdromance.com
Facebook: GinnyBairdRomance
Instagram: @ginnybairdromance